Bangkok in
Times of
Love and War

Bangkok in Times of Love and War

Claire Keefe-Fox

RIVER

BOOKS

First published and distributed in 2020 by
River Books Co., Ltd.
396 Maharaj Road, Tatien, Bangkok 10200
Tel. 66 2 622-1900, 224-6686
E-mail: order@riverbooksbk.com
www.riverbooksbk.com

Editor: Narisa Chakrabongse
Production supervision: Paisarn Piemmettawat
Design: Ruetairat Nanta

ISBN 978 616 451 041 8

Printed and bound in Thailand
by Bangkok Printing Co., Ltd

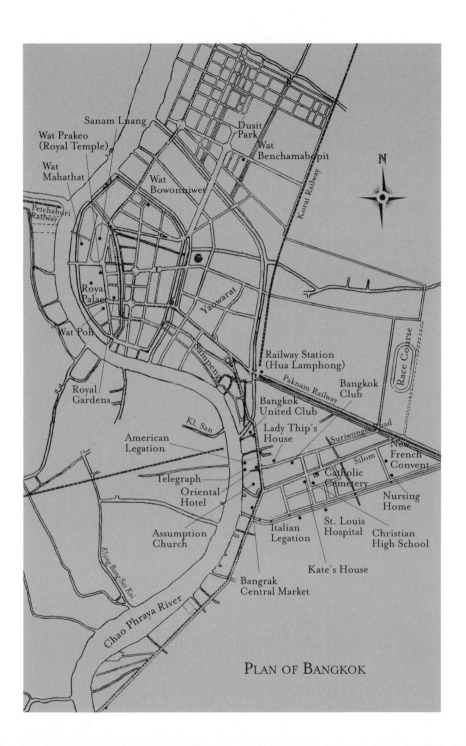

PLAN OF BANGKOK

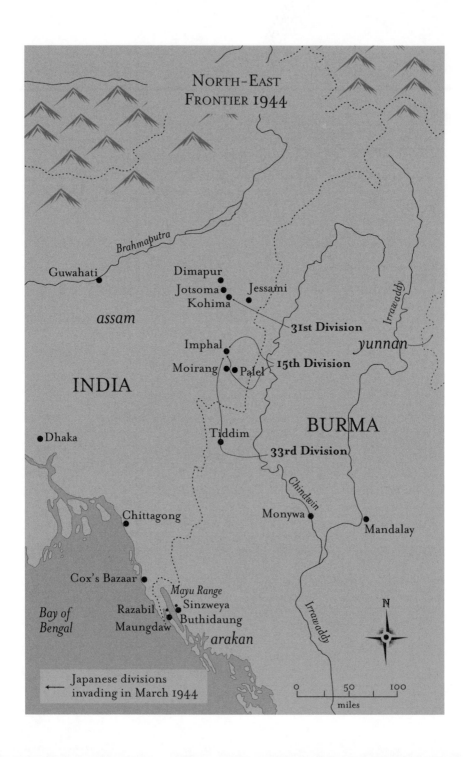

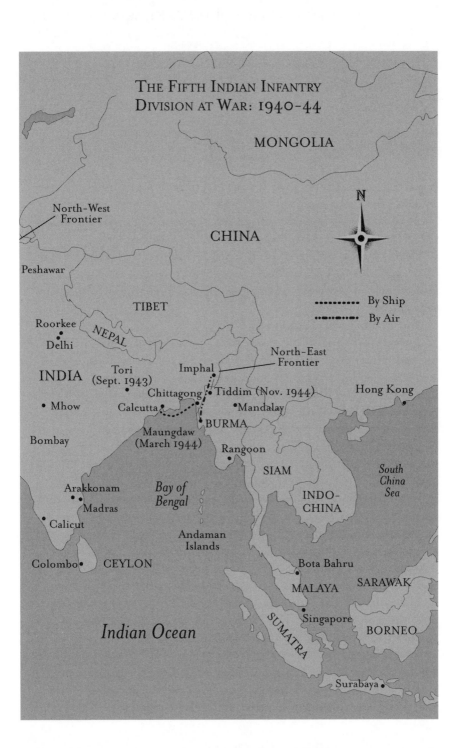

Bangkok, Siam
September 26ᵀᴴ1945

It was a hundred years ago, it was yesterday, it was all but a dream as it so often was, and he would wake up.

His mind reeling, he caressed the roughened, peeling wood of the great gate. It was no dream, and here he was at last,

Barely four years had passed since he had last stood before that door, and he had spent those years wondering if he would ever come back, if it would once again open to welcome him to the enchantment within.

But had *he* come back, truly?

He was no longer the same man, although the ghost of who he had once been walked in his shadow, unchanged and yet so foreign, speaking through the dark mists of memory to remind him with irony that his expectations and certainties of those bygone, magical times were now shattered forever, just as were, he supposed, those of the rest of the world.

Lawrence Gallet, SOE agent, former war correspondent, would-be novelist and veteran of the long march through Burma had finally returned to Thailand — or Siam, as one was again supposed to say, now that the kingdom had reverted to its former name, in the wake of the upheavals marking the end of the war.

Whatever it now chose to call itself, it was a haven, the only one he could conjure up after dark, bombed out London, his family home reduced to rubble, his family gone with it, no one left to claim his love and far too many to claim his pity.

Standing on the sidewalk in front of the big wooden gates to the house and its sprawling garden that led down to the river, he paused in fear of finding that nothing might remain.

Would there be anyone to remember him? Would his little pavilion tucked away behind a copse of banana trees still stand?

The man who edged the gate open and eyed him suspiciously was certainly unknown to him, and when asked for Khunying

Thip, he was told the Khunying had died a year ago.

Lawrence closed his eyes in pain – wise and worldly Thip gone as well – but jammed his foot in the door to stop it being closed in his face.

Khunying Busaba, then? Or perhaps Khun Fon?

The man frowned, motioned him forward and told him to wait there.

But after a moment, he heard rushed footsteps on the gravel and Fon, Khunying Thip's old major-domo, welcomed him with tears in his eyes and trembling hands as he performed the formal *wai* – "Khun Lo, it is you, I could not believe it at first, you are back, you are back! But so thin, so thin..." then spat a few vicious words to the doorman, how dare he make Khun Lo wait in the drive.

Yes, the Lady passed away, so sad, Khun Lo but Khunying Busaba, her daughter-in-law, was still here, though poorly, and young Khun Somchai her grandson, well — "he is still in England, almost six years now," he said sadly.

They all hoped he might announce his return any day, but ... nothing yet.

Did Khun Lo remember the farewell parties when Somchai left to study at Cambridge? and they both laughed together – three days of visiting friends, feasting and drinking, and Somchai, who, since his boarding school days in England preferred to be called Sam, was brought to the boat with a raging hangover.

"But Khun Lo, you said you would return, and you did," the old man said, "and your room is waiting for you.

"Old Lady Thip always made sure it was kept ready, even during the difficult days", but turned away when Lawrence inquired about the difficult days, and just asked, eying Lawrence's rumpled and stained uniform, whether Khun Lo was with the British troops that had arrived recently.

Well, yes and no.

He was not exactly in the army, but he still was in uniform – it was complicated, and Fon didn't ask why, nor as they walked down the paths through the trees to the pavilion, did he inquire about what had happened since the day – or rather the night – when he had come to warn Lawrence that he should slip away to avoid being arrested and interned by the Japanese.

He just pointed out the once lovely fret-worked sala, now sagging with its piles sinking pitifully into the river and its thatched roof half missing, and the leaves scattered over the grass and the overgrown borders, shaking his head — there was but one gardener nowadays, and he was a lazy youth — Lady Thip would never have stood for it.

Lawrence dropped his canvas holdall on the floor, looked around at what had once been his room, and thought that here, at least, nothing had changed.

He sighed in relief.

The mosquito netting was still hanging over the big Chinese bed, the lower branches of the frangipani tree outside still scraped against the screened window and the heady perfume wafted in just as it did in those carefree days before the world had been caught in a vortex, twisted and wrung and transformed forever.

His white dinner jacket and linen suits were hanging in the closet — "You still have your clothes here, Khun Lo" — the stephanotis shaving soap in its wooden bowl was on the washstand and he fingered it thoughtfully, wondering at the boy he used to be, a boy who considered such luxuries indispensable, along with the silk dressing gown the maid — a new young girl he didn't know, but as giggly as her predecessors — was pulling out of the drawer.

He put his portable typewriter in its battered case on the desk, and stopped suddenly, seeing the pile of stones there, each one a memory, picked in the garden or by the river or at the beach, and Fon mistook his silence for a reproach.

"Your papers are here, Khun Lo," and he tugged to open the desk drawer, which stuck, as it always did. "The Lady said they are important, the story of old times. "and pulled out a pile of typewritten, much corrected pages which he handed over with an air of ceremony.

Lawrence smiled.

Old times, yes, and new times, and he put them on the desk, weighted as before under the stones so the fan would not scatter them.

Fon and the maid withdrew, "You need rest, Khun Lo, but I will have tea brought to you. When Khunying Busaba wakes, I shall tell her you have come back" and he was alone.

Opening the door to make sure both servants had indeed left, he shook his head.

He was safe now, why would Fon watch him — would this habit of secrecy ever leave him?

Then pushing the bed aside, he opened his pocketknife to ease one of the wide floor planks up and felt with his fingers.

The package of notebooks wrapped in brown oilcloth jammed between two beams was still there, untouched, and he pulled it out.

He sat back on his heels, and breathed out, relieved. But he could not yet face the memories they contained and picked up his old manuscript instead.

When the maid returned with a tray, he was reading what he had written in kinder days, before he knew how to describe bodies torn by shells and gutted men begging for water, their mothers, or a merciful death, and he had slipped back into the skin of the man he once was.

For this was the story he should tell — someday. Someday he would.

What must it have felt to be the hope of a nation?

BANGKOK, THAILAND 1939

What must it have felt to be the hope of a nation?
Once the initial elation and pride of winning the Royal scholarship to study in France
had worn off, once they had shrugged off the entreaties of tearful mothers and the
embarrassment of being marched around by boastful and beaming fathers ...

Frightening, no doubt, when actually faced with the fact of stepping on the boat
bound for — where? Marseille, probably — and even more so to arrive and discover
a world known thus far only through books.

Was it winter, and cold and grey, with the rain and wind slapping their cheeks as
they were marched through customs with their fellow students, eyes straying beyond the
cranes and electric lines towards the city and the looming spire of the Cathedral above?

Did they have proper, warm, clothes, or were they shivering in their inadequate
jackets, rubbing their gloveless hands to warm them, and did this discomfort stain the
excitement at finally starting a new life?

His hands poised over the keyboard, he tried and failed to
remember being seventeen again, and about to enter the heady
world of adulthood, university and all of its implied promise.

Of course, for him, Oxford was a short train journey from home
and the promise was that of relief — from the boredom of school
with its appalling food and the distasteful company of hearty, hairy,
red-faced cricket and rugger players, from his mother's anxious
love and his father's unspoken disappointment in him.

Oxford meant like-minded conversation well into the night,
inspiring tutors, and, at last, freedom.

Freedom to read, to argue politics, to carouse — and avail
himself of those freedoms, he certainly had.

But what of those Siamese students bound for France, what
plans had they made, what hopes had they dared to indulge
in beyond returning home with a degree that would ensure a
brilliant future for themselves and the standing of their families?

All young men dreamed the same dreams, didn't they?

Glory, wealth, changing the world.

Women.

Well, as far as he could tell, women seemed to have been singularly absent from the ambitions of those young men...

It would have been nice, though, to know something of a woman, something to make them seem more human, if only to himself. Of course, not to marry, never to marry, the thought of returning to Siam with a French wife in tow did not bear thinking of, but still...

Surely, they couldn't have only been interested in politics, could they?

He shrugged.

After all, what mattered to him was what happened later in Paris, on the 27th of February 1927, when seven of these young Siamese students, those who were like-minded, who saw themselves as reformers, yes and patriots, gathered in secret in the room of a small — and cheap and shabby, no doubt — hotel in the rue du Sommerard, not far from the Sorbonne and agreed to change the course of their nation.

They called themselves "The Promoters."

They were most of them from aristocratic, Court-connected backgrounds, such as Prayun Pamornmontri, an army officer, formerly one of the late King Vajiravudh's pages, whose mother was German, and who had been exposed to views other than the traditional, archaic, ossified ones.

Or Luang Siriratchamaitri, a diplomat serving at the Royal Siamese Embassy in Paris, or also genial, unaffected Luang Tasnai Niyomsuk, who was already a cavalry captain and was liked by everyone.

But not all came from such exalted circles, and the two who stood out, the most charismatic, the natural leaders, had gained their scholarships to study in France on merit only.

One, Plaek Kittasangka, was a soldier, a silver-tongued charmer from a humble background with such military promise as a cadet that he had been selected to study at the artillery academy in Fontainebleau.

His reputation for fearlessness was as great as were his ambition and vanity, and it was said of him that upon graduating from the Military Academy, he chose to become an artillery officer because of the colour of the uniform.

The other, Pridi Banomyong, was the reflective unofficial

mentor of the group; he was a legal scholar who had written his doctoral thesis on what was probably the driest subject ever, the status and demise of corporate partnerships, but for whom the years in France had opened his mind to political theories, the plight of colonized peoples and the very idea of a modern, fair system of ruling.

He had debated all forms of political action, listened to some young Indochinese friends vaunt the cause of Marxist-Leninism and others of authoritarianism, but he was a moderate at heart, and knew that his people, the Siamese, land working, harmony-seeking Buddhists most of them, were not and never could be turned into Bolsheviks, and that attachment to the Crown was in their blood.

Therefore, constitutional monarchy, beneficial as it evidently was to Great Britain, Holland and Sweden, should no doubt also benefit Siam, should it not?

But to achieve this benevolent and enlightened form of government, it followed that Siam needed a constitution, one that would guarantee the rights *and* the obligations of her monarch and his subjects both.

Yes, constitutional monarchy was the way forward, at first at least.

And then and then.... even more thorough, overarching reforms could follow. But this was a view Pridi shared with no one. One step at a time.

Was it revolutionary?

For Siam, of course it was, and the young men asked to come that evening had been very carefully observed, and contacted in the most veiled of words...

Secrecy was of the essence, for Pridi himself had been accused of revolutionary tendencies by the Siamese Minister in Paris, autocratic and violent-tempered Prince Charun, merely for asking that the students' allowances be increased, and he had narrowly escaped having his scholarship revoked and being recalled to Siam.

Potential recruits were tested by a night of drinking and gambling in Paris, to gauge their reliability, and if they were deemed poor prospects, at least they spent a pleasant evening and were none the wiser.

Picture them, Lawrence told himself, coming in from the rainy, miserable Paris night, gathering around a wood burning stove, their coats steaming, perhaps brewing tea over an illicit spirit lamp smuggled in in defiance of hotel rules, unwrapping greasy brown paper containing something bought at the nearby charcuterie, bland but filling food that would never be either comforting or familiar.

The pleasure and ease of speaking in their own tongue, the news from home exchanged as one by one, the latecomers drifted in...

He checked his notes again and sighed, looking at the still unmade bed with its darned mosquito netting. The giggling maids knew by now that he was not to be disturbed once they had brought him his morning tea and bananas, but he could hear them chattering just outside the funny little house where he had been put up by an elderly friend of his grandmother.

He shifted a pile of pebbles to weight down the typewritten pages on the table, so they wouldn't be scattered by the maids or the whirring ceiling fan and forced himself back to the article he was writing in the hope that, at last, it might be accepted by a political journal he admired.

That's it, he told himself, his fingers thankfully following the image that had formed in his mind, there they were:

"coming in from the rainy, miserable, Paris night, gathering around a wood burning stove and rubbing their cold numbed hands, their coats steaming, perhaps brewing tea over an illicit spirit lamp smuggled in in defiance of hotel rules, unwrapping greasy brown paper containing something bought at the nearby charcuterie, food that would never be either comforting or familiar.

The pleasure and ease of speaking in their own tongue, the news from home exchanged as one by one, the latecomers drifted in, and sat down to engage in the planning, the drafting of a charter, the arguments, quiet, always, for losing one's temper was not the Siamese way.

And always, Plaek and Pridi, cajoling, convincing, teasing out agreements and quelling dissents.

Yes, Pridi and Plaek — known now as Luang Pradit and Phibul Songkram, Pridi the Finance Minister under Phibul, Prime Minister of this land which they contributed to shape, fated to have their lives always linked, for better and for worse, and growing to hate each other, each of their steps forcing a move from the other, as if they had been joined at the hip, like — he paused, and laughed out loud — yes, — Siamese twins.

He had his title: *"Siamese Twins"*.

PART I

Chapter I

The girl with coppery curls clanged the heavy, noisy, gate of the tiny porch and closed the enormous padlock with an equally oversized key as the two pyjama-clad old Chinese women who seemed to never leave the bench opposite returned her bright smile, muttering all the while, she was sure, about the colour of her hair.

She had learned enough Siamese to know that "daeng" was red, and "som" was orange, and she longed to be able to shout "Venetian blonde, ladies! Venetian blonde! Or plain run of the mill Irish!" but she just adjusted her starched pinafore with a shrug and strode down the narrow alley, dodging skinny cats dragging fish heads from the woven rattan rubbish baskets, and she wondered once again why there were no zinc trash cans like there were at home.

The alley was so narrow and full of palms in cement planters, blossoming shrubs in huge pots and even smaller plants growing in repurposed tin cans that she needed to flatten herself against a door to make room for the cooked food hawker who balanced his wares fragrant with coconut and turmeric in baskets hanging from a shoulder pole.

The smell was just an extra layer added to those that made up the strange chronology of scents punctuating the day in the alley, and Mary-Katherine Fallon, known as Kate, could have set her watch by them.

As she had written to her family, when she woke up, or indeed, returned home from a night shift at the hospital around six in the morning, the alley reeked of fish, from the dealer's who lived to the right of her funny little lodging, and who purchased it, she supposed, from one of the large markets on the river.

"Squid, mackerel and shrimp, nothing that a good Bostonian could object to. Early morning's the time when the monks from a nearby temple, wearing bright orange robes, come begging barefoot for their daily food, and the ladies from my

little street line up to put little packets wrapped in banana leaves in their bowls.

Can you imagine Father Mike dressed in orange and begging for food? although he did seem to manage to get himself invited somewhere to Sunday lunch almost every week! "

Later in the morning came the hawker and his spicy food, followed, when he left the alley, by the smell of steam, starch and ironed cloth from the tailor shop opposite. Noon was frying ginger and garlic. In the afternoons came the delicious aroma of grilled chicken, then some kind of sweet breads or rolls griddled over charcoal, and in the evening quiet, flowers whose perfume was piercingly sweet and so intoxicatingly heady their scent became cloying by nightfall.

Her letter had continued:

"What I first found strange here is that there seems to be no mealtimes. There are people eating at all times of day, not in restaurants or luncheonettes or drugstore counters like us, but squatting on low stools out on the sidewalks, with little carts — a bit like our hotdog carts, actually, cooking everything from noodle soup to fried chicken or grilled pork or other things I don't recognize.

It smells really good, but the nuns have told all us lay nurses that we never, never, never should have any of it, it's sure to kill us. Though why their food hasn't killed any of the Siamese yet is something none of us dare ask.

Another thing that sends the good sisters into fits is the fact that there are little dollhouse-sized temples in front of every house or building, and the Siamese put little doll sized meals there.

And did I tell you that all year round it's hotter here than Boston in July?"

The fishmonger, his rubber apron glistening with shiny scales, shouted a greeting, and like every morning, made to flick some blood-tinted water at her, and laughed gustily, when, like each morning, she dodged it with a dutiful grin, wishing that someday, he might desist, although, after three months, he had not yet tired of it.

She could feel the stiff cloth of her uniform stick to her shoulders from the sweat and grimaced — to hell with economy, she would hail a trishaw on Sathorn Road instead of walking ten minutes or so to Saint Louis Hospital, although she always felt embarrassed at having a poor thin man heave on his pedals to weave through the traffic of automobiles, other trishaws, and the occasional old-fashioned pedicab.

But then, she reflected, she was much lighter than many of the large ladies laden with parcels, bags of rice and squawking chickens who made up the usual passengers of the trishaws, and whose eyes swept over her red hair and flushed face with a curious or disapproving look.

As usual, there were at least a dozen trishaws clamouring for her custom — *farangs*, as westerners were called, were all known to be wealthy and no good at haggling over the fare, and this one would be a feather to carry — and as usual, she wondered whether to chose the strongest looking so as not to be too much of a burden, or the oldest who possibly needed the fare most; as usual, pity won, and the elderly man wheezed his way down the avenue, over the rackety bridge spanning the canal, or *khlong*, and into the graceful entrance to the gardens of the hospital, now occupied by tents, food hawkers and people sleeping on straw mats.

Who told all these people that here they would be taken care of for little if no money, and that despite the forbidding look of the nuns in their wimples and habits covered by blood-stained aprons, they were sure to be given some food, some succour and hope?

It wasn't just the hospital that was overrun with refugees from China fleeing the war with Japan, it was actually most of Bangkok except of course, for the rich, leafy areas where mansions hid behind curtains of trees and the wealthy hid behind armies of servants.

The men, the women, the children came in ragged, battered droves, she had seen them at the port when her own ship from San Francisco had docked, and watched the long lines of bent, thin, bowed down people.

Some, the luckiest, carried small rattan baskets, most had their few possessions tied up in cloth bundles.

They must have heard that their brethren who had had the foresight to come to Siam years ago would help, and if not, well, it was better than being slaughtered or starved, doing, she imagined, what her own grandparents had done when they sailed from Ireland.

She alit from the trishaw, handed over the agreed, exorbitant fare with a resigned shrug — Nuch, one of the Siamese hospital staff, had briefed her on the maximum amount she should accept to pay, and this was twice as much — and picked her way between the children running around, the elderly staring with empty, patient faces, and the women kneeling by the sick and the infirm, mopping faces with rags and glancing up at her uniform, hoping that here was someone who might stop and help.

Each time she crossed the hospital grounds, she remembered the words on the Statue of Liberty: "Give me your huddled masses", or at least something like that.

Huddled masses... Yes, she now knew what that looked like.

Shaking her head with apologetic smiles right and left, she hurried to the maternity ward, pausing briefly to cross herself before the statue of Saint Louis that was, as usual, bedecked with garlands of flowers, and with a sigh, bundled up her curls into a rough chignon before covering it.

There seemed to be more and more people every day, people in need of help, or a few words of advice —" don't let your child drink the water from the khlong!" — but she dared not be late.

Mother Melanie was a dragon, and a stickler for timeliness, along with obedience and neatness, and if there was one thing she could not abide, it was hair sticking out from under the starched coif all lay nurses wore and which made them look like nuns.

A far cry from the perky little cap she had worn during her training in Boston.

In the ward, things were both chaotic in appearance — women writhing and panting in the throes of childbirth, new babies wailing, orderlies rushing around bringing boiled water and clean linens — and completely under the control of Mother Melanie who paced between the beds with piercing eyes scanning everywhere and everyone.

She greeted Kate with a curt "You've taken a trishaw, I see, you're not dripping with sweat. Heavens, you Americans are soft!

"Go wash your hands, then deal with the woman in bed eight.

"It's her first, and it's a breech. Call me when she's near delivery, but she's got hours to go," before turning away to examine a newcomer and palpate her belly with surprisingly gentle hands.

When she was annoyed, her accent was stronger, and Americans came out as *hamerreeecaanss* and Kate gritted her teeth.

"I've known Melanie for years," Mary-Katherine had been told by Mother Felicity, the Reverend Mother of the Holy Cross Nursing Home in Boston in her usual rambling way when she had offered her this job in Bangkok last year. "She's not a bad sort. Prickly, yes, but then, you know, she's French, they tend to be difficult.

"I met her when my convent in Dublin sent me to Paris to train in midwifery; she was the best of our group of nuns. We both wanted to be sent to China – well, the good Lord had other plans for us.

"Just as well, I suppose, given the horrors happening in China nowadays and that we couldn't have helped – still, we kept up, and she needs a maternity nurse, no French nuns are being sent out to Siam nowadays, they all go to Indochina, and Melanie needs someone, and you need a job somewhere away from here.

"You can't spend the rest of your life here nursing a broken heart.

"You'll be put up at the hospital, fifteen dollars a week, a room with an electric fan no less, trip paid for and all that and no expenses, lovely exotic country, one day off a week, so what do you say?"

She'd said yes. What else could she have done?

As she examined and attempted to reassure the young Chinese woman who was gasping with pain, her mind wandered, as it often did, to the letters she would write home. This time, it was to Mother Felicity, whom she would tell that, well, Mother Melanie had perhaps not been entirely truthful – no, strike that, nuns didn't lie – not entirely accurate, perhaps?

Although, to be fair, by the time she had arrived in Siam a month ago after a long journey, the hospital was already overflowing with refugees from the war in China, the nurses' rooms had been turned over to patients crammed in with barely enough room to walk between the beds and the Western nurses were all housed where lodging could be had for them.

"In my case," she wrote in her mind, "I was assigned to share a sort of windowless damp old shop front that belongs to some elderly Chinese Catholic woman, with a tiny, tiny, tiny, porch that is entirely enclosed in bars up to the second floor.

"It's like walking out of a cellar and into a birdcage, and that's where Belinda — she's a Dubliner, and her real name is Bridget, but she hates it — and I put out our two chairs in the evening and sit with our knees squashed up against the bars when we want to get some cooler air.

"We stare at the Chinese ladies in pyjamas who sit all day long, it seems, on the bench opposite, and they stare back.

"There is of course no electric fan — there is no electricity at all, and we need to use an oil lamp whatever the time of day because it's always dark inside. There is no running water either so to wash, we scoop water with a wooden dipper from a huge jar that a nice little Siamese man comes by to fill every evening with a jerry can he carries from the communal tap at the entrance of the street."

No, she wouldn't write that, and anyways, she had grown to rather like her cave of a room. At least it was peaceful, and Belinda-Bridget, who had arrived only a month before Kate after losing her position at a hospital in London, was a friendly soul who constantly begged for stories of life in America and was unstinting in her admiration of Mary-Katherine's accent, independent spirit, make-up and clothes.

She did not appear to believe that growing up in South Boston was, as far as Kate could tell, much better than being a child of the poorer neighbourhoods of Dublin and refused to accept that life in America was a far cry from what she saw at the movies — but she didn't say movies, she said "fillums".

"But the Irish have it made!", she countered, her accent veering between the Irish lilt that Kate knew of old and a nasal twang that she assumed was due to the year Belinda spent in London.

"Look at Joe Kennedy!" and Kate could only agree that yes, some Irish had made it — just not the ones she'd grown up with.

Yesterday evening, fingering a green silk dress with white polka dots Kate had fought other impecunious girls such as herself to acquire in Filene's bargain basement, Belinda had sighed with envy. "See, a frock like this, I never could have bought anything this nice in Dublin — or London. Not that I would go anywhere posh enough to wear it."

Her face took on a cunning, greedy expression. It wasn't attractive.

"Could I borrow it tomorrow evening?"

Kate had raised her eyebrows. Was there anywhere "posh" enough in Bangkok to wear it?

"Oh, I was going to tell you, but old po-faced Melanie was on the warpath, and afterwards our shifts clashed so I never found a moment.

"I met a young man, last Friday, on my day off, British, a clerk in a law firm here – you know a superior kind of clerk, not a dogsbody, at least that's what he says – I was browsing at Whiteaways and..."

"Whiteaways? I didn't know we could afford anything there," Kate interrupted in disbelief, recalling her single visit to Bangkok's only Western-style department store, where everything cost over a week's worth of wages, and clients appeared to glide about on clouds of wealth and perfume, shutting out the Siamese chaos and clatter of New Road.

Not unlike Filene's dress department, or even Saks Fifth Avenue that she had visited during her one and only trip to New York with Brendan when she had entered that temple of sophistication and luxury in the same reverent spirit that Brendan—he who had broken her heart – had brought to the Metropolitan Museum.

Belinda shrugged.

She had only been browsing, as she said, and enjoying the fan-cooled air. Didn't cost nothing to browse, did it? Not that she needed anything.

At least, in this heat, there was no need for things like stockings, or woollen jumpers, and there was enough peroxide at the hospital to do her hair, but where was she?

"Yes, the fella I was telling you about. We got chatting at the stationery counter, and he asked my opinion about a fountain pen. Me – can you imagine? As if I knew what a good pen should feel like – anyways, he said there is a dance tomorrow at the British Club, it's near Silom Road I think, and he invited me. Can I borrow it, so?"

Of course, she could, she was welcome to it, Kate replied, thrusting the garment in Belinda's hands.

She didn't know why she had even packed it, except that it *was* her best. But she never would wear it again, that was for sure.

"Oh –" Belinda had put her hand out in sympathy – "reminds you of a fella does it?"

Yes, Kate had answered, opening up for the first time.

It reminded her of Brendan, and of so many other things — the evening she'd worn it for the first time, unpacking it shyly in their hotel room in New York, when everything was bright, and shiny and — "possible, you know?

"Everything seemed possible then.

"Okay, I was still a lowly nurse in a Catholic lying-in clinic, but things were going better for all of us — Francis had been ordained, Da didn't seem to be drinking so much, he'd managed to use his union connections to get Joe.Jr on the force, so that was one worry less, little Eddy got a job to apprentice as a mechanic, my kid sister Maura was training as a school teacher...

"We may not have been Kennedys, but we were fighting our way up..."

She smiled sadly.

But all that was before Brendan had decided to join the International Brigades to go fight in Spain. "Spain! I ask you, what did *we* have to do with Spain?"

"Nothing, I suppose." Belinda replied hesitantly.

"Exactly, nothing!

"Mother Felicity had warned me, I'll give her that.

"Brendan O'Malley is an Irishman looking for a fight, she said.

"He talks a lovely story, and he's a gorgeous man, but for all that he's got himself a job with the *Herald,* he's still a mick like all the rest, and an angry one at that, she said.

"Don't get involved with him, she said, or you'll end up like your mother, with a baby every year and a black eye every Saturday — except, of course, that my Mam died in childbirth before she was forty,"Kate exploded, adding a with a disbelieving shake of her head that when the Mother Superior had been unable to talk her out of following Brendan to New York over Easter, she'd slipped a forbidden little package in her hand.

"I can't condone it," she'd said with her lilting voice lowered to a whisper, "but I couldn't bear to have you come back pregnant and forced to marry that *sleeveen.* The lesser of two evils, you know?"

Mouth open, Belinda stared, looking both envious and scandalized. "You mean, you've done it?"

With a grim smile, Kate nodded.

"And where's your fella now? In Spain?"

Kate nodded again. Yes, he was in Spain, the devil, and in his second letter, he'd written that he met another woman, an Italian, who cared about the same things as he did.

"You're welcome to the dress," she repeated. "In fact, you can keep it."

Belinda bundled up the emerald coloured silk. "Thank you, Kate. But —" she added with a blush, "— tell me you've confessed, haven't you?"

Kate had stood, pinching her mouth.

No. She hadn't.

She would have had to reveal Felicity's role, and also, frankly, what business was it of fat old Father Mike's, what she did?

Did Father Mike stand up for the poor women who came in year after year to deliver the babies who would grow up poor?

Did he try to stop the bar owners who kept pouring whisky down the throats of men who spent all their dollars there instead of buying milk and bread for their kids? In fact, more often than not, he could be seen at the bar downing drink with the rest of them.

"So, no. Don't talk to me about confession."

Shaking herself, Kate came back to her surroundings and gazed down at the young Chinese woman who was straining and gasping with pain and wiped her face with a damp cloth. "Soon, now, soon, don't fret," she murmured reassuringly, and cocked her head towards Mother Melanie, then stepped aside to let the midwife work.

It was weeks, no months, since she'd even said Brendan's name and Holy Mother of God, why, why had she poured it *all* out to bottle blonde silly Belinda?

Still, she felt better for it, although the anger that had come simmering up had startled her. But at least, it was anger now, not heartbreak.

It was probably getting rid of the damn dress, and she wished Belinda luck with it.

"Fallon now. Wake up, Fallon. *Now!*"

Melanie's voice cut through her abstraction, and she proffered the readied towel to receive the red-faced baby, and quickly cleared its nose and mouth and waited for the squall. She laughed with relief when it came and smiled at the mother who was raised on her elbow, trying to see. "She's fine. You see? Fine!" she repeated. "A girl, a beautiful girl!" but the woman fell back on her pillow with a stricken look.

Kate and Melanie sighed.

It was always like that when the Chinese had girls.

All they wanted was sons, sons, and more sons. As if there were no need for women to keep the human race going.

"If this child makes it to her first birthday, it will be a miracle." the French nun muttered. " At least she won't be smothered right away, now that I've managed to keep mothers-in law away from the ward — oh yes —" she replied to Kate's gasp" — I've suspected it time and again, and I've stopped it more than once, believe me!

"And maybe the mother will get attached, who knows? It's in the good Lord and His Holy Mother's hands now."

She placed the wailing child into the listless woman's arms and watched as Kate helped it find the breast and gave a half smile as the mother's arm tightened instinctively around her baby.

"Perhaps..." she murmured, "perhaps... Now come, Fallon, there is work to do."

Screams, blood, the never-failing rush of delight at a new life coming into the world even knowing all the risks and travails a child would face in these cruel times, and the powerless anguish at watching an older woman haemorrhage to death, straining and failing to give birth to stillborn twins.

"If only," Kate had dropped despairingly, "If only we had the surgeons or the training ourselves to perform Caesarean sections... What a waste..."

And Melanie had reminded her matter-of-factly that it was all God's will and that the babies wouldn't have survived anyway. But she added with barely concealed venom that although the Good Lord knew that she agreed with Kate about Caesareans, His Grace Bishop Perros who headed the hospital and Doctor Hermet, who was a fool in more ways than one, would never let women do surgery in a Catholic hospital and real surgeons here in Siam didn't work for charity maternity wards, not even Doctor Sumet who, though he wasn't even a Catholic, was otherwise a good man and a good doctor.

So that was the way it was and there was no time to be wasted complaining about what could not be changed.

At six, her dress and coif limp and sweaty and with her pinafore splattered with the poor woman's blood, Kate was counting the minutes before she could pass on her duties to Sister Marie-Marguerite, an older French nurse with merry eyes and a surprising love of Siamese food, chillies and all, and heaved an enormous sigh when she saw her come in flapping her leather sandals and munching on some strange brownish floss.

"*Allez*, go, my girl, get some rest. I will see you at mass, tomorrow?"

Perhaps.

She tugged off her bloodied pinafore and dropped it in a laundry basket, then unpinned her coif and shook her hair free as she walked heavily back to Sathorn Road and waved away the trishaw drivers — the evening air was cooler and she wanted to buy some fruit on the way to have back at home — she'd hardly eaten all day and although she found it difficult to feel hungry in such heat, some sliced pineapple and a banana would be nice — that such luxuries cost next to nothing was a daily marvel to her.

She had forgotten Belinda's plans for the evening and started at seeing her attired in the bright green dress, primping at the small mirror over the single chest of drawers, her brassy hair wound up in metal clips and carefully outlining her lips with scarlet lipstick in the dim light of the oil lamp.

"Here you are! I thought you'd never get back! How do I look?"

She twirled and fluttered the emerald silk skirt with crimson tipped fingers and gave Kate a guilty smile. "I hope you don't mind, but I borrowed your nail polish. Mine is almost dry, and the price of it at Whiteaways — Highway robbery! Anyway, you never use your polish, do you?"

Kate threw herself on her narrow bed without even kicking off her shoes, still clutching her purse and her sticky, leaking, paper parcel of fruit.

"Fine, you look fine," she muttered wearily. "Better than I ever did. Have fun.

"Holy Mother of God, what a day.

"You know, that older woman, Sinmei, the one who was

expecting twins?

"She died. The babies too.

"What a waste."

She closed her eyes, debating whether to give herself a makeshift shower or eat her pineapple first.

The clammy heat and the discomfort of the sweat-soaked uniform were far stronger than her hunger and she raised herself, stripped off her dress, dropping it to the floor with a moan of relief, and headed naked to their bathing area.

"Say, Kate?" Belinda suggested as she unfastened her hair clips, shaping curls around her fingers, "Why don't you come with me tonight?

"After all, tomorrow's Sunday, we're both off. What do you say?"

No.

This young man hadn't invited her, he would be embarrassed, she was exhausted, and she had nothing to wear.

She emptied the dipper over her bare shoulders with a final shake of her head. No.

"Come on, do say yes," Belinda wheedled. "They never have enough girls to go around, this fella says, and you could do with a change, so. And you do have a dress, what about your blue one?"

Kate shuddered.

The cheap blue rayon dress printed with tiny flowers, with that girlish white lace collar and the bow at the back she'd worn to Bernadette Moynihan's wedding, bought at Kennedy's store with Maura to advise her.

"Very proper," was her schoolmarmish sister's assessment, and proper it certainly was. Becoming it was not.

Memories of that wedding came flowing back, Bernadette smug and visibly pregnant in her tightfitting white satin —"Your turn will come some day, Kate," she'd simpered, holding for dear life onto to red-faced, sweaty and terrified looking Michael Boyle's arm, Da getting drunk and Joe Jr. trying to drag him away from a fistfight with Frank Neal's father, the hawk-eyed Mammies watching over the girls, and the pain of being alone, missing Brendan, knowing that they all knew about the Italian woman, and feeling a fool. All better forgotten.

"I look like a nun's older sister in that thing," she finally said, realizing she had already given in.

"Well...," Belinda unhooked the dress from behind the curtain where they stored whatever clothes they had and considered it. If they unstitched the lace collar, and removed the bow at the back, it wouldn't be half bad. They could buy some flowers near the Indian temple, and Kate could wear some in her hair.

"Come on, it will be grand," she said again, grabbing her nail scissors and attacking the collar. "You need to have some fun."

Chapter II

A dinner dance at the British Club would usually be the last thing to tempt Lawrence Gallet, but he had spent the day staring at his typewriter, trying to find the words that would convey to the editors of the Journal of the Royal Institute of International Affairs why the fraught relations between the Prime Minister and the Finance Minister of Siam not only were of interest, but should matter to an Empire that after all shared the Kingdom's Western and Southern borders.

His little pavilion was starting to feel claustrophobic, and, judging from the shrill giggles of two maids below his window, no one was at home to quell them.

Old Lady Thip, he knew, was at the beach house in Hua Hin, along with Fon, her trusted major-domo, Pichit, her son was in Singapore on business, as usual, Lady Busaba, her ethereally beautiful daughter-in-law must have been out with friends, and who knew what Somchai, known as Sam, the adored young man of the house was up to and where — enjoying his last weeks of freedom before he was shipped off to Cambridge.

He remembered hearing about the dinner dance at the club, and anything, anything, including the conversation of the stuffy British business-wallahs, was better than sitting at the blasted typewriter for yet more frustrating hours and he wasn't in the mood for the sophisticated ambiance of the Oriental's bar.

A pint, a plate of chips perhaps — and there was sure to be a journalist or two to discuss the situation in Europe — that was what he needed.

Of course, he realized it was a terrible idea as he entered the relative cool of the dark wood-panelled club's bar.

A group of elderly Englishmen, all ruddy faces and bristling whiskers, were deep in conversation and gave him a withering look as he approached, and, with a chastened nod, he took his drink up the wide stairs to the ballroom then paused--the mix of bad music and high-pitched conversation made him want to flee.

Nonetheless, beer in hand, he stood at the doorway and

watched a group of flailing and dishevelled dancers attempting an energetic jitterbug to the haphazard beat of the Siamese musicians who looked on, bemused, at the antics of the *farang*.

The smoke and the stench of sweat and fried meat, onions and curry coming from the buffet were overpowering, and he wrinkled his nose.

In Siamese gatherings, and he had been to many, nobody smoked, somehow nobody seemed to sweat, and he noticed a few young Siamese men, probably recently returned from Oxford or Cambridge who were propped up against the walls or gathered by the open windows, gazing uncomfortably at the clash of their worlds.

Of course, the men outnumbered the women, three or maybe four to one, and the two dozen or so women there were all *farang*, most certainly the daughters of English employees of law firms or business houses, because, as far as he knew, there were no other unattached women in Bangkok, except, naturally, for missionaries.

Club members knew better than to bring their native girls — and he would wager they all had at least one — but as he scanned the room he noticed a redheaded girl in blue standing alone by the drinks table, clutching a glass.

She looked as he felt, as if she would rather be anyplace else, and he saw her cringe and shake her head with a self-deprecating laugh at a moustachioed young man who approached her with outstretched hand to drag her into the jitterbugging fray and went back staring at her feet when he turned away with a defeated slump.

When Lawrence walked up to her, she raised her head.

"It's no good you know," she smiled, "I've had a hard day and I'm too tired to dance."

"How very lucky", he replied lightly. He had come to rescue her.

"We can move outside," he gestured to the wide, balustraded terrace opening off the landing, "or, better still, sit down in the bar below, where it will be less noisy.

"I have it on good authority," he said, "that after the jitterbug, the band will play a Lindy Hop, which is actually worse."

She considered him for a moment and shrugged gently. Why not?

When she sat opposite him, she looked around shyly. She'd wanted to come and sit down here for the past hour, at least, but hadn't dared enter alone. Were women even allowed on their own?

"Probably not. We British are very strange that way. And you, I take it, are American?"

She nodded, face down towards her drink. Boston.

Boston Irish, she added defiantly, looking up, giving him his first real view of her greenish-grey eyes and her freckled nose.

"That's all right.

"We don't all despise the Irish, you know. And most of us secretly envy Americans though we would never admit to it."

She smiled and looked down again, drawing circles on the polished wood table with her finger.

She definitely wasn't like the American girls he'd met in London, all peppy ways and free, flirtatious grins.

On the other hand, all the American girls he knew were rich, which this one certainly wasn't, not with that plain, ill-fitting dress and ringless fingers.

And she did not seem used to society, which was his mother's way of describing his lower-class, left-wing friends from Oxford.

Who ever said the Irish were talkative?

He could hear the elderly businessmen discussing the situation in Europe —

"We could do with a few more like Herr Hitler at home, I'm telling you" — the swish of the overhead fans and the squeak of the barman wiping glasses, as well as the music coming from upstairs, and still she remained silent.

"Well, now that we're here, we should make conversation, you know," he finally said in a firm tone. He took off his glasses and polished them with his handkerchief.

"I shall start, and ask the usual questions, then you can.

"Okay, as you Yanks say?"

She grinned shyly and nodded.

"I'm very good at making conversation," he assured her, put his glasses back on, and proceeded to tick off his fingers.

Question number one. What did she do to make her so tired of a Saturday? Oh, a nurse at Saint-Louis Hospital? But he'd thought the nurses there were mostly French.

They used to be, she answered, but most now went to Indochina, apparently. The nuns, of course, were all French, and there were a few Irish nurses and herself, the only American.

Did she live at the hospital?

Yes, he agreed, much better to have a room outside, uncomfortable as it sounded. There were surely too many germs floating around.

And to have those French nuns always watching you...

It didn't bear thinking of.

"This is when I offer some personal information," he then announced, "I'm actually half-French myself, my father was French — no, he isn't dead, he was brought up in London and became British to fight in the war.

"He's a surgeon, so in the same line as you. Now, it's your turn to ask questions. See? It's easy."

Kate obliged with a laugh. What did *he* do?

No, she'd never met a writer before — well, she amended with a wry twist of her mouth that wasn't really a smile, she knew a guy who *wanted* to be a writer... He was fighting with the International Brigades in Spain, now. Probably not writing a line, just parading around with a gun and drinking red wine, if she knew him.

The war in Spain was obviously a magnet to would-be writers, he commented dryly — that's why he was in Siam, in fact. "We all want to be the next Hemingway, you know...," but she gave him a blank look in return, so he just added that in his case, it was his father who had pushed him to travel the East just to keep him away from Spain. Anyway, he couldn't picture himself parading around with a gun.

And what was *he* writing?

Lawrence grimaced.

Next to nothing, despite sitting down at his typewriter and trying, every day.

"I finished a book last year. It just poured out of me so naturally ...

"It was my grandmother's story, she lived in Bangkok as a young woman, and my father was born here.

"I imagined that it would be just as easy — no, I don't mean easy, exactly, but.... It wasn't easy writing about my family, although,

33

Bangkok, in my grandmother's day, it was... extraordinary. The events she witnessed...

"Anyway... when I started this new thing – I thought it would be a book, but now, if I'm lucky, I might be able to make it into an article, for a political journal, and they would give me assignments for other subjects."

You're babbling, he told himself. You lost her with Hemingway.

Stop, she's getting bored, get to the point.

"So, I had an idea, the story of the Prime Minister here, and his Finance Minister, who were friends when they were students in France, revolutionaries in their own way, and actually together started a movement that put an end to absolute monarchy in 1932 – that was just seven years ago, can you imagine? – and now they hate each other."

Kate shrugged.

Politicians.

What did he expect? They were all the same, caring only for themselves, and never for the little guy – at least, that was what her Da always said.

She could tell nobody here cared for the little guy, that was for sure.

There was an uncomfortable moment of silence again, and she swallowed nervously.

She didn't want to offend this young man who had rescued her away from that awful dance, she actually found him nice. And she could tell he came from money, so maybe his family was the kind that cared nothing for workers and he didn't want to be reminded of it.

She looked up at him and offered dutifully:"I suppose this is when I'm supposed to say that I really understand nothing about politics here, I arrived only a month ago."

He nodded approvingly. "Very good!"

If she knew more, she continued with careful courtesy, she was sure she would find it very interesting.

She probably wouldn't, he smiled.

"Enough of politics. Not a proper subject for conversation. Have you visited the city yet?"

He was easy to talk to, Kate discovered to her surprise, not at all intimidating, despite his clothes and style – even her untrained eye could tell that cream linen suit was not bought off the rack, and she was impressed by the offhand way he had in summoning the white-gloved waiter — that was the manner of a rich guy, and the waiter knew it as well as she.

Everything about him looked expensive, even the way his hair was cut, the loosened knot of his heavy silk tie, and those horn-rimmed glasses.

"If that is the house punch in your glass, stop right away.

"Let's get you a proper cocktail, shall we? Or no, better, a glass of Champagne?" — and he would not hear her protest. "You've never had Champagne? How wonderful.

"Please don't deprive me of this opportunity to introduce you to one of life's greatest pleasures."

Oh my God, just listen to yourself, Gallet. Stop it. Who do you think you are? Fred Bloody Astaire?

But she did not seem to mind, or perhaps that what was she expected from an Englishman and continued to talk about her first impressions of Bangkok. "It was all pretty exciting at first, you know?

"Just like a movie about the mysterious Orient.

"The bicycle rickshaws, the way people dress, the boats on the canals selling food... Those pagodas...

"Of course, once I started working, it was just the hospital and then back to my room. I've hardly seen anything except for one temple."

When she described being taken there by a French nun, "That pagoda with a big statue lying on its side? Do you know it?" he refrained from saying it was called the Temple of the Reclining Buddha or Wat Pho, and that everybody knew it, and laughed with her, as she described being shown the impressive bronze reclining figure with its serene, compassionate face and hearing the nun say disapprovingly "This, this is what we have to compete with.

"No suffering, you understand. No suffering at all! How can we save them, if there's no suffering?"

But were they nice, the nuns, nevertheless? he wanted to know. She shrugged. Nice enough.

And the girl she shared with, Belinda, she was an okay sort —

actually, Belinda got the invitation to come, and she just tagged along.

Belinda was Irish from the Old Country, and the way she talked about it... "well, sometimes, I wonder what my parents emigrated for, you know?

"Okay, things are getting better after some really bad years, but... forget it, let's not talk about that."

Lawrence smiled and said quietly that from what he gathered, people emigrated out of hope.

Kate shrugged. "You must be right. Heaven knows, where I come from, they haven't got much more than hope, but that, they have.

"The women, especially, hope their sons won't grow up to be drunks, that one of them will turn out to be a priest, and that their daughters won't get pregnant at fifteen.

"Anyway, I guess now is when I ask you where you live and all that, is that right?" and when he mock applauded her, she gave him an apologetic smile.

"You know, I do know how to talk to people, we sometimes even have conversations in Boston, but..." she waved around at the wood-panelled bar, with silver salvers on the wall and uniformed staff, "... this place is pretty overwhelming."

Lawrence followed her gaze around. "You think? I guess I'm just used to it. So, where do I live? Well, now that's a story."

He had just come back to Bangkok from Chiang Mai last year — "it's a city up North, quite a journey," where he was visiting an elderly cousin, no, she shouldn't ask why he had a cousin living there, too long to explain — and he went to a party at the British embassy —"Willy Wilkes, a friend from Oxford had joined the Foreign Office and been posted here."

"You people —" she couldn't help saying, striving for a teasing tone to mask the strange resentment she suddenly felt,"— you have friends everywhere, don't you?"

He cocked his head in thought. If by "you people," she meant the British, yes, he supposed they did.

"It's the Empire, you see," he added lightly. "The sun never goes down on it, as they say, so obviously, we get scattered. Anyway, do stop interrupting, I was getting to the interesting part."

At that party, he was introduced to a Siamese gentleman —

"one of those who actually speak better English than we do, you know?" — and she shook her head with a laugh, commenting that no one like that ever set foot in Saint Louis Hospital. "Although," she amended, "there's Doctor Sumet, one of our two Siamese surgeons, he studied in England I think. His English is pretty good, but, you know, foreign sounding. Oh, sorry —" she shook her head in apology, seeing his patient smile, "I interrupted you. Go on."

He nodded and continued to say he explained to this man that he was researching a book about his grandmother who had lived in Bangkok and actually taught French to ladies of the Royal Court, and the man, whose name was Khun Pichit, said his elderly mother had been brought up at the Palace and been taught French by a very nice lady.

Perhaps it was his grandmother? What was her name? He would ask if she remembered.

"And guess what, the very next day, I was asked to go and meet this old lady, Khunying Thip — her title is actually Mom Rajawongse, it's maybe like a countess, I think, but she's addressed as Khunying. I call her Lady Thip.

"She remembered my grandmother very well, and still could sing some songs in French that she was taught more than forty years ago."

And so, upon hearing he was living in a hotel, she simply ordered him to come and stay at her house — well, not really a house — it was more of a strange baroque half-timbered English manor in a huge park, with little cottages dotted over the grounds, and he was given one of them, and had been living there for over a year, now.

It was so much nicer and friendlier being with a family than at the Oriental, which would have been a bit expensive in the long run. Also, he could practice his Siamese with the maids.

"The Oriental?" she raised her eyebrows.

"A 'bit' expensive in the long run?" She could well believe it, it seemed to her too expensive even in the short run, even for five minutes, and had never dared enter, not even to look around, afraid of being chased away by the turbaned guards at the door.

"I'll take you there for tea," he promised expansively, then looked up at a dishevelled Belinda who was lurching towards their table with her British clerk in tow, her careful curls nothing but a sweat plastered memory now, and both their faces flushed with the combined effect, Kate imagined, of the jitterbug and the house punch.

"Here you are, Kate!

"I was looking all over for you, I thought you'd given up and gone home." she exclaimed and plopped herself down on a chair that the observant waiter had rushed over to pull out for her, with what seemed, to Kate, a slightly disapproving look as Belinda kicked off her shoes and wiggled her toes.

The emerald silk dress was stained with reddish smears, perhaps from the curry stew served at the buffet, but what do you care, Kate asked herself, it's her dress now, isn't it?

"Cor, I'm not half fagged! And what's that?" she added, leering at Kate's glass, "Bubbly? Ooh — Grand!"

The clerk, with more restraint and probably less painful shoes, remained standing until Lawrence got up and extended his hand.

"Do join us, please. I'm Lawrence Gallet."

"Edward Giles. Eddy. I'm with Tilleke and Gibbins'."

Lawrence smiled easily. The law firm? Yes, he knew of it.

So, Kate thought. His name was Lawrence.

They hadn't even introduced themselves, and yet she already knew about his grandmother, his father, how difficult he found writing his new book, and he had promised to take her to tea at the Oriental. How strange.

Meanwhile, Belinda was still giving her that knowing smirk and Kate found herself giddily explaining how Lawrence had rescued her from the noise and heat of the ballroom.

Even to her ears, she sounded silly, laughing too much, speaking too high, too fast, as if to cover some sense of guilt or shame. But shame for what?

For thinking herself better than her fellow nurse for disdaining the crushing crowd of the dance upstairs?

Or for imposing upon this obviously upper class young man the presence of this pair of unwelcome interlopers.

But Lawrence came to her rescue once again, offering Champagne "to get rid of the taste of the house punch. They always make it too sweet."

"I'm more of a beer man myself," Eddy said, "and wouldn't

say no to a pint. How about you, Bel?"

Bubbly would be very nice, thanking you kindly, was Belinda's reply and she proceeded to interrogate Lawrence, was he from London — yes, she knew London, she had lived in Kilburn — what he did, where he lived, how long had he been in Siam, punctuating every question with high-pitched giggles.

Lawrence laughed.

"Kate," he smiled at her to let her know that he too had registered her name, "had practically to be forced to ask me even half of those questions. We were talking politics, weren't we, Kate?

"But I do know you share lodgings in a funny little Chinese shop front."

And Belinda, as Kate knew she would, started complaining and exclaiming about their pokey little house and never seemed to notice Lawrence had replied to none of her questions.

Unaccountably, this pleased her. Very much.

Chapter III

He never used to keep a diary, thinking rather disdainfully that it was an activity better left to schoolgirls or bored spinsters, but ever since his cousin Michael had given him the notebooks in which his grandmother had described her life and the events she lived through in Siam, he too had started to put down on paper the fabric of his days in Bangkok.

Of course, he admitted to himself, more often than not it was limited to

"Bad day. Stared at the typewriter all morning." or "Spent two useless hours at my desk and when Sam came to drag me to a party, I accepted with relief.

"But if I go on like this, there will come a point when I can no longer introduce myself as a writer without feeling ridiculous, or worse, like a fraud."

Still, there were other entries he was rather pleased with, an account of a funeral prayers service to which he had escorted Khunying Thip because Pichit, her son, was in Singapore on business and Busaba, her daughter-in-law, was indisposed and also, as she drawled in that weary manner of hers, "not overly fond of the old bat who was being bid farewell".

The elderly Khunying was delighted to have him along and showed him off much as she flaunted her pearl necklace and diamond pins.

He was prodded by claw-like elderly hands dripping with rubies, his hair was tugged — "gold, gold, and curly, just look, Tukkata!" — and when Lady Thip explained that he was the grandson of the famous Teacher Julie who used to give lessons at the Palace when she was a young girl, another old lady swathed in tawny silks tottered up to him on unsteady bare feet, grasped his arm for balance and waveringly said that she too remembered Teacher Julie well, peering up at him with milky eyes.

"Always laughing, and her little son? Father of you? Yes, yes, same hair."

And there was also his description of the Siamese New year

celebrations, Songkran as it was called, when you gently poured water on the forehead, hands and feet of your elders, asked for their blessing, then went off to join Sam and his riotous friends for a party when after they partook of far too many gin and tonics, splashed each other with big cool buckets and ended up soaked in great gales of laughter and jumped into the river.

He had copied that entry into a letter for his father, who answered with more feeling than Lawrence had ever known him to express, saying he well remembered Songkran and that Lawrence, for a moment, brought him back to the Bangkok of his childhood.

"You are a gifted writer, my dearest son, and in reading your letter, I was there, feeling the heat and could almost smell the mix of flowers and spices I thought I had forgotten. And better still, you took my mind away from the awful foreboding I feel in watching Germany readying herself for another war and remembering the horrors of the last one."

His mother, meanwhile, expressed her usual worries about his health and admonished him to keep away from spicy food and not swim in cold water when his body was overly heated.

He picked up his fountain pen and smoothed out the page of his notebook, because, out of affectation — or affection? — he wrote longhand in ink in yellow-papered notebooks and endeavoured to imitate his grandmother's diary keeping as much as he could.

SUNDAY, MAY 21ST 1939

I woke at dawn, fired with good intentions and the desire to write and find myself, as usual, facing my typewriter with nothing to say, so picked up my notebook instead.

So. Last night's party, if one could call that a party

It was as dismal an occasion as one might have imagined — frightfully Somerset Maugham, with the full complement of florid-faced old codgers lifting their noses up from their pints only to mutter to each other, the earnest law firm clerk in a white duck suit, obviously his best, who shook my hand too vigorously and the chirruping bottle blonde nurse who swilled her Champagne as if it were cider.

All that was missing were planters in what Maugham described as "double brimmed hats" — I always wonder what they could have looked like — or a visiting company of second-rate downtrodden actors who had just performed Shakespeare badly being cold-shouldered by the proper, upstanding members of the Club.

And of course, there was that little copper-haired American nurse, who looked like a stray and frightened kitten when I first spoke to her but turned out to be interesting?

Quick, with bursts of spikiness — her "you people" remark, or "no one here cares for the little guy" — but at other times, very fragile and guarded, as if she had been hurt rather badly. Nice eyes, and although her dress was appalling, she seemed in a completely different class from her blatant friend who was wearing the most eye-watering green silk of which she seemed very proud as she kept smoothing it over her knees with great pleasure.

The nurse's name is Kate, I never learned her family name, but I imagine she cannot be too difficult to find.

I shall make good on my promise to take her to tea, her confession of not even daring to enter the Oriental for fear of being chased away broke my heart. But should it have?

How many working-class London girls would dare enter the Ritz, and upon daring, would they not be asked to leave?

But somehow, I expected Americans to be impervious to such snobberies.

And now, tempting though it is to write more about Miss Kate, I must return to Plaek and Pridi, the Siamese Twins.

How to find out more about them?

Might it be possible to meet either?

They are here, so near, yet I know that if I asked to interview them, I would be rebuffed. Perhaps through Pichit, although he professes great contempt for the People's Party and is even more conservative than my late grandfather, which is really saying something. Or maybe there are others, from that Paris group, whom I could talk to?

It would be interesting to hear about returning to Siam after the heady political ambience of Paris, when everything seemed possible, and coming back to face the unyielding apparatus of an absolute monarchy.

But of course, besides the novel I am attempting to write, I must remember my prime objective, which is to produce an article to give myself an entry into the journalistic world, and so, all the psychology I am attempting to divine should take second place to the facts.

What are the facts?

After their days of planning and plotting in France, they returned to Siam and of course, of course, their foreign diplomas and knowledge of the world meant they were assigned rather important positions, with money, prestige for themselves and for their families, and which even endowed them with titles: Pridi, now known as Luang Pradith Manutharm, joined the Ministry of Justice with an obligation to teach at Chulalongkorn University, the then, and now still, most prestigious in Siam, which afforded him the opportunity to shape minds and discover promising students.

Plaek, promoted to captain in the Siamese Army decided to call himself Phibul Songkram, and by virtue of sporting his attractively coloured uniforms and the French manners acquired by watching his fellow students at the Fontainebleau Academy had now been appointed equerry to one of the Princes in the Supreme Council.

Luang Tasnai Niyomsuk returned to the cavalry and discreetly, gently, began to spread the view that perhaps, perhaps, Siam might be governed differently?

Another officer, a late-comer to the group, was a plum recruit indeed.

Sindhu Somkrachai was a naval officer, and brother to an admiral, and who knew what he might whisper into his brother's ear?

No, no, no! Lawrence moaned in despair, feeling like banging his head on the desk, or, even better, against the wall.

What absolutely ridiculous prose. Ridiculous and boring. It was as entrancing as the examination paper of a mediocre sixth form student.

Head in hands, he stared down at the paper.

Had he not written in his diary "What are the facts"?

Well, the fact he needed to face was this: he was a novelist, not a journalist. He couldn't write about dry, objective events and make them interesting.

He needed to understand the people behind.

So for instance, if he were to write about Pridi standing on the deck on the boat that brought him home late in 1928, watching as the red, swollen waters of the Bar of Siam stained and churned the deep azure of the gulf, his mind still full of the nights spent talking with Indochinese students who wanted to put an end to French rule over their land, and brimming with the headiness of the hopes and ideas he had patiently, logically, softly imparted to his fellow Siamese, yes, he, Lawrence could feel it was right, it was good writing, and that he in some way was connected to Pridi.

And also, when he imagined that dark face, so familiar now through countless pictures in the Siamese papers, was there not in it — yes, yes, that's it, he crooned to himself as his hands began shaping the words on the keyboard —

"a trace of fear, fear that he might be tempted to let himself be eased into the life of privilege his doctorate in law, all that studying, those countless hours reading by lamplight in a chilly room, his very knowledge, entitled him to?

If not he, what about his friends, charming, vain, bombastic Plaek, ambitious, calculating Prayun, or easy-going Tasnai?

Would they not consider that it was easier to wait, would they not think that the time had not yet come and in the meanwhile, why not amass some riches, enjoy the rewards they considered they deserved, and as they said, as they all said, even he, Pridi, that the Siamese people, uneducated farmers most of them, were not yet ripe for democracy, for the lofty principles set out by what they had all agreed to call the People's Party.

Khana Ratsadon.

A beautiful name, but what if it were to be nothing but a pipe dream, much, he feared, as was the idea of an independent Indochina that so entranced them all In Paris?

And then, after the rejoicing at being home, all the familiar, comfortable faces, tastes, smells, the heady pleasure at being shown to his office at the Ministry of Justice and the almost physical gratification, which, despite himself, he felt coursing through his blood when he was wai-ed with a respect bordering on reverence by the myriad of clerks, underlings, secretaries, office boys, and messengers as he paced the corridors of his new domain.

Was he then so vulnerable to flattery?

But he knew, he knew how to hold his dream fast, and little by little, a whisper here, a nod there, or an allusion to the way things were run in the more advanced countries, he learned to choose the men who flocked to him, in silence, under the pretext of walks through the halls or discreet, covert meetings for tea at the home he had found in the area where the newly wealthy lived.

For such was the way all revolutions started.

Quietly, a murmured expression of sympathy here, a knowing smile, a nod, a bit of sycophancy there, that turned his stomach but were effective, so nauseatingly effective.

Yes, that was the way revolutions started, with no one, no one at all noticing.

Softly, softly, catchee monkey… Until the great wave came to sweep all the tired, unfair, old world away."

And "Oh, my God! — *Softly, softly, catchee monkey…*", Lawrence exclaimed, aghast, reading what he'd just written.

"I'm losing my mind. Time to stop. And I suppose, while I'm at it, time to go and hunt down that sweet little American nurse."

Nothing had prepared him for the scene in the gardens of Saint Louis Hospital, and he looked with astonishment verging on horror at the rows of straw mats on the scrabbly lawns, the moans of the sick, the wide eyed, questioning looks of the children. An old woman tugged at his trouser leg, obviously convinced that a western man in a white suit must be a doctor or had a way to help her. But when he crouched down to her, she shook her head in hearing him ask in Siamese what he could do and flopped back in discouragement.

Picking his way through, careful not to step on anyone's possessions, he entered the main door, and, much as he had expected, it was not difficult, using many smiles and an apologetic manner, to get a tired looking orderly to put down his bundle of dirty linen, wipe his sweaty face and say that of course, he knew the nurse with red hair but he could not say where she lived, all he knew is that sometimes she walked and sometimes took a samlo.

But, he pointed to the chapel, as it was Sunday, most certainly, she was to be found at the *pithi tham*, the ceremony — "Mass" he enunciated carefully, there, in the farang *wat*.

Lawrence hesitated; but after all, why should he not enter?

He was a Catholic, and he had never visited this chapel before.

Actually, he had to admit, he had not attended Mass for several months, a fact that was brought to mind each time he guiltily avoided the Bishop when he saw him in the narrow *soi* leading to Assumption Cathedral, so inconveniently located a few steps away from the Oriental's bar.

The doors were open, the smell of incense wafted out, he could hear a familiar hymn sung in Latin, the warbling, high voices of more women than men, and once he had entered the candlelit darkness, memory took over and he automatically sought the font to cross himself with holy water.

Communion was just about over, and he decided to remain standing at the back to be as unnoticed as possible and watch; he saw several Chinese, more than he expected, kneeling at the altar rail. The nuns were all sitting to the front, the other farang, French, probably, behind them, then Asians at the back.

And then he spotted her from behind, wearing a straw hat, in the same pew as a couple who looked familiar. Of course, Doctor Hermet, and his wife.

Finally, the priest, Father Perroudon he seemed to remember he was called, said the " Ite missa est" marking the end of the service and gradually, the faithful filed out, the Chinese talking at the tops of their voices, as was their custom, and the French, pausing in front of the chapel to exchange Sunday greetings and wishes, followed by the nuns who advanced with their eyes downcast and their hands tucked inside the wide sleeves of their habits.

Kate passed by him without the merest nod, but he heard her whispered hiss "Outside" before she stopped to speak to a tall youngish woman, one of the other nurses most probably, who wore a hat piled with red roses and he found himself waylaid by Doctor Hermet who pumped his hand and Madame who exclaimed was such a pleasure to see him here, and did he attend Mass at Saint Louis often?

No, no, he smiled, it was the first time, he had long intended to visit, lovely service, yes, inspiring sermon, yes, yes, he did understand French, all the while acutely aware of the stares that seemed to come from everybody, even from the group of nuns who were circling the priest for a final blessing.

He lifted his hat, "Goodbye, yes, au revoir Madame, Doctor!" and made his way as unhurriedly as he could towards the gate and posted himself well out of sight on the sidewalk behind a huge banyan tree wrapped in ribbons to honour the spirits who lived within its roots.

Fanning himself with his hat, he waited in the shade until he saw her appear, walking fast.

"Well, this is unexpected!" she snapped, tearing off her hat and shaking her hair loose. "Did you come for me, or to attend the service?"

For her, of course. He had stopped by the hospital to inquire about her address, so, he added teasingly, attending Mass was an extra bonus. And by the way, where was Belinda?

In bed, nursing a very bad headache, which she richly deserved. Why did he want her address?

He took her arm and walked her up Sathorn Road towards the river.

"Do you not remember we have a date?

"Tea? At the Oriental? It is just past noon, and if you took communion, you've had no breakfast and must be starving, so how about lunch, instead?"

She stopped in her tracks, speechless.

Lunch? The Oriental Hotel?

This was too much.

First, he turned up at Mass, and almost made her look bad in front of Melanie and the other nuns — she'd noticed that Sister Perrine, that termagant, was pursing her lips while scanning the face of the unknown young man — not to mention the awful teasing she'd had on the way back home from Belinda, who, thankfully, was too hung over this morning to be at Mass too and would therefore have seen him pursuing her.

And now, lunch? Who did he think he was?

Furthermore, who did he think *she* was?

No, no, that wasn't possible, she finally was able to say. She wasn't dressed for it, waving her hand at her plain cotton print dress. And anyway, he hadn't mentioned anything about having tea today.

"No, I hadn't, but it just occurred to me that there's no time like the present. As for your dress, well, if it's good enough for God, it's good enough for the Oriental. Do you want to take a *samlo*?"

A samlo?

He looked at her patiently. Samlo were what *farangs* — she did know what farang were, didn't she? — called trishaws.

"Here, let's take one, shall we? We could walk, but not in this sun."

He did not have her scruples and helped her into the shiniest, newest samlo with the youngest, strongest looking driver, but then surprised her when he admitted, after settling back on the cushions, that he always tried to pick the older men, who needed the fare most.

She pulled her skirt modestly over her knees. "Me too, I always feel guilty at having someone pedal me around, so I try to ... I don't know, turn it into a good deed."

"As do I, but you see, although you're as light as a feather, I'm not, and today, there are two of us. So just this once, let's get to our lunch without all the heaving, coughing and usual dramatics they engage in, all right?"

Going through New Road, he pointed out the places he said she might enjoy, Whiteaways' of course, a few silk shops, a general store and next to it the British Dispensary, "although, I'm sure your need for headache pills must be taken care of at the hospital, but they do sell toiletries and they're not as expensive as Whiteaways'."

Further along he showed a lady in a kimono walking along under a coloured parasol "and here you have all the new Japanese places.

"There seems to be new businesses every day, and I've noticed at least twenty Japanese restaurants opened in the past six months. Haven't you?"

She answered that she really hadn't been around Bangkok much and couldn't say.

"But back home," she added, "we have quite a few Japanese too, not so much in Boston, but in California, there are lots of people from Japan, not as many as the Chinese, though."

"It's funny," he mused, " there's a chap at the Club, Sparrow, his name is, he has a real bee in his bonnet about the Japanese. Says they are here in such large numbers because they're preparing to invade the country.

"And every time he sees one, smiling and bowing, as they do, you know, they're always so very formal and polite, he says that thing from Lewis Carroll about the crocodile, welcoming the little fish with smiling jaws.

"I heard him do it at a party at the Embassy, once, when he was being introduced to a Japanese general and the Ambassador was very embarrassed.

"And here we are!"

Once they reached the grand, forbidding entrance of the Oriental, she was assisted off the samlo, as she decided she might as well call it, by one of the turbaned, impressive doormen and nodded uncertainly as he greeted her with a bow and a resounding "Welcome, sir" and Lawrence grinned.

"Don't mind the 'sir', everybody gets called that. See? No one has asked you to leave yet.

"So far, you're in, and you're safe."

He was easy to be with, as easy as she recalled from the evening before, and she dismissed that uncomfortable feeling that this was a man who did as he pleased and expected everyone to comply with his plans. She supposed most rich guys were like that anyway, and that he was used to getting what he wanted.

And, she had to admit to herself, he *was* nice, showing her the bar, walking out with her to the terrace to look at the river, and asking a waitress to lead her to the restroom so she could freshen up.

She could have spent half an hour admiring and stroking the shiny brass faucets and enamel washbasin, sniffing the scented soaps and seeing herself reflected in the beautiful gold-framed mirror but an attendant, a mere girl of fifteen or so was offering her a linen napkin so she dried her hands, fixed her hair and adjusted her hat, squared her shoulders and gave herself one last disparaging look before joining Lawrence in the dining room and tried not to think that all the diners in the elegant room were staring at her plain dress and cheap shoes.

The table was laden with silver and glasses and orchids in small crystal flutes and she hoped she would not disgrace herself and embarrass Lawrence by knocking something over or using the wrong fork.

He rose and waited till a waiter had pulled out her chair and smoothed a heavy linen napkin on her lap before sitting again.

"Mother Felicity would approve of you," she commented drily. "She always said manners make the gentleman."

His grandmother said the same, no, not Julie, Julie, from what he remembered had very little regard for most conventions, it was his maternal grandmother who said that.

"She disapproved of Julie heartily, and heaven knows she had reason: French, divorced, married three times, and she didn't know the half of it.

"But I'm pleased I'm up to Mother Felicity's standards, whoever she may be."

"A friend of my mother's, her only friend, actually, from the Old Country. They knew each other as girls.

"She's a nun, and a midwife, and it's thanks to her I was able to train at the Holy Cross Nursing Home.

"She more or less took Maura, Teddy and me in at the convent when our mother died in childbirth. There was this kind of home for children, sort of an orphanage, but there were other kids like us, whose parents couldn't take care of.

"My brother Francis — he's the oldest — he was already at the Seminary, he was ordained a few years ago — Joe Jr. was sixteen, I was fourteen, and Maura was ten. And little Teddy was six.

"There were two babies after him, but they were stillborn.

"The doctors said, Felicity also said that Mam shouldn't have any more children, but Mam listened to what the Church said..."

She paused and shook her head. "Da was unemployed at the time, but he got odd jobs because he was in the stevedore's union, but it wasn't much, so you can imagine how tough it was with four kids at home.

"He kept Joe Jr. with him — well, at sixteen, he was too old to live at the convent — and managed eventually to get him to join the force.

"Every Irish American's dream, one son a priest, another one a cop."

"Your brother is a copper?"

"Well, we say 'a cop' but yes. Playing cops and robbers for real now.

"Most cops in Boston are Irish, and most bad guys are Italians, where I grew up."

She picked up the menu, scanned it then put it down, looking defeated.

"Listen, will you choose for me? I don't understand half the words."

It was just fancy names in French for ordinary food, he reassured her, but chicken was a nice Sunday lunch in his home, so how about that?

She smiled. "That sounds just like Melanie, the Lady Superior, who runs the laying-in ward of the hospital. Putting French names on ordinary things, like 'Fallon, Fallon, get a "*chiffon*" to mop this blood off the floor right now.'

"Chiffon is not the stuff you make ball gowns out of, which I'd always thought; it's a piece of cloth. A rag."

She toyed with the second bread roll she'd been given after devouring the first and only pride stopped her from eating it whole now — bread!

She'd not eaten bread in weeks. They were given rice at the hospital, even at breakfast.

Melanie wasn't too bad really, she admitted, she ran a ship-shape ward, and was always doing battle with Doctor Hermet and the Bishop to let midwives and nurses do more.

"How do you stand it?" he asked with real feeling. He had no idea, no idea at all what it was like at the hospital. All those poor people...

"Those poor people are the lucky ones," she replied matter-of-factly. "They got away from the war in China."

The things she had heard...

Some spoke a bit of English, they'd learned from the mission schools in Shanghai and other cities. Rape, torture, bombings — famine of course...

She thought she knew what war could be like.

"I heard the stories of the men who'd fought in France in the Great War, still this seems different, somehow. Women, children... That human beings can treat each other like that — when you're faced with it, it's a shock. But you get used to hearing it, you get used to children screaming and screaming when they hear an airplane above — though, thankfully, it doesn't happen that often here, and, like I said, they're the lucky ones and they know it. But it's not what I signed up for when I came here; I had no idea either."

How did she decide to come to Siam?

Well, there was a need for nurses, and she wanted to get away.

She was tired of watching all her friends get married, get babies, get trapped, and she was determined — and also, Mother Felicity was determined — that it wouldn't happen to her. Felicity knew Melanie from long ago and that was that.

"You know what annoys me here? It's being called 'Sister'. That's what you English call nurses too, right? I guess that's where the Irish got it — it makes me feel as if I've become a nun myself. In the States, we're called 'Nurse this' or 'Nurse that'. Thankfully, Melanie just calls me Fallon..."

She smiled her thanks at the waiter who deposited her dish before her with a flourish, and picked up the silver cutlery, surprised at its weight, and tasted cautiously: it was not simply, as he had said, a plain roast chicken but a flattened cutlet of tender white meat, with a sauce of mushrooms and cream and wine, and it was delicious.

"So that's what an 'escalope Normandy' is.

"Nothing like the Sunday lunches *we* were given at the convent, even when there *was* chicken, which wasn't that often.

"Listen to me, I sound like an orphan out of Dickens, and there's no reason. Why are you looking so surprised?

"Because I've actually heard of Dickens? Most Americans have.

"They do teach literature over there, you know, and we do read books."

She laughed when he protested and buttered her roll before continuing.

"They were kind to me, the good sisters, in Boston. They looked after Maura and Teddy when I had to study, they helped me with homework, and when they had some they helped with money to buy clothes, so we wouldn't have to dress out of the charity box all the time, and all of them were so proud when I got my nursing degree."

She bit her lips.

"Do you miss them?" he asked, sympathetically and was taken aback when she shook her head with a faraway, determined, look.

No. Not at all. She was glad to have left all that behind, but of course, the problem was now, what was ahead?

"Dessert," he announced, "dessert is ahead. Ice cream?"

"I had a lovely time, really, and thank you," she said as she shook his hand before parting at the end of her funny little soi so as not to risk encountering Belinda. "I'm sorry I was so... unwelcoming ... at first."

"I had a lovely time as well and you were quite right, it was thoughtless of me not to realize I might get you in trouble.

"What will you tell Belinda about disappearing for three hours?"

"That I was browsing at Whiteaways. She'll believe that."

He hesitated. " Would you like to see a film, some evening?

"There are a couple of cinemas that aren't too uncomfortable, and it could be fun. Shall I send you a note at the hospital?"

She smiled. No, at home. Any mail that came to the hospital ended up on Sister Perrine's, the administrator's, desk — "I wouldn't put it past her to open and read it, she's a holy terror, that one."

There was no street number that she had seen, but it was easy to find the house opposite a bench where two old ladies in pyjamas sat all day doing nothing but eating sunflower seeds and spitting the husks.

And if they weren't on the bench, well, just look for the pile of husks.

LAWRENCE'S DIARY
BANGKOK, MAY 22ND

Whoever said a good deed never goes unrewarded knew a thing or two about life, as I am sure Kate would say in that funny Yankee way of hers, because having taken the girl to lunch I now find myself wanting to see her again.

But she is busy all week, she says, and besides, she pointed out, shouldn't I be writing?

Therefore, write I shall, but not before finding out what's playing at the Sala Charoen Thai Theatre.

"TUESDAY, MAY 23RD
Dear Kate,

I am dropping this off myself, as somehow, I could not face asking Fon, Lady Thip's butler, to have someone bring it to a house that looks like a birdcage fronted by piles of sunflower seeds.

Furthermore, I don't know how to say sunflower seeds in Siamese, though I suppose I could have found out.

Sala Charoen Krung is showing "The thin man", with William Powell and Myrna Loy — please say you haven't already seen it.

Ring the number below — there must be a telephone at the hospital — to say which day of the week suits you, and I will pick you up at seven in the car at the corner of Silom Road where we parted Sunday. I thought we might have dinner before as there is a showing at nine. I promise I will have you safely back in the birdcage before midnight.

Meanwhile, I am doing as you ordered and rarely leave my desk. I shall tell you about it.

Yours,

Lawrence"

Kate looked at the note she had luckily been the first to find slipped between the bars of the porch and thought she would need a new way to communicate if Lawrence wanted to keep on inviting her — or she could quite simply tell Belinda and tell her as well to keep her teasing and sly smiles to herself and mind her own business.

She read it once more. A butler? Butlers were for movies, not real people. Who had a butler nowadays?

Friday, she decided. She was doing three night shifts this week, so had both Saturday and Sunday off. She had actually seen "The Thin Man" already, more than two years ago, but that didn't matter. What a pity she had given her green dress to Belinda, although maybe not, it was unlucky.

If Lawrence was working as hard as he said, he would be pleased to have a change, no matter how she was dressed.

SIAMESE TWINS

Conspiracy, conspiracy...

Even when your intentions are pure, precisely because *your intentions are pure and you have only the good of the nation as your motive, does it not, somehow make you feel belittled to watch over your shoulder all the time, to be careful whom you speak to and when?*

Did Pridi not feel this? He must have, or was he simply caught in the excitement of the great Plan?

And the wary courting of those who could be helpful when the time came, the slow, careful, skilful convincing when the righteousness of the cause was so manifest, did he not find that exasperating?

Sidhu Somkrachai, for instance, a naval officer who had studied in Denmark and who had been able to see for himself what a functioning constitutional monarchy could achieve, and whom they had finally been able to win over to the People's Party had wavered and demurred at length. But he had a brother who was an Admiral; so, a useful recruit, obviously, for it dawned on all of them very early on that the small, though growing, group of Promoters could achieve nothing on their own and that they needed support at the highest level.

Barring the Court, obviously, there was only the armed forces.

But what of the Siam they found when they returned one by one from Europe?

The years they had spent abroad had not been kind to the Kingdom.

The Treasury was empty, the late Sandhurst and Oxford-educated King who had died in 1925 had tried some reforms, no doubt, but had ultimately abandoned them in discouragement and preferred to indulge his taste for literature and building lavish palaces.

The worldwide economic collapse at the end of the decade had crushed an already fragile economy, sending the price of rice sky-high, and creating a backlash of enmity against the Chinese rice merchants who were accused of hoarding.

All this Pridi knew for having lived through difficult days before he left for France, and then later, from what his family wrote to him during his years in France.

But this new King, his father also wrote, his friends newly arrived from Bangkok said, everyone said, this new King was different.

Even the Army, who had been so angered by the creation of the Wild Tigers by his predecessor King Vajiravudh, a paramilitary corps that threatened not only the prestige of the Royal Siamese Armed Forces, but their very role and honour, was now pacified by the fact that this monarch chose to serve in their midst upon returning from his training in England.

He had not expected to become King, he had always thought that the title of Crown Prince he carried would be passed along to his brother's firstborn son, he only wanted to serve his country.

And when the mantle of absolute power was thrust upon him as his brother died with no male heir, he vowed to continue to serve his country and not himself.

Lawrence grimaced. That last sentence was a bit over-prosy.

Still, he felt sympathy for the man who was now living out his life in exile in an English manor, caught in the clash of a Revolution he probably secretly approved of. It was said he had become fond of gardening.

Never mind, go on.

Pridi had mixed feelings.

Of course, on the one hand, it was best to have a King sympathetic to the fate of his people, but on the other, wouldn't an absolute, authoritarian one, command greater support for the cause amongst society when the time came?

For society approved of the young King's earnest good will, his modesty, his acknowledgement that he could not govern alone.

At first — but not for long — all applauded His Majesty when he set up the Supreme Council of State and manned it with those competent members of his own family who had already proved their worth, such as Prince Damrong, who had served so ably under the widely revered King Chulalongkorn.

And his reforming efforts did not stop there.

The King, who had himself lived and studied in England for many years, had been brought to understand that in those kingdoms he most admired, England, the Netherlands, Denmark, Sweden, a government operating under a constitution was the best recipe for peace and stability, and thus, prosperity.

And given the fate of the Russian Imperial family, so close in friendship to his own, he also came to realize as well that absolute monarchy was no longer compatible with modern times.

His older brother, King Rama the Sixth, had tried to modernize the Kingdom and endow it with a constitution, but the resistance he encountered was such that he finally gave up in discouragement.

But now that that fate had placed the Crown on his head and the future of the Kingdom and the happiness of its subjects in his hands, he was determined to succeed where his predecessor had failed, and to do so even contracted the services of an American advisor, Raymond Bartlett Stevens, to assist him in this task.

It was said that the King, along with two younger brothers also newly returned from studying in England, spent days working on the draft constitution with this Mr. Bartlett Stevens only to see it rejected by the Supreme Council, whose aim, His Majesty could only conclude, was to continue to live and govern as in centuries past...

"So much the better," cynical Plaek had said. "The constitution shall be our legacy!"

Naturally, Pridi, despite his important position at the Ministry of Justice, was never invited to attend any of the Council's sessions. But he heard things and what he heard encouraged him.

Plaek, who now insisted on using the title name he had chosen for himself — Phibul Songkram, meaning "total war" — was equerry to one of the Council members, and overheard or was even told that the State treasury was in such dire straights that His Majesty had proposed that all the Siamese should be taxed on their income and property.

This outlandish idea was met with anger and outright refusal by the Council members. Why should they, and their families, suffer for the rest of the country?

Instead, the civil service payroll was to be cut.

Whilst wincing, no doubt, for this affected him directly and he was not wealthy, Pridi must have rejoiced at this further step to create general dissatisfaction amongst the still small, but rising, bourgeois classes whose greatest dream was to have their son become a civil servant or to have their daughters marry one.

But sorely as it was felt, such a measure was not enough to alleviate the Crown's finances, and the military budget was slashed next.

His Majesty, fully aware of the dissatisfaction this would generate among those, who, after all, were entrusted with defending the Kingdom, convened a meeting of the top-ranking officers to put the situation before them.

Surely, with their pledge to support King and country, who could better understand the need for this drastic measure?

Picture them, in their spotless uniforms, epaulettes crusted with gold braid, buckles, scabbards and insignia gleaming, standing before their monarch, eyes trained on he who had worn their uniform and served amongst them, unable to read anything from his downcast eyes, hoping against hope that he would announce that the decree was to be rescinded only to hear him say:" I myself know nothing at all about finances, and all I can do is listen to the opinions of others and choose the best...If I have made a mistake, I really deserve to be excused by the people of Siam.

Imagine them, their eyes trained to the floor so as not to betray their disappointment, and yes, their anger.

Leaving in silence, looking neither right nor left, for indeed who might have dared challenge a Royal decree?

But then, in the safety of their offices, or their homes, railing against the Princes who cared for their own lavish lifestyle more than for their Kingdom, some, perhaps, finally spat out their rage.

The King is weak, they must have muttered angrily. If he is not willing to give us the means to guard the country and people of Siam, we must take the matter in our own hands.

And then, and seemingly from nowhere, in markets and teahouses, in the corridors of the Ministries and the exercise yards of military barracks, came whispers of an old prophecy, which no one had dared mention for many years.

It was now resurfacing, albeit in secret, and offered hope to those who despaired: when His Majesty King Rama the First decided to move his capital across the river from Thonburi to Bangkok so as to put a final end to the last reign and attempt to erase the memory of the previous monarch, he decreed that the soul of his new City would be embodied in a Pillar to represent the divine foundation of his rule.

After determining the most propitious location and the most auspicious alignment of the stars, the Royal Geomancers and Astrologers selected the exact place, by the riverbank, the exact moment, immediately after dawn on the ninth day of the waxing moon of the sixth month of the year of the Tiger, and the Court assembled to partake in this ceremony, which was to establish the Duang Muang, the City's Fortune.

In the hazy light, all gazed down at the hole dug the evening before and which now glistened red and muddy. The Chief Astrologer knelt before it and laid down four stones, symbolizing the four guardian spirits protecting the city in the four cardinal directions then carefully placed atop of them a parchment on which he had written magical incantations.

The moment had come, four Brahmin priests chosen amongst the strongest and most devout, raised the Pillar, the trunk of a Javanese cassia, over the hole, poised to plunge it in place to mark the joyful advent of a blessed future.

A gong was rung, then in the following silence, only a swish was heard, and then a gasp of horror and fear: fours large snakes wove their way between the feet of the assembled courtiers, Brahmins and astrologers, and slithered deep into the hole at the exact moment the Pillar was thrust in and down, and the snakes were crushed and killed.

It was a terrible omen, which blighted all hopes for the very future of the City and even the Reign, and the ceremony which was to mark a joyful beginning left a pall of foreboding and fear.

Was this not, people whispered a few years later, the cause of a fire which destroyed the Throne Hall in the Royal Palace, and thus, imperilled the very symbol of the monarchy?

But the astrologers offered a reprieve: because His Majesty had commissioned a new translation of the Tripitaka, the Buddhist scriptures, angels had interceded and offered to delay the inevitable demise of the dynasty by a century and a half. "My line of Kings will last one hundred and fifty years," His Majesty proclaimed.

The ninth day of the waxing moon of the sixth month of the year of the Tiger was the 21st of April, 1782…

Yes indeed, said those who were spreading the rumour…

Exactly one hundred and fifty years ago.

"But is the rumour about this curse enough to make people believe the time has come?" Pridi wondered.

Phibul shrugged. Of itself, no, probably not. But given the mood in the upper ranks of the Army…

One of the malcontents, he surmised, was Colonel Phya Phahol Pholpayuphasena, the Deputy Inspector of artillery.

Colonel Phya Phahol had studied in Germany in his youth; he must share their views. Truly, he must.

Prayun, as a German-trained officer himself, agreed. The Colonel was known for his vexation at the dominating role Princes played in the armed forces.

He had been heard to say, Prayun knew, that in the Imperial German Army, no doubt many aristocrats were commanding officers, but they achieved their rank thanks to their loyalty, training and competence.

Perhaps, was Pridi's reply, remembering not to call his fellow Promoter Plaek.

But if not, if the Colonel's loyalty to the Crown were greater than his dissatisfaction, what then?

He was too important to be approached unguardedly. One misstep, and the Cause, their careers, their very lives would be destroyed.

They thought at length, Pridi, with his eyes half-closed, turning a pencil between his fingers, and Phibul pacing and muttering as was his custom, repeating that if they could not get Colonel Phya Phahol on their side, then it was useless — do you hear me — useless, to go on.

The Party needed the top echelons of the Army to get things started.

This was not France where an uprising of farmers and workers could be organized.

The Army and Navy were their only hope.

"So basically", Pridi noted dryly, "not a revolution. A coup d'état. *"*

He articulated the last two words in French as there was nothing in Siamese that could render the very, unthinkable, concept.

"Call it what you will, it won't happen if there is no one but the middle-rankers involved," Phibul retorted, before Prayun ventured an idea.

He remembered, oh, it was some thirty years ago, he was a child still, Mutti, his mother, had given Colonel Phya German lessons before he left for Berlin to study.

"Why shouldn't I try to meet him, discuss Germany, how he felt when Siamese forces left for Europe prepared to do battle with Germany, and discuss how one feels when one comes back home?"

Why not, indeed?

It seemed safe enough, even for Pridi's caution.

Of course, Phibul could not refrain from gloating when he was able to report that Prayun's careful sounding had proved what he, Phibul, knew all along.

He was right and, and, the good Colonel was not alone in joining the Party. Who did they think was coming with him?

None less one of his fellow students in Germany, Colonel Phya Song Suradet.

Pridi did not indulge in effusive expressions of joy, for such was not his way.

He closed his eyes, briefly brought his crossed hands before his mouth, as if making a thankful prayer, and sighed in relief.

They all knew, and admired, Colonel Phya Song, Director of Education at the Military Academy, considered the best military mind in Siam.

"I think," he whispered as he looked up, "I think we may prevail."

And now, Lawrence thought as he stretched before pulling the cover over his typewriter, all the pieces are in place, and we can start the Revolution.

Chapter IV

When the lights went out in the movie theatre, Kate was finally able to sit back in the plush, slightly musty smelling seat and breathe a sigh of relief.

So far, the evening had been overwhelming, enjoyable, yes, in a way, but ... unsettling.

When she was waiting at the assigned time and place, oblivious to the stares she was getting from passers-by, mopping her forehead and hoping she wouldn't look too sweaty and shiny, she scanned the busy avenue. She didn't know what to look out for — not a samlo, perhaps, but a taxi? — and ignored the long chauffeur-driven car that glided up to the curb while the usual traffic parted respectfully before the gleaming silver hood until it had stopped in front of her and she jumped in surprise when she heard herself called.

From the bits of knowledge gleaned from hearing the talk between her brother and his car-crazy friends, she could tell it was a Packard, the very symbol of luxury on wheels, but before she could catch her breath at that, and at the fact it was driven by a chauffeur for that matter, Lawrence had jumped out and was easing her inside onto the grey leather cushions.

"We aren't late, are we? Have you been waiting long?" He nodded towards a Siamese teenager sitting in front, next to the driver, who bobbed his head shyly as the door closed with barely a sound, cutting them off from the noise and smells of Silom Road, and enclosing them in soft perfumed cool air. "And this is Somchai, but he prefers to be called Sam. He loves going to the cinema — well, the movies, as you call it.

"Say hello to Miss Fallon, Sam."

He dropped his voice to a theatrical whisper, "He's in love with Myrna Loy, but don't tell anybody."

Somchai — Sam — grinned and shook his head and said, in the most perfect English accent she had ever heard, better than Lawrence's, even better than Leslie Howard's in *Berkeley Square*, "actually, I prefer Merle Oberon. Have you seen *The Scarlet*

Pimpernel, Miss Fallon?", and he glowed with pleasure when she said she had and loved it. "But call me Kate, please."

She sat back against the soft leather and looked around in amazement at the little bouquets in crystal vases fastened between the car windows.

"Is this your car?" Sam and Lawrence both laughed.

"No, it belongs to Sam's grandmother, Lady Thip, she insisted that we take this one — she said that you would be more comfortable, what with the air cooler."

Kate shook her head in awe. "I didn't know you could have air conditioning in cars."

Sam nodded proudly. "It's the first in Bangkok, a special order, all the way from New York. My father rode in one in America last year, and immediately ordered one for my grandmother. Now she takes a ride every day.

"We were going to take the Buick, because I love going around with the top down, but I think she doesn't really trust me to drive in Bangkok."

"And rightly so," Lawrence added drily. "So, Kate, dinner - have you ever eaten Chinese food?"

Naturally, she retorted archly, pleased to hear they would not be going anywhere too fancy for her dress.

The Chinese restaurants she had seen here looked cheap and friendly, although she'd never dared enter one — and would these two even consider the kind of place she had in mind?

"We *do* have several Chinese restaurants in Boston, not that I often ate there — and I did visit Chinatown in New York with... with" — she hesitated — "with a friend."

Her voice trailed off, she was fascinated by the street scenes as they made their way though a tangle of carts, men bowed under huge loads, bicycles, samlos and a scattering of women with baskets, outdoor kitchens with smoke billowing above cooking stands and stalls piled with fruit, flowers, some clothes on hangers...

The market seemed to spread all over, occupying the road as well as the sidewalks, and banners with Chinese writing hung from windows and tattered canopies. People were sleeping on mats or directly on the sidewalks, children were playing next to vats of frying oil...

"Wow, I thought New Road was busy..." she murmured, but

Sam corrected her gently.

"Actually, this still is New Road – we call it Charoen Krung. It's just a different neighbourhood from Bangrak, where your hospital is.

"Of course, it's busier around here, nowadays, with so many new arrivals from China. And...," he signalled to the driver to stop, "here we are."

The chauffeur rushed out to hold the door and, cap in hand, help her on to the sidewalk, and she stood there, unsure where to look, sniffing at the many smells, sizzling prawns, frying oil with garlic, pepper, ginger, camphor, incense, and many others, some less pleasant, she couldn't recognize.

Lawrence took her elbow and guided her towards a tiny shop front. Strange reddish things were hanging in the window, and at just behind the door, a very fat man in a stained apron was crashing a vicious looking cleaver onto a board.

"This is it. What, you're surprised?" he teased when they entered the dark, and thankfully, fan-cooled room, that was cluttered with round marble-topped tables and mismatched chairs.

People seemed to be concentrating on their food and gave them not a look. The floor was distinctly dirty, littered with bones, rice and fish heads, and the table, when they sat down, was smeared with traces of brownish gravy and stuck to her bare arms.

On the wall, a stopped grandfather clock was set to half past four forever and a tattered photograph of a former king was so flyblown one could barely make it out. "You were expecting the Oriental?"

Well, not really... She didn't know what to expect, she admitted, shifting back to let a waiter flick a filthy rag over the tabletop. But not this.

He laughed. Neither had he, when Sam's father first brought him here.

"It's one of the oldest Chinese restaurants in Bangkok, and duck is their specialty. Do you like duck?"

She'd never eaten duck before; and the extent of her knowledge of Chinese food was fried rice, sweet and sour pork and chop suey.

Sam looked puzzled. He'd never heard of chop suey.

"But is duck all right, Miss Fallon, sorry, I mean, Kate?

"Shall I choose for all of us?" and beckoned over the owner, a fat, smiling bald man who wore a filthy singlet and showed off all of his gold teeth as he nodded his approval of what Sam was ordering.

Please. She couldn't handle the menu at the Oriental, so Chinese...

It was nothing like the food she'd had before, bewildering, but good, she supposed. Not overly spicy, unlike the stuff the Siamese orderlies had offered her tastes of.

She rather liked the duck despite its gamey taste, and the waiter provided her with a fork and spoon after seeing her pick up her chopsticks and look in dismay at the huge grilled prawns on the platter.

"Which restaurants here do you enjoy, Kate?" Sam asked, and Kate began to explain that she'd only been to one actual restaurant, the Oriental, and really couldn't afford to eat out when Lawrence cut her off, as if sensing her embarrassment.

"Kate is much too busy saving lives, you see.

"No time for gallivanting around restaurants and such. Just like your life will be when you go to Cambridge in a few months."

"Cambridge? Cambridge is next to Boston, that's where I come from. Why are you going to Cambridge?"

Lawrence shook his head. It was another Cambridge, in England. He sighed in mock disapproval. "Why he decided to go to University there is beyond me. Oxford is the only place, really. Poor boy. He's about to waste the best years of his life. Well, he can't say I didn't warn him."

Sam slurped his soup noisily and shrugged. His father went to Cambridge, his closest friend was going to Cambridge, and the headmaster of his school in England had insisted, so....

"What are you going to study?" Kate asked.

"Chemistry. I'm not quite sure what that will lead to, perhaps engineering.

"You know, my family has rubber plantations in the south, and I'm sure that my training could be put to use."

"Well, I'm sure that your training will make you a very boring young man, and what use will that be?" Lawrence quipped.

"More boring than if I studied philosophy and history, like you?

"Not likely!" Sam retorted.

Kate listened to their banter absent-mindedly, suddenly

consumed by a sense of sadness and envy she was unable to repress.

How lucky they were.

If Joe Jr. or Teddy had been able to go to college — or if she had, for that matter!

She could have been a doctor, a surgeon, instead of watching in frustration while women died, and she remembered Brendan always speaking bitterly of "those university fellas who think they're so much better than me," who got the plum reporting jobs at the Herald, and because of whom, he believed, he never got the breaks he felt he deserved.

Furthermore, who studied philosophy, for heaven's sake? Only a guy who knew he'd never need to earn a living.

"Kate? You're a million miles away. Don't you like the food?"

She shook herself. It wasn't their fault they were born into those kinds of families, and it wasn't hers she was not. Life was what it was.

Still, she couldn't refrain from saying she wished she had been able to go to college herself.

"But it never occurred to me, or to anyone else, for that matter, that we were the kind of people who go on to college.

"You learn a trade when — or if — you graduate from high school, that's what you do — and there just wasn't the money, you know?"

Sam cocked his head in surprise, but Lawrence merely nodded and asked what she would have studied.

"Not philosophy, I can tell you that!" she replied with a laugh. "Medicine.

"Yes, I would have tried for medical school — I feel I could have been a good doctor," she added wistfully.

Sam pursed his lips. Wasn't being a doctor too difficult for a woman? Too — how could he put it? — too trying, physically and mentally? Was it even proper?

"Heavens, but you're an old-fashioned dolt, do you realize that?

"My father always says there may be bad doctors, but not one of them is a woman!", Lawrence exclaimed, "Do you think what Kate does isn't trying?

"I, for one, think she would have made a great doctor — but of course, she would not have been sent to Siam and I wouldn't have met her, so that's the only good thing to come out of this really, really unfair world…"

He stopped suddenly, as if in surprise at his own outburst and looked at Kate who stared back, unsure of how to respond, and they both glanced at Sam who was too busy selecting a piece of duck to have noticed the awkward moment.

"Yes, well…," Lawrence muttered, "silver lining man, that's me. I can't be sorry you're here, that's all. I mean — well, you're a very impressive girl, and I've never met anyone like you, so … and I do think you would be a great doctor and it's the world's loss that you aren't."

"Also," Kate replied, striving for a lighter note, "I never would have eaten duck. And maybe someday, I can go to medical school. Who knows?" She smiled and shrugged.

Sam, who had finally put his chopsticks down, volunteered brightly "Find a rich husband, and he can pay for university. That's my advice."

Kate burst out laughing, and Lawrence groaned, — "Lord, you *are* old-fashioned! " — then looked at his watch. "We should go, now."

LAWRENCE'S DIARY
SATURDAY, MAY 27TH,

Interesting evening, yesterday.
Sam discovered that not all Americans are rich, and Kate discovered that some Siamese are.

At one point, I feared that somehow, I may have given her the wrong impression about my reason for inviting her out — twice, admittedly! — when all I am trying to do is to give the girl a bit of fun in her pretty dreary life.

Although — she herself does not seem to find it dreary.

Frustrating, certainly, not to be able to help the poor women she cares for as much as she might wish, but, in fact, exhilarating. She feels useful, and I guess I envy her that.

However now the problem is, I cannot just stop inviting her, that would be rude and I do find her company more pleasing than, say, her friend Belinda's

She is plucky, and forthright, and has no false shame about

her family.

And truth be told, I *am* rather starved for female company. Sam friends' sisters — gorgeous as some of them may be — are either shy and retiring or just a bit too forcefully "modern" and shameless flirts.

Well, when I say starved for female company, am I not being disingenuous, even to myself?

But in all honesty, would it be fair to call "female company" the thrilling, guilt-laced, stolen hours in the night when Busaba slips into my room?

She tiptoes in, drops whatever wrap she is wearing and slides into my bed, with hardly a word exchanged between us.

The only time we really talked was when she had too many pink gins taken and was rather tearful and angry and told me that her husband cares more about the Russian mistress he keeps in Singapore than for her, to which I replied with a sincerity I now regret that I could not understand anyone preferring another woman to her, and that she was the most beautiful creature I had ever seen.

We were alone in the sala looking at the moon, and the next thing I knew, she took my hand and pulled me back to my pavilion.

Somehow, I have the feeling that everybody in the house knows — except for Sam — and that nobody really cares.

I know I am behaving like the worst kind of cad, sleeping with my host's wife — It doesn't bear thinking of, and I must, I must put an end to it.

It was amusing to hear Sam pointing out the amenities of the cinema, Bangkok's most modern and opulent — "Have you ever seen such chandeliers?" — and Kate assenting politely, whereas I am convinced that Boston has several just as luxurious, if not more so.

I would go back to my book about the Revolution of 1932 but need reply to my father's last letter — full of forebodings about the situation in Germany. He is convinced there will be another war, but then, he always believes there will be another war.

To be fair, Cousin Michael told me in Chiang Mai last year that he believes the same, but I do not know — I loathe the very idea of Hitler naturally — God, those disgusting rallies in Nuremberg, appealing the sickest instincts of people's souls — and I am appalled by the plight of Jews in Germany, but I think that Chamberlain and Daladier are too weak to stand up to him and will watch him swallow up Poland as he did the Sudetenland and not lift a finger.

We just need hope that Poland shall prove enough to sate his hunger.

Part of me wants to go back home and be there to fight for King and country if the need arises and feels that I am wasting my time here, writing about events that no one seems to care about, and the other part is far too tempted to give into Father's entreaties to stay here and be safe.

So, and for the time being… the Revolution it is.

SIAMESE TWINS

Colonel Phya Song, the most recent and prestigious member of the Promoters group understood military tactics better than any of them, and the aura conferred by his reputation, rank and experience were such that when he sketched out his plan for what Pridi still insisted was a coup d'état, all deferred to his views — although Phibul was prone to muttering that for a late comer to the revolution, the Colonel was now acting as if it were all his idea.

Still, even he admitted that the safety precautions taken thus far were laughable, and that they had been extremely lucky not to have been found out.

But now, as Colonel Phya Song reminded them, the police were on the alert: it was known that disaffection among the military was rampant and, thanks to the rumour the Promoters had been distilling, royal circles were acutely and nervously aware of the 150th anniversary of the dynasty.

They must all be above suspicion, Colonel Phya Song insisted.

No gathering of more than eight persons at one time — eight was his lucky number, he shrugged — and they must always have a pack of cards already dealt and visible, for who would suspect a party of gambling officers?

And if, by chance, the myriad servants, maids or sweepers were questioned, what could they say but that the officers had met for a card game.

To seize power in Siam, Bangkok was the key: the rest of the country did not matter, and troops garrisoned in the provinces, being removed from the seething ranks in the capital, were likelier to be more loyal to the Crown. Avoiding bloodshed was paramount, if they were to ensure the support of an essentially Buddhist society.

Nothing, nothing, he repeated, was to be committed to paper, and the number of those in the know of the plan was to be kept to an absolute minimum. — "Yes, but —"

— "Don't you think?"

Phibul and Prayun had both jumped to their feet at the same time, but Prayun yielded to his more forceful friend.

"If we tell no one," Phibul reasoned impatiently, "we shall be cutting ourselves off from potential supporters — especially the younger officers who are seeing their hopes for advancement curtailed. The higher ranks already have money, but the second-lieutenants, or those who have recently been made captains — they have younger families, they're ambitious — and probably greedy.

"I know I was," he concluded somewhat defiantly.

The colonel twisted his normally impassive face into a cynical smile.

"Ah, yes. Greedy and ambitious, you say you were, Luang Phibul Songkram.

"So, tell, us, please.

"If you had heard of such a shocking, unthinkable plot, when you were a young, ambitious second-lieutenant with no money, no family connections to speak of, and a reputation for being, perhaps, rather self-serving — Oh yes, I had heard of you well before you won that scholarship...," he raised his hand to stop Phibul who had flushed an angry red and was sputtering furiously, "Would you have not gone to your commanding officer to denounce this plot and gain the notice of the higher-ups, and an immediate path to advancement, with, most certainly, an appointment to serve close to the Crown?

"Would you have not?"

Phibul sat back down, pursed his lips and did not reply while all the others nodded reflectively.

But Prayun was still not convinced. "What about those who are idealists, and sincerely want only what is best for our country?"

"I don't trust them, no more than you should," was the curt reply, met with a gasp from all but Pridi who, hands folded before his mouth, was listening intently.

"Why should we?" the Colonel continued.

"Those who have not travelled, who have never seen how other countries govern themselves, who have been told forever that the King is all wise and all powerful and is akin to a God....

"Well, who will their idealism and their loyalty go to? The Crown.

"And, therefore, they shall report us."

Meanwhile, as all those present reported, the mood of the city, among the general ranks of the armed forces, and the civil service, was ripening. Not to mention the upper echelons of the government itself.

Even in the most exalted circles, amongst those Princes whom the Colonels, Captains and others were railing, dissatisfaction and rivalry were roiling.

The former Minister of War himself, Prince Borowadet, after sharp words with the Minister for the Interior, Prince Boriphat, had submitted his resignation in protest at the sharp budget cuts, believing that his friendship with His Majesty would enable him to prevail.

Instead, he was thanked for his service and, seething, sought like-minded officers to assist him in taking revenge for this blow to his pride.

Amongst those who could best help in stirring discontent within the military, he reasoned, were those who had trained abroad, and decided, as had the Promoters, to discreetly approach Colonel Phya Phahol.

"But I turned him down, courteously, of course" the Colonel announced with a shrug.

"He seeks only to advance himself, and all the other princes would be bound to find out and act against him — and therefore us.

"However," and Colonel Phya Song nodded his smirking approval as his friend spoke, "... If we were to make it known that His Highness is plotting something, it might divert attention from our own purposes."

And of course, the prophecy was now being mentioned every day, by everyone, and the Court was on edge, because of the prophecy itself, and because of the effect it was having on the population.

"I heard that His Majesty was constructing that new bridge to counter the effects of the curse," Prayun offered with a satisfied smile.

Yes, they had all heard that.

Well, of course, not only was the King born in the Year of the Serpent, but his four closest aides were as well.

The four serpents.... Come back to seek revenge.

Phibul, who had his entries in princely circles, added that those four aides were actually using Red Cross donations to construct a new medical building dedicated to the four martyred snakes.

Pridi shook his head in dismay.

When would the Siamese learn to rid themselves of such foolish superstitions? he asked, but both Colonel Phya Song and Colonel Phya Phahol frowned, Phahol defiantly crossing his arms covered in sacred, protective tattoos, his open shirt revealing a string of sacred amulets hanging from his neck.

The prophecy was not foolish.

Just because Luang Pradit had studied abroad, he could not dismiss the weight of the omen handed down by divine intervention.

How, pray, could he explain the fact that it was this year precisely that the plan to overthrow absolute Royal rule would come to pass?

And just because the Promoters had all made sure that all circles of society, whether high or low, were reminded of the curse, did not mean that it was untrue.

Chapter V

Kate put down the typewritten pages on her lap and wrinkled her nose.

"I don't know," she said finally. "But why ask me?

"I don't know about books, especially political ones. There must be somebody who could give you better advice."

Lawrence took the sheaf of paper from her, and she crossed her legs and leaned back in the rattan armchair, gazing around at the lovely open sided and fretted pavilion and its huge blue and white china urns with tumbling sprays of purple and white orchids, then turned her eyes towards the busy river rushing swift and red towards the sea.

Threatening monsoon clouds were billowing overhead, and the skies were darkening with a promise of rain.

"This — what did you call it? — it's kind of like a gazebo—anyway, it's really pretty," she smiled. "The whole house is swell, actually.

"I've never seen anything like it — It was very nice of Lady Thip to invite me to lunch, I really enjoyed being in an actual Siamese home.

"And by golly, Lady Thip and Lady Busaba speak amazing English.

"Okay, Lady Busaba went to an English boarding school, she said, but Lady Thip learned it with a governess and has never set a foot outside Siam.

"I can't believe it!"

"From what I've heard her speak, her French still is quite good as well — not only from what she learned from my grandmother, she also had another French teacher afterwards, at home, when she left the Palace before she married," Lawrence replied, leafing through his manuscript with a rueful look.

"Girls of that circle were then — and are still now in fact — a lot more marriageable if they spoke foreign languages and were 'westernized' and therefore modern. Funny, isn't it?

"And this is called a 'sala'. Most houses have one to sit out and catch the evening breeze. I always think of bad brass music when I hear the word 'gazebo'."

At the old lady's suggestion, they had moved to the sala to have coffee, but before, while Sam took Kate for a tour of the house, drowning her in explanations about antique pottery and paintings and imported furniture, Lady Thip noted drily that the young American whom they could hear praising everything with sincere sounding admiration was quite charming — but terribly defenceless.

"So, do not break her heart, young Lawrence. Yes, yes," she cackled, "I know what you shall say — she's just a friend."

Lawrence raised his eyebrows and smiled. Kate was actually a lot tougher than she looked. "It may well be the other way around."

He had been surprised when Lady Thip suggested that he ask his "new friend" for Sunday lunch — "Lawrence", she had said quite firmly, "you have invited this young lady to lunch, dinner and the cinema many times. You see her several times a week.

"Somchai says she is very pleasant and, aside from you, knows no one in Bangkok. Would it not be the polite, and indeed, the kind thing to introduce her to a Thai family?"

He had rather suspected her — rightly, he was sure — of ulterior motives, such as delicately pressing home to Busaba the very hopelessness of their affair and that Lawrence was to engage with his own kind — younger, Western, and single.

If so, he, Lawrence, could only approve, and was markedly more attentive to Kate than he had been ever before, even suggesting that she read his manuscript after lunch.

Kate, rather overwhelmed by Fon, the butler, and by the procession of maids proffering dishes of Siamese specialties prepared with a farang palate in mind, was busy expressing her delight in the food and effusive in her gratitude at being invited and she had accepted his offer with a cursory "Sure. I don't mind", totally unaware — as of course she would be, how could she know he never, never let anybody read what he wrote until he was completely satisfied?

Busaba, besides raking over Kate's dress with a slightly amused look, was thankfully her usual languid and aloof self, but not unfriendly.

Pichit, of course, was in Singapore, which meant that Sam, absent his father's critical presence, was ebullient and chatty under the adoring gaze of his mother and his grandmother.

He was poking fun at what was called a "cultural mandate" issued by the Prime Minister the day before and in which it had been announced that the country's name had been changed from Siam to "Thailand".

"What's the point?" he chortled. "We've always called our country 'Muang Thai' in Siamese — That means 'Land of the Free', he added for Kate's benefit.

"But that's Phibul's specialty — coming up with grandiose ideas that make him sound as if he's saving the nation, while all he's doing is forcing banks and stores to change their name — did you hear the Siam Society itself is now supposed to be called the Thailand Research Society?

"Really, who cares what other countries call us?"

"You really think that's all he's doing?" Lawrence asked.

"Muang Thai doesn't just mean 'Land of the Free'. It also means 'Land of the Thai' — not of the Chinese. And to prove his point, he's closing Chinese newspapers in Bangkok, and most Chinese schools, not to mention imposing crippling taxes on Chinese businesses."

Sam shrugged, "I still think it's a ridiculous idea", before Lady Thip interrupted with a question to Kate about the hospital and gently encouraged her to describe her first impressions of Siam — "or rather 'Thailand', I suppose I should say now." she added with a laugh.

What, Kate had never been to the beach since she'd arrived?

They would invite her to the house in Hua Hin.

"The beach there is lovely," Busaba contributed. "Do you have beaches where you come from?"

Kate nodded, somewhat wistfully.

The Cape — Cape Cod, she clarified, very close to Boston... It was lovely there too, she said, her eyes going very bright with unshed tears.

Lady Thip, noticing, took her, patted her arm. "It's normal to be homesick, sometimes. I'm sure Somchai will be very homesick when he gets to Cambridge."

Sam grinned, "I won't, Khun Ya! Never, ever! But I'll miss the food here!"

So, Lawrence reflected, watching Kate turn her eyes once more upon the river, this lunch he had somewhat dreaded when the idea was mooted, had gone better than he had hoped – except of course for the fact she did not like his book.

"Tell me – no, don't say you know nothing about books, just tell me what you think is wrong, besides the fact that you find it boring."

"Well...," Kate pursed her lips. It wasn't boring, exactly.

"I mean, it was kind of interesting to read about these people going to study in France, and how they met in secret, and all that...

"The snakes' curse, too, I enjoyed that bit.

"It's just that when you write about them, they're just... well, they seem dead, you know."

Lawrence winced.

She really knew how to cut deep. But she was right.

This girl, who claimed to know nothing about books, had put her finger right on the problem with just one word. His characters *did* seem dead.

"And all those names...," Kate continued, oblivious to his grimace. "Prince Boro this, and Prince Bori that – They're just too confusing.

"Those colonels – well, their names are pretty alike too, so it's hard to keep them apart.

"And the man, the officer who liked nice uniforms, he's the Prime Minister now, right?

"The one Sam and you were talking about at the table, the guy whose picture is everywhere? We even have him on the walls of the hospital."

Lawrence laughed and nodded.

Indeed, in the past few months, all public buildings, banks, and schools had taken down the official portraits of His Majesty King Rama the Seventh, and instead of replacing them with a picture of the very young King Ananda, Rama the Eighth, who was now studying in Switzerland, Phibul had decreed that his own saturnine likeness should be displayed to preside over practically every public space in the city.

"So he's pretty much alive, isn't he? And the other guy?"

"Pridi?"

"Yes, him. He sounds nice enough, like he cares for the people here, but, in your story, they're not real, you know? Make them real.

"And when they decide — all the plotters, the two scary colonels — to go ahead and make a move, tell it like it is, make me feel it, like I'm there with them. What did the King say, what did he do?

"I mean, if it were a movie, it would be exciting, wouldn't it?

"The card game, acting natural…

"Talk me through it, just like you're telling me about a movie."

He frowned in concentration and leaned back in his armchair, tented his fingers and took a deep breath.

"All right. I'll try. Here goes."

SIAMESE TWINS

Finally, the day Siam was to be transformed for ever was nigh.

His Majesty was away from Bangkok, in Hua Hin, at his recently constructed seaside palace which he had named Klai Kangwon — "far from worries" …

His timing was perfect, as all agreed during a meeting a few nights earlier, because one of the major disagreements among the plotters was the need to take the King captive, which was Colonel Phya Song's original plan.

No, no, no, it was impossible, unthinkable, most of the Promoters said.

One could not treat a King that way. "The King? Prisoner?"

It was an insult to the Crown.

In fact, it led Colonel Phya Ritthi Akaney, commander of the First Artillery Regiment and Phya Song's closest friend, to walk away from the project, claiming that although he agreed with the Promoters' aims, any attempt to take the monarch into custody would lead inevitably to violence and might endanger His Majesty's life.

"And that is something I am not prepared to risk," he stated in final tones. "Until you find another solution, I'm out."

Pridi tended to agree, but not for the same reasons.

He believed that in a society still imbued with the values of respect for the monarchy, the move could only backfire.

"Well, the question no longer arises," Phya Song retorted, "but we must act speedily. The plan is in place, and we can proceed. Two days from now, June 24th. 5 am? Approved?"

In the lamplight, he scanned the faces of the seven others.

Pridi was as usual impassive, Phibul was biting his lips and nodding, Sindhu had nervously joined his hands over his mouth. Prayun's eyes were downcast and he was toying with the cards that he had been dealt in accordance with the usual excuse for their meeting.

All the members of the Promoters' inner circle were trembling in anticipation, and excitement — and for some, with a fear they were attempting to hide.

Who knew what their fate might be two days hence?

Prison, certainly, if they were to fail. The loss of … everything. Their lives, possibly. Their families dishonoured, imprisoned as well, if history were a lesson… But…

But… If they were to succeed! Their names would go down in history!

The Colonel rose heavily from his chair and began pacing the room as he once more sketched out the various actions he had planned, and as always, Pridi marvelled at the organizational and military genius of the man, who kept the list in his head and seemed to have thought of every detail, every possible obstacle and the ways to counter it if it arose.

"The Navy's involvement is essential.

"I have already made sure there would be warnings about a Chinese uprising to have it in a state of alert, along with the Army, the order to be ready to move will be given tomorrow night.

"Sindhu, please, tell us the naval watch officers know what to do."

Sindhu nodded. The watch officers — most of them were junior, and friends of his — would wait until the senior officers had left for the night, and they would begin.

One of his friends was in command of a gunboat, and he would have it slip its moorings, move upriver, and in the dark, position himself to train his guns on Prince Boriphat's palace, if necessary.

Meanwhile, he, Sindhu, had mobilized 500 sailors to empty the Arsenal — except of course, it would not be to quell a Chinese uprising but to use the weapons to capture the Throne Hall at dawn.

Colonel Phya Song nodded.

He himself had arranged to bring all his cadets to the grounds in front of the Throne Hall at 6am. to participate in a training exercise, along with troops from several military units, claiming they were needed to provide practical demonstrations.

"Prayun? The Post and Telegraph office? Is all ready?"

The answer was yes. With the help of the Navy, he would commandeer the Post Office, and make sure all the Palace and Ministries' telephone lines were disconnected.

Pridi added that various groups of civilian Promoters would be told to keep watch *in front of the Princes' palaces, to prevent escapes.*

"Yes, well," Phya Song replied somewhat dismissively. "No harm in that, I suppose.

"But this is a military operation. It's not that I don't trust the motives of civilians, I don't trust their discipline.

"Tasnai, I want you and your team to come here on the 24th at 4 am to be given your final orders.

"And now, it's time you all left, in small groups. Don't forget to talk loudly as if we'd just had one of our usual drunken card games. We can't afford to give rise to suspicion now."

Who talked?

Was it a servant, a fellow Promoter who'd had a change of heart? No one knew. Despite Colonel Phya Song precautions and cult of secrecy, word got out somehow that something momentous was afoot.

Who to blame? None of the eight who met on the night of the 22 of June, certainly.

But someone betrayed them.

In the late evening of June 23rd, the Director General of the Police submitted to Prince Boriphat, Minister for the Interior a request to arrest persons included in a list he presented along with a note describing the "strong possibility of a conspiracy against the Throne".

Although the list did indeed include most of the names of the inner circle of the Promoters, there were no details as to what was to happen, when it might happen, or indeed if it might happen.

The Minister perused the list, raised his eyebrows at seeing some of the names, well-known, well-connected. "How could those men be immediate threats?" he asked.

He looked down at the list of names again and frowned.

Certainly, there must be some mistakes there, he pointed out in a cutting tone, and there was such a thing as being over-zealous.

One should not see a revolutionary under every bed.

Yes, granted, he conceded, some of the younger officers returned from Europe might have acquired subversive political ideas, such as this Pridi Banomyong, or Luang Praditmanutham as his title now went.

A most capable man, or so he heard, but one to be watched carefully.

The Director General nodded, but having been rebuked once, refrained from voicing an opinion as Prince Boriphat continued from the list, his voice acid.

Colonel Phya Song...

Surely, the Crown had no more loyal servant.

Yes, he held card games in his home. He was a gambler.

Well, who wasn't?

Or Major Phibul Songkram, who received the title of Luang from His Majesty — Impossible. Everybody knew he was far too ambitious to ever get mixed up in anything seditious.

Young Tasnai Niyomsuk — now he was a different matter.

Why, furthermore, he mused, did one always say "young Tasnai Niyomsuk"? He must be at least thirty-two or thirty-three, by now.

But he still had that boyish manner... A follower, not a leader. Easy to see how he might be steered the wrong way.

The Prince sighed and shook his head.

All these promising men, the hope of the nation, celebrated for their abilities, and sent to study abroad by the Crown, so as to enable them, once they returned home, to better serve the Crown.

Could any of them be so disloyal, so... so ... ungrateful?

"Perhaps, Your Royal Highness, perhaps. If we could question some of them, we could make sure."

Prince Boriphat pursed his mouth and considered.

It was getting late, he was tired, and the monsoon rains had been unrelenting all day. He wanted nothing more than to get back to his palace and rest.

Very well, he decided. Certainly, this Pridi must be called in to be questioned. Perhaps Tasnai as well.

Tomorrow.

There was clap of thunder, a spiralling wind rose, and the rain began to batter the thatched roof of the sala, splashing the orchids and Lawrence, who had been pacing around as he recounted the last moments before the revolution pulled an armchair away from the cascading water.

The skies were so dark and the rain so heavy that Kate felt they were enclosed and hidden in the shelter of the sala, cut off from the house, in a separate world, and even more so when Lawrence lowered the split bamboo blinds that began to rattle in the gusting wind.

"So," he asked, "how am I doing so far?"

She cocked her head. "Better. I still don't really ... well, feel it.

"But I'm impressed you remember all the details, you're like that Colonel, everything at your fingertips."

She rose to push a blind aside, the river was almost invisible behind the curtain of rain, and the house had vanished. All she could see were the frangipani trees twisting in the wind.

"Wow, I don't think I've ever seen it rain like this, there's been the odd storm since I got here, but no worse than we get at home. Is this the famous monsoon they all talk about?"

"Yes, it was a bit late this year.

"And now, it will probably rain every day, usually in the evening, until November, and you had better get used to carrying an umbrella with you at all times. "

He took off his glasses and wiped them on his shirt.

"That's better. I can see you now. My specs always get misted up when it rains.

"We may as well stay here until it stops, we'd get drenched if we tried to run to the house. Let's pull your armchair closer to the centre, there's still some rain coming through."

"Shall I go on, you're not bored?"

She shook her head, no, she wasn't bored, and as she rose to help pull the armchair their eyes met and suddenly, he cupped her face in both hands and kissed her hard on the mouth.

Then before she could say anything, ignoring her gasp, he released her, began pacing again, and announced: "Okay, now it's happening. Listen."

SIAMESE TWINS

The Promoters were lucky.

It was not raining that morning of June 24th, which would have been a bad omen, and Tasnai, reporting to Colonel Phya Song's home in the dark before dawn, breathed the fresh, cool air with pleasure.

All fear had gone, what would happen would happen, and it this were to be his last morning of freedom, so be it.

He and his team of cavalry officers were told of the latest reports of the situation in the various points of the city and received the final instructions, and if some of the younger officers found the Colonel terse and forbidding, they were in too much awe of him to think it out of the ordinary.

The meeting point was to be near the barracks of the First Cavalry Regiment of the Royal Guards, which served as a depot for most of the armoured vehicles in Bangkok.

"No," Lawrence explained, before she could ask, "they didn't use horses anymore, except for ceremonies and parades."

The barracks were an essential target, and Tasnai and his team charged in, shouting about a Chinese uprising further down the river.

The officer on watch was sleeping and received a virulent dressing down — "You were asleep? How dare you be so derelict in your duty, when the city is threatened with violence! I shall report you to your commanding officer!" screamed Tasnai, trying to repress the nervous snigger he could feel bubbling in this throat — while the soldiers of the regiment, driven from their sleeping mats by the bugle call, began to mill around, still dazed and confused, putting on their uniforms and gathering their weapons.

The gates were opened, and Phya Song and other Promoters rushed in, all shouting about the Chinese uprising, as Phya Phahol, who had brought metal cutters, broke the padlock of the arsenal.

"No, no, wait. What is this?

"On whose orders, Colonel, are you taking control of my men?"

The commander of the regiment, still buttoning his tunic, pushed his way up to Colonel Phya Song. And they stood facing each other, almost nose to nose, while the officers present held their breath.

Phya Song did not bother answering. He just nodded towards a fellow instructor at the Cadet Staff College, Colonel Phra Prasat Pittiyayuth, who stepped forwards to announce to the commander that he was taking him into custody and that any resistance would be useless.

Those who knew him well, and Phya Song, who was his closest friend, in particular, could hear the note of nervousness in his voice, a tension they all shared.

Arresting a fellow officer who was doing his duty of protecting the realm was the first true act of treason of the day, and Tasnai no longer felt like laughing.

A moment of silence, a pause while the future of the country hung in the balance.

Then the commander nodded, and surrendered himself while Phya Phahol resumed handing over pistols, ammunition and shells and the soldiers, trained to obedience, fell in place behind Tasnai and him and climbed into the armoured cars to make their way to the Throne Hall.

There, all was confusion.

The news of the uprising was being circulated, but no one had confirmed it, and the cadets mingled with the troops who had been brought under the excuse of providing practical demonstrations and the wildest rumours were whispered, contradicted and embellished by the Promoters.

The sun was almost high, and it was already getting hot when Tasnai and Colonel

Phya Phahol alit from their car.

Tasnai ran a finger under his tight, high uniform collar and swallowed.

"What now?" he whispered, almost to himself, but Phya Phahol heard him, and gave him a withering look.

"Follow me!" he barked in his parade order voice, and, moving towards a tank parked at the forefront of the grounds, he clambered upon it, raised his arms, and waited for silence.

Gradually, all the voices hushed and still, he waited, smiling, and Tasnai could only wonder how, how he managed to bring that unruly, worried crowd to hang on his, as yet unsaid, words.

"Soldiers of the Kingdom! Listen to me!

"I am bringing the most important news you will hear in your lifetime!

"Absolute monarchy has come to an end!

"We shall continue to honour and serve our great king, but no longer shall His Majesty be given every power to rule the Kingdom.

"There shall be a Constitution, ensuring all Siamese enjoy their rights!

"Rejoice with us!

"Long live the King, long live the Constitution!"

Several Promoters, strategically scattered in the crowd, raised a cheer which was followed, timidly at first, then resoundingly, although Tasnai, standing at the foot of the tank, overheard a soldier mutter to his friend that he didn't know what a "constitution" was.

"Cheer anyway", his friend advised. "You don't want to stand out, might get in trouble."

Phya Phahol came down from the tank and mopped his sweaty forehead.

"That was the biggest bluff of my life, and it went better than I expected," he admitted ruefully. "Now let's just hope things are going well elsewhere!"

Elsewhere, the situation was still evolving.

The Post Office had been overrun, and the telephone lines disconnected.

No alarm could be raised that way.

Phra Prasat, along with several senior promoters had commandeered drivers and cars to carry out what was probably the riskiest move yet and arrest Prince Boriphat and other Ministers.

They knew all of the men they wanted to take into custody would be armed, no doubt, and protected by their personal bodyguards. On this confrontation depended success or failure.

The civilians Pridi had assigned to watch in front of Prince Boriphat's palace nodded in silence when the command car pulled up. All was quiet.

No one had tried to come in or out.

The guard posted at the gates, awoken by Phra Prasat's hammering on the wood, peered through the eyehole then swung the doors open and bowed, assuming no doubt that the officer in his dress uniform and decorations could only be coming on official business.

His Serene Highness emerged in a hastily knotted phasin, —

"That's what you would call a sarong, the cloth they wear around their waist." Lawrence explained, noticing Kate's questioning look

— and seeing Phra Prasat standing there, without bowing or wai-ing and with his hand on his pistol in its holster, went pale with anger, then flushed a dusky red when he heard he was under arrest.

"It is I who should have had all of you all arrested last night, when I was warned about the plot," he spat venomously. "To think I trusted in your loyalty to the Crown."

"Our loyalty to the Crown is not in doubt," Phra Prasat replied, pulling himself up to stare the Minister of the Interior in the eye, further enraging the Prince who was unused to such flagrant and brazen disrespect, "but our loyalty to the Kingdom and its subjects is greater."

The Prince returned his stare with contempt.

"Will you at least allow me to go put on some clothes, or do you want me to go almost naked?"

Phra Prasat smirked. He had long waited for this day and was fully enjoying the humiliation he was inflicting on the once all-powerful man.

"Do you imagine I would let you leave the room to try to escape?

Have your servants bring clothes, and dress in front of us."

As the Prince fumbled with his buttons he kept on staring at the Colonel balefully and, once he was fully dressed, he pronounced himself ready to go.

"Remember the French revolution," he said finally, turning to walk down the stairs, "and as went Marat, Robespierre and Danton, so shall you go.

"Mark my words, Colonel.

"Revolutions turn against those who instigate them."

"Marat, Robespierre and Danton were French revolutionaries who finally got caught up in the violence they unleashed. Robespierre and Danton were guillotined, and Marat assassinated." Lawrence clarified for Kate's benefit, and the contrast between his everyday voice and the thundering and threatening tone he had used to speak as Prince Boriphat made her stifle a giggle as she nodded.

"I'm sure I should know that. Go on. This is getting exciting."
He grinned, took a breath and continued.

Although some forty persons were taken into custody that morning and brought to be kept under guard at the Throne hall, one however, Prince Purachatra, Minister for Communications, did manage to escape, make his way to the railway station, and once there, though gasping for breath, attempted to show by his behaviour that although it might appear somewhat unusual, he was doing nothing untoward.

He commandeered a railway engine with its engineer to slip away to Hua Hin, a journey of almost ten hours by train, to warn His Majesty after trying fruitlessly to raise the seaside palace on the telephone but finding his call cut off after his first, confused words.

And by eight am, it was over.

The promoters had won, Khana Ratsadon had carried the day, the People's Party was now the governing body of the realm.

And as did Tasnai when he arrived that morning on the grounds before the Throne Hall, all were wondering: "What happens now?"

Not so Pridi.

This was what he had wanted, this was what he had dreamed of, and prepared for all those years, beginning in that cold and damp hotel room in Paris. This was a new Siam.

He had gone to his office perhaps somewhat earlier than usual, but still making sure his behaviour appeared normal, and once there, he sat, head in hand, waiting for a message to be brought to him.

He knew the telephone was not working, but in itself, that would raise no alarms in Bangkok, where at best, telephones were unreliable, more so during the monsoon season.

He could hear a bird screeching, and outside his window, the white squirrels that seemed to inhabit most of the trees in the city were dancing on the branches and electric lines.

Finally, he was brought a note scribbled by Phibul, who had been put in charge of detaining the princes and Ministers at the Throne Hall, and, who, as he wrote with glee, was fully enjoying the task.

"Set the distribution in motion!" the note continued, and, with a deep sigh of relief, he had his office boy bring notes to other Promoters to trigger the elaborate system devised over the past days to hand out leaflets informing the people of the end of absolute monarchy, and which were to be distributed throughout markets, near the main temple gates and all other places where crowds congregated.

And as he sat and waited, he recited to himself the words on the leaflet, the

'Manifesto of the Khana Ratsadon' as it was called, into which he had poured his soul, for just as he knew that Colonel Phya Song was the undisputed master in creating the conditions for this coup, he knew that he, Pridi, was the master in shaping the words to ensure its acceptance by the people of Siam, and he believed, no he knew, that in the end, words were the most powerful weapon.

All of his training, all of his passion — and, he admitted to himself, all the lessons learned in a France still deeply influenced by her own revolutionary rhetoric — had flowed in the message of the Manifesto which proclaimed that the King had failed his people, by appointing incompetent relatives, "who treated the people as servants and slaves to sweat blood".

His Majesty could remain on his throne, it continued, if and only if, he accepted to cede power to a constitutional government.

Otherwise, and the threat was clear, and this was also the part which had given rise to the most vehement debates amongst the Promoters, leading some to actually wash their hands of the whole affair — "the King would be considered as a traitor to the nation and the country would then have a head of state who would be a commoner elected for a limited period of time."

"Wow!" Kate breathed," Really? What did the King say?"

"Pretty inflammatory stuff, isn't it?" Lawrence smiled. "Amazing he got away with putting that in a leaflet that was distributed throughout the city."

He raised a blind and peered out. "Look, it's not raining any more, shall we go back to the house?"

Kate shook her head.

No, she wanted to hear what the King said. "If we go back to the house, Lady Thip is sure to be there, and Sam, and they'll talk, and I'll never get to know.

"Okay, you'd tell me someday, but I want to hear now.

"Please?"

She mock-fluttered her eyelashes at him and pretended to pout.

"Well, wow, as you'd say... I feel quite overwhelmed by your enthusiasm. So, my guys, still to quote you, are no longer dead?"

Kate looked at him sternly and tapped her foot. "I'm waiting."

"No, you're not, just now," Lawrence retorted, "you're flirting with me, Nurse Fallon.

"Not that I mind, you know, but as it's the first time I wanted to point it out..."

She was startled, and blushed, embarrassed. "I most certainly was not."

"You were so.

"And you're obviously out of practice."

She tossed her head, annoyed with both him and herself.

"You're right about that. I haven't flirted in years, and you're the last person I would I flirt with, anyway, so don't get any ideas.

"Now can I hear the end of the story?"

"You're sure you wouldn't rather keep flirting with me?

"Oh, all right, if you insist."

"I do insist," she replied shortly, still surprised and displeased with herself.

Had she really slipped back into a behaviour she had vowed to put away for good, and which led only to heartbreak?

And with someone like Lawrence, who was so out of reach for a girl like herself? What had got into her?

It must be the heady feeling of being invited to this amazing house, and the rain, and all the wealth and easiness, she thought.

And of course, that kiss.

But it meant nothing, she was sure. He was just excited at performing for me... or perhaps... well, she didn't know.

Anyway, stop it.

He mustn't get any ideas, just because he's rich and I'm a poor nurse, it doesn't mean I'm easy or cheap.

"The King?" she prompted him, and with a laugh, he obliged.

His Majesty was playing golf in Hua Hin, and he'd just reached the eighth hole —

"No kidding? she asked. "There was a revolution going on, and he was playing golf? "

"No kidding. Remember, he didn't know. And his palace was called 'Far from worries', so he wasn't worrying. Stop interrupting, now."

The people with him were all enjoying the beautiful day and the cool breezes, and there were calls of "Oh, good shot, Your Majesty!" when a servant from the palace rushed up, running at top speed up the greens, with an urgent message.

Something had happened in Bangkok, a phone call had come through somehow, but nobody knew more than that.

The King and the two princes who were with him returned to the Palace, attempting to call the various ministries, Prince Boriphat's house, everywhere...

All they got was a busy signal.

"Possibly, the phones are out of order," one prince ventured.

Or disconnected, another added, in a worried voice.

All they could do was wait.

Someone tried the usual "No news is good news" saw everybody offers in such cases, and they wandered aimlessly throughout the ornate, airy rooms, gazed at the sea shimmering in the midday haze, picked at the food that was brought to them, and waited and wondered.

For hours.

Until a car pulled up and Prince Purachatra jumped out, dishevelled, sweat and soot stained and with such an ominous face that suddenly, they all understood, and his tumbled, breathless words only confirmed their worst fears…

"A counter coup, that's what is needed! Give the plotters no mercy, and retake control of the army," shouted one of the princes.

"No point," sighed another, "all the senior officers control the troops.

"My advice is to flee to Malaya, Your Majesty. Remember what happened to the Russian Imperial family.

"The British would doubtless offer you protection."

But the King remained silent, and in a state of shock. How had his Kingdom turned against him?

He had had only the best intentions in assuming the Crown.

How had this happened?

An hour went by, and another. And finally, a messenger from the Hua Hin Post Office was shown in, eyes downcast, clutching a telegram that none of the palace servants had wanted to relieve him of.

He was quickly shooed away as His Majesty opened it and scanned it at length then handed it to a prince who read it out loud in a disbelieving voice.

After announcing the end of the absolute monarchy, the message said that if the King were not prepared to remain on the throne under a constitutional form of government, another royal prince would be appointed in his stead.

A gun-boat was being dispatched to Hua Hin to bring His Majesty back to Bangkok if the offer of Khana Ratsadon were accepted.

It continued by stating that if any member of Khana Ratsadon were to be injured, the princes held hostage would suffer the consequences.

And it was signed by Phya Phahol, Phya Song and Phya Ritthi, who called themselves the Bangkok Military Command.

"Traitors!" someone muttered viciously, and there was a general gasp, except from His Majesty, who remained deep in thought.

Constitutional monarchy…

Of course, he would remain on the throne!

Had he not always aspired to endow the country with a constitution and had he not himself attempted to have one drafted with the help of his American advisor, Mr Bartlett Stevens, only to have it rejected by the reactionary princes of the Supreme Council?

But to have it forced upon him...

Was this not an insult to everything he had done thus far, and if he had failed, well, was it his fault or that of a country not yet ready to hear him?

"I shall reply that I am happy to remain as constitutional monarch, as this is what I have always wanted," he announced finally. "But I shall not, no, I shall not return to Bangkok by gun-boat.

"I am not the prisoner of Khana Ratsadon, and I shall return to Bangkok as I came, by train.

"They say tomorrow, I say the day after tomorrow.

"I am still the master of my time, although, it would now seem, of very little else."

After declaiming those last words in the bitter and resigned voice he'd used to play the part of the King, Lawrence wiped the despondent look off his face, took off his glasses, grinned and bowed, hand on his heart, then threw himself into the armchair as Kate applauded.

"That was great!

"But is that how it happened?

"How do you know what the King said, or anybody else?"

Lawrence stared at her, surprised.

"I don't. I just — well, imagined what was said.

"I mean, I know what happened, the facts, but to come up with what people said, or thought, I just apply... logic.

"What would someone like the King say when he was presented with this ultimatum, forcing him to accept what he'd wanted all along, but making him look weak?

"And the same for Pridi, or Phibul..."

He sat down next to her and attempted to explain.

"You develop this ... image about the characters you're writing about, and they begin to become ...," he hesitated, " they become real, for want of a better word.

"Or at least, real to me, not that they're not real, but it's as if I know them. Does that make sense to you?"

She nodded uncertainly.

"For instance, if I were writing about this afternoon, this is what the Kate in my book would be thinking," he said, teasingly, "I can't be sure, of course, but part of her would be wondering why I kissed her.

"Does he think I'm easy, she would be asking herself, or was he just carried away, and now is he regretting it?

"Why did she flirt with him, did she give the wrong impression — and may I add that you're pretty bad at it, Miss Fallon, leave that kind of behaviour to girls like your friend Belinda, it doesn't suit you — and what happens next?"

She frowned and blushed, then looked down at her feet.

"It would never occur to me that you might regret it, and I don't know how good a writer you are, but as a mind reader, you could probably make a living at the fair," she replied sharply. "And what did happen next?

"Why is the King in exile now? It's the same one, right? Did he refuse at the last minute, and did they choose someone else?"

He took her hand. "What happened next is a subject for another time.

"Don't be angry.

"No, I don't regret kissing you, and why I did is because you just looked irresistible.

"You're a very attractive girl, Kate Fallon."

She shrugged and swatted his hand away. "Don't make fun of me, please.

"Anyway, it's time I went home."

She got up and busily began to raise all the blinds and picked up her purse from the low table. "Can I get a samlo around here?"

He stopped her with his hand on hers again.

"Listen, I'm sorry. I never would make fun of you.

"You haven't known me long, but still, I think you would have realized that by now?

"Come, I would like to show you my little pavilion, then I'll drive you back."

Her face still sullen in her embarrassment, she nodded. "Yes, I'm sorry too.

"I know you're not that kind of guy. Let's not talk about it anymore."

LAWRENCE'S DIARY
MONDAY JUNE 26TH 1939

What have I done?

I've spoiled it and hurt Kate.

I may not be the kind of man who would make fun of her, granted. But still — did I know all the time, as we were walking to my rooms, was it indeed so inevitable that I would try to push further?

And am I *that* kind of man who finding himself alone with a woman in his room would consider her fair game?

It would seem so.

We kissed again — or rather I kissed her, and she surprised me by responding. And surprised me again when she pushed me away and told me quite firmly that this made no sense, then asked me to drive her home.

I'm afraid I sulked somewhat."

Sulked somewhat?

Be honest, he told himself.

In the car, when she'd attempted to explain herself, "Listen, it's hopeless. Guys like you don't get involved with girls like me," he barely unclenched his teeth, except to drop contemptuously, "What is that supposed to mean?"

She sat back in her seat, crossed her arms, and responded, staring straight ahead, "Don't pretend you don't understand.

"We come from different worlds, and I don't belong in yours. I don't have the right manners, or the right clothes for it — oh, I don't know, the right background, okay?

"Didn't you see how Busaba looked at my dress, that I wasn't sure which fork to use?

"I know there aren't many available girls in Bangkok, and I'm sure that's why you've paid me such attention, but ... in a few months, you'll go your way, I'll go mine," and then her voice had trembled somewhat, "and I won't be your good time girl in the meantime. I'm not ready to have my heart broken again."

When he stopped the car at the entrance of her soi, she took a deep breath, and said as she opened the door, "You've been very nice to invite me over the past weeks, and I'm grateful. But please leave me alone, now," before adding in a brittle voice "I didn't get to say goodbye to Lady Thip and thank her for lunch.

"Don't worry, I'll write her a note.

"Felicity was very particular about sending bread and butter letters."

And she got out, walked away and didn't look back.

Chapter VI

The rains came gushing down with boring and depressing predictability every evening. Except that some days it poured in the afternoon, and some days, it drizzled for hours with a grey and gloomy sky, which perfectly matched, Kate reflected, what her mood had been these past weeks.

Everything, everywhere, memories of times spent with Lawrence intruded.

The stall at the top of Silom Road manned by the old lady who grilled pork and chicken on skewers, which she had been dying to try but hadn't dared because of all the other nurses' warnings about cholera, typhoid fever, dysentery and worse.

He laughed at her and bought a dozen which they ate seated at a ramshackle table on the sidewalk, dipping the meat into a spicy peanut sauce as delicious as chocolate fudge.

Walking on New Road, she now always looked at the graceful arched covered passage bordering the street, and at the stucco decorations and lovely curved eaves on many of the houses which she had never noticed until he pointed them out to her one afternoon, when he had taken her to the only Western style bakery in town, after she had confessed her craving for bread.

At least, because of the rain, she did not have to avoid the outdoors neighbourhood Chinese movie showings he had insisted they spend an evening watching, munching on peanuts, sipping lukewarm beer, making up a story that drove them to fits of helpless giggles, with the picture flickering on a makeshift screen made of a sheet and the audience groaning or cheering, eating and drinking, and children mesmerized or playing at their parents' feet, babies rocked in baskets, and all around them, the smell of charcoal and sizzling fish.

It was worse than the days after Brendan had left, except that she did not feel the shame of having given herself away too easily.

Although she often felt regret that she hadn't...

She thought of Lawrence each time she remembered to take her umbrella before leaving the house, she thought of Lawrence each time she selected the most dismal samlo driver, she thought of Lawrence each time she walked near the soi leading to the Oriental.

She both hoped and dreaded bumping into him in all those places they had been together, but never did she sight a tall man in a white suit whose tousled gold hair stood out above the crowd.

And the thoughts of him haunted her most when she was in her room listening to the rain dripping outside, alone more often than not because Belinda spent most of her evenings out with Eddy.

Belinda didn't mind being the law clerk's good time girl, apparently, although she did entertain hopes of becoming something more.

"He's here, and I'm here, and we have fun together. And who knows what might happen? He thinks I'm swell." she retorted defiantly when Kate urged her to be more careful. "And anyway, I *am* being careful. He hasn't had his way with me yet, and the longer I hold out, the better my chances are.

"That's where you went wrong with your Brendan,"and she whirled away in one of the bright new dresses she'd had made by a little Indian tailor and returned bleary-eyed in the wee hours.

At the hospital, she was careless and snappish with fatigue and often earned a tongue-lashing from Melanie, though perhaps, Kate thought, not as virulent as it might have been, after Belinda one day threatened to resign.

Melanie couldn't afford to lose a nurse, difficult and headstrong as she might be.

For the situation at the hospital, from being chaotic before, had turned almost impossible once the monsoon had started in earnest and the all the people waiting outside, sleeping on mats or under makeshift tents had been moved to any available space, the front hall, the covered galleries at the side of the building.

Those who could sit up even waited in the stairways and Melanie had tried in vain to enforce a rule of not letting families in.

At work at least, Kate was kept too busy to allow thoughts of Lawrence to intrude after Doctor Hermet had told Melanie in despair, that "although the refugee women seem to have more babies than ever, I need your nurses to help out in other departments.

"With the rain and the heat, every cut or wound turns septic, every cold turns into pneumonia, and I'm not even talking about malaria and dysentery or the risk of cholera!"

"You exaggerate, Doctor, as usual." Melanie replied tartly.

Nevertheless, she was prepared to make Nurses Fallon and O'Grady available when — and only when — they were not needed in the maternity ward. "Although, I wonder whether O'Grady would be much help. Heaven knows she's not much use to me these days."

As a result, when there were no difficult deliveries to require her presence, she began to assist the physician during surgeries, handing him instruments, compressing arteries, and stitching incisions.

"You have good hands," the Frenchman remarked one day, as he watched her. "Pity you've not had the right training."

The backhanded compliment meant little to her, she didn't even feel like replying that she was a maternity, not a surgical nurse and only on loan because there was no one else to assist.

She felt numbed, like an automaton, doing her job, replying "yes, doctor, no doctor," reassuring patients, asking "does it hurt?" and never thinking to ask herself the same question.

Her world just felt as grey and hopeless as the sky and she could barely bring herself to write home because she didn't know what to say, and when she did, her letters were short and lifeless.

Felicity was perhaps the only person who realized something might be wrong — "When are you coming home? You sound as if you're homesick..."

No, she wasn't homesick.

She was bored, and exhausted, and lovesick.

She knew she should make some effort to seek a new job, a new life, a new beginning, just as she had when she had accepted the offer to move to Bangkok.

And look how well that went, she told herself.

Was she fated to always be the one standing on the outside looking in, the child without a mother or even a home, the only unmarried girl at twenty-five in Boston, the only American nurse here, a foreigner to everybody in every way?

Each time she had a sense of belonging, with Brendan and their unspoken plans for the future, or with Lawrence and those three months of his magical Bangkok, something happened to pull that feeling from under her feet, and she was left behind, battered and aching and bleeding.

But as the weeks went by, she managed to steel herself to look to the future. Stay put for now, save as much money as you can, and get over that stupid crush.

Things will get better, of course they will.

Won't they?

One afternoon, waiting outside the doctor's office to brief him on the fever an old man was experiencing after a boil had been excised from his groin, she picked up a copy of *The Bangkok Times* that had been left lying on a chair and stared in amazement at the huge black headline " War in our time?"

She sat to read about the German ultimatum to Poland, comprehending little. She knew, of course, about Hitler and the situation in Germany, but she thought any talk of war had been silenced, remembering that last year at the movies – she'd gone with Maura and Teddy to see *Robin Hood* – and in the newsreel always shown before the film, the British Prime Minister, whatever his name was, was clutching an umbrella and proclaiming, "Peace for our time!" and people in the audience had clapped.

What happened since? How could she have been so involved in her own misery that she had just shut her eyes and her ears to the outside world?

What was this alliance with the Soviet Union?

When Doctor Hermet came down the hall in his usual important, hurried way, she raised her eyes and showed him the front page.

"What's happening?"

He sat down heavily next to her and sighed, all his overbearing manner and bustling gone. "Yes, my child, I fear our world is going mad again.

"If it's to be war once more, between France and Germany... I don't know.

"I was too young to fight in the last one – just – and I remember it well.

"But can one let this madman continue unchecked?

As a Christian, as a patriot, as a... human being?"

She stared at him, wide-eyed in dismay at hearing this all-knowing, always so certain man sound so dejected.

"I don't know," she whispered.

"No, you don't, and you don't need to know."

He rose from the chair and looked down at her, replying with an edge to his voice, "This doesn't really concern you, does it? Your country has voted to remain neutral many times over the past years, hasn't it?

"Come, let's go see Mr. Chin Liu."

Melanie just glared when Kate came to her for reassurance.

"What is to happen will happen. I put my trust in the Good Lord, and in the wisdom of France's leaders. As should you."

"But if there's a war?" Kate insisted. "What does it mean for us?"

"For us, nothing," the nun answered brusquely. "We are on the other side of the world, and those who are fleeing another war are our concern.

"Get back to work."

But her words rang false to Kate, and she felt that Melanie was masking the same fear as Doctor Hermet. And if there were to be a war, what would it mean for Lawrence?

In the following days, Kate always took the time to go buy an English language newspaper at the general store on Silom Road and read it carefully with mounting anxiety.

Hitler had invaded Poland — where exactly *was* Poland, she fretted, and berated herself for not remembering a thing about the European geography she'd been taught at school.

But the following day, a map of the invasion route was displayed on the front page, with an even more ominous headline about a British and French ultimatum to Hitler.

"Why do *you* have such a long face?" Belinda demanded, flouncing into the room and finding Kate sitting on the bed, staring despondently at the picture of a column of armoured cars triumphantly flying pennants with the Nazi eagle. "It's me that should be worried, not you!

"Eddy says that if Britain declares war, then he'll leave Bangkok to go join up. And then...," she sat next to Kate and picked up the paper, her voice trembling. "And then... well, I'll be left behind.

"He said the Ambassador has called a meeting at the Club this evening for all the men here, and they will be told what happens if England declares war."

She looked up. "Maybe I could suggest we might get married before he leaves, if he does leave? What do you think?"

Kate shrugged. "The way I see it, you've nothing to lose."

Belinda sighed. "Unless, of course he gets me pregnant, and then gets himself killed.

"Well, let's set what happens tomorrow. Hitler might cave."

There was to Lawrence a curious feeling of muted excitement, almost of elation amongst the men pressing at the bar of the British Club, eager to have a pint and a smoke before hearing the news that might change their lives.

Everyone had come, the bankers in white linen suits, the manager of the Bangkok General Stores in his shirtsleeves, diffident looking missionary teachers and whiskered, weather-beaten old Siam hands who were fanning themselves with their straw hats. Some were very old, or perhaps, Lawrence reflected, they only *seemed* old, as they looked with compassion at the tender-skinned, sunburnt young law clerks and junior employees of logging firms and insurance agents who were noisily claiming their intention of signing up to serve their King and returning to Bangkok "once we've taught the Hun a lesson, which shouldn't take long!"

And this evening there were none of the bombastic "We could use a man like Herr Hitler!" talk that he remembered from his last visit to the Club six months ago...

He spotted Belinda's friend Edward and nodded before climbing the stairs to the ballroom where the Ambassador, Sir Josiah Crosby, was already waiting behind a baize-covered table on the dais.

Behind him, the Union Jack and the tricolored flag of Thailand — still the same as the flag of Siam, Lawrence noted — were deployed against the wall.

Waiting until the general hubbub, the scraping of chairs, the greetings and high-pitched, nervous laughs had quietened, the diplomat gazed at the men facing him, his bland, waxy face quite unreadable.

Lawrence found a seat next to Gerald Sparrow, a Judge-

Advocate detached to the Siamese Ministry of Justice, whose true passions seemed to be his Siamese mistress, the racehorse he kept at the Royal Bangkok Sports Club, the intricacies of the opium trade, and the threat Japanese imperialism posed for the British Empire.

He always enjoyed the man's genial manner and tales of the more bizarre cases he had to try, but for once, Sparrow had lost his eternal gambler's smile and his face was dark.

"They say," he murmured, "that Crosby knows the Siamese better than anyone. Then how come he hasn't seen the Japanese are poised to take this country over and that Phibul is opening his arms wide to welcome them?"

The Ambassador coughed, and in the sudden silence, only the whirring of the overhead fans could be heard, and Lawrence shivered, suddenly.

"Friends, Englishmen, I have gathered you here," Sir Josiah began and paused to cough again, as Sparrow muttered viciously "Ha! Shakespeare's Marc Anthony speech! Borrowed eloquence!"

Lawrence who was thinking the same had to stifle an irreverent laugh into a sneeze, while hisses and "Quiet!" came from behind them.

The Ambassador resumed, in a stronger voice, "I have asked you to come this evening, because the situation is most grave.

"You all know, I am sure, that the Prime Minister and the Premier of France, Monsieur Daladier, issued a joint ultimatum yesterday demanding that the German Army evacuate all the Polish territories it has invaded.

"This ultimatum is due to expire at eleven in the morning London time today, that is…," he checked his watch "just about now.

"I also wanted – nay, I needed to inform you that His Majesty's Government, has ordered the general mobilization of the British Armed forces as well as the conscription of all males between the ages of 18 and 41 residing in the United Kingdom.

"This, of course, does not apply to any of you here, and we shall also need to hear what is to be required of our Imperial Dominions.

"I am sure you have many questions, just I am sure I shall be able to answer very few of them — but...," he raised his head, starting, as an embassy aide rushed towards the dais, clutching an envelope.

The Ambassador took it, opened it and unfolded the flimsy sheet of paper it contained and read, then closed his eyes briefly and nodded.

He sighed, deeply, turning to face the audience.

"I had hoped and prayed I should never need to impart such news.

"The deadline for the ultimatum has expired, and Britain has declared itself in a state of war against Germany."

He raised his hand to quell the sudden outburst of exclamations and questions.

"I shall be informing the Royal Government of Thailand of this and urge this country to remain neutral in this affair. I am convinced that Prime Minister Phibul Songkhram in his wisdom shall see that this is the advisable — in fact, the only course.

"And for us... We must do our best, hope for the best and prepare for the worse."

A wavering voice was raised, low at first, the voice of an old man singing the first words of "God save the King", and others joined until they were all singing, and Lawrence shivered again.

"We are at war", he thought, but beyond the words, he felt nothing, nothing but surprise at feeling so little.

"I want a brandy," Gerald Sparrow said. "Join me?"

In the bar, the Siamese waiters were smiling as usual, taking orders and seemed completely unaware that the world had changed in the last hour.

All the young men were talking excitedly, jostling each other to call out for more drinks, and the old men looked stunned.

One of them had tears pouring down his cheeks. "My Jimmy" he kept saying, to no one in particular, "my son Jimmy is twenty-five..."

Lawrence gulped his brandy and put down his glass. "First drink of the war," he said, still trying to get used to the word.

Sparrow laughed, bitterly, and toasted him. "Well, there'll be plenty more.

"What are you going to do?"

"I'm going to have another brandy. And after that...,"

Lawrence looked around, and declared in bemusement, "...you know, I have absolutely no idea."

LAWRENCE'S DIARY
BANGKOK, SEPTEMBER 4TH, 1939

First day of the war, and I start it with a hangover.
I got back last night, rather late, and rather drunk.
All the lights were blazing in the big house, so I knew that Lady Thip was waiting for me.

Of course, she and Busaba had heard the news on the wireless, and they wanted to hear what the Ambassador had said – Sam is in Cambridge and they are worried.

Today, I received a telegram from my father, beseeching me not to do "anything foolish. You are safe where you are, if you value our peace of mind, please remain there."

But to repeat what I told Gerald Sparrow last night, I have no idea of what I *can* do.

He looked me up and down and said, very quietly, that I might want to meet somebody.

"Friend of mine from Malaya," he said. "He has some interesting ideas for someone like you."

"Someone like me?" I asked.

Well, yes, he replied, university graduate, good at languages – "You are good at languages, aren't you? " he asked.

I told him I speak French fluently – my grandmother Julie and my father both saw to that – and that my Siamese is good enough to get me by.

Aside from that, I'm trained for nothing, short-sighted, I've never held a gun in my life and nobody could seriously trust me with one.

Also, judging from my school experience, I don't enjoy being in all-male company and I'm not very good at following orders.

Not a very promising recruit for the Army – or Navy, or Air Force, for that matter.

"I've a degree in philosophy, for heaven's sake!"

He clapped me on the shoulder. "Sounds just like the kind of man he'd be interested in meeting. He's coming to Bangkok next month. I'll be in touch. But all of this is rather hush-hush, so don't discuss it with anyone, all right?"

And he melted away, probably to go back to that spectacular Siamese mistress of his.

Whatever his friend's "interesting ideas" are, I'm open to hearing about them. I only know that my spending my days writing about this Siamese Revolution when the real world is preparing for a clash of civilization seems petty, irrelevant and utterly unimportant.

But what do I *want* to do?

I want to see Kate.

And that is what I *cannot* do.

Chapter VII

She was slowly walking up Sathorn Road, her exhaustion visible in her downcast head and dragging feet as if each step were an effort.

He got out of the car and waited for her to raise her eyes and see him.

When she did, and stood there, arms crossed, just staring at him, he was shocked at how drained and pale she was.

"I was waiting for you." he finally said, feeling foolish.

She nodded. "I see that. Why?"

He sighed. "I don't know. Because I needed to. Because ...

"Will you get in the car, so we can talk?"

She shook her head.

He opened the door, and said, more impatiently and angrily than he would have wanted, "Don't be silly. Get into the car and I'll drive you back. Heaven knows you can use a lift, you look about to collapse."

He was surprised when she accepted with a sigh, probably more out of sheer fatigue and relief at not having to walk any further, he thought, than out of the pleasure of being with him.

"Drop me at the corner of New Road, then.

"I need to buy some chicken skewers and fruit for dinner."

She settled back in the seat and closed her eyes. "The air conditioning feels good,"she said softly. "I've missed feeling cool."

"I've missed *you*," he replied. "No – no wait – " he said as she made an annoyed face and began to open her door. He reached across her and pulled it shut.

"I tried. I tried for a long time. It's been almost two years since..."

"It's been seventeen months," she interrupted.

"You counted? Well, it felt longer to me," he replied.

She raised her eyebrows. "It's perhaps because I've been busier than you. What *have* you been doing since the war broke out?"

Couldn't they go for a drink, or dinner, somewhere? That was precisely what he wanted to talk about with her.

She gave an exasperated snort. "Look at me."

He did, noticing she was still wearing her crumpled, sweaty, stained nurses' uniform.

"I don't mind," he smiled. "It suits you."

She exploded. "You still don't get it, do you? I do. I mind.

"I can't go into someplace fancy like you do and think I'm good enough and who cares what I look like and who I am.

"Even if nobody else cares, I care."

She paused after her outburst, seeming relieved at having vented her feelings. "We talk in the car, or you drive me straight home."

Or, he offered, he drove her home, she changed, and then they went to dinner.

"I can't have the engine running for the air-conditioning in the car for hours," he explained, "it's supposed to be dangerous. And what I have to say will take more than ten minutes."

She relented. She would change. But then, "Nowhere fancy, okay? Not the Oriental. Someplace like the British Club would be all right, I suppose."

He grimaced and shook his head as he started the car.

He didn't go to the British Club much, these days. "I get funny looks.

"You know, all these men whose sons who were either killed or evacuated from Dunkirk — or are fighting fires in the blitz, and I'm here, doing nothing, just swanning myself living in luxury with natives."

She scanned his face, keenly. "You don't look like you've been doing nothing. You're sunburnt, and somehow, I don't know... you look — different."

He nodded. "Anyway, it's all part of what I wanted to tell you."

"I know, we'll go to the Trocadero Hotel. It will be quiet on a weeknight, and we can get some chips and eggs."

She smiled, at last. "Chips — that's French fries, right? — and eggs would be wonderful. With catsup."

How had he known she would be coming off duty, she asked.

He'd been by her house, and seen Belinda. "She showed me your room, it's really awful."

She laughed, bitterly. "That, it is. And you should have seen it during the monsoon. Humidity running down the walls, and our shoes getting all mouldy. Wait here, I won't be long."

The Trocadero Hotel was quiet, as he had hoped, in the dark, cavernous room only one table was occupied by a lone diner engrossed in a book.

They gave their order, and she looked at him, chin held high.

"What was it you wanted to tell me?"

He pushed his glasses back up his nose and rubbed his face, wondering where to start.

"You remember the day the war started?

"Well, the Ambassador called a meeting at the British Club to inform us all."

She nodded. Belinda had told her Eddy was going to attend.

"She was going to suggest they got married before he enlisted, but he's still here, they're still not married. And she's still hoping."

Lawrence grinned.

He knew. Well, not about Belinda hoping for marriage, but that Eddy was still around, propping up the bar at the Club. He'd been declared medically unfit.

"He's even more short-sighted than I am, has flat feet and I don't know what else. A living medical textbook case.

"It broke his heart, or so he says."

But anyway... That evening, he had been, as one says, tapped on the shoulder for something else.

He looked around to check if a waiter might overhear and lowered his voice.

"This chap, I may have mentioned him, he's the one who has a thing about a Japanese threat, well, he suggested my name to someone from Imperial Chemicals.

"I thought that was really funny, can you see me working for Imperial Chemicals?

"But that wasn't it at all.

"It was just to gauge my — well, fitness, and interest, I suppose — to train for...." He sighed, flustered, and ran his hand through his hair.

"Oh God, this is hopeless, I can't really say anything much.

"Well, this man suggested me to someone else — I can't say who, I'm not even supposed to know what his name is.

"Anyway... I was sent to this school in Malaya, to train."

He stopped speaking while their plates were put before them and she frowned, stabbing at her fried egg. What kind of school?

Some kind of secret school. "Some of the inmates call it 'The Convent.'"

More a camp than a school, in fact. He wasn't really sure where it was in Malaya, in the jungle, near some mountains.

Train for what?

Psychological warfare, he supposed it could be called.

Propaganda.

Writers were good at that kind of thing, creating a reality out of nothing, or changing the way you look at reality.

"Having lived with the Siamese for years, it was assumed than when the war comes here, I would know how to..."

Her eyes went very wide. "What do you mean, when the war comes here?" she yelped.

He winced and held up his hand to silence her. "Shh... Not so loud."

"Thailand declared neutrality over a year ago. Even I heard of it," she whispered obediently.

"Don't whisper either, it's more noticeable. Just pitch your voice low."

She looked around the restaurant and raised her eyebrows. "There's nobody except us, now."

He shook his head. "Still. The waiters might notice.

"Yes, I know, they declared neutrality, and there was also the non-aggression pact between England and Thailand signed some months ago, but it won't hold, it can't hold when the Japanese attack us in Malaya and Singapore.

"The war *is* coming here, believe me.

"Maybe not next month, or even next year, but it's coming, and when it does, Thailand is going to have to choose between Japan and us.

"Who do you think it will be?

"The Japanese have taken over French Indo-China, they're in Hanoi, you know that, don't you?"

She bit her lips and nodded, shaking catsup over her chips.

When Melanie heard, she'd cried for two days straight.

"How could she feel that Indo-China was part of France?

"France is on the other side of the world.

"I just don't get it... I mean, maybe if her parents had settled in Indo-China and she'd been born there...

"I didn't know Indo-China was French until I came here, and I'm pretty sure most Americans don't know...

"But since the French there surrendered to Japan, things have been difficult for her, Doctor Hermet and all the French, really, because Thailand thinks that now it can get even for some war they fought a long time ago.

"We have the police coming by to check our papers, and Doctor Hermet's medical degree, and apparently, many French people want to leave, but they just don't know where to go...

"All that to get back land France took over a hundred years ago."

He sighed.

"Actually, it was less than fifty years ago, and people have long memories when it comes to their country. And it's always good for a politician to create enemies of the nation, and to whip up hostility.

"You see," he explained, "when I was talking about propaganda, that's what it's all about. That's what Phibul is doing.

"He's using the old resentment to better control his people, so he can accuse his opposition of being traitors.

"Furthermore, the Thai army is strong, its air force even more so, so he will be tempted to use it someday soon, and not just for half-cocked skirmishes at the border as he has so far."

She cocked her head at him. He has changed, she thought.

There was none of his usual light-heartedness, his way of seeing life as a charming comedy. He was making an effort, she could tell, but he seemed far more ... sober, perhaps, and pessimistic.

And quite surprisingly well-informed.

"This training school, is it dangerous?" she asked, "Cloak and dagger kind of dangerous?"

He laughed.

Writing propaganda wasn't dangerous, he reassured her lightly, not mentioning the other aspects of the five months of training he'd received, the armed, and more importantly, unarmed combat, the landing on the beaches with rubber rafts, jungle night marches and survival skills, foraging for food in the dark, menacing rain forest that challenged any sense of direction, climbing slippery hills trying to cling to mosses and ferns and slide through bamboos, plants that seemed to tangle themselves around you when you stopped for a minute to catch your breath, eerie animal calls, buzzing of insects, the leeches that managed to attach themselves to the smallest bit of uncovered skin and that you had to burn off with a cigarette, and, his own personal terror, the ever present threat of being attacked by a tiger.

"No, it was fun, actually," he said, and realized that it had been.

He picked up a chip with his fingers and ate it thoughtfully.

He hadn't realized how lonely and dissatisfied he was until he met with Sparrow's mysterious friend from Imperial Chemicals and was induced to leave his life, his book and his future behind for the moment and devote his talents, such as they were, to something else.

In the wake of his argument with Kate all those months ago, he had signified to Busaba that their affair was over and was both relieved and annoyed when she agreed it was for the best, saying "We were getting a bit bored with each other, weren't we?"

Daunting and exhausting as they were, those months spent in Malaya were also fascinating and exhilarating.

"It was like boarding school, only so much better."

He'd made friends, "other misfits like myself. There was an archaeologist from Burma, and a trader from Borneo who collects orchids... Not good armed forces material, which is probably why we became friends."

The idea, when the Japanese invasion came — and that was a given — was that they — he, and the others who trained with him — would stay behind.

"Now that, however, was a crazy notion. None of us looks remotely Asian, except for one chap whose mother was Chinese Malay.

"Furthermore, the Governor of Singapore considered that besides being crazy, it was also defeatist — the very idea that the Japanese might win! — so he ordered the school disbanded. And here I am."

What would he do now?

Well, the people running the training, they had connections everywhere in London. Foreign office, Fleet Street. Big firms, such as Imperial Chemicals, and banks...

He wasn't fit for anything commercial, but that's not what they wanted out of him.

He'd been given some newspaper work to do by a press agency, writing articles highlighting the danger of the Japanese troops massing on the borders of Siam, Phibul's increasingly aggressive demands for Siam to recover territories lost to the French fifty years ago, that kind of thing, morale in the Thai army and the population, Phibul's gradual slide into a Mussolini type of rule.

"Some are completely straightforward and published under my name, which officially makes me a journalist and gives me the standing to meet with politicians, and army officers and the like.

"The others, the ... well, the slanted, or propaganda ones are published under an anonymous by-line, so as not to get me into trouble. Or Lady Thip, for that matter, if it were to become known she is harbouring someone who writes those articles for British and American papers," he added, not mentioning what he also wrote for some underground Chinese or Thai papers.

"American papers?" she asked, impressed.

What she wouldn't give to read an American newspaper...

"You're homesick?"

Yes... No... She was just tired. Bored.

She set her mouth and shrugged. She was not about to tell him how lonesome, broken-hearted and miserable she felt.

"How *is* Lady Thip? And Busaba? Is there any news of Sam?

"I think of him each time I hear about the bombing raids over England. And what about your family?"

Sam was still in Cambridge, which had been spared altogether. So far, at least...

But it was difficult for letters to get through, what with the U-boat attacks, now that half of France was occupied meant the Atlantic was increasingly dangerous for shipping from England.

His family... he hadn't heard for a few months now. His father — "he's too old to be mobilized, of course" — was busy caring for blitz victims.

"I've only just found out what 'blitz' means," she remarked. "How incredibly arrogant of Hitler to believe he could win the war quickly."

He shook his head with a wintry smile.

"The first time *I* heard it, I thought it was German for 'obliterate'...," he confessed, adding that his mother had become an ambulance driver.

From what he'd gathered, she had never been happier, feeling useful, at last.

If anything had happened to them, he'd have been told.

"I have an aunt and an uncle and assorted cousins who know where to send me a telegram," he went on quietly. "And what about you?"

She shrugged again.

She worked. She went home — if one could call that place home. Yes, she agreed, she knew she should find someplace else, but it was close to the hospital and also, more importantly, she paid no rent.

"I can't really afford anything much better, you know, and I'm trying to save money."

The hospital was no longer so overrun by patients, now that the flow of refugees from China had dried up, what with the anti-Chinese laws adopted in Thailand last year.

"The Prime Minister's anti-French policy hasn't helped.

"Many people avoid coming to us. So, it's fairly quiet, with the usual Thai-Chinese patients, many of them Catholics. Less babies. Of course, a few French, who get preferential treatment, but the French nuns deal with them...

"I assist Doctor Hermet for some surgeries now, and I really enjoy that. I've learned a lot."

Her voice trailed off.

Finally, she looked and him and said in a brittle voice. "I understand *what* you wanted to tell me, but I still don't understand *why.*

"Why tell *me*? We haven't spoken for seventeen months.

"Why now?"

They were alone in the restaurant now, the waiters had gone outside on the sidewalk to enjoy the evening cool, and they both stared at the branch of orchids in a pink vase between them on the table.

"When war was declared last year," he said very low, "I wanted nothing more than to come to you."

"When war was declared, I hoped for days that you *would* come," she whispered back. "And then I stopped hoping."

Yes, she knew what she'd said, and it still stood.

She would not be his good time girl, or "your little bit of comfort on the side, or whatever you guys call it."

He traced the rim of the vase with his finger, then looked up at her.

"What if I asked you to marry me?"

LAWRENCE'S DIARY
BANGKOK, FRIDAY DECEMBER 6, 1940

I did not know what to expect when I asked Kate to marry me, I hadn't actually expected to ask her, although the idea *had* crossed my mind, but never did I think she would burst out laughing.

Why should she do that? she asked.

"Because I love you and you love me, I suppose, would be the obvious answer," I replied.

She didn't challenge that, which was a relief.

She kept on shaking her head. "It's crazy. You're crazy.

"Guys like you don't marry girls like me."

If she married me, I said, that would disprove her statement.

No, no, no, it wasn't possible, she repeated, getting very agitated.

What about my parents? What about her work?

What about...

I told her that my parents could only welcome her (my mother, however, but I didn't say, might take some convincing, but by the time we make it back to London—*if* we ever make it back to London — she will have had time to warm to the idea) and as to her work, would anything change?

If Melanie insists on having only single women as nurses, *and* if she herself insists on working, then the British Nursing Home on Convent Road would be delighted to have her.

But she could also stay home and be wife to an anonymous journalist.

"Listen, you're just casting around for excuses." I finally said. "Can't we grab a chance of being happy?

"There's a war on.

"Who knows what will happen?"

She leaned back in her chair and told me that she'd always been amused at hearing me describe myself as short-sighted.

In the States, she says, I would be called near-sighted.

"Except that you're also short-sighted in the American sense.

"It's precisely because there's a war on and that we don't know what will happen, that we shouldn't do this."

Why? I demanded again. Why not be happy when we can?

Or was it that she didn't love me?

She sighed. "Oh, I love you. That's not the problem. Or rather, it is. What if you meet someone else? An English girl from a better background?"

"What a snob you are.

"What if you meet a big handsome Yank who actually does something useful with his life?" I retorted.

She smiled, I don't know if it was at being called a snob or at the idea of the handsome Yank.

I hate this non-existent man, and I made him up myself.

Oh, the power of words to whip up passions, as we were told, repeatedly, at that place in Malaya.

She gave me an arch look. Well, what if she did?

"I'd kill him," I said very firmly.

Of course, she has no idea that I could, or at least, I think I could, very discreetly and silently, by crushing his windpipe.

"Say yes. Please."

I think I'd never wanted anything so much in my life.

She looked at the ceiling, at the table, and finally at me.

"All right. Yes."

Chapter VIII

Never had a bride created so many problems before being taken up the aisle was the central premise of Lawrence's speech on their wedding day.

"And never did a groom deploy so much ingenuity in solving them," he added to laughs from the small group of their guests at the reception which Lady Thip had insisted in hosting in her house.

"There were the papers, and the bans, and oh yes — her patients!

"I am so very grateful that both Doctor Hermet and Mother Melanie took my side in considering that perhaps her wedding could take precedence over a case of measles."

Doctor Hermet raised his glass and Melanie bowed her head slightly, trying to hide her satisfied smile, as if, Kate thought, watching her from her seat next to Lawrence, she had actually organized the match herself.

When Kate had come to her, biting her lips and twisting her hands in apprehension saying that she was intending to get married, the nun just stared piercingly, gestured her into her private office and sat her down.

"I know Felicity has served as your mother for many years, so I will ask you the questions she would ask.

"Who is this boy? Is he a Catholic? What does he do?"

And when Kate had finished explaining, and assured her that indeed, Lawrence Gallet was a Catholic, that his father was French and a surgeon in London, she just said. "I see."

"But Mother Melanie, do you think I should go ahead with it?

"I don't know, the future is so uncertain, with the war and... He could marry anybody — he is rich, you see. And he studied philosophy!"

Melanie nodded. "I see," she said again, "although philosophy is usually not a hindrance to happiness. I suppose he loves you, otherwise he would not have asked you to be his wife. But do you love him? Yes, I can see you do."

"Is he kind?"

Kate thought about it.

Yes, she supposed he was. He rescued her at that party at the British Club because he could see she was having a miserable time. He always chose the oldest and poorest looking samlo driver...

"Should I marry him then?"

The nun got up and considered Kate with her usual impatience.

"My girl, he loves you, he is rich, and kind, and a Catholic. And half-French.

"You would be a fool not to.

"Get back to work now.

"Tomorrow, I shall help you for your wedding dress."

She opened the door to her office and walked down the corridor, all the while taking long sideways considering looks at Kate.

"Ivory peau de soie, I think, if it can be found here, and a high neckline... Ivory is better than white for red hair."

Taking a few running steps to keep up with her, Kate hesitated, twisting the button on her blouse.

She had thought that perhaps Belinda's Indian tailor...

Melanie stopped and turned to face her, with an offended glare.

"You would trust an Irishwoman to advise you with your gown?" before declaring with considerable hauteur that she may be a nun, "but I am also a Frenchwoman.

"There is a shop, opposite the British Legation, run by a compatriot, one Josephine," she sniffed, "a rather fast woman I believe, but, I hear, a talented seamstress. We shall go there."

"Mother, please, stop!" Kate grasped the nun's embow.

She could not afford a dress in whatever that ivory fabric might be, and a French seamstress sounded much too expensive.

Melanie raised her eyebrows. "Did you imagine I would let you pay?"

Belinda was seated across from Melanie, with Eddy by her side, doing her best to impress upon him the wisdom of a hasty marriage in wartime, but she also seemed somewhat awed by the house and the silver and the servants, and Eddy could not detach his eyes from Busaba long enough to converse with Rose, one of the other Irish nurses who kept staring at everything in wonder.

Sister Perrine, the hospital's terror, was for once smiling contentedly and gazing at the garden view, and Doctor Sumet, Kate's favourite among the Thai surgeons, turned out to be the son of one of Lady Thip's childhood friends and was greeted with cries of delight.

"You're so lucky, and I am so happy for you, and the dress is beautiful," Belinda had exclaimed generously when she helped Kate into her gown.

"Say what you want, Melanie has good taste," Kate had agreed, considering herself in the mirror. "Pity she insisted that I have long sleeves," she added, buttoning the tight cuffs. "I know it's the style, but I'm so hot already."

Belinda sat on the bed of the room at the Oriental Hotel that Lawrence had reserved for them both over Kate's protestations, arguing they needed someplace nice to prepare during the week before the wedding.

When they were shown to their room, Belinda rushed to the balcony to admire the view on the river and squealed, before bouncing on the bed, barely waiting for the porter to leave, then bustled around examining everything with cries of rapture.

"A bathroom! A bathtub and a loo!

"Holy Mother Mary, would you look at this, Kate? I've never been anywhere so posh! A fan!"

By the morning of the wedding, she had finally calmed down, although she frequently moaned that she could never go back to the little house in the soi.

"All I need now is for Eddy to give in, and we'll be all set," she sighed, as she settled the short veil over Kate's hair and tweaked a silk flower that had slipped from her headdress.

"Do you realize we never could have had frocks like this back home?"

She fingered the silk of her own pale blue dress, a gift from Lawrence, who told her that it was his thanks for taking Kate to the British Club that evening.

"I never would have met her without you," he had said. Melanie had also sternly decided on the style and fabric.

"You are very lucky," she repeated wistfully. "He's a lovely fella, your Lawrence."

Yes, Kate said, twisting the ring with the big ruby set in diamonds that Lawrence had slipped on her finger the day before, yes, he is.

And now it was done, they were married, and the following day had departed for Lady Thip's seaside house for a week's honeymoon.

During the long and leisurely ride as the train puffed its way south through farmland and jungled hills and down to the coast, they had spoken little and exchanged shy looks as if still trying to come to terms with the change in their lives.

Kate was quiet, fingering her ring, gazing outside the window while Lawrence tried to draw her out of her silent, uneasy mood by offering comments about the reception, the guests — "Mother Melanie and Lady Thip got along like a house on fire. They'll probably be fast friends from now on," and "Father Perroudon ate as if he feared it might be his last meal," or "What is the name of that nice nun who kept on kissing me and called me 'mon enfant'? Marie-Marguerite? Is she the one who loves Siamese food?" until he finally took her hand.

"Regrets?" he asked.

She shook her head.

"No. Never. It's just that...

"Well, I don't know if I'm up to all this, your lifestyle, your family, your friends...

"It's just beginning to sink in and I'm kind of scared and I wonder if *you* might not have regrets, now that it's the day after, and you've saddled yourself with a wife.

"Now that you have the old ball and chain as the guys used to say after a wedding, in Boston."

He laughed. "Do you want us to have our first married tiff? Do I need to tell you once more that I love you? That last night was — what is the word I'm looking for? Listen to me, supposed to be a writer — exquisite, extraordinary, fantastic, wonderful?"

"No, I know. Perfect."

"Truly?" she smiled at last.

"Truly."

For the rest of the journey, Kate looked at the slowly unfolding scenery of rice fields, grazing buffalo and small villages and homesteads with thatched roofs while Lawrence unfolded the newspaper he had bought at the station and read, and closed his eyes, endeavouring to hide his distress at the terror and devastation the blitz was inflicting on London and Manchester.

Snatching whatever bit of happiness, he thought, *was* the only sensible thing to do while the world circled down into madness.

LAWRENCE'S DIARY
THURSDAY, DECEMBER 26TH 1940

I am writing this as Kate is absorbed in the letter she is to send to her family. She is prompt to defend them when she thinks she hears a hint of criticism, and I suppose she must be right. How am I to judge what it must be like to find oneself unemployed with five motherless children?

Still, I find them strangely distant for not wiring the merest of congratulations after receiving the cable in which she announced our impending wedding.

Felicity, the nun who looked after her, wrote a telegram that was as Irishly lyrical and loving as a telegram can be, but still, the brother who's a priest — a priest!! — might have stirred himself somewhat to send a message on behalf of them all.

It's not as if they were huddled in bomb shelters, as opposed to my parents.

They, however, did send their love and best wishes and in no way could I detect in the, necessarily terse, telegram any note of caution or disapproval. Perhaps my mother's work as ambulance driver has led her to believe, as do I, in the virtue of being imprudent and of living for the moment.

I shall attempt to send a letter in the hope it reaches them to say how enchanting my wife of two days is.

She is finally beginning to lose that stray kitten edginess and to believe she will not be cast out by morning.

And I find it possible for hours on end to believe that we shall go on peacefully, me writing my books, she nursing her patients, and that we shall thus happily grow old wherever life decides to take us.

But I know better.

And sometime, soon, I shall have to tell her.

After splashing in the tranquil silky waters of the gulf of Siam, they walked on the beach for hours, watching the ghost crabs scuttling before them, until the sun set in its short-lived frenzy of orange and red, before returning to Lady Thip's sprawling house and retiring to the huge bed draped in netting to whisper stories of their childhoods and promises for their future.

"You said you would tell me the end of the story some other time," Kate murmured, "don't you think the time is now? I've waited over a year, you know."

"Which story, my darling?"

Lawrence was stroking her back. "How extraordinary you are. Your skin just glows, and you have the loveliest bones in your spine. Each one is different."

"I think I have a bit of sunburn — that's why it glows. It comes with the red hair — and the bones are called vertebrae, and they *are* all different. I can tell you each one's name — actually, it's a letter and a number — if you like, if you stop distracting me by kissing them."

"You learned that in nursing school?

"I did. And I shall list the whole spine for you if you don't tell me the story of the King, and the revolution. As we're in Hua Hin..."

"Ah... that story."

Lawrence sat up and plumped the pillows behind his head and put his glasses on. "Talking about Phibul and Pridi and the revolution of 1932 is not the way I expected to spend my honeymoon," he complained. "You wouldn't rather tell me about when you realized you were in love with me?

"Oh, all right, you hussy.

"But I warn you, I haven't done any research or any writing about it for over a year, so it's going to be sketchy."

She grinned.

It probably would still be too detailed for her, she said, and he bit her shoulder, gently.

"And pull that sheet up. You're too beautiful, and I can't think when I see you like that.

"Get ready, the revolution is about to march on."

SIAMESE TWINS

His Majesty returned to Bangkok, by train, as he had said and every mile the train chugged towards the capital was a mile closer to the new Siam and, he thought as he watched the farmers at work in the flooded rice fields, that for all its proclaimed ideals, the new Siam might be no kinder to them than the old Siam had been.

With a sigh, he looked around at the plush, ornate saloon of the Royal Train car, the gold ornaments and painted china — he would keep all this, at least, all the trappings of kinghood.

But those had mattered little to him...

He was expecting to find his city in turmoil, but no, it was as if no one had noticed that suddenly, the very foundation on which the country had been based for centuries had ceased to exist.

Some, perhaps, had been a bit surprised when at the end of a cinema performance they did not hear the royal anthem and a new, recorded nationalist song was played — and they did not realize that Pridi and his skill in stirring emotions was to thank for that.

The song was also played over and over on the national radio and it was perhaps through radio broadcasts that people began, gradually to understand the tremendous scope of the change for the kingdom.

"What is the point of a revolution if nobody knows about it?" Phibul asked in exasperation at the seeming indifference of the population and even of the civil service who had been informed, in the afternoon of the 24th, of the new form of government which His Majesty had endorsed.

To think they had planned, schemed, and met in secret just for this.

He paced the room, his elation at the morning's events fizzling away with fatigue and disappointment.

"I said, I always said, didn't I, even in Paris, that the people were not yet ready. You remember me saying it?

"I was right."

Pridi stared at his friend, suddenly realizing that not only did he dislike him now, but that he always had, ever since those days in Paris listening to his bragging and watching him swagger as if he were so much better than them all.

He checked the cutting words he would have loved to use. There were more important things to do today than argue.

"Yes, you did, yes, we remember. Yes.

"But what were you expecting?

"To have the people take to the streets with pitchforks?

"This is Siam, not France." was his quiet, controlled reply.

"So, what do we do now?" Phibul demanded, spinning around and drawing himself to his full height in his uniform.

There was a moment of silence.

"Now," Pridi said finally, realizing that although the colonels of the Bangkok Military Command had the might of the armed forces behind them, his was the mind shaping the future, "now we wait for the King.

"When he speaks, when he endorses Khana Ratsadon, the people will listen, and know, and understand."

"Then why are you looking so nervous?" Tasnai wanted to know, watching his friend drum his fingers on the desk, and constantly cocking his ear to hear the approaching steps of an office messenger.

Pridi sighed impatiently.

Did they not remember the French and the English, so close to them, at the Kingdom's very borders?

What of them? The affairs of Siam were of no concern to them, Tasnai replied, bridling.

Had they not taken enough of Siamese lands in the past?

Indeed, Pridi replied, and they might be tempted to take more, if there were the slightest breath of a danger to their nationals, or the merest unrest, they could see their way to step in, to "restore order" and then never leave.

"Did you not understand what His Majesty replied in his telegram?

"That his fear of not having the new government recognized by the world was why he accepted to remain on the throne. And he is right.

"I am now waiting from telegrams from London and Paris acknowledging the new forces in Siam."

Pridi kept his face down towards the papers on his desk and shuffled them to mask his disappointment.

Phibul may have been disenchanted at not seeing the stirring revolt he had hoped for, but for him, Pridi, his dream of making of Siam the first enlightened republic in Asia had been dashed.

At least for now, and probably forever.

His Majesty immediately called a meeting of the senior group of the Promoters at the Palace, and as they waited in an anteroom, they huddled in small, nervous clusters, under the stern, angry eyes of the helmeted and beribboned guards in front of the gilded and painted arched door.

Phya Phahol whispered that he had been told that the King had read the Manifesto and was exceedingly angry.

"It is true that the words were over strong, and that he has cause to feel insulted by your tone," he remarked in a biting, chiding voice.

Pridi had been nursing a headache all morning and was as tense as the others.

"Perhaps," he snapped, "but the Manifesto was meant for the people, not for him.

"And may I remind you that you all read and approved what I wrote."

Phibul, who was more accustomed than them to court circles and to the subtleties required, raised a calming hand to intervene.

"Yes, we did. But that was then, and now is now.

"Apologize to His Majesty. Do not antagonize him now, when all depends on his good will."

He would think about it, Pridi replied brusquely. In any case, he promised himself, he would not go down on his knees.

The days of kowtowing were over.

Then the doors were opened, and they were ushered into the royal presence, an honour quite extraordinary for them who had seen their monarch only in large receptions, and never, never to speak to.

Pridi noticed the silence, above all, at first.

Nobody seemed to even breathe, and he couldn't even hear a bird sing, or a breeze ruffle the branches of a tree outside the window.

He noted the papers scattered on a big table, his Manifesto on top of the pile, next to an empty cup and a plate of fruit and felt surprised at seeing that the King's desk was not unlike his own, the ordinary things of a man at work.

His Majesty was seated in the centre of the room, not on a throne, of course. Important, decisive as it was, the meeting was a political one, not a state occasion.

There was an uneasy moment, as the Promoters wondered if they should kneel, or bow.

What was the protocol for stripping a monarch of his absolute powers?

The King took a deep breath, steadied himself on the arm of his chair and stretched up, very slowly, in acceptance of the new order.

"I rise," he said, "I rise, in honour of Khana Ratsadon."

Did he hear them gasp as he stood, when they all dropped to their knees, hands joined before their faces?

Never before had a King of Siam risen before his subjects.

"Come," he said, "be seated, let us talk of the new Siam.

"I believe that you, Luang Praditmanutham, have been one of persons in the civil service who has crafted the plans for our country?"

Pridi heard Phibul behind him hissing "Apologize! Now!"

While his friends took chairs, he cleared his voice, as he stood before the King, and against any rule of protocol and custom, did not cast his eyes downwards.

The King stared, and he stared back, struck by the resigned dignity with which this man was facing the end of his world.

"Your Majesty," he said, his French-trained lawyerly manner coming back to him just as when he had faced the examination boards for his doctorate in Paris, "the message we have attempted to convey to the people is that all power resides with the people.

"Perhaps I used words that were stronger than they wanted to hear, and if so, I profoundly regret any distress these words have caused."

The King nodded and replied something, but Pridi did not take it in.

Through his throbbing headache, he heard himself and others speak, he heard that the Royal anthem was to be reinstated, he heard that the princes who were still hostages were to be released, except for Prince Boriphat who, Phra Prasat insisted, they all insisted, was to leave the country, he heard the King accept and then, in a daze of migraine and disbelief and joy, watched him sign the document that he had drafted, and which proclaimed that Khana Ratsadon was now the government in power in Siam.

The provisional constitution which had been submitted, His Majesty said, required only a few amendments to his mind, but was, all in all, acceptable.

Acceptable…

All of his royal power stripped away, forced to submit any decision to the yet-to-be-appointed People's Committee and People's Assembly, denied any right to veto any action taken by them…

The childless monarch was even refused any right to nominate his successor.

Pridi barely heard what amendments were suggested, he saw his fellow Promoters nod, awed and mesmerized as was he by the mere fact the King was speaking to them as equals almost, negotiating with them, and not challenging in any way what the son and grandson of the great Kings who had made Siam could only view as the abolition of the monarchy except in name.

He did not see the King rise to signify the meeting was over, he didn't remember leaving his chair or bowing very low and filing out behind the others.

They found themselves in the anteroom once more, chattering and elated and relieved.

But when Phya Phahol suggested a celebration, he declined.

"We have just witnessed the end of an era," he said, "and I think I had rather go home."

"And that is the end for today," he announced, stroking her hair. "Did I put you to sleep? You really know how to puncture my vanity."

She smiled and stretched. "Did I have you worried? No, I was just listening with my eyes closed, it's easier to picture it all.

"So, what happened after that?

"I mean, I know the King didn't die, Melanie told me he is living in exile in England."

"He is. He had to leave, because this revolution, or coup d'état, didn't go as smoothly as they had expected. You can't change the soul of a nation overnight.

Although," he added thoughtfully, "Hitler did."

They both remained silent for a moment, until Lawrence shook his head, and got up from the bed.

"Let's not think about this now, all right?

"Thip made sure there was plenty of Champagne for us, and I'm going to ring for a bottle to be brought up."

She giggled. "Champagne? In bed? That's a bit... decadent, isn't it?"

"Champagne in bed. We're on our honeymoon, after all. Time enough to return to our austere, virtuous ways when we get back."

Chapter IX

Kate walked slowly out of the gate of Saint-Louis Hospital, holding a wreath of jasmine blossoms and was about to hail a samlo when she saw Lawrence waiting, leaning against lady Thip's long dark green Buick convertible and gave him a delighted wave.

"What are you doing here? Smell," she held up her wreath of flowers to his nose. "A new father brought me this when he came to take his wife and son home. If it had been a daughter, he probably wouldn't have bothered, obviously."

He sniffed and leaned over to kiss her, but his face was somber.

"I wish I could say you smell far nicer than the *phuang malai* but actually, you smell of Dettol and worse."

"I'll shower it off as soon as we get home," she promised, settling into the car. "Phuang malai? Is that what those garlands are called? I never knew that."

He nodded, started the engine and waited for a taxi to pass before pulling out into Sathorn Road.

She shook her hair loose to better enjoy the cool wind and sniffed the blossoms again. "It's heaven driving around with the top down. I could almost wish it took longer to get home."

When he didn't answer, she turned in her seat to look at him. "Is something the matter? Is that why you came? We've been married two weeks and you're fed up already, is that it?"

"I was worried about you. Haven't you heard?"

Why? Heard what? What happened?

"There's been a battle between the French and Thai armies in Laos and Cambodia. It's been going on for a few days now, and so long as the Thai were winning, I thought there wouldn't be any problems at the hospital.

"But they've been pushed back out of Cambodia, so I worried that there might be some hotheads taking some kind of revenge on a soft French target. I heard talk of some anti-Catholic movement going there to demonstrate.

"It's been quiet all day?"

As hospitals go, yes, she smiled.

"Kate," he said very firmly and seriously, "I don't want you going back there. Things are only going to get worse."

Her eyes narrowed, and she did not answer.

"Did you hear me?"

"Oh, I did, I certainly did," she replied quietly after a moment, when she seemed to be trying to control her temper. "But that is not your decision to make."

"You're my wife, and I want you safe."

"I am your wife, and a nurse, and the hospital needs me.

"If there is indeed a war, then they will need me even more. Can't you understand that?"

He was sullen and angry, and changed gears with a screech of metal and dodged brutally to avoid a man tottering on a bicycle overladen with baskets and parcels as he turned off Surawong Road into the soi leading to the house.

"Need you more than I, you mean?" he demanded at last, honked impatiently to have the gardener pull the gates open and parked the car.

He switched off the ignition and turned to her, defying her to answer.

She put her hand on his arm. "You see, that's one of the reasons I love you. Your English is so much better than mine. You say 'more than I', when I would say more than me."

He sighed, defeated, "That's not funny," and walked through the garden behind her towards their pavilion.

When she emerged naked from the shower, she came up to him and put her arms around his neck.

"I love it when you go all lord and master on me," she whispered in his ear as he thrilled to her touch, "and you try to order me around. It's very sexy.

"But you didn't actually expect me to obey, did you?"

CHAPTER IX

I had to be content with that, and also that my straight-laced Irish Catholic wife from Boston has revealed herself as somewhat of a wanton.

But she will not be moved by my entreaties, she returns to the hospital, albeit for the shorter hours I managed to get Melanie and overbearing Sister Perrine to accept – but for half pay, which is what that martinet of a nun then exacted in exchange – and she laughs at my fears.

And I have discovered an unforeseen aspect of seizing love and happiness – I now worry constantly that I may lose them.

Yesterday morning, a French naval squadron sank two Thai torpedo boats off Koh Chang after an attack they launched on land backfired and forced them to retreat.

The pro-Phibul papers – which is to say all Thai newspapers – have somehow managed to report on the battle without saying that it was a crushing defeat which has destroyed most of the Thai navy.

Anti-French *and* anti-Catholic sentiment is very high in Bangkok these days and I've no idea if the authorities here will allow the hospital to continue to operate.

When I told Kate, she just replied that they wouldn't cut off their noses to spite their faces and went off to work.

Meanwhile, I am working with two translators, one Thai and one Chinese, who manage to include my anti-Japanese anti-Phibul articles in underground, clandestine newspapers that are sold, or just distributed for free in the Chinese neighbourhoods and around the station and universities.

I have no idea of the risks for those who hand them out and those who are caught reading them, but I imagine they would be dealt with harshly.

I meet the two translators separately at cinemas or in other places where farangs can mingle with the Thai without giving rise to suspicion, and I don't know their names or anything else about them.

They were sent to me by this curious network of people who appear unexpectedly by my side at the club or elsewhere and give me instructions on whom I should try to interview officially and what I should write for the underground.

Lately, a tall, rather sunburnt country-type came up to me and jostled my elbow, spilling my drink over my suit.

"Sorry, mate," he slurred in a rough, uneducated voice, "just off the train from Butterworth, dead tired, makes me clumsy."

He apologized and volunteered to buy me another then brought it to a quiet table and apologized again — "Wasn't aiming for the suit, got a tad carried away,"— in one of the crispest upper-crust tones I've ever heard, and I had to laugh.

He looked the part, I told him once he'd sat down, the wrinkles, the shabby, slightly grubby linen suit, I absolutely fell for his rustic planter act.

"Emmanuel, Cambridge. Anthropology.

"Amateur dramatics on the side. Afterwards, SOAS, Chinese." he said with a grin.

When I asked 'Footlights'? he nodded, surprised, until I said, by way of an explanation, "The other place. Balliol. Philosophy. Shifted scenery at OUDS."

He acknowledged that with a raised eyebrow. "I didn't know. But then we're told very little.

"And I really do have a rubber plantation near Ipoh," he added, tapping his nose.

If this was sign code for "It's all pretence," he was being pretty obvious.

I suppose I was looking somewhat sceptical because he felt the need to explain. "I inherited it from an uncle... My Malayan is fine, it's just my Chinese that needed working on.

"Still does, actually. Haven't spoken it since I was a lad, and as I'm off to Shanghai to help train some of the Chinese communist groups..."

"Should you be telling me all this?" I wondered out loud.

He just shrugged and pointed out that he had chosen to meet at the quiet hour between tiffin and the first stengah, making sure the bar would be empty. "Nobody can hear us."

At the school, I said, they kept on insisting on total discretion, need to know, what you don't know you can't tell, etc.

He just gave me another foxy smile.

Those precautions, it seemed to mean, don't apply to people like us.

I have also been told that in May or thereabout, I should

report to someone in Singapore if I could find a way of leaving the wife behind, before being complimented on having married. "No one would suspect a newlywed of being SOE."

"I'm not SOE," I argued, wondering if he had the wrong man.

"Oh, aren't you?" was the answer I got with a knowing, cunning, look, and was offered another pint.

When I asked what SOE stands for, I was told "Special Operations Executive."

"They've taken over that little group you were part of in Malaya."

Oh. I asked whether I would be expected to engage in more training. "Possibly. Things seem to be heating up. Probably need a refresher, I know I do now and then," he remarked.

Special Operations Executive sounds harmless enough, but so was the description of the training school I received before I went there.

I shall go and pick up Kate at the hospital this evening. I know she would prefer me not to, she is embarrassed at being seen getting into one of Thip's shiny big cars, that she is well-known and liked in the area for being a nurse, and people here are kind.

But still...

Kate had lingered over breakfast and was running late. She gratefully accepted the chauffeur's offer to take her to the hospital, although she asked to be dropped a block away, and felt like royalty being ferried to work in a gleaming Packard.

How easy it was to get accustomed to luxury, and how very little time it had taken her, barely a few weeks, to stop marvelling at having her laundry done, dinners served on china in the big house or brought to her in the pavilion, and to no longer work those gruelling hours in the ward.

"But I'm on half-pay," she wailed to Lawrence when he told her of the deal he had struck on her behalf.

" It's the price to pay for spending more time with you," he sighed. "Although, arguably, the one paying the price is you.

"Well, we'll just have to manage and eat nothing but rice in the future.

"I *was* relying on you to help pay my rent to Thip..."

And when she had given him a stark, panicked look, he gathered her in his arms. "I'm joking, darling.

"My rent is next to nothing, just enough not to make me a free-loader.

"And I certainly can afford it. It's ill-bred to say such things, but I am rather rich. And while we are on the subject of money," he pointed at the suitcase she was unpacking holding only her three dresses and some shoes, "you need more of these. Let me get you some clothes.

"You wouldn't let me pay for your wedding gown, but now... No, don't argue. You *do* need more dresses, and, remember, you can't afford them now," he reminded her with a triumphant smile. "And you always claim you haven't the right clothes each time I want to take you somewhere. Now you'll have no excuse."

She moved around the room, picking things up and putting them down, as unsettled as a cat, opened the big teak wardrobe and paused in surprise. He had more suits, shirts, dinner jackets and ties than anyone she had ever met, possibly more than all of them put together.

"Where do you wear this?" she demanded, unhooking a striped flannel jacket on its hanger and thrusting at him, and he frowned. "I'm not sure. Fancy dress ball, perhaps?"

She shook her head in amazement and went to the bathroom then came back, holding his wooden shaving bowl.

"Stephanotis? What's stephanotis?" and laughed when he said that it was the Greek word for bowl. Or maybe shave. Or maybe soap.

"No, even I know that."

She smelled. "It must be some kind of flower. Now this..." she unhooked his navy-blue silk dressing gown from behind the door. "This is beautiful," she sighed, holding to her cheek.

"Take it. It's yours now, at least until I buy you a new one."

No. She stripped off her skirt and blouse and draped herself in the dark, shimmering robe that came down to her ankles.

"You get a new one for yourself. I'm keeping this one."

Smiling at the memory, she asked the chauffeur to stop there when she spotted Belinda trudging her way up Sathorn Road, her dishevelled hair signalling that yet another evening with Eddy had lasted into the wee hours.

Running a few steps to catch up with her friend, she put an arm around Belinda's shoulders.

"Another late night?"

Belinda gave a hoarse laugh. "You always can tell, can't you? Let's hope Melanie can't. Hullo, what's this?"

Three army cars and a truck were parked in front of the hospital's main entrance, and two armed sentries were standing on each side.

"Oh, not again," Belinda groaned. "What are they going to want to check this time? Our nursing degrees? Our papers?"

"There seems to be more of them, this time." Kate pointed at a group in uniform who were huddled in the shade, laughing and smoking.

They both fished out their stamped documents from their purses and approached the first soldier posted at the foot of the stairs who barely glanced at the papers and waved them through, looking bored.

"Whatever they want, it's nothing to do with us." Belinda remarked.

"No. It's not us." Kate replied seeing Melanie and Doctor Hermet who were arguing with a civilian in a hallway leading to the surgical ward.

Next to them, an officer was glowering and barely seemed to be able to contain his impatience, his hand on the handle of the glass door.

"And no," Doctor Hermet was saying angrily, moving to stand so as to block the way, "I repeat, you cannot disturb my patient. He has just been operated on."

Doctor Sumet was hovering nearby, rubbing his gloved hands, his gown still blood spattered, and translating his French colleague's words for the officer, who kept shaking his head.

The civilian man was insistent, looking at both doctors, and showing Melanie a paper which she pushed away with an ingratiating and insincere smile, repeating, "Infection, infection. Dangerous..."

Finally, with a muttered curse, both the civilian and the officer left, their irate footsteps thundering on the wooden floor.

When they were gone, both surgeons exchanged a look of relief, and opened the door to the ward.

Melanie, catching sight of the two girls, ordered them tartly to go to the maternity ward.

"You are not needed here. Go, go.

"In fact, you are not needed at all today. Go home."

Then, catching up with them as they left, whispered urgently, "You have seen nothing. Understood?"

"What was that about?" Belinda asked. "You have to tell us, Mother, if you expect us to lie," she added slyly.

Melanie sighed, fingering her rosary.

"A French soldier, who was wounded the other day in Thai territory, and somehow bribed his way to us. Except someone talked, of course."

"What happens when they come back to get him?" Kate asked.

Melanie sniffed.

There would be another Frenchman just recovering from surgery in his bed. She believed there was a young employee of the Banque de l'Indochine who could very easily do without his appendix.

"Astonishing!" Lawrence exclaimed in admiration. Who could have expected that from Melanie?

"Although I'm not sure they'll be fooled, even if they cannot prove anything.

"And it means the hospital will be watched from now on. Now will you believe me when I say you shouldn't work there anymore?"

They were sitting in the sala and watching the sunset behind the river. She leaned back in the rattan armchair and smiled at him, rather nastily, he thought. "What about you?"

"Me?"

She raised her eyebrows. "You really are a lousy actor, aren't you? No wonder they kept you shifting scenery. You think I don't know what that ... that school was all about?

"I have no idea what they — whoever 'they' are — are making you do, but you are much busier than you used to be. You go places you don't tell me about and you meet people and don't say who.

"I may be less educated than you, but I've probably seen more movies, and I'm not a fool.

"You see, you don't know what to answer."

She got up and walked away, turning her head to give him a hard look, over her shoulder. "So, don't you talk to me about danger, all right?" And then, her voice turning to velvet, she went over to him and pulled him out of his chair.

"Now let's go back to our room."

Chapter X

On the train somewhere between Butterworth and Hat Yai.

We are passing through jungle-covered hills, and what would have seemed, until a bit over a year ago, a beautiful, lush scenery, I now see as dark and ominous, alive with buzzing insects, shrieking monkeys, and, most threatening of all, the silent dangers, horrible centipedes, disgusting leeches, red ants and their aggressive cousins, the aptly named fire ants, and deadly spiders. Snakes, huge snakes.

And, of course, malaria...

But at the same time, I also remember the shimmering, green light filtered through giant ferns and dancing on the dripping mosses and rainbows thrown onto the rocks, bursts of coloured flowers hanging from vines with Monarch butterflies studding them like jewels and the magical sight of a sun bear with her cubs basking on a log before scampering off.

Our instructor, a hard-bitten, foul-mouthed, retired Indian Army sergeant, who, for all his years in Malaya still berated us with a Yorkshire accent, gave us a very rare and grudging smile.

"Good. Shows you crept up on her silently," before adding that of course, the Nips would be less easy to surprise, "because they wouldn't be distracted by having their young with them, now would they?"

Before I was dispatched to the euphemistically called "refresher course" in the jungle, I reported to a dingy, dusty office, located behind a shipping company near the port, and met a delightful, erudite, and terrifying man who, when he greeted me at the door, announced what he had in mind for me — code and radio training in the Cameron Highlands before a stint in Merapoh. He tapped the map of South East Asia hanging on the wall to show me where Merapoh was.

"You'll love it," he assured me, "best climbing in Malaya."

I asked, trying to copy that crisp, biting way British officers have of speaking, omitting most articles and pronouns, "Do much mountaineering yourself, sir?" not noticing that he had a cane by his chair. He showed it to me and replied "Hardly" in a dry voice and tapped it on his leg. It rang of metal.

"Of course," he added pensively, "there are those who swear by the Cameron Highlands. Just like Kent, or so they say. Can't say I set much store by Kent, myself."

I assured him I was open to both.

"At some point, there should be time to lay on some decent bangs as well."

I found this very embarrassing and was about to say I was not interested until I realized he was talking about the use of explosives and sabotage, not prostitutes, and nodded enthusiastically.

"Good lad." He clapped me on the shoulder. "Now down to brass tacks."

Lawrence gazed unseeing out of the window and put down his pen, reliving that unsettling interview.

The man, who for all his cordial welcome, had omitted to introduce himself, picked up a file and perused it.

"Hmm, Balliol, philosophy and history. Yes." He looked up. "You're a runner I see. Bit of rock climbing. Where?"

"Lake District, mainly. Once in the French Alps."

"Hmm. Good. Though I'm told mountains in Asia tend to be a bit different. Still, a mountain's a mountain, what?

"Hmm. No cricket, no rugby?"

When Lawrence replied shrugging, "Easily bored, sir," he looked at the paper again, humming "Yes, yes...," as if in approval then cocked an eyebrow. "Poor marksmanship, what?"

"Poor eyesight, sir."

But, the man continued, as if Lawrence hadn't spoken, good at unarmed combat, good jungle skills, yes, yes, good team spirit.

He frowned.

Recently married? Why?

"Love?" Lawrence offered in reply, and the man grunted.

He would need to dispose of the wife somehow, he realized that, didn't he, when the balloon went up here?

"It *is* going up, you know, it's a matter of months.

"Even the Yanks have finally accepted that, well, Roosevelt has at least, and pretty soon, they are going to have to get off their arses and join in.

"But they haven't yet, and in the meantime, we shall have to defend the civilized world on our own.

"Now, this is where you come in.

"Brooke-Popham — you've heard of him?"

Lawrence grinned.

Everybody had heard of Air-Marshal Sir Robert Brooke-Popham, Commander of the British Far Eastern forces.

"You probably know that the training school which you were invited to attend last year was disbanded, for several reasons, one of the main ones being that it was considered defeatist by the Governor of Singapore, and also because Supreme Command of Far Eastern Forces thought we were a bunch of bumbling amateurs, well-meaning no doubt, but not to be trusted, assuming that only the military arm of intelligence is in a position to collect information and be trusted with various operations.

"Well, Brooke-Popham has finally overcome his mistrust of civilians and realized that it's people like you and me, the engineers, the planters, the teachers and the missionaries, the intellectuals, the dabblers in Buddhism, or archaeology or Sanskrit, or whatever, you know who I mean, the men who make up British civil society in the East, who can take the pulse of a country and act accordingly to help when needed.

"Therefore, there is finally money and facilities to train you people properly, provided it is done by military instructors."

Lawrence raised his eyebrows.

"You make us sound like characters in a short story by Somerset Maugham, sir. Not that I object, of course, I've often thought of all of us that way."

He received a piercing glare in return.

"Ha! I can tell you're a scribbler, in fact, that's been your task so far, I see.

"Pretty good at it, judging from what came out in the British press about nationalism and irredentism in Siam."

"Actually, it's Thailand, now, sir."

The man peered at him through his glasses and snorted.

"Call me Bill, it's not my name, but it will serve... Just like Thailand for Siam.

"Always be Siam, though, as far as I'm concerned.

For that matter, remind me what irredentism is."

Wondering if he were being tested, Lawrence cocked his head.

Simply put, it was when one state claimed back land that either was part of its territory, sir, or — interesting distinction — was *considered* as having been part of it.

"Hmm, not bad." was the answer.

Bill pushed himself away from the desk and crossed his hands behind his head.

"What do you think of Major-General Phibul?

"Will he side with the Japs when the time comes?"

Narrowing his eyes, Lawrence considered, feeling increasingly as if he were back at university sitting for an exam, aware that the man opposite already had his own opinion.

It was difficult to say, he finally began, choosing his facts carefully.

Left to himself, more than probably.

For starters, it was necessary to understand how immensely popular Phibul was.

He had been whipping up nationalist sentiment for the past couple of years, to great success, using the war with France as a rallying cry, at least until the cease-fire the Japanese imposed in January.

"He, and his Minister for Propaganda, Wichit Wathakan, are very talented at manipulating public opinion.

"Most of the anti-French demonstrations in Bangkok turn into pro-Phibul parades - they're hardly spontaneous, you realize, everything is very carefully orchestrated.

"They rope in the Yuwachon, an ultra-nationalistic youth organisation, very like the Hitler Jugend, if you like. Uniforms, slogans, salutes, the works.

"Besides the Yuwachon, university students have formed a secret 'Thai Blood' party, the name is probably derived from the title of a play that Wichit wrote and he is generally assumed to have founded the party himself.

"Certainly, he inspired its ultra-nationalistic aims and objectives which is to be re-united with what they call 'left-bank Thais'. Left bank of the Mekong, that is, French Indochina, is what they mean.

"As I said, it's supposed to be a secret party, but actually, everybody knows about it, and there's a good deal of pressure on students to join."

He paused, trying to express the forebodings shaped by all these disparate facts gleaned during the past months, debated whether to call the man Bill, then decided against it.

"I'm sure some are true believers, but for the others — a lot depends on joining, better grades at examinations, perhaps the possibility of a promotion for the father, mothers who think it's a safe way for their sons to spend their time, the influence of friends, also just the appeal of the uniform.

"It's difficult to separate the pressure put on students or the members of the Yuwachon to join those groups from the real — and justified — bitterness about the territories lost to France.

"Last year, the Ministry of the Interior printed maps of *all* the lost territories, not just those taken over by France, but also including the Burmese and Malay states ceded to Britain, and they've been distributed in schools throughout the country. I think every household has one.

"Have you heard of *mo lam*?"

"No, I can't say I have. What is it?"

Popular music, songs, from the Isan region in the North-East, which directly borders Laos and Cambodia, Lawrence said, warming to his subject.

Last year, the Propaganda Minister, Wichit, had produced a Book of Songs, each one about a territory or province lost to the French.

"They're sung everywhere, now, sir."

Settling forwards again and pouring a glass of water, Bill barked a bitter laugh.

"Gifted at propaganda indeed!

"You've told me something I didn't know. And what can be done to counter that, in your opinion?"

Lawrence leaned back and sighed.

"Very little, although, I think, perhaps... irony.

"Make him ridiculous in the eyes of the public.

"Phibul claims he wants a return to some ideal of 'Thainess' freed of all Western influence?

"Make fun of him imitating the Mussolini fascist salute, and also of his preposterous cultural mandates, such as forcing people to abandon traditional dress, wear hats, — I mean one cannot ride a tram if one is not wearing a hat, and there's a thriving trade of hat rentals at each tram stop, you pay to put one on and hand it over when you get off.

"And that whole business of ordering men to kiss their wives in the morning before going to work. Everyone finds that tremendously silly, actually.

"His passion for Italian films, perhaps...

"But, I have to admit," he spread his hands out, "there's not really much to go on. Except for one thing, and that's really important.

"The Crown."

The fact that Phibul was seen as attempting to erase any trace of the monarchy except in name, could and probably would backfire.

"If there were to be rumours circulated that he was trying to create a republic, or still, even better for our purposes, that he wants to depose the present King and get himself crowned instead... He has his portrait hanging in very public building, bank, hospital and shop, replacing the portrait of the King.

"The people resent that, even those who support Phibul.

"The people of Thailand are still very attached to and respectful of their King, even when the King is a young man still at school," he explained.

There was also the mitigating influence of the Finance Minister, Pridi Banomyong, who was the true intellectual leader of the People's Party, Khana Ratsadon, and who loathed the Thai Blood party — he was also the rector of the University of Political and Moral Sciences — and repeatedly warned his own students against it.

The Deputy-Foreign Minister as well, Direk Janayama, whose sympathies were far more with the Western powers, as was the case, it would seem, of the Thai Royal family.

"Plus, the thing is, as a rule, the Thais don't really like what they know of the Japanese, in part because of the war with China — not that they're necessarily pro-Chinese — Phibul has made sure the Thai resent the hold the Chinese have on commerce and banking.

"But the Japanese in Bangkok, especially those who are newly arrived, and they arrive in droves, well... they tend to be arrogant towards the Thai, treating them as –," he hesitated, then decided to tell it as he had seen it himself, and heard it described by his contacts, "–they treat them as we treat natives in our colonies. The Thai are very sensitive to respect and manners, 'face', if you like.

"Also some people, those who are better informed, if you will, are getting suspicious of all this Japanese activity, 'companies' that open all of a sudden and don't seem to do much, the 'engineers' who turn up in mining towns, the photographic expeditions... and of course, the two new Japanese consulates opened in Songkhla, in the South, near the border with Malaya, curiously, and Chiang Mai in the North, where there are actually very few Japanese people living.

"I've written about it for the underground press.

"Finally, a lot depends on the armed forces, some are pro-Allies, and others, such as Prayun, one of the original officers behind the coup of 1932, well, his mother was German and he's rabidly pro-Axis.

"So, it's a bit of a tug o' war between both tendencies, with the armed forces as a wild card, sorry for the mixed metaphor, sir."

How the power would play between the two factions was anybody's guess.

"And of course, the Japanese have just forced a Peace Treaty in Tokyo between Thailand and France, returning some territories to Thailand," the older man mused. "But surely not as much as the Thais wanted."

Lawrence was surprised. "I hadn't heard, sir."

"Happened yesterday, while you were en route, I expect.

"Quite a feather in Phibul's hat, except for the fact that they also have to pay the French four million baht as an indemnity.

"Given the state of their economy, it must have been a blow, and I'm sure the people haven't heard.

"Do slip in that fact, will you, when you get a chance, for the underground press, of course, but also officially, under your name. Not bad to call things out for what they are.

"We bankroll *The Bangkok Times*, so they will publish anything you write along those lines."

Then veering to the personal again, "Keep a diary? Yes, I

thought so.

"You writers all do. Think everything in your life needs to be recorded for posterity.

"Well don't.

"Destroy the ones you've written so far, unless, of course," he drawled sarcastically, "they deal only with your love life.

Now,…" he got up, to signify the meeting was over. "I have a few papers for you to sign, pay – it's not much, but from what I gather, that's not a problem – pension, next-of-kin, that kind of thing.

"Basically, you belong to us, now.

"You will be told where to go and when, you need to learn radio and code, and combat in different types of situations."

He turned back to the wall and pointed at the map, and Lawrence came to stand by him, as he traced the Northern borders of Thailand with his finger.

"The mountains in Merapoh are a poor substitute if you need to get out through Burma, and the Cameron highlands aren't really much like the areas around Kunming, if you get out through China, but it's the best we can do."

"China, sir?"

"Well, yes, Yunnan. Easier than hiking through the hills in Burma.

"You might need to hitch a ride with our Yank friends from China. There's some kind of daft American aviation base in Kunming. From there, of course, you'll need to report to India.

"Meerut.

"Yes, India, eventually." he grinned at Lawrence's expression of disbelief and walked him to the door. "Delighted to have met you, old chap.

"Drinks tonight at the Tanglin Club? We can talk about German philosophy, if you've a mind to.

"And remember," he raised an admonishing finger. "Nothing in writing unless we tell you to. Oh! – I nearly forgot –" he pretended confusion, and Lawrence had the eerie feeling something truly frightening was about to come up.

"Yes, by the way, your name was on a list that the Kempetai got its hands on in Shanghai a few months ago.

"Obviously, one of our men there appears to have been rather careless, what? So far, the Japs don't seem to have taken the group very seriously, probably because our own government didn't take us very seriously until a couple of months ago.

"But when they get into Thailand, you may find yourself singled out... See you this evening. Six."

He was alone in his sleeper compartment and there was no one to see him or attempt to read over his shoulder. He picked up his pen, determined to ignore his instructions and continued to write.

"I was terribly worried at first, then the feeling gradually wore away, replaced by more present fears, centipedes, scorpions, tarantulas, snakes, etc.

"Besides finding myself rather talented at coding — our sergeant admitted resentfully that he wasn't surprised — 'all youse intellectual types take to it — you all think it's a game, you do.' True, it does somehow seem a game — I was given an extremely useful tip, to have several pairs of spectacles made — having lost a pair whipped away by a branch when we were climbing in the jungle — thankfully, Gerald, my friend the archaeologist from Burma had a spare, but a bit strong for me.

"I intend to act on that wisdom as soon as I get back and have half a dozen made.

"Meanwhile, yet another worry.

"In the dark panelled bar of the Tanglin Club, my host dropped as if in afterthought, which seems to be his way of imparting unpleasant facts,'By the way, when the Yanks join in, and assuming, as we all do, that Phibul will throw his lot in with the Japs, your wife will be an enemy alien.' "

I pointed out that there were many women and children in Malaya and Singapore.

"For one thing, Fortress Singapore will not fall.

"We have evacuation plans ready for civilians to get here from Malaya. We have none from Bangkok.

"Get her back to the States as soon as possible. That will be one thing less on your mind."

I have no idea how Kate will react to *that*.

She may surprise me, after all she occasionally lets slip a bit of nostalgia for Boston winters, for her family — who finally came up with a letter sending their best wishes — and for treats such as

Hershey chocolate bars and Coca Cola.

But I think not, and that she will dig her heels in. She has shown herself to be quite stubborn.

Kate, in fact, became quite angry at the prospect of being sent back to Boston.

"Do you think I could leave you? Or leave my job?"

She stormed out of the room, muttering darkly that she didn't want to discuss this anymore, then returned, eager to continue the argument, saying he had spoiled her pleasure at his return.

"It's been six weeks! And that is the first thing you had to tell me? That you want me gone?"

He caught her in his arms and whispered that he had missed her so much and never did he want her gone, but "Listen, I'm just passing on a warning I was given, it does make sense for you to leave. I want you to be safe."

She was trying to twist out of his hold, and he could tell she was close to tears. He finally released her to dig into his pocket, and extended a small velvet covered box. "Look! I got this for you in Singapore"

It was a pair of jade and coral earrings set with small diamonds, but instead of the raptures he was expecting, she gave him a knowing, cynical look, after glancing at the opened box in her hand.

"Oh, I get it.

"I have three brothers, you think I don't know how men's minds work?

"No! No, no, NO!

"Don't think for a minute you will get your way by sulking and giving me jewellery.

"I am not leaving," she declared firmly, as she fastened the pendants in her lobes and watched herself in the mirror, swinging them left and right.

"Oh! Oh my! These *are* beautiful, though," she exclaimed, fingering them in awe.

"Almost as beautiful as you. Jade for your eyes and coral for your lips," he smiled, delighted at her pleasure, but determined to make her see reason.

She looked up at him, her eyes still over-bright.

"They will be so lovely with a new dress I've just had made to celebrate your homecoming — grey chiffon and halter neck.

Rather low-cut… When you see me in it," she added slyly, "you'll never want me to go."

He smiled again, instead of answering, thinking all the while, "We shall see."

LAWRENCE'S DIARY
BANGKOK, WEDNESDAY, JUNE 25TH,

She wore the earrings in bed that night.

And the following evening, when we went to dinner at the Royal Hotel and never had I found her more enchanting with the grey dress revealing the skin of her shoulders and her long neck, and the jade that matches her eyes.

And never have I been more determined to spring her loose of the trap that Bangkok may become.

The first night, when we were both lying naked in bed with the sheet thrown off to let the cool air from the fan dry off our sweaty bodies, and the monsoon rains beating and whipping against the shutters, she propped herself on her elbow and with a gentle finger, traced the scars left by mosquito and ant bites, and the scab from a deep cut on my arm from a parang, the long bladed machete used to clear paths in the jungle. I hadn't moved out of the way fast enough and the chap next to me slashed a bit too far.

"Does it still hurt?" she asked, running her forefinger on the purple, swollen line.

Not enough to mention, I replied, although it had hurt like the devil, not when it happened, the blade is so sharp I barely felt it, but afterwards, at first when I poured iodine on it, and then, even more so, when it turned septic.

"The sergeant had some kind of powder that he sprinkled on before he bandaged it, and it healed in a few days," I blurted out before catching myself, dreading the question that would follow, "What sergeant?"

But she just nodded, saying knowledgeably, "Sulpha powder. Yes.

"I wish we had more at the hospital, but it's difficult and expensive to get hold of, so we keep it for the cases when other anti-bacterials don't work."

I did not tell her I have a ready supply in the escape kit I was given in Penang, before I caught the train back, along with quinine, balls of opium and a roll of bills and gold coins sewn into the lining of my bag to bribe my way out of Bangkok. And a Webley MK 38 revolver.

Meanwhile, I am keeping busy writing an incendiary piece on the enormous indemnity paid to the French to regain a mere fraction of the lost territories, calling Phibul's leadership into question.

The target, this time, is the nationalist faction.

How and where it is to be published, I do not know, I no longer meet my two translators, it's too dangerous, and I receive instructions slipped into my locker at the Club to drop my paper in a conveniently placed basket at the feet of a woman selling mangoes at Bangrak market, or at Wat Mahathat when I go there for my Thai language class, or indeed in the towel hamper of the Club's changing room.

I have been having regular meetings at the British Club with Andrew Gilchrist, who is nominally second secretary at the Embassy here but actually in charge of propaganda, one of the strange crew of people who sidle up to me regularly and drop messages or instructions or just, as it were, take my pulse and make sure I am not getting overly jittery about what I am asked to do.

He is a Scot from Lanarkshire, with a ginger beard and an accent which Oxford did nothing to dispel, and a laugh that honks like a goose and though he is my senior by ten years or so, we have become quite friendly.

He is also my boss, or as he put it, my commanding officer, "although we're both civilians, any instruction I give you is an order, get it?" which is how I realized he too must be SOE.

He passes on subjects for articles, snippets of information to dig into, between our discussions about life, love, comparisons between Trinity, his college, and Balliol, the Thai language — his knowledge of it is better than mine and he often makes fun of what he calls my plummy aristocratic accent — "Where did you learn it, with monks from Wat Mahathat?

"Or French priests from Assumption School?" and when I said "Both", he honked in triumph.

This evening, when we were sitting over our pints, he quietly dropped that I might be surprised to hear that Phibul was secretly making overtures to the Allies through Crosby, the Ambassador, asking about British support in case of a Japanese invasion of Thai territory.

"Wipe that astonished look of your face, will you?" he snapped irritably. "It's visible miles away.

"Yes, indeed," he added with a huge smile to give the impression we were discussing pleasant, personal matters in case anybody was watching us, "but at the same time, he has meetings with Tamura, the Japanese attaché, behind the Japanese Ambassador's back, mind you, about strengthening Thai-Japanese military cooperation.

"Have you ever met Tamura?"

I shook my head, I only knew of him, and grinned to still create that impression of a cheery, friendly conversation between two beer-swilling Oxonians.

"Well, he's a crafty one, I can tell you.

"Cultivates this persona of a drunk and dissolute number, but he's a spy's idea of a spy.

"Perfect English — he grew up in Hawaii, lucky bastard, bound to be warmer than Lanarkshire. Apparently spied on the Yanks in Manila, went to China in 38 — now what does *that* tell you? — and he's here and obviously has instructions outside of the Embassy's reach.

"What do we do now, you might ask?

"We wait. We — and that includes you — try and find out more.

"Our friend Field-Marshal Phibul — have you gotten used to calling him Field-Marshal, by the way?

"It seems that only last week he was still Major-General — the man's a complete Gilbert and Sullivan show to himself, well, the esteemed Field-Marshal has also been complaining to Crosby about the number of Japanese military operating in secret in Thailand and suggesting that we bring in more agents of our own.

"Does that make any sense to you?"

"No, it doesn't, except that Phibul is playing one side off each other or hedging his bets. Thinking about it, in fact, yes, it does make sense when you know Phibul.

"So, are we?" I asked.

Are we bringing more agents? I meant, but was told that was no concern of mine.

What I did need to do was to try and befriend one Shoji Yunosuke, a Japanese journalist whom the Embassy would like to keep tabs on.

"As fellow scribblers, you can probably moan together about the idiocy of governments. Heaven knows you wouldn't be wrong."

I am told he favours some of the more dubious watering holes on Sri Phaya Road, which means more evenings away from home, and that does not much appeal and will not be easy to explain to Kate.

Although she knows better than to ask about my activities, I see this strained, anxious look on her face when I leave the house after dark, and I too, feel the weight of this secrecy between us.

Neither have I told her yet — though I shall need to, someday soon — that I have made provision for her in case, well, just in case, but mainly because Andrew Gilchrist told me to.

I wrote a will, feeling slightly ridiculous, filed one copy with the Embassy here and sent another by mail to my parents, asking them to inform me by telegram when — if — it arrived, and shall keep on sending copies until one ship carrying mail gets through and they tell me it has been received.

The process, distasteful and depressing as it was, has at least taken one weight off my mind.

Yesterday was National Day, and there was a huge parade with rather amusing floats to represent the theme, which was "Progress" and there were also tanks and armoured cars and young men in uniform, and watching the smiling, happy faces, the families with young children, and everybody laughing, cheering and eating sweets and grilled squid on skewers.

We had made an outing of it, with Belinda and Edward, and people smiled at the no doubt charming sight of two young couples of farang lovers, Kate looking radiant in a flowery frock and a big white hat with flowers on the brim, and the children wai-ed her and she wai-ed back to everybody's delight.

I could not believe these cheerful people are seething over a map of the lost territories hanging on their kitchen wall nor reconcile this spectacle with the description I gave in Singapore last month.

Yet both are true.

Chapter XI

Dear Mother Felicity,
I have just received your letter, with all the news from home, and I am sorry I haven't
taken the time to write in months. It was good to know that Maura is now a full-
fledged teacher and is dating a good man. What you wrote about little Teddy — well,
he isn't so little any more, and the fact he has gotten involved in dubious businesses,
with the smuggling gangs... I just hope he doesn't get into too much trouble.
    I'm also very happy and relieved that Da is getting enough work, and that Maura
and Joe Jr. are looking after him. None of them write, ever, so could you please
remind them that they still have a sister, and that even though I live on the other side
of the world, I still care about them.
    Now for my own news: first, to dispel any of the worries you mentioned and those
you didn't — I am fine, and happy, and no, there is no baby on the way.
    Today is Thanksgiving, and I'm feeling a bit homesick...

Kate paused.

What could she say without raising fears?

Certainly, she shouldn't mention the Thai-Blood organized demonstrations in front of the hospital demanding that the French bishop, priests and nuns leave the country, nor that a bloodied and battered Italian priest, Father Gavalla, had turned up last month at the hospital for treatment, and haltingly told of how he had been dragged by a mob from his house next to the church in Tha Kwian, a small town not very far, Mother Melanie said, from the Cambodian border.

He had been kicked in the head and clubbed and punched and then tied naked to a tree.

All his possessions, his watch, papers and money had been taken, his house was ransacked. The headman of the town affected to know nothing of the attack and then forced the poor man to sign a statement blaming the Catholics of his parish.

No, she couldn't write that.

Nor that the city seemed on edge, hardly any traffic at night, and that markets were beginning to look bare as the farmers from the other side of the river hesitated to cross over to Bangkok to sell their vegetables, and the usually smiling Thai were nervous and sullen with fear.

For the first time, last week, a samlo driver had refused to take her to the hospital, raised his fist at her and muttered something threatening she thankfully couldn't understand.

For that matter she hadn't told Lawrence about it either.

He was already far too worried after hearing of Father Gavalla's ordeal, and once again, had tried to convince her to return to Boston.

"And then what?" she demanded. "I can't go back to the convent, and if you knew what my father's house is like, you wouldn't want me living there.

"And what about you? I won't leave without you."

But he had just turned away and vanished for hours.

She went back to her letter, at a loss for any news that would not worry the old nun.

There's a lovely holiday here, held on the full moon of November, where you make little baskets of flowers with incense and candles, and once you've lit the candle, you float them away on the river, to carry all the bitter thoughts and sins of the year with it off to sea.

It's a beautiful sight, all those brave little rafts of flowers with their flickering, bobbing flames, flowing downstream under the moon.

Until now, the nuns forbade us to take part, we were only allowed to watch but this year, Lawrence and I celebrated it from the landing of Lady Thip's garden, but I still miss Thanksgiving, though.

Of course, people here know nothing about it, and I have given up trying to explain.

Even Lawrence, kind and loving as he is, can't seem to understand that it's almost as important to us as Christmas, though he has promised to take me to dinner tonight to the best restaurant here, to be followed by "Gone with the Wind" which has just arrived in Bangkok, so we shall make our own celebration.

I feel so lucky being married to him that I still pinch myself to make sure I'm not dreaming. I hope one day we shall be able to visit Boston and then you will meet him.

She frowned.

Now why had she written that? "*Some day visit Boston*"? she asked herself, imagining Felicity's voice lilting in surprise. Why, she will wonder, wouldn't they?

Did Felicity also live with this threat of war looming over any moment of the day? Did the sisters talk about over dinner?

Perhaps, although the refectory of the convent—she could still conjure up the combined smell of cabbage, corned beef and furniture polish — was not a place where the outside world was given much space to intrude.

Much like us, she sighed.

Each time the talk turned to the war, it always ended with her crying, Lawrence getting angry — he did not shout or slam doors but went cold and silent, so that they finally had reached an unspoken agreement to discuss it no longer.

But then, it was difficult to know *what* to talk about... All subjects were dangerous and full of pitfalls which brought them back to arguing again.

She didn't want to bore him with the little events of the hospital and it was out of the question to tell him about the major, frightening ones, or how distressed Doctor Hermet, Melanie and the other nuns seemed to be, and that only last week she had found Mother Melanie packing up a small case and bedroll.

Seeing her, the nun had taken her hand and sat her down, saying that it was necessary to face facts, and that she, Father Perroudon and the others may most likely be forced to flee soon.

"But to go where, Mother?"

That, she did not know, the Lord would show the way. Perhaps India, if at all possible.

"Listen, my girl. Either this country sides with Japan, and therefore as French we would be enemies — not that we are much loved at all, these days — or they do not, and fight the Japanese, and what chance do they have to win, unless the British step in?

"But it still means war, one way or another.

"Of course, if there *is* a war, we will be needed more than before, and of course we shall do our duty to take care of those who need us.

"But we may be given no choice."

She laughed softly. "And I shall tell you a secret, which is that this is my little superstition: if my case is packed, with some family photos, and the like, then I shall not need it."

Then more seriously, she added, "You, however, have a husband who is British, and the British look after their own. I do not worry for you. And I know that if I am forced to go, you will stay as long as you can and continue our work.

"So, do not look sad, and do not tell anyone, please, especially not O'Grady.

"I don't want that flibbertigibbet running around and saying that I have lost my nerve."

She had promised, but keeping silent to Lawrence was a burden, and he, for his part had given her to understand that he wanted no questions about the articles he wrote or the people he saw when he vanished for hours, coming back reeking of smoke and alcohol merely to say he had been to the movies but couldn't recall which film he'd seen.

It was only in bed that there seemed to be no strain between them.

Finally, last night, when they were lying under the mosquito netting, she put her head on his shoulder and whispered that he had never ended the story of why the King left Siam to go to England.

Stroking her hair, looking up at the shadows of the frangipani that the moon threw on the ceiling he smiled. "That's true, I never did... Do you want to hear it now?"

She thought about it for a moment.

"Yes, but somehow.... What that's story, Arabian Nights? When the girl never ends the tale, so she won't be killed?"

"So, maybe if you always leave a bit out for the next day... then you won't go away..."

He laughed softly in the dark.

Somehow, he didn't see himself as Scheherazade, but he was willing to give it a try.

"Although, you do realize, my darling, that I may have to leave... If — and bear in mind it's only if — if I do, then you must promise me..."

She sighed. "Promise you what? Not that again."

"Yes, that again. If I am no longer here, what's to keep you?"

"How many times do I need to say it?

"My work, for one. I shall go on living here and wait for you to come back."

"All right. But if – once again, only *if*, the hospital is forced to close, and you know that *could* happen – *then* would you promise me to go home?"

Home... She had never thought she would feel that way, but this was home now.

She sighed again, choosing her words, remembering what she had promised Melanie, that she would stay and continue working as long as she could.

"All right.

"If – *if* – I can no longer work, I'll go back to Boston and wait for you there."

She settled more comfortably against him, plumping her pillow, confident it would never come to that. In times of war, hospitals were more useful than ever, weren't they?

"You really won't take no for an answer, will you?" she murmured playfully, but with a slight edge to her voice. "I noticed that right away, in fact, I remember thinking it when you dragged me off to the Oriental for lunch."

He held her close and chuckled, relieved at having at last exacted her acceptance. "Did you? You may be right... My mother always says so as well.

"Now, do you truly want to hear about what happened after the revolution?

"You don't want to tell me instead how irresistible I was?"

"I thought you were just a rich guy who always had to have things his own way.

"And yes, I want to hear the rest of the story."

Anything, anything, to stop talking about either of them leaving. It didn't bear thinking about.

Siamese twins

The thing about power is that it's different when you actually get it, Lawrence began, thoughtfully, *and that is what the King knew all along, and Pridi, Phibul and the others discovered very soon.*

Once the King had signed the provisional Constitution, Pridi set about what he had always seen as his mission, dreamt of, laboured all those long years for: creating a democracy.

But how do you explain democracy to those whose whole lives, and that of their parents and grandparents and countless generations before them had always been ruled by monarchs whom they venerated almost as gods?

And when you begin the process of nominating members for the People's Assembly, how do you weed out those who are solely motivated by personal ambition?

For that matter, he mused, how do you separate personal ambition from the public good, when you know, as he did, that you are the one to carry out the reforms the nation was so sorely in need of?

Were the people of Siam, on the whole, ripe for democracy as it is known in Europe or America, was the question the Promoters always asked rhetorically.

No, not yet, all agreed, they needed, as those foreign nations had, years of step by step guidance.

The Colonels, Phya Song and Phya Phahol had very definite views on who should sit in the People's Assembly which was entrusted with exercising power on behalf of the people.

Although, as Phya Song ruefully admitted in one of the many, flurried meetings immediately following the entry into force of the Constitution, it's not as if they had that many potential candidates to choose from.

A mix of Promoters, yes, but then...

Nobody from the provinces, they had been kept outside of the whole movement, and besides, how could the loyalty of those of whom one knew very little be verified?

Members of the Assembly would be drawn from Bangkok only and nominations would need to include senior officials who had proven their worth in previous administrations.

The Chairman of the Peoples' Committee, Phya Phahol proposed, should be Phya Mano.

A most suitable choice, most agreed, an English-trained lawyer, who had provoked the ire of the princes, some years ago, when he suggested a cut to the Royal Privy purse and thus found that his ambition of becoming Minister of Justice had been thwarted.

But he was nonetheless a Court insider whose wife was lady-in-waiting to the Queen and had never joined the Promoters, probably in fear for his career.

"Plus ça change...," Pridi muttered, finding, as he often did, that French was the best language to express cynicism.

"Yes," Phibul cut him off impatiently, "the more things change, the more they *stay the same. Did you think that all of a sudden, a new politically enlightened class would emerge?"*

Pridi sighed.

No, of course not, but he had hoped for better than this life-long, self-serving... "I don't even know what to call him. Hypocrite, perhaps?"

Phibul pursed his lips and gave him a knowing look, seeming to imply that Pridi would have hoped for the position himself, and the two stared at each other at length, daring the other to speak.

But this was no time for quarrels, while other challenges were becoming evident, and the backlash of public opinion was one none of them had reckoned with.

The press, revelling in its new freedom latched on to the message of the Manifesto and published stories of princely extravagance, entrancing and infuriating the common people who gathered in coffee houses to read the most sensational articles out loud and exclaim in disgust at often fabricated details. A few somehow believed the new government was to abolish all taxes and stopped paying them.

But the conservative newspapers, those read by the elite, stoked fears of having the kingdom in the hands of rabid revolutionaries who, not content with stripping the beloved monarch of all powers were now intent on establishing a Communist form of government.

What had happened to the beloved kingdom, they asked?

Rumour had it that several princely families would have their wealth confiscated.

Leaflets were mysteriously distributed throughout Bangkok and five provincial capitals calling the people to rise and impose a Soviet Siam.

A diplomatic letter of congratulations to Khana Ratsadon from the Chinese Kuomintang was transformed by stories whispered at first, then openly told and repeated, into a message of support from the Comintern.

"What's the difference?" Kate demanded, in a slightly annoyed voice.

The Kuomintang was the Nationalist Party of China. The Comintern was the movement that wants to establish world communism.

"It's easy to remember – Communist international – therefore Comintern."

She raised herself on one elbow and brushed her hair away from her face.

"See, that's where you lose me. Too much detail.

"I don't really care about who was on the assembly or whatever, although," she added waspishly, "you obviously do. Just tell me what happened to the King."

Lawrence took a deep breath. "I was trying to," he replied patiently.

"No, you weren't. You were just – Oh, I don't know.

"You were showing off your knowledge. You were making me feel stupid. You were being – what's that word you use all the time? Oh yes – condescending."

Lawrence sat up and turned on the light to look at her, shaking his head in disbelief.

"That's incredibly unfair, and it's just not true."

He punched the pillow and lay back down, speaking to the ceiling between clenched teeth.

"All right, you want to know what happened to the King?

He thought the Promoters were going too far, everybody thought Phya Mano was turning into a dictator, the princes tried a comeback, there was another, actually several coups, I'll spare you the details as you don't want to hear them, the King went abroad and abdicated and never came back, a new King was appointed, but as he was still a child at school in Switzerland, he stayed there, there were the usual plays for power, Pridi was accused of being a communist, forced to leave in exile and go back to France, then he came back because, hate him as he did and still does, Phibul needed him, and Phibul became Prime Minister and the strong man he had always wanted to be. Happy?"

Kate gave an exasperated hiss, turned her back and pulled her pillow over her head.

The following morning, neither mentioned the argument and Lawrence announced he had reserved a table at the Oriental – "for old times' sake" – and also seats to see the long-awaited *Gone with the Wind*.

Kate stared at her cheerful letter to Felicity.

She was still rather ashamed of her childish outburst over the Comintern last night and determined to be smiling and loving and not the snappish harridan he must have thought her to have become.

As you see, she resumed writing, *my life is a dream, well, even better than that, I never could have even hoped for anything so marvellous.*

You know, before, when I arrived, Belinda and I used to go to the only real department store here and just watch the rich ladies shopping, because we couldn't afford anything there. Now, I'm one of those ladies.

How right you were to advise me to come to Bangkok, and how grateful to you I am, for that and for everything else you have done for me.

Your ever loving,

Kate

"And that," she said firmly out loud, sealing and addressing the envelope before she was tempted to tear it up and finally write the truth, feeling that everything in this letter was a lie except for her love for Lawrence, "is that."

Chapter XII

The time had come.

Earlier in the day, Lawrence received a phone call from Gilchrist ordering him to come to Christ Church on Convent Road. "Now."

This was unusual, as they had met a couple of days before at the British Club, to discuss what Lawrence had heard from Shoji, the Japanese journalist he had been instructed to cultivate, about some incident at the Cambodian border, where a Thai diplomat had apparently been insulted and arrested as a Kuomintang spy by a Japanese officer.

"It's a bit of an interesting mess," Lawrence had reported, "Phibul is furious, understandably, Shoji claims Tamura is furious, wants the officer punished, most severely, he said, and that the ambassador will apologize immediately."

What caused the incident, Gilchrist had wanted to know, did Shoji have any ideas?

Lawrence shrugged. Shoji had said that perhaps the officer in charge had recently come from China and was nervous and trigger-happy, or perhaps drunk, or perhaps Thanat, the diplomat in question, was actually spying on the troop movements.

"Listen, I rather like the man.

"He's a real journalist, and he's quite friendly, and well read. In fact, I enjoy spending the occasional evening with him, except that he can drink me under the table.

"But I didn't believe a word of it. Except for one thing — spying on troop movements. Doesn't that sound to you like there actually is something to spy on?"

Andrew had grinned broadly though his beard and said nothing, getting up to leave.

"You're a regular Cheshire cat, you know that?" Lawrence complained. "You could at least tell me if you think I'm right."

Gilchrist tapped him on the head with his rolled-up newspaper.

"Don't you think you're a bit old to go fishing for compliments, laddie? Keep on fishing, but for something useful."

Christ Church was deserted during the mornings, and inside, it was dark and pleasantly cool and smelled of tuberose.

"Finding religion in your old age?" Lawrence quipped, when he finally spotted Andrew at the far end of a pew, hiding in the shadows.

The Scot snorted. Hardly. Although if there ever were a time to get friendly with one's maker, this was it. He didn't have much time, so they should get down to business and stop talking theology.

There was word of troop movements on the Indochina border.

"Just as I suspected...," Lawrence whispered.

"Yes laddie, just as you suspected. You and others."

"Don't you go imagining you are the only one keeping watch. But you did well.

"Now.

"We hear also that the ever-two-faced Field-Marshal has vanished, nobody knows where, and also hear that the Thai armed forces are going to resist the Japanese invasion.

"The Japs are coming through the Cambodian border at Siem Reap, so that's where the fighting is going to be."

Lawrence frowned.

Why had Phibul gone awol? Unless —

"Oh, of course. He got word in advance, didn't want to get the blame either way this turns out."

Gilchrist sat back in the pew, gazed at the altar and nodded grimly.

"Yep. Until last month, he was still demanding to know how we would react in case of an invasion and how Thailand should respond to such an event.

"Well, we encouraged them to fight the Japs if they invade in the North and offered some very nice words indeed.

Makes you proud, doesn't it?" he sighed, adding "Of course, Phibul was disgusted with us, and we never really informed him of Operation Matador, which may still save the day. We didn't trust him not to go squeal to his friend Tamura."

Seeing Lawrence's inquiring look, he explained that he might as well inform Lawrence, now the balloon was going up.

"Operation Matador is Brooke-Popham's brainchild, a plan

to intercept Japanese troops just inside the Thai borders with
Malaya if they land in the South near Songkhla or Pattani.

"It's top secret and Crosby only heard of it last week."

Lawrence took off his glasses and rubbed them on his shirt.

"What do you want me to do?"

Andrew turned to face him.

He – they, SOE – wanted him to get out.

"Or at least, prepare to. Today. Pack a bag. Have your escape
kit? Papers? Your revolver? Nice and clean?

"Repeat your story and your route to me.

"It's unlikely your papers will get checked, I think the Thai
police has other fish to fry at present, but you can never tell."

Lawrence took a deep breath.

"My name is Edward Shaw, I'm a teak-wallah, I work for the
Borneo Company, and I've been sent on an inspection tour.

"Train to Chiang Mai – yes, I know, you chaps would prefer
me to get off at Lampang, but I prefer trying Chiang Mai. It's a
bigger town, with logging firms and it fits my story better.

"If possible, I'll hide at my cousin's there. Then, over the
border, Burma directly if possible, or China, whichever is easiest."

"Your wife?"

Lawrence made a face.

That was the difficulty. She wasn't easy to budge.

In fact, she was impossibly stubborn. She felt needed by the
hospital and would leave only if she could no longer work.

"That's the problem with redheads, argumentative. I should
know.

"She's probably safe enough for the time being. Did your
parents finally get your will?"

Yes, the telegram had come last week, at last. "My father
promises he will deal with it. My mother sent a separate one,
begging me not to do anything hasty.

"Hasty like what? Get killed?"

"You'll not get killed, laddie, we've trained you too well for
that."

The older man got up and looked down at Lawrence. At least,
Kate wasn't pregnant.

"No," he replied in a toneless voice. "The advantage of
marrying a nurse. Access to all sorts of things. Even in a Catholic

hospital, surprisingly."

He stared at his feet, his eyes welling and shook his head. "We were going to celebrate our first anniversary in three weeks."

Getting up as well, he scanned the other man's face. "When will you let me know?"

Tomorrow evening, at the latest, probably before. Possibly tonight

"Don't leave home in the meanwhile."

Lawrence sniffed. As if he would leave Kate on what might be their last night together.

"It's a pity, though. Shoji invited me – well, the Japanese press corps invited all the foreign journalists in Bangkok – to a dinner cruise on the river tomorrow evening. A 'bury the hatchet party,' he said it was going to be, and promised lots of sake."

Andrew honked his usual loud laugh. "They want you guys too drunk to cover the invasion. Not a bad idea.

"Right, I have to go. I've a few more chaps like you to dispose of in various ways, and I have to get back to the Ambassador – he's in a right state, as you can imagine. Don't envy the man his job."

He stretched out his hand. "Gallet, it was a pleasure working with you. We'll meet again after all this is over, and get royally drunk, and not on sake."

Lawrence grinned.

"Of course we will."

And now he was in his pavilion, checking his bag and selecting and discarding clothes. A change of shirts and trousers was all he needed, along with the pairs of glasses he had had made, never believing, somehow, that it would come to this and that he would ever need them. His false identity papers were in the breast pocket of his jacket, and the real ones sewn into the lining of his bag, along with the gold, dollars and opium balls he might need to buy his way out.

Kate wasn't due back for another hour, so, heavy-hearted, he took all of his diaries and wrapped them in the brown oil cloth he had chosen to match the colour of the floorboards.

He pushed the bed aside, eased out one of the wide teak floor planks with his paper knife, and lying down on the floor felt with his fingers for the crevice at the join of two beams and jammed the package in, making sure it could not slip out, and wondering if he would ever come back to get them or if someone would find them when the pavilion finally collapsed and chuck them out without reading them.

"So that's one part of my life over," he muttered.

Now, before Kate returned, he had to take his leave from Lady Thip.

The elderly lady had aged in the past few months. Her skin was grey, and she had lost weight, her once round and jolly face sagging and the rings hanging loose from her fleshless fingers.

But there were still diamonds and rubies in her ears, her hair was carefully done up with jewelled combs and her eyes were keen, and she listened to Lawrence without a word, fanning herself.

He told her very little, only that he was leaving to serve his country, but not in the military.

Finally, she put down her fan, and took his hand.

"I was very happy to have you here over these past years, although," she chuckled wickedly, "I can't say you didn't give me cause to worry at times."

Lawrence blushed. "I'm very sorry."

"Don't be." She shook her head. "It was certainly an education for you and who knows, it may have averted worse things.

"Given my daughter-in-law's personality... and her state of mind at the time, she was bound to retaliate.

"I make no excuses for my son, except that Siamese men have always behaved that way, and Siamese women have always put up with it. But now with these modern-educated girls...." She sighed. "At least, she misbehaved at home, and didn't shame us publicly. But she gave me my grandson, and because of that I forgive her anything."

Her eyes very bright, she tried to smile, but couldn't and squeezed his hand.

"You know I will look after Kate to the best of my ability.

"It's probably best if she moves in to the big house and is not alone in your cottage, do you agree?"

Yes. It was best. He did not want to think of her alone.

"Will she be all right for money?"

Once again, he nodded.

She drew money from his account, as he had arranged soon after their marriage. Not that she had ever taken much.

He looked around at the big, familiar room, with its priceless antique pottery and the rather indifferent English landscapes on the walls and the lovely verandah looking towards the river.

"I've been very happy here. You gave me a home and a family in Bangkok."

Drawing him close, she put her hand on his forehead, her gold bracelets chiming.

"Then I shall speak to you as if you were my son.

"Go with my blessing, and please look after yourself, be safe and come back. Your pavilion will be waiting for you."

And now, Kate.

Would it not be better if they just spent an ordinary evening, not spoil it with good-byes, and tears, and instead make love without this horrible feeling of it possibly being the last time?

He quickly slung his bag in the wardrobe to hide it, tugged open the stiff desk drawer to put away the manuscript of "Siamese Twins" — who would ever read this now? — and pulled a sheet of paper to him, thinking of her face when she read it, set his mind and began.

"My darling, my Kate, my beloved,
If only I were not such a coward...

But he had not reckoned with her sensitivity to his moods.

When they were lying under the mosquito netting, enclosed in their own world, she turned towards him.

"Were you going to tell me?"

There was no use pretending he did not understand.

No, he wanted their last evening together to be perfect.

"I wrote you a letter, though."

"Yes. I imagined you would. I'll read it once you're gone. When?"

Tonight. Tomorrow morning. Very soon.

"Listen, when I'm gone, Thip wants you to move into the big house."

Yes, she would prefer that.

"Now, no more words, all right? Just hold me. Don't worry about me.

"I'll be brave."

He knew she would.

Chapter XIII

My darling, my Kate, my beloved,

If only I were not such a coward... I cannot bear the idea of parting from you, and I could not bear the idea of telling you.

So this is it, my goodbye letter.

Shall I dispose of the boring but necessary things first?

I have opened a bank account for you in New York, you will find the papers in a file in the desk marked, obviously, 'Bank, New York, HSBC.'

There is enough money for you not to have to live in your father's house and to see you through quite a few years, and I'll be back long before that.

Just so you know, if this war lasts and I cannot make it over to America as soon as I would like, there is enough also to pay for medical school as well if you still want that.

My parents have a copy of my will (it's SOE rules, I hadn't thought of it, and truly believe there is no need, but there you are, a rule's a rule) and everything I own is yours. When you get back to Boston, please let my parents have your address.

Now, the important things.

I love you, I love you, I love you even when you argue with me, I love you when you are stubborn, I love watching you in the morning when you stretch and at night when you sleep, and I am eternally grateful to all the gods that we have had this perfect year together.

Please do not worry if you do not hear any news for some time ... and believe me when I say that I shall return to you and shall think of you every hour of every day.

She read the letter at first with tears pouring down her face, then again because the words were blurred, then again and again in the greyish-pink light of dawn.

The call had come just when the night was at its darkest, a scratch at the door and few soft words from Fon. "Now. Hurry."

She had not slept, nor he, and she watched as he dressed quickly in the oldest of his duck suits, slapped a battered straw hat on his head, grabbed his bag and typewriter and leaning over, kissed her hard.

She had tried to smile, and he kissed her again, without a word, slipped quietly down the steps and made his silent way over the grass.

Then, mopping her face, she dressed in her uniform, folded the letter and slipped it inside her bodice, then sat on the bed to think.

It was important not to betray anything about Lawrence, that she understood instinctively.

Why he had to leave, to go where and to do what, she did not know.

His letter mentioned SOE, so she assumed that was the outfit he belonged to and that had assigned that mysterious "propaganda work" he did.

He was needed elsewhere, his country was at war, and he was doing his duty.

Millions of women were like her, what was the word for it, yes, grass widows, waiting and worrying, scared to death and sick at heart.

She clenched her teeth, to stop the tears from coming again, straightened her shoulders and got up. Although her country was not at war, she too had duties, and she set off for the hospital.

Today was Sunday, and she would begin her day by attending mass and praying for Lawrence.

When she returned in the evening, she felt spent from the sleepless night, the effort of smiling at patients, pretending to Belinda that all was well, and commenting as had all the nurses and doctors, that although it was a three-day holiday, Constitution Festival, the streets were deserted, and how very unusual that was and nobody, nobody at all mentioned the nerve-jangling, eerie feeling of a Bangkok poised on the edge of disaster.

Melanie was surly and abstracted, the Thai orderlies whispered amongst themselves, many were absent, and finally, Doctor Sumet came up to Kate as she was taking a moment to chat with Belinda over cold tea, and, removing his blood-stained coat, announced that he was leaving early.

"I want you to watch that old woman with the infected foot for several days to check if there is any spike in her temperature, please", he asked in his careful English. "I fear it might turn into blood poisoning."

His eyes met Kate's for a brief second and she wondered fleetingly if he knew about Lawrence, or worked with him, and she turned her head away.

"Are you not coming tomorrow?" Belinda asked cheerfully, "Have plans for the Festival, do you?"

The surgeon smiled and shook his head at her blithe manner. No plans, no.

All her things had been taken from the pavilion, although Lawrence's clothes were still hanging in the wardrobe, his tennis racket was propped up against the wall, and his maroon silk dressing gown was hanging behind the bathroom door.

Burying her face in it, she closed her eyes, but she was so tired the tears would not come.

"I promised you I would be brave," she whispered, and turned away, leaving this room that she loved and walked slowly over to the big house where Lady Thip was waiting.

No one spoke or ate much at dinner, neither Busaba nor Pichit asked after Lawrence or commented on Kate's move to the main house, and, although Lady Thip did her utmost to keep some kind of conversation going, the meal was a tense and melancholy one.

The phone rang, jarring them all and Pichit jumped, rushed out to answer, and returned to the table looking relieved.

It was only his old friend Suthiphand, he said almost giddily, cancelling a card game for tomorrow.

"He's cancelling because Japanese troops are massed at our border, that's why," Busaba snapped.

Phibul would stop them, Pichit replied confidently. "He's a cunning man, and he'll find a way. The Thai people want us to remain neutral and would never stand for giving in to the Japanese."

Busaba shrugged and stabbed at her fish viciously. "He's so cunning he'll tie himself in knots."

Kate wasn't listening, besides this was an argument she had heard over and over, including at the hospital, including from Melanie, and when the three others gathered around the big polished wood wireless radio to listen to the BBC news service, as they did most evenings, she went up to the room she had been given facing the back of the house.

"This was — is — Somchai's room. You don't have such a nice view," Thip had apologized, when she had shown her there earlier, "but it's quieter, you won't have the birds singing their heads off at dawn, and you won't have to share a bathroom."

Kate stood silently, looking around, her brush and comb had been put on the dresser, the dressing gown that had been Lawrence's was draped on the bed next to her nightgown, and her shoes were neatly lined up by the wall. She felt her tears coming back.

The old lady took both her hands in hers and shook them slightly. "He is coming back, you must believe that."

Kate nodded. Yes, she believed that. "But I miss him so."

Thip sighed. She knew what it was to miss one's love.

"Listen to me," she said very softly. "You will find I have had Lawrence's personal papers, your passport and marriage certificate, bank statements, your jewellery and the like removed from the desk, and I have them in my safe.

"Of course, you can have them anytime, but I advise you to leave them with me for the time being.

"Do you understand?"

Kate bit her lips and nodded. "Yes, okay, I guess."

"Good. It's best to be careful.

"Come now, take off your uncomfortable uniform, change into something pretty that Lawrence would have liked, and let's go down to dinner."

And now she was alone, and threw herself on the bed, without undressing vowing to close her eyes only for a moment before taking a shower.

She was startled out of her deep sleep hearing loud knocks at her door and looked around, surprised to find herself still clothed and trying to understand why Busaba was telling her to come down, quickly.

Lawrence!

Lawrence was back!

Pierced with almost unbearable joy, she opened the door, but one look at the face of the sarong-clad and tousled Busaba killed her brief elation and she slumped against the doorjamb.

"What is it?" Her voice trembled. "Not Lawrence, no, please, no."

Busaba shook her head. No, it wasn't Lawrence, nor Sam.

"Come. It's news, on the wireless"

She gave Kate a strange look. "You're still dressed?"

"I fell asleep with my clothes on," Kate replied impatiently "What time is it?"

It was five-thirty in the morning.

Following Busaba down the stairs, she found Thip also swathed in a sarong with her grey hair tumbled down her shoulders and Pichit in pyjamas in front of the radio. Thip had her hands joined before her face and was swaying back and forth as if in pain.

Fon was there too, and the cook, and other servants, crouched in the doorway.

Pichit was translating into Thai what the English language news broadcast was saying, and Kate had to come nearer to try to hear.

"... several waves of bombers ...reporting live... impossible to tell what damage ... most of the fleet...at this time the attack is still going on..."

"What does it mean? I don't understand."

Pichit took a deep breath. "I received a call from a friend.

"Japanese planes are bombing the fleet at Pearl Harbour. Hawaii."

She looked up at him, uncomprehending. "Hawaii? But – but that's America! They're bombing *American* ships?"

He looked back, his face stark. "Yes. The United States are now at war with Japan."

He paused, swallowed, and added that he had been woken up by a call from a friend. "They have also invaded Thailand, and our forces are resisting at the Khmer border. The wireless says that convoys of Japanese warships are steaming towards Malaya and that there have been landings at several points in the South, including Songkhla. Where our rubber plantations are.

"We too are at war."

"And possibly ruined," Busaba added, her voice shaking.

Kate felt dazed and sick.

She grabbed the back of an armchair, lowered herself into it and put her head in her hands, trying and failing to take it all in, while the newsreader's voice droned on, announcing that the American air base in Manila was also being raided, and that

President Roosevelt had ordered the general mobilization of the United States armed forces.

What did that mean for Joe and Teddy?

Francis was a priest, and priests didn't fight, did they?

They would enlist, of course they would.

Finally, she looked up. "What's happening in Thailand?"

"In the South, I don't know. We're fighting them in the East," Pichit replied tonelessly. "But we don't stand a chance.

"They'll be in Bangkok tomorrow or the day after."

He turned the knob to a Thai language channel and hunched over, listening, then shrugged. "It's still the official bulletin, over and over. We'll hear nothing new now."

He went over to Lady Thip, who had still not said a word and sat hunched and shivering, eased her gently out of her armchair and nodded to his wife.

"Come, Khun Mae, we'll help you up to your room."

Kate remained alone, as, heavy-footed and weary, Thip made her way upstairs, supported by her son and, one by one, the servants retreated.

Fon asked if she wanted tea, then, when she refused, plumping the cushions on the sofa, leaned over and murmured that he had heard that Khun Lo had reached Hua Lamphong station and was seen boarding the early train to the North, then when she started and was about to speak, shook his head and put a finger on his lips.

He wai-ed to her and left the room, leaving her dazed and trying to think.

What was she going to do now?

PART II

Chapter XIV

The night streets were deserted when Lawrence slipped into the samlo that Fon had told him would be waiting parked in the shadow of a tiny soi by the Portuguese embassy.

"Hua Lamphong?" the driver whispered, and Lawrence nodded, wishing the man had thought to oil his squeaking wheels, although the streets were deserted, and anyway, riding a samlo to the station just before sunrise was not forbidden — yet.

Peering around, he wondered when he would next come back to this city he loved, and despite his heavy, thudding heart, he was relishing every moment, every smell, the first cries of an irascible rooster and the dawn chanting coming from the nearby wat.

They crossed one of the small arched bridges over the khlong and the streets suddenly became busier.

Lights were on in the many godowns of the Chinese quarter, and the samlo paused to let fish be loaded off a truck near the entrance of the market.

Nobody seemed to notice, nobody was looking, a farang in a samlo near the station was a common sight.

The driver dropped him off, refused payment with a smile, softly said "Chok dee!" in response to Lawrence's thanks and squeaked off, soon blending into the crowd of other samlos, cars and lorries that congregated at the meeting place of Bangrak, the serene and wealthy part of Bangkok and hectic, gritty and industrious Yaowarat, Chinatown.

"Yes, well, I'll need to be lucky," Lawrence muttered to himself.

He had a bit over an hour before the earliest train North left, and his hat jammed low over his hair to hide the colour, he queued, showing the impatience and poor manners the polite Thai expected from a farang, peevishly kicking his bag on the floor ahead of him and sighing loudly. When his turn came, he pretended to speak only English, repeating, "Chiang Mai, Chiang Mai, first class sleeper, get it, man?", and collected his ticket, muttering unpleasantly when he was told there were no sleepers and that he was lucky to get a window seat — the train was almost full even in first class.

There was a soup vendor on the sidewalk outside, and he would have dearly loved some noodles and broth but strode into the dining-room of the O-Ping Hotel next door instead, and ordered coffee and eggs, right now, get it, now! then heard himself and winced.

Don't overdo the colonial idiot act, he cautioned himself, don't get noticed.

Remember what a terrible actor you are, remember Kate said that's why they kept you shifting scenery instead of being on stage, and just thinking her name stabbed in him the gut and he suddenly felt nauseated by the greasy eggs put down in front of him and he pushed the plate away.

While he was breathing deeply so as not to be sick, the Yorkshire tones of his sergeant came back to him.

"Don't think of the ones you love if you can. It's easier if you don't.

"Lock them in a box, and open the box only, hear that, *only* when you are absolutely sure that thinking of them can't distract you.

"Remember the sun bear we saw? She was too busy watching her young to hear you galumphing in."

"Come on, Sarge," someone complained, "we weren't galumphing. Even you said we were pretty good."

"I said, 'not bad'," the sergeant retorted, and continued, "Eat, pee and shit when you can, not when you need to, you never know where your next meal is coming from nor where you'll be next time nature calls."

So, he drowned the eggs and rice in a brownish gluey sauce, spooned it up and drank his coffee, focussing on the next hour, the next day, the next week.

He went to the newspaper rack and picked up a *Bangkok Chronicle*, but the paper was a week old, and returning it to the holder, he looked around as discreetly as possible at the three other customers, all of them farang, all of them focussed on their own newspapers.

The radio was on in the background, and he tried to listen, but didn't hear anything unusual from what he could make out.

Andrew was right, he probably had a day, perhaps two days, head start before Bangkok fell... The thought of Kate flickered briefly, no, no, no, don't think of that.

There were a few Japanese military types in the station, appearing to be waiting for someone, peering around, and looking annoyed as they were buffeted by the milling passengers, and the Thai policemen in their uniforms gave them haughty, unfriendly looks as they patrolled the area.

He hunched his head down, and for some reason, affected a limp, as he passed them to go through and didn't dare look back to see if he was being watched.

The platform was very crowded, and near the first-class cars, he spotted a few farang — two or three were missionaries by the look of them — and mainly well-to-do Thai and Chinese families, but none that he recognized, thankfully, several monks in their orange robes, a prosperous-looking portly Indian gentleman with many, many parcels surrounding him, who when the train doors opened, scrambled ahead of everyone to get on, directed his two porters to distribute his parcels in the overhead racks throughout the car, then settled himself down opposite Lawrence with a contented belch and fell asleep.

Lawrence pulled his hat down over his face and when he opened his eyes again, they were pulling into Lopburi and the Indian gentleman was gone.

He bought some cold tea in a bottle from one of the many vendors who swarmed on at each station and hopped off at the next, then dozed again, waking up very thirsty and drinking the dregs of his tea. Then he stared at the landscape, wishing he had bought a newspaper at the station, or some cheap novel, longed for a crossword puzzle and wondered where he'd be going next.

Around midnight, he bought some chicken on skewers and rice and more tea, poured hot this time from a thermos, and his eyes wide open, waited and counted the hours and the stations, listened to a baby crying and recited Latin verbs just to keep his mind off Kate, and failing.

His papers were never even checked, and when, bleary-eyed,

unshaven and dirty, he got off the train two days later in the cool morning of Chiang Mai, he breathed in deeply, looking at the sparkling spire atop Doi Suthep, the steep hill that dominated the city.

The first step of his journey had gone without a hitch.

That was a relief.

And it was even more of a relief when he opened the gate of the lovely house near the moat and first spotted Somboon, Michael's partner and the love of his life, kneeling in a flower bed, weeding, then Michael himself, sitting under a tree with a book on his lap.

Somboon squealed with joy and wai-ed deeply, and Michael rose with the trembling gestures of a very old man and opened his arms.

"The prodigal has returned!" and for the first time in days, Lawrence felt the heavy weight on his chest lessen.

No, he didn't send a telegram, he couldn't, he would tell all later, but was there any news?

Michael and Somboon exchanged a look, then Michael sat back down.

"You don't know?"

He had been on a train for three days. "Tell me."

Michael closed his eyes as he recounted Pearl Harbour, the United States at war with Japan, and Lawrence flinched.

"And Thailand?"

Somboon looked down, as if in shame, while Michael said, his voice flinty, "Field Marshal Phibul signed a treaty with Japan. He's just stopped short of declaring war."

But that wasn't all, Michael continued, Manila and Singapore were attacked by air, and Japanese troops landed on the beaches in Southern Thailand and were making their way down the peninsula.

So much for Operation Matador, Lawrence thought, his mind reeling.

It was too much to absorb, and it was too awful to believe.

"What about Bangkok?"

Bangkok was still, nominally, under Thai control, and life there, according to the radio, was normal.

"As normal as it can be, I suppose," Michael concluded bitterly, "when the Prime Minister is a raving dictator.

"Where is your wife?"

Lawrence sighed. She was in Bangkok, and close to being an enemy alien now.

Somboon clasped his hands to his chest with a soft moan, while Michael swallowed, seeking words, any words that might comfort.

"She's a woman, and a nurse. I've known and liked many Japanese, they are an enlightened people. The hospital is doing vital work, so I think you can assume she is safe where she is.

"Come," he added gently, "let's get you some breakfast. We can talk later."

"I take it you're SOE," he said matter-of-factly over coffee, and when Lawrence made a surprised face but answered nothing, shook his head in amusement.

"I may be ancient, but I'm not in my dotage, and remember, I was a diplomat myself at that same embassy, and I do keep up with people in London — those who are still alive, that is.

"They haven't evacuated you so fast because you're such a nice chap.

"God, to think we imagined that what we lived through then was earth-shaking... that was before the world went mad... We had nothing like SOE, of course, there was no need. We just had what Kipling called the 'Great Game' but it was all rather gentlemanly and civilized.

"You were very lucky you got out when you did, the Japanese have taken over the railways — how on earth did Phibul let them do that? — and therefore the route to the North from Bangkok is closed, according to the radio.

"Now, let me think."

He closed his eyes and Lawrence realized how frail the man had become, his skin wrinkled like tissue paper and the curly hair sparse and limp on his almost bald head, his voice wavering and breathless at times.

Somboon came in with more coffee, frowned, and stood, watching, then relaxed when Michael opened his eyes again.

"I'm fine, Somboon," he sighed, exasperated, "instead of hovering, send the boy with a chit to Khun Consul asking him to come here, as a matter of urgency.

"Yes, now." he snapped, when Somboon began to protest.

Then turning to Lawrence, "I wish Somboon weren't such an

old woman. Just because my heart flutters occasionally...

"Anyway, I think you may be in luck. Perhaps.

"Our Consul — he's quite a good man, and he would go far, I believe, if the Foreign Service promoted people on merit rather than sycophancy — well, he comes by some days, for tea or a drink, and he was telling me day before yesterday this strange story about a Chinese Air Force plane with an *American* pilot, mind you, that had an engine problem on its way to Kunming and made an emergency landing at the airport here. They couldn't order the part, so some mechanic was actually making it, I think.

"If that plane is still here... "

If the pilot was indeed American, Lawrence objected, would he not now risk being arrested, if the Japanese called the shots here as well?

Michael snorted. Not in Chiang Mai. The head of police was a good man, and hated Phibul.

"However, *if* the pilot is still here, he may be strongly encouraged to limp his way over the mountains to get the hell out.

"Now tell me about your wife. What is she like?"

Lawrence smiled.

Beautiful rather than pretty. Honest and strong, Irish working-class background. Hot-tempered. Delightful. He adored her.

"Your grandmother would have liked her," Michael mused, and made a face.

"I'm not sure your mother will, though. Ah, I can hear Ben's car. That didn't take long."

The British consul was a diffident, be-spectacled and slightly stooped man nearing middle-age, who looked Lawrence up and down with a huge smile.

"You made it, did you?

"Good chap! Had a telegram from Gilchrist yesterday, saying you were on your way. I was worried you might get pulled off the train in Pitsanoulok.

"Didn't even get checked? Well, it's not all that surprising, the Thai aren't that eager to cooperate, except for a few black sheep.

"I'll try to send a message back, but I'm not at all sure I will get through, given the situation in Bangkok.

"I'll tell you about that later, but let's see how to get you on your way."

He listened to Michael's idea and nodded.

He had had the same thought himself. "The pilot, Tex, as he calls himself — his real name is David, but he's from Texas, so..." he rolled his eyes heavenwards at American predictability. "He's part of that crazy American Volunteer Group that's providing fighter pilots and flies some of the Lend-Lease supplies from Burma to Kunming, for Chiang's Air Force.

"Of course, most of the stuff goes by lorries taking the Burma Road into China.

"Must be a hair-raising drive up and down those passes with loads of ammunition...

"Apparently, there are American-built bombers on the way too — ," he added with a sour look. "Bombers that were earmarked for the RAF, but for some reason, old Chiang Kai-Shek got his hands on them. Can't understand how Washington wants to help Chinese Nationalists over Britain, but...

"Tex is at the airfield right now, with his Chinese co-pilot, checking out on the repairs. I've put him up at my place, and I want to get him away as soon as possible, given the circumstances.

"I'll get a chit to him telling him he'll have a passenger."

He shook his head ruefully and got up.

"Major Chalit, the head of police, has officiously given me notice that the Consulate will be surrounded as from tomorrow, so as soon as I've dispatched you chaps, and dealt with other matters, such as destroying my short-wave radio, then I too shall make my way out somehow.

"I've been burning papers all night. Not quite sure why, but there you are."

He looked at Michael in concern.

"Will *you* be all right?"

Michael shrugged. He was an old man and harmless. As he had told his young cousin here, the Japanese were a civilized people.

"From your mouth to God's ears, as my nanny used to say," Ben replied not sounding convinced. "Right then. Come by the Consulate for lunch. I hope to have you on that plane very soon thereafter."

"*Will* you be all right?" Lawrence asked once the consul left.

A dismissive smile. Of course. What could they do to him?

"I'm just sorry I will have seen you so fleetingly.

"And by the way, I wanted to tell you how very much I enjoyed your articles. Good writing, and sound, informed views. Somboon clips them out and pastes them in a book.

"Now, have you any news from your family?"

A telegram, last week in fact. They were still weathering the blitz.

"Of course," Lawrence added, suddenly depressed, "I've just realized that now there will be no way to reach me."

"Nonsense," Michael was brisk. "Once you reach Burma, or even perhaps from China, you can communicate with them easily. Now, do go and clean up before we go to lunch.

"This may be wartime, but you must keep up appearances and the Consulate, after all, is the outpost of Britain."

When Ben greeted them, his face was sombre.

"I was on the telephone with Bangkok and passed on the news about you. All of the Embassy staff from the Ambassador down is locked in, and the Embassy is surrounded, but by Thai police, thankfully, not Japanese.

"And Gilchrist said...," he passed his hand over his eyes in despair, "My God, I just can't believe it. The *Prince of Wales* and the *Repulse* have just been sunk — or are sinking, Gilchrist wasn't sure, oh God, oh God — off Malaya. Not a naval battle. Bombed from the air."

Michael grabbed Lawrence's arm and bent over, winded, nauseated. "No, no, I'm all right, don't worry."

He staggered to a chair in anguish and closed his eyes, seeing it, hearing it, *feeling* it.

All those young, young men, the flames, the stench of oil, the dark waters engulfing them, the screams of the seamen and the cheers from the airmen who had destroyed these two symbols of the might of the British Empire.

"That's very bad news," he murmured, his lips becoming blue. "Along with all the other bad news..."

Yes, the consul sighed, dejected, sitting next to him.

"And you want to hear even more bad news?"

"Churchill gave a speech at the Commons after Pearl Harbour, imploring Phibul to remain on the Allies side, and swore to treat any invasion of Thailand as an attack against us.

"But Phibul apparently received it *after* he had signed the treaty with Japan.

"What a bloody mess!

"Although…," he bit his lip, "given our rate of success so far, I'm not sure it would have made much difference." He shook himself.

"I've tried to reach the Embassy again, but it seems their phones have been cut off. Not a good sign, that….

"Do you mind awfully if we skip lunch?

"I'm going to get you to the airfield right now.

"Tex is waiting for you, and I need you both out of Thailand fast. I've asked cook to prepare some sandwiches, I'll go get them now.

"Michael, I'll drive you home after the airfield,"

Michael stood up, still shaken. "No, send your boy to get me a samlo. Better still, send him to get Somboon, I'll wait here."

He looked at Lawrence, his eyes bright with an old man's tears.

"I don't want to watch you leave, I hate good-byes." He hugged him and whispered in his ear. "Julie would be proud of you. Be safe my boy and go with God."

The propellers were already whirring when Lawrence reached the airfield in the Consul's car, and a very tall man in flying helmet, goggles and a leather jacket was walking around the plane, making one last check.

"Meet Tex," Ben said, "your ticket out of here. Tex, this is Lawrence Gallet, newsman."

Tex pushed his goggles up his forehead, grinned and stretched out his hand. "Happy to be of help. Even happier to be getting away, this place is beginning to feel a bit too hot for comfort."

"I'm very grateful — sorry, what shall I call you? Are you a lieutenant? Most flyers I've known are — I don't really know much about American ranks."

"Call me Tex. I'm Chinese Air Force now, not US anymore, and I can't remember what the Chinese word for squadron-leader in Chinese is. That guy up there at the controls is Wen, my co-pilot, on loan from the Chinese pilots' team.

"Ever flown before? No?

"It's great. Best thing in the world."

He handed him a pair of goggles."I think there's a jacket in the plane somewhere, it's gets pretty chilly up there. This old Beechcraft ain't exactly your luxury air cruiser, you know.

"You'll have a seat behind us, like I said, not luxury, but it's not too bad.

"Ben, thanks for the sandwiches and the hospitality, and for getting the authorities off my back.

"I appreciate it, given how busy you must be right now."

Ben made a face. "Surprisingly un-busy actually. It's quite amazing how little there is to do to unravel almost a century of British presence here.

"Lawrence, Gilchrist said he'll get a message to your wife somehow.

"Safe journey and good luck."

"Same to you. And thanks for everything."

"All in the line of duty. Godspeed."

Ben seemed very small standing on the airfield and waving as the plane climbed suddenly and turned, wagging its wings in farewell.

Lawrence, his face pressed against the window saw him gradually disappear from sight and watched the ground below as they approached the slopes of Doi Suthep then soared over the temple, and through his depression and misery, could not help a feeling of exhilaration seeing the hills and jungle from above, with more shades of green than he'd thought existed.

"Okay so far? Not feeling sick?" Tex asked once he'd passed controls to the co-pilot and came back to sit next to Lawrence, shouting to be heard over the engines.

He unwrapped his sandwich.

"So, Larry, you must be one important newshound, if the Brits want to get you out so bad."

"Not really, no. More of a loose end."

"One hell of a loose end, I'd say, if they need it taken care of that fast. "

"Someone was careless, and the Kempetai has my name."

"Ouch." Tex munched reflectively. "Hear about those two British warships?"

"Yes. *HMS Prince of Wales* and *HMS Repulse*. Awful. Doesn't bear thinking of."

"Yeah." More chewing. "We'll get them in the end, though. You'll see.

"Ever been to Kunming? It's a dump.

"Now Toungoo, there's a place. Been there?

"Burma. It's a dump too, but I think it's paradise.

"We were first based out of Rangoon, and I thought the place was pretty swell, until I saw Toungoo. That's our base now. Flowers like you wouldn't believe, a real Garden of Eden. You'll love it.

"Okay, back to flying this bird. Sit tight now, it's going to get bumpy, when we start passing between the mountains, but don't puke in my nice clean plane. There's a paper bag under your seat, get it?"

Would he love it, really?

Would he love being anywhere so cut off from his own idea of paradise, Kate, their pavilion, the sala on the river, his books, his writing?

Everything Michael and Ben had told him, Pearl Harbour, the attacks on Singapore, the invasion of Thailand, the Pacific fleets of both Britain and America almost destroyed... Kate, Kate and her safety...It all whirled though his mind and he just couldn't think clearly or see his way ahead.

He watched as the deep emerald and celadons of the jungle gave place to the greyish yellow lichen-like scrub of the mountains. There was no sign of any human presence, but thin wisps of smoke emerged from the valleys, and Tex turned around and shouted pointing downwards: "Laos!"

Then pointing forwards, "China!".

The winds slapped the aircraft all of a sudden, Lawrence had the feeling they were dropped uncontrollably into a deep hole, the engines sputtered and stopped, then started again, he kept his eyes on Tex who was chatting to his co-pilot, but neither of them seemed to panic so he decided he would not either.

He shivered, wrapped the flight jacket more tightly around his chest and rested his head against the window.

So this was China... He had no idea of what would happen next, and instead of being frightening, it was somehow comforting to think he had no control over events. The noise of the engines as well was soothing, like an enormous cat purring next to you and he stopped trying to think, looking at the pattern of fields and towns below.

He felt a thump, his head hit the window hard and he realized they were on the ground, being jostled and bumped down a potholed and pitted runway, and the plane came to a complete stop.

"Well, aren't you the cool one, falling asleep on your first flight?" Tex called out to him as he cut off the engines, but the cabin door was suddenly yanked open, an irate woman put her head in and started screaming, "What's the rat's ass reason for this latest stunt, Tex?

"Do you think we needed this right now?

"Do you?

"What the fuck were you doing over Chiang Mai, anyway?

"Why did you fly East when your route was due North?"

Tex flipped off his goggles and put his hands up in protest. "I wasn't *over* Chiang Mai, I made my way *to* Chiang Mai when I got caught in a storm and my navigation went crazy.

"You know what this decrepit old bird is like, don't you? The oil line started leaking again.

"I was pretty damn lucky to get there. What are you so mad about?

"Anyway, what are *you* doing here?"

"You think I'm mad?

"Wait till you hear the Old Man, you'll know mad.

"Yes, he's here too. We flew in yesterday, after we heard the news about Pearl Harbour."

She spotted Lawrence who was unfastening his harness and smiled charmingly at him.

She was striking, dark, lush and beautiful, and she knew it. "Now, now, look what the cat dragged in."

Tex watched her with a knowing grin. "That's Larry, a fugitive newshound from Thailand, and *this* —", he pointed at the woman, "is Olga, the Old Man's — Chennault's — that is, secretary."

Olga smiled again, a slow seductive grin that lit up startling green-blue eyes and drawled, in an exotic accent he couldn't place "Well, hello, Larry.

"Welcome to China."

Chapter XV

They spent the following day waiting, gathered around the wireless, barely speaking.

No, Kate was *not* to go to the hospital, Lady Thip stated firmly.

It was too dangerous. She had promised Lawrence to look after his wife.

Mother Melanie, when Kate finally managed to get through to her on the telephone, said the same, in more forthright terms.

"Stay in my girl. You are not indispensable. Who might tell the perils today for a farang, even for a nurse, once the Japanese are patrolling the streets, which could happen any minute now? I do not want you raped or killed."

Kate, remembering the tales of horrors told by the Chinese refugees, complied with guilt-laced relief...

The BBC news was dire when reporting from Pearl Harbour but declared optimistically that Fortress Singapore would hold and that the invasion down the Malayan peninsula was being contained by the bravery and superior force of British troops.

The Thai bulletins made no such claim.

The Imperial Japanese Army was advancing towards Bangkok from both East and South.

After ordering the Thai forces to cease fire and let the advancing soldiers through, Field Marshal Phibul had closeted himself with his government, so as to, it was announced, best ensure the neutrality of the Kingdom.

Broadcasts recommended that people stay at home, and servants, sent by cook to buy fish and vegetables, returned to the house empty handed, saying that no one was to be seen on the streets and that all markets were deserted.

"At least," Pichit sighed, " our plantations won't be devastated."

In the evening, Lady Thip suggested a game of cards, but Kate declined.

After hours spent listening to the BBC, she found that the tone and accent of the newsreader grated on her nerves and longed for a familiar, American voice but didn't dare ask Pichit to fiddle with the knob and find an American station. She just wanted to be alone and think, although her mind kept going around in circles. Fears for Lawrence — was he safe? What was he doing? — and thoughts of Joe Jr. and Teddy were jumbled with visions of the destruction of Pearl Harbour and worries about her own fate.

She barely slept at all and woke up, bathed in sweat from a nightmare she couldn't remember, the awful events of the day before coming back to her.

But she had work to do, she told herself firmly, and rising, put on her uniform.

She went to the hospital early, despite Lady Thip's urging — what else was there to do?

"I just can't desert my patients, and I need to keep busy," she said, her head heavy, her eyes feeling hot and glazed, stirring her tea listlessly.

"And," she added, pushing away her cup, and trying to smile "Babies have this inconvenient way of wanting to be born even when there's a war on."

What she did not say is that she wanted — no, needed — to be with her own, Belinda and Melanie and the others, people who thought as she did, and feared the same things.

Pichit seemed convinced that the Japanese army would just traverse Thailand on its way to Malaysia, and leave the country to its shaky neutrality, but was he right?

And if he were wrong, what then, for all the farang?

Thip bustled around her, still disapproving. "Then take a car — No, no, I won't have you in a samlo, we have no idea what's going to happen on the streets today", and Fon was told to instruct the chauffeur in no uncertain terms that if he encountered any roadblock or sign of trouble on the way, he was to turn back.

But the streets were very quiet, many of the shops on New Road were shuttered, and only military motorcycles and automobiles whizzed busily up and down Sathorn Road, official pennants fluttering.

There was only one lone food vendor in the hospital gardens, an old woman who stood under her tattered parasol and waited for someone to buy the sliced papayas and pineapples from her garden, but nobody, neither patients, orderlies or nurses could be seen.

All the jasmine wreaths garlanding the statue of Saint Louis were wilted, brown, and rotting, and no new ones had been draped at the saint's feet with prayers for his protection.

Kate crossed herself and cleared them away, thinking that if ever there were a time to make offerings, it was now, and then she realized there was nowhere to buy flowers. Would there be other food vendors later on?

Probably not, judging from the deserted gardens – they usually arrived at daybreak.

She faintly heard voices raised in chant from the chapel and opened the door, seeing that only some two or three Catholic Chinese nurses were there, along with a few patients.

No nuns and no priest?

Surely, Mass could not be over yet?

"Oh Kate… They came to get them at dawn," Belinda wailed, coming in the chapel behind her.

Nai Khop, a genial orderly who often shared his special holiday food with the farang nurses, had seen it all.

All the nuns were marched out at gunpoint – "Gunpoint! Can you imagine?" she sobbed – "and Nai Khop swears he glimpsed the Bishop and Father Perroudon already in the truck – a canvas covered lorry – and when he ran to help them get on, the Japanese soldiers threatened him with bayonets."

She grabbed at Kate's arms and looked around in fear.

"What's going to happen to us?"

Kate held her tight, imagining Melanie clutching her little rolled up pack – her superstition had failed – jolly Marie-Marguerite, bossy Perrine and the others, poor Father Perroudon who had already served in the last war, and His Grace the Bishop… She closed her eyes and rested her forehead against Belinda's shuddering shoulders.

"We mustn't panic…" she finally said, uncertainly. "Nobody has threatened you?"

Belinda shook her head.

"Good. Me neither. So, it's only the religious staff they've taken, not the lay doctors or nurses."

Her breathing was ragged, but she tried to control it, and

Belinda released her at last, wiped her face and nodded. "Doctor Hermet hasn't turned up though. But he may have just stayed home."

"Maybe. Let's go up to the wards, okay? That's what Melanie would have expected of us."

Belinda tried to laugh but it came out as a coughing sob. "That she would have, old slave driver..."

And as they walked to the stairs, she added in a whimper, "I wonder what's happening to them... Dear Jesus, let them be safe..."

Thank the Lord, the wards were half deserted, thank the Lord, people were staying home, thank the Lord, two of the three Thai doctors had showed up and there were only a few patients to care for...

Throughout the day, those were Kate's only thoughts as she changed dressings, checked temperatures and comforted the old woman with the infected foot, trying to convince her not to return home quite yet.

Thank the Lord the hospital had reserves of rice to feed both patients and staff although there was nothing but fish sauce to add to it.

Thank the Lord I have this job to do and cannot think of Lawrence.

At lunchtime, they were sitting on a bench outside, spooning up their rice and gazing listlessly at the Japanese military convoys driving up Sathorn Road, and Belinda made a face, and put her bowl down. "What I wouldn't give right now for a nice steak pie...," she groaned.

Kate closed her eyes. "What I would like is a chicken sandwich. Lots of mayonnaise, toasted bread. Or maybe... Oh, I don't know.

"Anything but rice, really."

Belinda looked at her sideways. "Kate? I've been wanting to ask... Where's Lawrence? What is he doing?"

Kate shook her head, her mouth tight.

Gone. She wasn't sure where.

Belinda was shocked, and put her hand on Kate's arm, in sympathy and horror.

"What? He's left you?"

"No! Of course not. He didn't leave me — not like that. The British Embassy ordered him out. He said no more than that."

"Oh, you mean he's been mobilized?"

Yes, Kate sighed, she supposed so.

Belinda got up and shook out her skirt.

"Well, better that than being trapped here like the rest of us.

"Did you hear about the HMS *Prince of Wales* and HMS *Repulse*?

"Somehow, Eddy had the idea that they were going to land here and save us all...

"Cloud cuckoo land is where *he* lives, I sometimes think.

"He and a lot of the other blokes who propped up the bar at the British Club...

"I wonder where they all went."

Towards evening, Nai Khop approached Kate at the ward treatment room as she was washing her hands in preparation for leaving and, after having glanced around to make sure they were alone, slipped her a piece of paper, folded over many times and whispered, "For you, Khun Kate. Man give me. He say secret, important," before picking up a bundle of soiled sheets and backing away.

Her hands trembling, she opened the letter, and smoothed the creases. It was from Andrew Gilchrist, and she caught her breath.

"Dear Kate, I hope this reaches you. Lawrence is safe and is probably in China by now. I could not tell you myself, we are locked up in the Embassy, and are forbidden to communicate, but I am able to slip this to a friendly Thai man who brings us food. Sit tight. Andrew.

"PS, best if you destroy this."

She read it twice to be sure, closed her eyes, memorized every blessed word, then ripped up the paper and watched the pieces flutter into a pail of bloody compresses, then, to be sure, spilled a bottle of mercurochrome over it, staining everything scarlet.

There. It would all be burned later.

China... Why China, rather than Burma, which was closer and British?

She wiped away her tears of relief. Might she perhaps find a way of getting to China?

The following day brought more news, filtered in by the Thai doctors and nurses.

Doctor Hermet had been interned, possibly at the Trocadero Hotel, along with, it would seem, all the nuns and priests, not only from Saint Louis, but also the Catholic schools and parishes.

Others, British, American and Dutch civilians had been taken there and to other places as well.

It was said that the American Ambassador, Mr. Peck, had tried to arrange two trains to evacuate them and that Thai officials had agreed, only to find that the Japanese, now in control of the railways, had forbidden any evacuation — so there was no way for her to get to China, Kate realized despondently.

And now, Ambassador Peck and his staff were also locked away in their Embassy.

It was said that people were ordered to cheer when Japanese soldiers marched in the streets, and that although some complied enthusiastically, others preferred to stay indoors rather than obey.

It was said.... Indeed, what was *not* said?

Kate tried to close her ears to the rumours, but some, nonetheless, were repeated so often that they must be true...

She kept repeating, "Lawrence is safe, Lawrence is safe" and went about her work, grateful that an emergency appendectomy was brought in, and that although Doctor Sumet was not there to deal with it, Doctor Jingjai had accepted to come in his place.

Time in the operating room was blissful because she then became an automaton, watching, doing what she was told, passing instruments and sponging blood as the surgeon cut and stitched, and she closed off the outside world.

When she emerged, tearing off her cap and apron and throwing them into the laundry basket, Belinda was waiting for her, her face as pale as her coif, grabbed her and dragged her into the pharmacy reserve.

She could barely speak.

The Japanese, two Japanese officers had come, and demanded to see the foreign nurses.

"I was with Rose when they came, and Bernadette. They said we're okay, we're Irish, we're neutral, and they asked about you..."

Her heart in her mouth, Kate just stared.

"I said you're Irish too and were in the operating theatre. Rose and Bernadette, they just nodded.

"They had a Thai interpreter with them...

"They had checked with the hospital administration — Nuch, she was there, and heard everything. They looked at the books and saw our names. And the interpreter, he said — he said that nurses were always Irish or French, and that all the French were nuns.

"So, one of the Japanese laughed and said that that had been taken care of."

She swallowed. "I think they believed him. Kate, you've got to lose your papers."

No. No, it was too dangerous.

She turned wildly on her heel, she had to get home, now. Now.

Belinda caught her arm.

"You can't, stay until the coast is clear, they might be nearby.

"Anyway, who knows you're American? Besides us.

"Think. Nobody. The Thai don't care, we're just foreigners to them, they just know we're not French. Nuch wasn't even surprised he said that, for all she knows, you *are* Irish."

Shaking, Kate thought, trying to remember who she might have shared any memory of Boston with.

"Doctor Sumet, he knows..."

He was gone, Belinda interrupted impatiently. "Remember? He hasn't turned up for four days now, and anyway, he wouldn't turn you in. He helped with the French soldier... He's probably in hiding himself."

Yes. Beginning to breathe more easily, Kate nodded.

"Now." Belinda was trying to plan. "Whatever you do, don't go home in one of those huge cars. Maybe we can leave together, go to my room. Spend the night with me there.

"Hide your papers somewhere, here maybe, it's the safest."

Her eyes scanning the pharmacy, Belinda discarded any idea of it being a possible hiding place, too many people, nurses and doctors alike, had access.

"I know — there's a loose tile behind the bench in our changing room. That's where I kept my cigarettes away from Melanie's prying eyes.

"Let's go."

No.

She grabbed Belinda's sleeve, trying to think, to discipline her rasping breathing, applying the control she had dearly acquired in the operating room when a patient started haemorrhaging and the essential thing was *not* to panic.

"No. I can't be walking around with no papers. That would be crazy, and the best way to get me in trouble."

Belinda thought, and nodded slowly. What did the papers say? Did they even mention their nationality?

Neither had any idea, it was just those two flimsy and by now dog-eared sheets with writing in Thai script they carried around in their purses.

"Okay, this is what I'll do," Kate decided. "I'm going to call Thip and say she is not to send the car. Then, I'll leave on foot with you, and take a samlo around nightfall, when the streets seem a bit busier and there's less of a chance of being noticed."

Belinda considered her. Better keep her hair covered with her coif, then.

"Dear Mother Mary, you're right. It hadn't occurred to me."

She quickly twisted her hair up and anchored it with pins then fastened the hated veil-like starched linen securely at her nape.

"Have you heard from Eddy?" she asked when they left the hospital and walked out the gate, trying to look unconcerned as they made their way up Sathorn Road.

Belinda sighed.

Nothing in two days. But from what she'd gathered, Thailand was not at war with England, so he should be all right.

Kate was about to blurt out that the British Embassy was surrounded by the police, but she caught herself in time. If diplomats were cut off and treated that way, what would happen to the ordinary people?

"Sure, he is," she agreed, her heart sinking. "He'll probably come by tonight."

She ended up walking all the way through the deserted streets, cursing her white canvas uniform shoes that rubbed her heels and felt a blister break and start oozing. Tomorrow, with no Melanie to breathe fire if she caught sight of a nurses' toes, she would wear sandals.

There appeared to be no samlos, the sidewalk noodle stalls

and tea-sellers had all vanished and most shops were closed with steel shutters.

A cat trailed her down the soi, meowing pitifully — no food stalls meant no fish heads thrown to the sidewalk. "Can't help you, friend," she told it as she rang the bell, "I've got my own problems, but I'll try to remember you tomorrow, all right?"

The doorman opened the door just a crack, peered out at the soi behind, pulled her inside and slammed and bolted the heavy gate behind her.

"What?" she began to ask, but Fon came running down the gravel path.

"Come, come," he panted, and hurried her towards the house. What had happened? "Is it Lawrence?" she gasped.

No, Fon shook his head, catching his breath, no, all safe. "Come, quick, please."

He was holding her hand to rush her along, barely stopping to let her kick off her shoes on the bottom step.

Lady Thip was waiting at the top of the verandah stairs and enfolded her in her arms. "Oh, my child," she whispered. "We were so worried about you."

Was there news of Lawrence? what was the matter?

"Tell me, please!"

Busaba, standing pale and remote behind her mother-in-law, stepped forward and put a hand on Kate's shoulder. "The Japanese — they said they were Kempetai — were here this afternoon," she dropped in a cool voice that belied her worried face. "They were looking for Lawrence. They searched your pavilion and questioned all the servants."

Kate closed her eyes, feeling faint and grabbed the back of a rattan chair. "I need.... I need to sit down, I think," she stammered. "What did you say?"

Nothing. Nobody said anything more than what they all knew.

That Lawrence had left about a week ago, probably to visit his elderly cousin in Chiang Mai, to say goodbye before being mobilized.

They had gone through all the drawers in the desk, but there was only his manuscript, and they had left that, after scattering it around, along with all his clothes, but hadn't damaged anything.

Kate breathed in relief and was about to thank Thip for her

foresight in moving all the papers to her safe, but the old lady met her eye and shook her head slightly, while Busaba continued.

"The officer asked why we had this English spy living with us, and —"

"We said he wasn't a spy!" Pichit walked onto the verandah and interrupted his wife firmly. "We said he was just a journalist, not a spy, that his family in England was close to our Royal Family, and that is why ... The officer was very polite after that."

"Did they ask about me?"

No.

They didn't even seem to know Lawrence was married, and no one told them. Of course, as there were no women's clothes in the room...

Busaba snorted. The servants would talk, at some point, they would gossip with the neighbours.

"They certainly will not."

Thip was frosty. "Fon had forbidden them to say anything about the household if they were not asked," she added, settling heavily into a large bamboo armchair. "And now that the Japanese police has been here and seen that Lawrence has left, there is no reason for them to return."

She turned to Kate and took her hand.

"We were worried they might have gone to the hospital to look for you anyway."

"They have," Kate sighed, — well, not for herself, personally — and recounted that the bishop, the priests and nuns had been marched out at gunpoint to be taken who knew where — "I didn't want to tell you about it yesterday evening, I didn't want to worry you," — and how today Japanese soldiers had come to check on the remaining farang nurses.

"I was in the operating theatre, thankfully, and the other nurses vouched for my being Irish.

"So, tell me —," she fished her hospital papers from her purse and thrust them at Pichit. "Does it say here anywhere that I'm American?"

Pichit put on his reading glasses and scanned the document. "No. It just gives your name and says you are authorized by the Health Ministry to work as a maternity nurse at Saint Louis Hospital. Authorization number, visa number and so on. That's all."

"Holy Mother Mary, thank you," Kate whispered and crossed herself, then got up from her chair, smiling for the first time in days, it seemed to her.

"Thank you, all of you. And now, I need a shower, I think. I feel filthy, I walked all the way, there were no samlo to be had."

" Do you… Have you… heard at all from Lawrence?" Busaba asked tentatively, and Pichit threw her an unpleasant look.

No. Kate gazed guilelessly at all three of them in turn. No, for all she knew, he was in Chiang Mai.

"Well, he won't be able to stay there," Pichit muttered. "But how he is going to get out of the country, I don't know.

"We should be able deal with our foreigners ourselves, and if they want to leave the country, why shouldn't they?

"It's an outrage, really, the way the Japanese are treating us, taking over our railways and interrogating our people.

"We are allies, now, not enemies, and they are not occupiers."

Lady Thip raised her beautiful arched eyebrows. "Allies? Do you think so?

"Do you think this is not the beginning of an occupation, just like France, just like Belgium?

"I'm not so sure everyone agrees with you.

"The Japanese may be right, you know, in treating us like enemies.

"It seems to me we probably are."

Pichit snorted. "Khun Mae, you really should not be heard talking this way, and you know nothing of politics."

She pushed herself out of the armchair and turned to enter the drawing room, seeming very old and discouraged.

"That is true, my son. I know nothing of politics, but I do know my country. Mark my words. We *are* enemies."

Chapter XVI

Kunming, China,

The sun was sinking behind the mountains, and it was bitterly cold with sudden stiff gusts of wind that brought tears to Lawrence's eyes.

Shivering despite the fur-lined leather flight jacket, with his canvas bag and his typewriter at his feet, he looked around at the airfield, made up, as far as he could see, of a motley assembly of corrugated steel shacks and hangars surrounding the landing strip.

Chinese men in dun-coloured uniforms started to swarm around the Beechcraft, unloading crates and cartons and shouting in harsh guttural voices while Olga checked numbers on a clipboard.

There were several small planes lined up on the side of the runway, all of them painted with threatening grinning sharks' teeth opened on blood-red mouths.

"P.40 Tomahawks." Tex said proudly, standing by Lawrence's side. "Single-engine combat planes, four Browning machine guns, two nose cone-mounted, two wing-mounted. Beauties, aren't they?"

"They look — well, lethal," was the best Lawrence could reply through chattering teeth.

Tex laughed. "That they are. We hope. Say, you look pretty cold. Keep that jacket for the time being, and let's see what we can find to put you up."

There was only Hostel Number Two, Olga said, shrugging, giving Lawrence another long, considering look as they walked towards a jeep with a Chinese driver waiting. "But I'm not in charge of billeting."

"Not yet, you aren't,' Tex countered, "But I bet you will be before the week is out."

"Well — I'll see what I can do," she answered with a pleased smile.

"You may have to share," she warned Lawrence. "And that goes for you too, Tex.

"Colonel Huang, our quartermaster is a bit over his head, what with the bomb raid yesterday."

Yep, she said matter-of-factly, as she climbed into the jeep, Kunming was raided just before they landed. They flew in with a CNAC transport — 'Chinese National Aviation Corporation' she added as an aside for Lawrence's benefit — They'd had to circle away from the bombers. Pretty messy. Over two hundred civilians killed, and the Chinese population was leaving the city in droves.

"Hey," she grinned at Lawrence, "you're in the same predicament as I was. No cold weather clothes. We'll have to swing by Thieves' Alley tomorrow, we should be able to kit you up there.

"In the meantime, I have to tell the Old Man we have an unexpected guest, so we need to make a stop at Hostel Number One. That's where the Command offices are," she explained as the jeep stopped in front of a tall ochre-coloured, rather impressive building.

"Doesn't look Chinese, does it?" she said, as he gazed up at the vaguely Grecian pediment and columns. "They say it's French, actually, built when the railway from Indochina was opened."

She took them both down a dingy corridor to an anteroom reeking of cigarette smoke and kerosene and damp.

Lawrence halted, suddenly disconcerted by the familiarity of the smell — of course, the Senior Common Room at Balliol.

An oil heater glowed in the corner and he moved over to it gratefully, rubbing his numb hands. Olga nodded towards the beat-up chairs gathered around a tall lamp that threw a yellowish glow on the dusty and stained carpet.

"Okay, you guys wait here while I talk to the Old Man."

She had left the door half-opened behind her, and if at first Lawrence couldn't make out what was being said in the low-voiced exchange, he winced when he heard a man's voice raised in irritation. "A Brit? A newsman? Why the hell did he give a lift to a Brit journalist? As if getting here four days late wasn't enough, he saddles us with a fucking Limey journalist!"

Tex, leaning comfortably against the wall with his hands deep in his pockets, gave him a cheerful grin. "Don't mind him. Par for the course. He's actually a really nice guy."

Olga put her head through the doorway.

"Tex, then Larry."

Tex ambled in slowly, and Lawrence tried to stop listening to the voices raised in argument. The technicalities of the Beechcraft's problems were of no concern to him, and he tried to remember what little he had heard of Colonel Claire Chennault, Chiang Kai-Shek's air advisor and the man behind the American Volunteers in the Chinese Nationalist Air Force, that "crazy group" that Ben had mentioned.

Aside from that comment, and what everyone knew, that he had single-handedly convinced Washington to supply enough planes to Generalissimo Chiang Kai-Shek to continue to wage his own war against Japan, there wasn't much really. Andrew Gilchrist had told him that Chennault was "when all is said and done, a mercenary. A mercenary on the side of the angels, but a mercenary nonetheless."

Could such a man truly be a "really nice guy"?

He sighed and stretched out his legs.

Well, whatever happened, he couldn't be returned to Thailand, so somehow, he'd hitch a flight to Burma.

Tex emerged from the office, not looking the least bit chastened, and cocked his head at him. "Your turn. Keep your pecker up, Larry."

The man in olive drab uniform sitting smoking behind the desk looked him up and down without smiling and didn't offer a chair.

"I'm Colonel Claire Chennault. Who are you?"

Lawrence took a deep breath.

"Lawrence Gallet, sir. I'm a British journalist from Bangkok, and –

"Yes, I'd gathered that much. But what I want to know is, what are you doing here?"

"And speak a bit louder, would you? Can't hear that well."

Lawrence looked at Olga, then back at Chennault. "Would you mind awfully, sir, if we spoke in private?"

"Yes," Chennault replied, mimicking his accent. "I would, actually, mind awfully, so spit it out…"

Lawrence shrugged. "I'm sorry sir, but in that case, I suppose I'll just express my gratitude for getting me out of Chiang Mai and pay whatever expenses you see fit. Good evening, sir."

He turned away, but just as he was reaching the door, Chennault growled

"Okay. Olga, get out and close the door behind you. You, young man, sit."

And once the woman had left, he stared at Lawrence again through spirals of smoke. "So?"

"I'm sorry if I offended you, sir," Lawrence said again. "But I do not know the level of clearance Olga might have.

"She has no clearance at all." Chennault replied dryly.

Lawrence nodded.

"It's what I thought. I'm SOE, sir, escaping from the Kempetai."

And seeing the wry smile on the man's craggy features, he added that it was very easy to verify by contacting the SOE operations in Meerut, India.

Chennault made a note on the paper before him and asked him to spell out his name.

"I will verify, believe me."

"Please do," Lawrence replied coldly.

And when he did, could he possibly mention that Lawrence Gallet was trying to report for duty as soon as humanly possible?

"Listen, Colonel, as I said, I'm very grateful, and I'm sure you're as keen to get me out of here as I am to leave.

"From what I've understood, you operate flights between here and Rangoon. All I ask is to be put on one as soon as possible, and then I'll catch another flight to India and I'll be out of your hair.

"And once again, I can pay my way."

Chennault listened in silence, then grabbed two glasses and a bottle from the top of a filing cabinet. "Drink? It's whiskey, the real stuff, not Chinese moonshine. You look as if you need it."

He pushed the full tumbler towards Lawrence who took a gulp, feeling the blessed burn go down his throat.

"Well, for starters, son, we can't fly you to Rangoon.

"I've just evacuated our squadrons from Burma, with just one left in Rangoon working with your RAF. I'm not about to send a plane back there just for your convenience.

"You do realize, don't you, that the Japs are going to bomb Rangoon just like they are now destroying Hong Kong, Singapore, Penang, and — oh, just about everywhere you Brits thought the sun would never set.

"Yep," he added in response to Lawrence's stricken face, "Our side doesn't seem to be doing too well this week.

"We, as you no doubt know, no longer have a Pacific fleet.

"You guys have lost most of yours, with the *Prince of Wales* and the *Repulse*, so, if you'll pardon the lousy joke, we're all in the same sinking boat."

He paused to drink and to light another cigarette. "Like I said, son, we can't take you to Rangoon, but we can, possibly, take you to India. Depending."

"On?"

" What do you think? On planes coming in and on planes leaving," Chennault snapped irritably. "We lose some almost every week, and those we do have also have other cargo to ferry, human and otherwise."

Then, returning to his friendly manner, he smiled. "Get a night's sleep.

"I'll try to get through to your outfit — I suppose Calcutta command knows how?" Lawrence nodded — "and we'll keep you posted.

"In the meantime, enjoy Kunming between the Jap bombing raids — and watch out for the whorehouses. Most girls got the clap, but there are a couple, I hear, who have leprosy."

"Oh." Lawrence rose from his chair. "Good to know, sir."

"Yeah. Good to know. Tex and Olga will show you around."

The room Lawrence and Tex were to share was small and neat, with a washbasin, two narrow iron cots, a single dresser and a table.

"I suppose I could find a chair and use this as desk, if that's all right with you?"

Tex chuckled. "Can't see myself needing a desk, pal, so go right ahead.

"Come on, we're going to Rose's restaurant. We'll meet a lot of the guys there."

Rose's restaurant was a dark room in an old Chinese shop

front decorated with cheap coloured lanterns and pictures of pin-ups and planes on the wall, an upright piano in a corner and a phonograph loudly playing a scratchy Edith Piaf record. There were candles on the tables and the air smelled of beer and garlic.

"Lovely," Lawrence exclaimed. "An actual dive!"

"Yes, indeed," Tex agreed, "and here is Rose herself," nodding to a pretty woman no longer in her youth coming to greet them.

She shook her finger at Tex. "What's this, I hear? You been a naughty boy, playing hooky with the Old Man's plane?"

She stared at Lawrence with the measuring eyes of a professional flirt, "And you, handsome, you are the Englishman?"

"Your friend Olga talks too much," Tex replied cheerfully, spying her seated in a corner. She was wearing some kind of cowled jacket with a fur collar and was surrounded by several men who seemed entranced at the sight of her face thrown back laughing and her heavy earrings sparkling in the candlelight.

"No, Rose, we won't sit with them, we'll take that table over there. I think Olga has enough to handle for now. Have Sandy and Pete come?"

Not yet. What would they eat?

"What is there?"

Same-same as usual. Pork chops with garlic, rice. Beans. No chicken, all gone. No vegetables.

"Difficult to get vegetables with bomb raid," she explained.

"Well," Tex drawled, "you know what, Rose?

"I think I'll have the pork chops and beans. Two beers, two shots, Ok?

"You, Larry? The same?"

Rose was the girlfriend of an AVG trainer, Butch Carney, Tex explained.

"She's a great businesswoman.

"As soon as she heard about this base beginning to operate in Kunming, she came here to open a restaurant; she also has her own transport company — runs convoys up the Burma Road."

Lawrence drank his shot of whiskey and coughed — this was probably what Chennault had called Chinese moonshine.

When he managed to stop sputtering, he asked what the Burma Road operation was, precisely. "I mean, I've heard of it, but..."

Tex furrowed his brow, wondering how best to explain.

"What you need to understand is that it all started with the planes. They were shipped in parts to Burma, and assembled in Toungoo, where we train on them, and also train Chinese fighter pilots. I told you about Toungoo, didn't I?

"Best place on earth."

But Chiang Kai-Shek's war needed a lot more than planes, so the Burma Road became his army's lifeline.

Lend-Lease materiel, and that meant everything, from ammunition, bombs, shells, to medical equipment, jeeps and supplies, was shipped from the States to Rangoon — "with the Japs patrolling the Pacific, it's going to be a lot more difficult to get them there" — then it was put on freight trains and taken up to Lashio, near the border with China. It was then loaded on to trucks, and that was where the fun began.

"I don't know if you can imagine this, because I personally can't, this road used to be a mule track, so narrow and steep that pack animals used to fall off it. It's been used for centuries by smugglers, then when the Japanese went to war against China, Chiang had it turned into a kind of passable road.

"The story goes it took over two hundred thousand men to do the work.

"Then the Generalissimo — or more likely his wife — managed to convince Roosevelt to get him Lend-Lease supplies — and that's the only way to get them to him, here in Kunming, then onward to Chongqing.

"But of course, this is China, and it's a long road, and a lot of the stuff kind of vanishes on the way, or other stuff appears here on the market coming from Burma that shouldn't...

"Take Rose, for instance — I don't put it past her to do some smuggling on the side, but she's a good sort.

"Just wish she'd smuggle in some better food.

"Great friend of Olga's."

So yes, what about Olga?

"Ah, Olga..."

Tex took a swig of the second beer a giggling waitress had just brought, followed it with a gulp of the whiskey shot, wiped the foam off his mouth and spoke in a dreamy voice.

Olga.

Olga Greenlaw.

Wife of Harvey Greenlaw, Chennault's executive officer, old Asia hand. Chennault apparently dug him up in Hong Kong — he was the balding man in uniform sitting next to her.

Nobody knew that much about Olga... Some said she was Russian, some said she was Mexican, she sometimes implied some French Indochina past — "The records are all hers," — hence Piaf warbling "Mon legionnaire" in the background — but *she* always made a point of claiming American citizenship.

"The Old Man wasn't crazy about the idea of bringing a woman to Toungoo, but Harvey's nuts about her, so he said she came or he didn't. And that was that.

"She gradually took on various jobs for Chennault, she's in charge of the War Statistical Diary, and has her fingers in all the general management pies, but she actually does a pretty good job.

"She flirts — and more — with all the guys..." His voice trailed off and he stared at her, longing written all over his fresh boyish face.

Lawrence grinned. "And?"

Tex blushed then burst out laughing. "And all I can tell you is that there's only two guys who haven't slept with her and I don't know who the other one is."

He stared again. "She's what my missionary mother would call 'blatant' I think. She was always going on about blatant Mrs This or blatant Miss That."

Lawrence raised his eyebrows.

Missionaries in Texas? Who for, Indians?

Tex shook his head in mock disgust, and started to fork up his beans.

"God, the things you Limeys don't know about the States. We don't convert the Indians any more, I think that was taken care of a hundred years ago.

"No, my parents were missionaries in Korea, I was born there in fact, but we came back when I was a little kid, and my father became a church minister in San Antonio.

"Hey, here come the guys — Larry, meet Pete and Sandy."

The two airmen sat down in a clatter of thick flying boots, called for beer, looked at Lawrence's and Tex's plates and groaned. "Pork and beans, again!"

Then one of them — at this point with the beer and the shots of whiskey added to the generous drink Chennault had given him, Lawrence could no longer tell which was Pete and which was Sandy — asked "You the stowaway from Chiang Mai? Olga says you're some kind of big hush hush Limey spy."

Lawrence shook his head with an apologetic smile.

As Tex said, Olga talked too much.

No, he was just a journalist who published things the Japanese weren't very keen on, that's all.

Enough to get him in trouble with the Kempetai.

"Yeah, so why'd you want her to leave the Old Man's office before you talked to him?" the other one demanded.

Lawrence stared at him at length, desperately trying to think of a reason.

"Didn't want to get scooped," he finally said. "You know what it's like."

Tex nodded gravely, and either Sandy or Pete replied, after a long pull at his beer, "Nah, can't say I do, but I'll take your word for it.

"So, Tex, hear about the bombing raid here?"

Lawrence leaned back in his chair and let the flyers' talk of engines and patrols and navigation malfunctions wash over him. He looked around the room with half-closed eyes, the coloured lanterns, the flickering candles, overcome with a sense of strangeness and dislocation compounded by whiskey and the raucous American laughs and the accordion warbling to Piaf's voice.

What was he doing here? Was it only this morning he'd got off the train in Chiang Mai? He closed his eyes.

Come on, Gallet, get a grip. You're here, you're safe, and you must not, repeat not, even think of Kate.

LAWRENCE'S DIARY
KUNMING, CHINA
SATURDAY, DECEMBER 20TH, 1941

So here I am in Kunming, Yunnan province, China, and these are the first words I write of my new life.

I am now an actual war correspondent, on loan to AP from the SOE.

Colonel Chennault, having checked, was satisfied that I am indeed who I claim to be, and when he had me called into his office three days after I arrived, told me while I was in Kunming I was instructed by SOE Meerut via Calcutta to start earning my keep and write propaganda. No byline.

"Something about our heroic boys, I suppose," he added with disgust.

"Holding out single-handed to help China fight for freedom, homeland and whatever...

"But remember this, young man, when you write — I've heard how you Brits have been grousing about Chiang getting so much Lend-Lease equipment.

"Well, you just better let your readers know that the Burma Road needs to stay open to let all that Lend-Lease materiel though, and keeping it open is your — the British Army's — job.

"The more trouble China gives the Japs, the less trouble the Japs give you guys in Malaya and Singapore and India.

"China's not just a country with funny little yellow people, it's fighting a bloody, awful, war against our common enemy, and it's been doing it alone for the past three years.

"Got it?

"Also, you go only where I say you can go, you keep out of everyone's way when trouble is brewing, and I want to check everything you write before you give it to Communications to send out. Are we clear?"

We were.

He then told me they had no provision for war correspondents' uniforms, and that he was blasted if he knew what rank I held.

"Likewise, Colonel," I replied which made him look even more disgusted.

As to a uniform, I found some trousers and heavy jumpers

at Thieves' Alley and a thick, rather dashing brown fur-lined Chinese jacket that may have belonged to a warlord for all I know. When I left his office, Chennault scanned my outfit and dropped, in his bad imitation of a British accent, "Far cry from Savile Row, what?"

I think he doesn't care much for us Brits.

I have now been here a week and I am gradually getting used to being called Larry, and to the eternal pork chops and beans although I have found one affordable Chinese restaurant here — most of the others cater solely to profiteers, I suppose. It is filthy, but surprisingly good.

What I do find difficult is to become accustomed to the overall unsettled, anything-can-happen-at-any-time atmosphere.

I suppose it is the fate of all people who live their lives in wartime, but it is so far from my slow, lazy, sensuous existence in Bangkok that my nerves jangle each minute of each day.

It is nothing like the months at the training camps — there, it was — well — training, and I think none of us actually believed we would put anything that we learned to use.

It was, to quote our Yorkshire Sarge, a game.

This morning, Olga took me to visit the city which is, or rather could be, lovely if it were not war scarred, stinking of burst drains and overrun with refugees from other regions of China who eke out whatever life they can in the rubble that clogs the streets. Some parts are worthy of a Chinese ink painting with cloud-draped craggy mountains in the background and the obligatory temple next to the obligatory picturesque lake. Beyond the cold, it is strange to be in winter again, to see the trees bare of all leaves and an icy mist over the lake.

The air raid siren sounded as we were returning to the hostel, and we scrambled to get cover in a cemetery behind the mounds of freshly dug graves, abandoning the jeep by the roadside. Lying side by side with our noses in the dirt, we must have made a rather ridiculous picture. "Well, if the worse happens," Olga muttered, "they won't have too far to go to dispose of our bodies." Then, as we saw no incoming Japanese planes, we jumped back into the jeep and rushed to the airfield.

When we arrived, a red flare was fired into the air, which, according to Olga, was the signal to the pilots to take off in their various formations.

The propellers on the shark-toothed planes were already spinning and as each roared down the runway, Olga read the tail number and whispered the names of its pilot, names I knew for having met most of them, but I couldn't reconcile the image of these terribly young men with whom I share beer and beans and who look barely out of adolescence — and behave like it — with the warriors at the controls of those killing machines.

Olga ran into the Control shack, and I, at a loss, not knowing what to do or where to go and trying, as ordered, to keep out of everyone's way, just sat on the ground against the wall of a hangar, wondering how I would behave when bombs started falling around me or low-flying enemy fighter planes began to strafe the airfield and all those there.

I wanted to be brave, nonchalant even, but could I?

Nothing in life, not even SOE, prepares you to face real danger.

I had no idea where the actual threat was, and scanning the sky saw nothing and could hear nothing.

The planes came back, in drips and drabs of two, then two more, then three.

The first group, I heard later, was confronted with heavy bombers and lost its nerve, "buck-fever" is what they call it, as they admitted shame-facedly when they climbed out of their planes walking heavy-footed in dejection to face the Old Man.

The next squadron was not able to overtake the bombers so returned to base as well.

I could just imagine them sitting around in silence, dreading the chewing up Chennault would give them, all the while waiting, as we all were, waiting, waiting for the sixteen other Tomahawk P.40s fighter planes still up in the sky somewhere.

Jack Newkirk, a big, aggressive New Yorker came to join me and sat and smoked in silence, and it was the very first time I had seen him not shouting, cussing, drinking, or daring his fellow pilots to do something foolish or reckless.

He flies with the 2nd squadron, also known as Panda Bear Squadron — the 1st is Adam and Eve, the 3rd is Hell's Angels, and the somewhat silly names are matched by equally silly decorations on the body of their aircraft alongside the vicious shark teeth.

Jack was leader of the first group to go out, the one suffering from buck fever.

I didn't know what to say, so I said nothing, and heaven knows, given my wondering a few moments before whether I'd end up curled into a whimpering ball, I felt no judgement at all, only sympathy and wonder at how they got up in those planes in the first place.

"Goddammit!" he finally said getting up and grinding his cigarette under his heel.

But then there was a rumble in the air, and the tall, dried grasses by the runway started whipping around. Jack put his head back and shielded his eyes with his hand.

"Well, I'll be damned," he shouted. "Here they are!" and he jogged towards the edge of the runway as fast as his heavy boots let him. Chennault and his team came rushing out of the dugout Control shed, all of them surrounding the returning pilots who were whooping in triumph.

Three confirmed bombers down, probably more.

I would have loved to join the general celebration in the hut, to be part of the joy at this so badly needed victory, but dared not and stayed put, feeling very lonely.

So, I am now back in my room, hoping that when the Old Man has finished debriefing them all, someone, Tex – probably, who has appointed himself my best buddy here, as he says – will come and get me to engage with them in "conduct unbecoming officers".

KUNMING, SUNDAY DECEMBER 21ST

I spent quite a bit of time yesterday evening at Rose's asking the pilots about themselves, as preparation for my propaganda article, before the general high spirits along with liquid spirits made them somewhat incoherent.

I found most of them rather arrogant in an adolescent way, but I suppose you must need to be, to believe that your skills will keep you aloft in one of those flimsy canvas and steel planes.

They are happy to answer questions, to talk about "back home", and pull out dog-eared photos of their girlfriends or wives –

some of them are actually married and one is already divorced. None of them, as far as I can tell, is the least bit introspective, and when asked why they left the US Air Force to join the AVG, they usually look puzzled at the stupidity of my question. They wanted to fly, they wanted to fight, they wanted adventure and greater freedom from military discipline and they wonder at those who don't share those feelings.

They are the modern equivalent of the heroes of myriad American novels, the men who settled the West, who wanted wider and wider skies over their heads.

Also, they are promised big bonuses for each Jap plane they shoot down.

Olga is not the only Western woman here, although she behaves as if she were, and she *is* the undisputed queen of Kunming.

There are also two nurses and several other girls in the general staff.

As luck would have it, one of the nurses, Emma, is a redhead, nicknamed Red (of course) and she is engaged to one of the pilots, Pete Petach. They hope to marry very soon. She is nothing like Kate, she is much taller with very blue eyes, but listening to her sweet girlish voice swoop for emphasis the way Kate's does was agony. She speaks Chinese well, was a political science exchange student to Canton several years ago, then studied nursing when she returned to America.

When I told her that my wife was also American, a nurse, a redhead, and, as far as I know, still in Bangkok, she gazed at me in bemusement.

Why had she not come with me?

Nothing could keep her away from Pete, she says, and she seems to blame Kate for not escaping with me.

Part of me blames Kate as well, for not leaving when it would have been so easy.

In two days, it will be our first anniversary.

KUNMING, STILL...
DECEMBER 25[TH]1941
CHRISTMAS DAY

Rangoon was attacked yesterday.

More than fifty Japanese bombers swept over the city and Mingaladon, the airfield.

Many RAF planes were destroyed, as well as several of the AVG Hell's Angels squadrons still stationed there.

Although, by all accounts, the AVG gave as good as they got, the mood here is somber and tense. They have lost two friends in combat.

The mood at Rose's was despondent, brittle, and ugly.

Too much drink taken, leading to some half-hearted fistfights that Olga stopped with a word.

Chenault is sending several Panda Bear squadron flyers to Rangoon to bolster their forces.

Another major battle over Rangoon today.

DECEMBER 26[TH]1941

Chennault called me in today and told me in no uncertain terms that in the piece I am writing, I am to make sure to stress that the AVG – he calls them the "sharks" – have been doing most the work for the RAF and that the officer in charge of the air defence of Rangoon has been sending them on suicide missions.

I was careful to speak very calmly.

"You know I can't do that sir. My piece is for readers in Britain, well, perhaps it might make one or two American wire services if I'm lucky, but basically, I write for the British.

"Also, not an insignificant point, I *work* for the British.

"SOE asked me to do a piece extolling the invaluable contribution to the war effort made by AVG, but I simply can't throw in any accusation against the RAF. For one thing, it wouldn't get past the censors."

He glared at me. "It's the truth."

I had no reason to doubt it, I replied. But still...

"Anyway," he thrust a paper at me, "More fodder for you.

"As you know, the Japs returned to Rangoon yesterday, and your RAF shot down seven planes, lost six men and nine of their Buffalo aircraft." He gave me a huge, triumphant grin. "We lost two and are credited with twenty-eight kills."

I took the paper and grinned in return. "I shouldn't cheer against my side, sir, but — oh hell, I will! Hurray!"

"Now" he added, "I hate to be a killjoy, but do you want news from Thailand, seeing as how you hail from there?"

The Thai-Japanese Alliance was signed officially and formally, at the Emerald Buddha Temple, "if that means anything to you?"

"It's the most revered place in the country, Colonel," I replied, "and attached to the Royal Palace itself.

"Symbolically, it couldn't be greater, I added with disgust, "but Phibul, the Premier, is a master of propaganda."

The Thai cabinet has been reshuffled, and Pridi has been ousted. He is now co-regent with Prince Wan.

"That's a pretty big deal, isn't it? From what I gather, Pridi's one of the good guys."

It could not have been a bigger deal in terms of political impotence, I said. "He's been sidelined. As to Prince Wan — he's always been somewhat of a cipher to me, one of those diplomats whose thoughts are impossible to guess."

Then Chennault slid some aerial photographs across his desk for me to look at.

"Eric Schilling took them on a reconnaissance mission yesterday.

"Recognize this?"

I didn't at first, then I saw the distinctive patterned roofs and spires of the Royal Palace and the curves of the river. Bangkok. He nodded.

"Look closer." He ran his finger down the river towards the docks. "Those ships there are Japanese troop carriers — see the soldiers being marched down?"

And crates and crates and crates of what was probably ammunition, and vehicles and who knows what else being unloaded. The docks looked jammed and at least two more ships appeared to be waiting downstream.

"Now this. Don Muang." The airport, such as it was.

I couldn't really make much out, but Chennault told me there were ninety-six — ninety-six! — aircraft parked wing tip to wing tip.

"You know where they're headed?"

Malaya?

No, The French airfields in Indochina were more convenient for Malaya and Singapore.

"West. Rangoon. The Burma Road."

If only he had a few bombers, he'd clean that airfield up. They'd been promised, but that was before Pearl Harbour, so....

"The RAF refuses to bomb Bangkok —," he once again affected his high-pitched fake British accent, "We're not at war, it would be an unwarranted act of aggression." Then, returning to his normal voice, he added that for want of a few planes a kingdom would be lost, "to misquote Shakespeare," he added.

"Thailand?" I asked.

No.

England.

"KUNMING, CHINA"

The unlikeliest angels.

They hail from Texas, Missouri, New York or California, places whose names embody all you ever dreamt about America or places you've never heard of.

They are young, they are brash, and they came to China to fight in a war that was not theirs and that the enemy's treachery has now brought to them.

They are the unlikely angels who decided to stand on the side of freedom and peace when no one else was lifting a finger because "it was the right thing to do, you know?" as one of them said simply.

When on the ground, they are no different from any man separated from home and family, some read, some laugh, some pray, some play cards. All are friendly, as this reporter who has shared countless pints with them has been able to experience himself. But when the signal to ready in formations comes, they become remote suddenly, godlike, enclosed in a world that only other flyers can penetrate, and they soar up in their flying machines with shark teeth on blood red mouths painted on the cockpits.

They are the heroes of our boyhood adventure books and of all the films we have thrilled to, they are the cowboy, the explorer, the sheriff who marches into Dodge City to restore order, the big-hearted rebel who redeems himself for love, the daredevil who marches into glory.

They are the men who put themselves at risk so that we may be safe.

They were always our friends, now they are our allies.

"*It was the right thing to do?*" Chennault asked, furrowing his brow, "Can't imagine any of them saying that."

That was because no one did, Lawrence replied briskly. He had just extrapolated from his interviews and decided to put the best possible gloss on whatever was said.

"The prose is awful, you need not tell me. But it serves the purpose."

The Colonel shrugged and handed the paper back.

"Actually, I rather like it...

"Anyway, kid, you need to pack your bags. You're leaving tomorrow."

Lawrence's face lit up. Calcutta?

Chennault grunted. No. Rangoon, believe it or not.

"Here are your orders.

"And from what I gather, you can sell that nifty war lord jacket back on Thieves' Alley, you're going to be put in uniform."

Lawrence scanned the flimsy telegraph sheet.

Meerut had no use for him at present and was loaning him out.

He was henceforth an Associated Press accredited correspondent and told to report to the Press Relations Office at the Ministry of Information in Rangoon.

Cable once there, etc, etc.

The Old Man rose and stretched out his hand.

"Good luck, kid. You're going to need it."

Chapter XVII

During the first days after war came to Thailand, the depleted hospital staff unthinkingly kept to the schedule set out for them by Sister Perrine; the single programmed surgery and the emergent appendectomy were taken care of, the expected birth yielded a healthy seven-pound boy, and all seemed well.

Ten days after they were rounded up and forced into trucks at gunpoint, Monsignor Perros and Father Perroudon were released from the Trocadero Hotel where they had been interned with Doctor Hermet and many of the American missionaries who taught and worked in Bangkok.

"The crowding was terrible," His Grace the Bishop told them when he came to Saint-Louis, and Father Perroudon nodded, adding "There was barely enough food, there were babies crying, women moaning..."

And then, with a sombre look, the Bishop told them the true reason for his call to the hospital.

Mother Melanie and the other nuns were not allowed back to their work, they were to remain confined at the Order's Motherhouse, on Convent Road.

"No, I was not able to see them before we left, they were taken away at night and I believe that the Motherhouse is guarded by soldiers.

"But I trust you all to continue the work that the Lord has entrusted us with, and I believe the Reverend Mother would say the same.

"It must however be, despite it all, a relief for you to know that they are safe."

He had tears in his eyes when he gave the nurses his blessing, Rose and Bernadette were sobbing openly and Belinda looked stunned.

Kate felt nothing when His Grace's sweaty hand touched her forehead, neither relief nor succour, nothing but fear of the future.

But as the days went by, in the strange semblance of a return to normal life, she too, began once more to be able at times to laugh, and even, in her dreams, to hope.

The farmers, trusting in the obsessive announcements of peace and amity between Thailand and Japan repeated hourly on the radio, began to bring their chickens, eggs and vegetables to the city once more, food was delivered from the market and there was more than rice to eat, although Kate often brought a packed lunch prepared by Thip's cook which she shared with the other farang nurses.

They ate sitting on a garden bench, fantasizing all the while about the meals they would have when they went home, and Rose told them again and again how she made her soda bread.

"She not a bad sort, really, Rose is," Belinda finally conceded one evening, "when you get to know her — although when I got here, she and Bernadette, they barely spoke to me, thought I looked fast. Worse than the nuns, they were. Bernadette especially. She's an old sourpuss, that one.

"Why do you think Melanie assigned you to room with me?

"Nobody else wanted to."

Kate laughed.

She couldn't imagine sharing a room with either of them.

"They always seemed so... not really unfriendly, but... I don't know. Superior, maybe? I thought they didn't like Americans.

"Especially Bernadette. Now, I think she's probably just shy."

Belinda looked critically at the mangosteen she was peeling.

"Nah, she was jealous of you being a Yank.

"I know I was. Then marrying money... Not that they could hope to marry, old biddies that they are. Rose is thirty-five if she's a day. Bernadette is even older, and a face like an old boot.

"But I think they got used to you being the lucky one. Anyways, what does it matter now?

"Look at us, all trapped here like mice."

Kate shook her head in despair.

Although she still went home most nights, she was more and more fearful of who she might encounter on the streets and no longer used the car anymore, even avoiding all the samlo except those who, knowing her, asked for her custom to feed their families. "The Japanese only give us half of the proper fare," one dared to complain, "and my friend got beaten for insisting on receiving what he was owed."

"Trapped like mice is right," she sighed. "I just don't know how long this can go on…"

They barely realized it at first, but life was unravelling, little by little, thread by thread ….

What they first noticed was the laundry or rather, that there were no clean sheets left – nobody had seen to the wages to have the linen, bandages, towels, surgical gowns and uniforms boiled, washed and ironed, and the service just stopped with no warning.

Food and pharmaceuticals, even cotton wool and rubbing alcohol, were not re-ordered, nurses had no idea when to begin their shifts, there were squabbles over appointments made and not kept, and more importantly, who was going to pay the sweepers, the suppliers, the nurses and the doctors?

No one was left to keep the system working, Nang Lek, the accountant explained. She herself made out the orders for supplies along with the pay slips, "But Sister Perrine had to sign them all and disburse the money, so…"

And, as Belinda wondered out loud, when they all met to discuss what might be done, "Where did all the blooming money come from, anyway?"

Nang Lek reflected at length before attempting a reply.

"The charity cases, well… those were paid for," – she corrected herself," – not exactly paid for, because no one paid, after all… it was part of the doctor's, or surgeon's fees or nurses' salary that they should cover those for free. The medication was provided at cost.

"But could the paying patients' medical fees have covered the rest?

"The food, the laundry, the cleaners, the…." Rose ran out of other categories to mention.

No, of course not. It was the Holy Church that paid for everything else, and that money had slowed down over the past year, since the beginning of the troubles and now….

"And now it's over," Belinda completed the sentence. "So, it's basically what we can charge patients now if we want to go on?"

Nang Lek nodded.

Yes.

Which was why no more charity cases were to be admitted.

She, along with Nang Wanida, Sister Perrine's secretary, gathered the Thai staff to suggest some tentative form of organisation for the administrative tasks and asked Doctor Sumet who had reappeared with no explanation after a week's absence, to please do the same for the medical staff.

Rose was put in charge of the pharmacy, Bernadette of the general wards, and Belinda of the maternity ward — "Just think what Melanie would say about that," she tried to cackle gleefully, but only managed to sound both despondent and scared.

Kate would be surgical nurse, and she accepted with a shrug. If the hours were longer, what did it matter?

She had no one to come home to anymore.

"Although, you all realize," the surgeon said, "we have few patients and shall have even fewer, I think."

And after Christmas, which they celebrated with Father Perroudon to say Mass but no joy in their hearts, life settled into a depressing but predictable pattern.

Seeing the few patients in the mornings as they lined up in the shade of the colonnaded porch, doing triage for the two remaining Thai doctors and Doctor Sumet, the single surgeon still operating at Saint Louis, keeping their eyes open for any sign of measles or chicken pox or any other potential epidemic, then treating those who only needed a few words of advice — an expecting mother, or a colicky child, or an elderly neighbourhood resident too ill-informed to realize that the Catholic Hospital was viewed with suspicion by both Thai and Japanese authorities or too stubborn to care.

Of course, there were no Chinese refugees crowding the gardens anymore, or well-to-do French demanding the best doctor, the best nun, the best food.

The refugees were lying low in Yaowarat and all the French, except the Bishop, priests and nuns, had been deported to Indochina two months ago and not heard from since.

Mother Melanie was able through Father Perroudon to send a brief and encouraging message at New Year — "I pray for you daily, and know you are all living to carry out your calling to heal" — but nothing was heard after.

Japanese soldiers and police never came back to the hospital, and were not even seen that often on the streets, but rumours were rife of farang being rounded up and arrested, and taken to mysterious prisons, but there were always rumours, and who to believe?

The fishmonger's wife who had heard from a second cousin that the farang living in the big house across from their sisters' neighbours had been arrested?

Or the kindly monk from Wat Yannawa who whispered to Nai Khop that he was helping some British people leave the city in a truck belonging to his nephew?

Or Wanida who claimed there were farang mems still just as proud as ever at Whiteaway's?

But maybe not English or French, she amended. Perhaps Germans and Italians.

The Bangkok Times, now taken over by the Japanese as their mouthpiece, exulted daily in the triumph of Asia's peoples "finally throwing off the yoke of the colonial oppressors" and surely, that could not be true.

Or could it?

They hated reading it, they resented the few satang it cost to buy, but they couldn't resist.

Every day, in fact, the newspaper tauntingly distilled tragic news of the advance throughout Malaya, the fall of Penang, then Kuala Lumpur, then Malacca.... Singapore was resisting, the paper said... but not for long. There was no water left and the cowardly British would soon scrawl out to beg for a drink.

There were warnings of impending air raids on Bangkok from the Evil Forces of Colonialism, there was news of victorious bombings of Chinese towns, of downed American and RAF planes, and Kate felt her heart twist with every cruel word but did her best not to believe it.

Surely, she would feel it in her bones if Lawrence were dead....

Only once did the air raid siren go off, early in the new year, but as nobody had told the hospital staff what they were to do or where to go, they just went out to the garden and scanned the sky for RAF planes, trying not to cheer, but saw nothing and went back to their duties.

The Thai nurses said there were no reports of damage or casualties on the radio, and *The Bangkok Times* screeched about the *"inept and cowardly Allied pilots who preferred to unload their bombs on poor farmers' rice fields and flee rather than face the fierce and well trained Zero fighter pilots."*

A few weeks later, on January 25th, when they came back from eating their lunch in the shade of a large frangipani tree, they saw the Thai orderlies and nurses and even Wanida, who in replacing Sister Perrine had also acquired her martinet manner, huddled in corridors, whispering.

They met the farang nurses' questioning looks with downcast, ashamed faces and scuttled away, and Doctor Sumet motioned them towards the pharmacy, muttering something about stock taking.

"Something has just happened today," he whispered. "It is very bad for my country.

"I want you to know that I, along with many of my countrymen, support you. You will remember that?"

Belinda shrugged. "Sure, I will. We all will, won't we?"

She looked around at the others who nodded, uncertainly.

Good, the surgeon sighed, and shifted a carton of compresses away from the wall.

"I hid a radio here last week," he breathed. "I was afraid my servants might hear me listening to English and report me to the police.

"Join me here at nine this evening, Wanida and the others will have left."

He paused and cocked his head.

"It's not that I don't trust them but…," he paused. "I don't know *if* I *can* trust them. And, please, this evening, do be careful nobody follows you here."

Once Rose and Bernadette tiptoed in to join them, Doctor Sumet turned off the overhead light − if the watchman in the garden noticed it through the window, he might wonder if there were a thief in the pharmacy and rush in….

Kate sat cross legged on the floor, her back to a cardboard box of surgical gowns, and Belinda and Rose crouched next to her.

As the oldest, Bernadette was given the only chair and wiped a tear when she heard the familiar chimes and voices of the BBC.

"You know what," Rose suddenly realized, "with this wireless, we don't have to buy that accursed paper again!" but then, as they all did, she gasped and paled when she understood what the newsreader was saying.

Thailand had opted to stand by Japan and the Axis powers and declared war on the Allies.

They exchanged stricken looks, realizing that their world had changed...

"I am truly an enemy alien now," Kate whispered, while Rose stared straight ahead as if in shock, Bernadette repeatedly crossed herself, and Belinda shook her head, biting her lips.

"So is Eddy... and how do I explain to a police patrol that I'm a neutral?

"Any farang face is bound to be suspect.

"And anyway, I don't feel neutral in the least, how *can* we be truly neutral in our hearts?"

Kate swallowed. "I think we should all stay in the hospital now, heaven knows there are enough rooms. I'm sure Wanida will agree.

"Let's get our things tomorrow morning, while we still can."

"Kate," Belinda muttered as they left, "you'd better get your money from the bank. We may need it."

And, Kate thought with a shiver, it may well be confiscated as enemy property...

"Please, please," Doctor Sumet urged them as they turned to leave, "please remember we are not all at war with you."

RAF bombers flew over Bangkok all night and the orange skies and dull thuds coming from the port area were noticed this time.

"Eight Blenheim pound Bangkok!" the BBC announced with jubilation "and inflict great damage on the docks and military targets."

The Bangkok Times said nothing at all.

The gardener and the watchman spent several hours painting a red cross on a sheet and stretched it on the roof, tying it down as best they could.

"Won't survive a storm when the monsoon comes," Rose said critically, "but maybe the war will be over by then."

The bank employee was just as optimistic when he smilingly showed Kate where to sign the withdrawal form, but could not give her all she had requested...

Oh no, no... there were new rules now, and in fact, he whispered, he should not be giving Madame Gallet anything at all… But they all knew and liked Khun Lawrence at this branch, and the war would be over next month, he was sure of it, she would see…

Of course, it would, Kate smiled back, blinking back tears of disappointment and fear. She gathered up the hundred ticals he'd allowed and promised she would tell her husband about his kindness today.

The teller nodded.

"Remember I am friend. When war is over," he whispered, then cut off his secretive manner as the manager came close. "Madame birthed my brother's boy," he explained loudly, showing her to the door. "We all give thanks at temple for you."

Belinda and Kate moved into one of the unused ward rooms the day after.

It was for their own safety, so as to be on the streets as little as possible, but also, as Kate explained tearfully to Lady Thip, for her household's safety as well. She knelt at the old lady's feet and held both her hands very tight.

"Someone someday soon is going to report on you, and I can't have that.

"I promise I will come and see you."

"Not too often," Busaba interjected shortly, and while Thip turned on her daughter in law with a hiss of anger and Pichit glared, Kate nodded.

"She's right. What would be the point if I came back often?"

She rose to her feet and looked around at the lovely view.

"I am very grateful to you for having kept me with you although you knew it put you in danger. I shall miss you all −" her voice broke − "and miss this view…

"I will go up to get some things, now, but I won't need much, really.

"And please, just call me a samlo, you don't want me to be seen in your car."

There was a petrol shortage, anyway, Pichit dropped despondently.

He took samlo as well these days.

When she leaned over to kiss Thip, she asked her in a whisper to please keep everything that was in the safe. "I'll write. Keep well."

Thip gave her a grim smile.

"I think not. I think I shall develop a complaint that will need to be treated at Saint Louis Hospital."

"You will do nothing of the sort, Khun Mae," Kate heard Pichit scold as she went down the veranda steps with Fon holding her suitcase.

"I shall send message, Madam, if needed. Please do same."

Yes, she would.

Then she gave the embarrassed butler a quick and heartfelt hug and turned away.

During the ride back, she fought the feeling she would never be back — how silly, she kept repeating to herself — why, all your papers and even your passport are there... But still...

When she arrived, Belinda was in a state, pacing the small room, shaking, twisting her hands.

Eddy had been picked up at his lodgings by the Japanese military police, rounded up along with just about all the other British, American or Dutch men and women who had not managed to flee Bangkok in the first few days after Pearl Harbour. They were to be taken as prisoners to the University, she sobbed.

Kate grabbed her shoulders and sat her down.

"How do you know?"

Belinda gave her a wild look. "I was there. I'd gone to see him, to tell him that we were moving to the hospital, and suddenly..."

She'd seen everything. She was in a samlo, gone to tell Eddy about the move to the hospital, but Sriphaya Road was blocked by Japanese motorcycles and a big truck was parked in front of the house and she saw Eddy, and the Pritchards, the family who rented him his rooms above being marched out, a woman, her husband and their child, all carrying suitcases.

The woman was begging and crying, where, where, and one of the Japanese soldiers said University and then the samlo driver got scared and turned around and....

"Where *is* the University?" Belinda hiccupped finally, wiping her eyes.

Kate shook her head. She wasn't sure.

"We can find out. Maybe they'll let you go see him."

And now, a week later, they knew no more about Eddy's and the other farangs' fate.

Nai Khop told them the University was on Sanam Luang, the large green near the Royal Palace — too far to walk, especially after dark, which is when they now only dared leave Saint Louis to go purchase some fruit from vendors they knew.

"That's where we went to see the National Day parade, remember?" Belinda sighed, pushing her rice and fried egg around her plate.

There was food available these days, now that things seemed more settled — the market at Bangrak still opened and the Thai orderlies bought them fried fish or pork skewers to make a change from the daily rice porridge which was all they now could afford to feed the patients.

"I wonder how long we can hold out here," Rose muttered. "The pharmacy supplies are running low, and Wanida says she is not sure she can get more ether and sulpha powder. And how we can pay for it…

"Apparently, the Japanese have opened their own hospital for their soldiers and they have taken whatever is to be had."

"But where will the Thai go to be treated?" Bernadette wondered.

"The Japanese are offering to treat the Thai for very little money… In exchange for some show of support, Wanida says, or maybe even not… Nobody she knows has dared so far."

Then came the dreadful news that Singapore was falling and for those women whose lives now were circumscribed to the wards and corridors of Saint Louis Hospital, it seemed their world had come to an end.

Evening after awful evening, they gathered in secret and followed without really understanding the advances and retreats, names of unknown places and officers, Bukit Timah and Pasir Panjang, General Percival and General Yamashita…

But they understood only too well the descriptions of dwindling water and food supplies, of mounting civilian casualties and of women and children being evacuated on ships that were then torpedoed and sunk.

"Thank you, dear God, for having Eddy where he is," Kate overheard Belinda pray at night.

But for herself, she found she could no longer talk to God…

Hands clenched together, her face white, she listened to

the BBC describe the horrors of the battle for the Alexandra Hospital, the bayonetting of the wounded soldiers, surgeons and nurses, and could only stare at the mustard yellow tiles of the floor.

"Is it very bad of me that I'm thankful Thailand gave in when it did?" she whispered to no one in particular.

In hearing of Britain's unconditional surrender of once impregnable Singapore, Rose sobbed.

"All my life, all my life, I was told by my Da to hate the British. And now I'm crying for them and I'm sure he is too."

The crushing of Singapore, *The Bangkok Times* announced with glee, was only the first great Japanese victory of this war, but it was to be the lodestar for the Imperial Armies future campaign.

Henceforth, the city was to be called Syonan-To.

Several days later in the worst of the afternoon heat, two Japanese cars, an ambulance and four motorcycles pulled up in front of the hospital, and three officers strode in, with a young civilian in tow. Two soldiers carrying a stretcher with a heavily bandaged man followed.

Wanida ran out of her office, bowing, cringing, and smiling, and when the younger officer barked at her, bowed again as the civilian translated, "We need surgical nurses. Where?" and offered to have them called.

The nurses, she explained, were in the wards, upstairs.

"No. Doctor want see at work. Go up."

Rushing ahead, Wanida prayed the farang nurses were neither asleep nor doing anything forbidden such as listening to the foreign radio.

She knew fully well it was there, indeed, nothing, nothing, happened inside this hospital that she was not aware of.

Thankfully Doctor Sumet was sterilizing equipment with Kate, thankfully the operating theatre was ready, and the younger officer looked the surgeon up and down.

"Do you speak English?" he asked, and Kate almost dropped the retractors she had just pulled from the autoclave.

The man's accent was pure American and as Sumet nodded and replied quietly that he did, she pretended to busy herself checking the order of the blades, keeping her back to the doctors.

"I'm Captain Ken Akira."

"Doctor Sumet Suthichirat — well, just call me Sumet.

"What can I do to help?"

"Show me how your English-speaking nurses work.

"I'm a US-trained surgeon and I can't work with the Japanese military nurses here. Different method.

"Somebody said you have Irish scrub staff."

Yes, yes, Wanida said eagerly, Kate was their best surgical nurse.

Doctor Sumet bit his lips and looked away. "She's actually a maternity nurse we trained ourselves to pitch in for emergencies... I don't know if..."

"Listen," the Japanese surgeon cut in impatiently. "Can she tell a scalpel from a retractor?"

"Of course, she can."

"Then you both get prepared to work with me and let's see if I can save this general's son's leg."

Sumet eyed the Japanese surgeon doubtfully. He wasn't sure they had the necessary supplies. "We have chloroform, still, but we'll need ether."

They had brought ether. And sodium pentothal and sulpha powder, and everything else that could be needed.

"I am so sorry, Khun Kate," Sumet whispered while they were scrubbing.

"But I had no choice."

No. Kate shrugged. She could not hide forever.

Perhaps this US-trained surgeon might not be able to distinguish between the accents of Kerry and Massachusetts.

But she very much doubted it.

The Japanese surgeon joined them as they were donning masks and gloves and began scrubbing himself.

"Can you believe it?" he demanded to no one in particular, just venting his frustration. "I had to order those two officers out of the operating room. Because the patient's an oh-so-important general's son, they claim they can't have him out of their sight.

"They only backed off when I said that if he got septic and died, I'd pin it on them. Okay, let's go. Every minute counts now."

At first, she remained in the background, and realized that despite her fear she was beginning to get interested in the discussion between the surgeons about use of the injectable anaesthetic.

"You mean you still use a chloroform mask here?" Akira asked in contemptuous disbelief.

This was not America, Sumet replied defensively.

"Yeah, well, I wouldn't use sodium thiopental myself either — quick loss of consciousness, but short lasting, and very low level of analgesia," the Japanese replied, eying the hypodermic he was about to sink into the moaning patient's vein, "but that's all I have here, which means we have to keep using ether along with it.

"There, see, he's out like a light."

He removed the bandages and compresses on the patient's thigh and grimaced. The flesh was puffy and oozed pus and blood.

"They claimed they treated him on the spot. Look at that. Butchers!

"Nurse, clean the field."

Kate hesitated.

Although the worse of the lacerated skin had been roughly stitched, and the artery seemed not to have been touched, there was still shattered bone showing in another gaping wound and she had no idea where to start.

"Let me," Sumet stepped closer, leaning in to take a closer look.

"As I said, Kate is a maternity nurse we trained ourselves, and she's never seen such a surgery as this. But, from what I can see, it's not a gunshot wound?"

Akira shook his head. "Motorcycle crash. The idiot was drunk. He's badly concussed, as well."

Sumet sniffed. "Sepsis is setting in, you realize?"

"Yeah, due to the so-called treatment he got on the spot. They probably didn't even bother to wash their hands." Akira replied in a tense voice.

"I'm going to have to ... well, start with cutting those stitches, and then..." he hesitated, peering down at the mess of bloody flesh. "Nurse, retractor. Then clamp, there. Yes, like that."

Kate watched in fascination as the Japanese surgeon worked quickly to remove bone fragments and held out an enamel dish to collect them along with bloody compresses.

She saw sweat running down his face and, unbidden, offered a dry clean towel. "Your forehead? Shall I mop it, Doctor?" she asked, mimicking Belinda's accent as best she could, and he nodded his assent with a grunt.

Sumet seemed as mesmerized with the man's technique as Kate was. "I've never done anything this complex," he admitted.

"Neither have I," Akira replied with a rueful laugh. "You're good, though. Where'd you train?"

London, Sumet answered. King's College.

"But I only do general surgery here. Appendectomies, hernias, gall bladders and the like... You?"

Akira sighed. "God, an appendectomy would be a dream right now, wouldn't it? I trained in San Francisco. University of California.

"That's where I'm from."

He glanced up from sprinkling sulpha powder liberally over the incision he'd just made to reveal more of the bone and began to attempt to set the shattered shards of the femur. "Yeah, I know what you're thinking.

"American, Japanese uniform?"

"I'd gone to Nagasaki – hold it, nurse, just there, yes – It was a graduation gift from my parents, to see Japan, meet my grandparents, a huge deal, you know?

"Then I found myself drafted into military service, even though I was born in the States, I'm still considered Japanese in Japan. So ... Here I am."

He sighed and muttered, "Bangkok. Not part of my plan. Well, as my mother always says, *shikata ga nai* – it can't be helped."

"It must be rather uncomfortable." Sumet said in a soft voice.

"It is." Akira replied shortly.

"Less and less, though, from what I hear about the way people like us – I mean, people of Japanese ancestry – are getting treated in the States, rounded up and lynched in some cases. 'Yellow Peril', they call us" he added in a bitter voice. "And you know what? My Japanese isn't good enough to speak to nurses and orderlies – I speak it like a kid, they say, which isn't surprising – as I never used it, obviously, in medical school.

"Which is why they wanted English-speaking scrub staff for this very important patient."

So how did he manage for other operations, Sumet wanted to know.

"I'm assisted by an English-speaking colleague, and I learn fast."

He worked in silence, then, only issuing terse instructions to increase the ether in the mask or ask for instruments.

He finally stretched up and rolled his shoulders to ease the tension. "Okay, I'm done. We're going to immobilize the leg with a splint, and just cover it up for now and hope for the best."

He looked down at his patient.

"Can you guys put me up for the night? I think I'd better not leave him."

Kate saw Sumet furrow his brow behind the surgeon's back and felt a chill herself.

They didn't want this man, and probably also his two officers and the interpreter poking around the hospital.

"Wouldn't it be better to transfer him back to your own wards? We are very under-equipped here," Sumet finally suggested.

Akira paused and thought, removing his mask.

"Yeah, you're probably right.

"And if he dies here, it'll be on my head alone, whereas at the Military Hospital...

"You can keep what's left of the ether and sulpha, and everything else."

He waved away Sumet's mumbled thanks.

"We have no shortage, and it looks as if you guys might need it.

"We'd better get going now, then, before he wakes up.

"Thank you for your assistance, Doctor ... Sumet, is that it?", then, turning to Kate, "And you, nurse... What's your name by the way?

Kate swallowed, hoping her voice would be muffled by the mask she still wore.

"Fallon, Doctor. Mary-Katherine Fallon."

"Mary-Katherine Fallon," Ken Akira repeated with a grin." Well, doesn't get more Irish than that, does it?

"You're not bad either, Mary-Katherine Fallon. A bit nervous, but, hey, it wasn't an ordinary surgery, was it?

"And if I need assistance again, I'll know where to come ask."

Sumet and Kate watched the stretcher being carried back down the stairs, and once they were out of sight and out of earshot, Sumet whispered that he certainly hoped Doctor Akira would not need their help again.

Kate tore off her mask at last and wiped her forehead with it.

She shook her head, feeling relieved, confused and apprehensive all at once.

The so familiar way Ken Akira spoke, and his easy American manner had made her feel strangely comfortable, and with this comfort, she knew came the risk of betraying herself.

"So do I, Doctor, believe me. So do I."

Chapter XVIII

"The civil-defence of this country is a bloody fucking mess, and I intend to report it, unless you give me a reason not to."

Those were the first words Lawrence heard as he entered, transfer and order papers in hand, the office of Major Hewett, in charge of press relations at the Ministry of Information, which was rather improbably located in the former teacher training college, above a regimental mess.

He had already had to run the gauntlet of road blocks, was forced to dismount from his cycle rickshaw, then to walk past sentry booths, officious and suspicious guards at various points, be questioned as to his lack of uniform and then, each time he said, "Press correspondent", be sneered at, and the last of those who halted him as he reached the last landing of the stairs at the barracks, a young lieutenant who could have been no more than twenty five curled his lip.

"Oh, another vulture. You're the fourth today," and pointed to a door. "Go in there and give your name to Major Hewett's secretary, Sergeant Rutledge."

He did as told and was waved towards a heavy teak door by the harassed and twitchy Sergeant Rutledge who barely gave his papers a cursory glance.

"Just go in," the sergeant muttered, "he'll be relieved to deal with you."

Nonetheless, feeling it more prudent, Lawrence knocked, and receiving no answer, pushed the door open, just to hear those words about it all being a mess, and he could not have agreed more, having seen the havoc and destruction of Rangoon since his arrival the day before.

He couldn't see the face of the man who had just rapped them out as he was hunched over a desk, but the American voice was familiar. United Press correspondent Darrell Berrigan, he of the flamboyant manner and dress, was a fixture of the Bangkok press circuit.

"Darrell? You made it out?" he asked.

Berrigan turned around and grinned.

"Lawrence! Our very own golden boy of Bangkok. What brings *you* here?"

"Same as you, I imagine."

The officer seated behind the desk stared, obviously relieved to no longer be in Berrigan's firing line. "And you are?"

"Lawrence Gallet, sir. Associated Press. I apologize for barging in, but your sergeant outside said…"

"Yes, yes. As I see you know Mr. Berrigan here, you'll understand why the good sergeant wanted to cut my meeting with him short. You have your accreditation papers?"

Lawrence handed them over. "I assume you'll find them in order, sir."

Hewett perused them, then raised his eyes to Berrigan who was still fuming as he stood by Lawrence's side.

"That'll be all, Mr. Berrigan.

"You cannot, repeat, *cannot,* tell your readers it's a fucking mess, not that I disagree with your colourful assessment, but because it's a matter of morale.

"Write it, it will get canned by the censors.

"And as you depend on our system to get your despatches through, I advise you to stay on our side before we suspend your wiring rights entirely."

He smiled charmingly. "I think you don't want that? No? Neither do we.

"Now run along and go join your friends Stowe and Gallagher at the bar of the Strand and moan together and let me deal with young Mr.…," he looked down at Lawrence's papers, "yes, Mr. Gallet here. Good bye."

Berrigan shrugged. "Meet us at the Strand bar this evening, Lawrence.

"We'll put you in the picture."

Once they were alone, Hewett pursed his lips and stared at Lawrence.

"I've been told to expect you. So. You are basically, but on a temporary basis, accredited to Associated Press to cover this area. But…"

The man rose and began pacing the area behind his desk, sighing all the while.

"But SOE Meerut may recall you whenever it suits their purposes. You know that?"

Lawrence nodded. Yes, of course.

"As for the time being, there is nothing, nothing, nothing, coming out of Bangkok except for those blasted Jap Zeroes, you are in all respects a normal journalist, with the proviso that you also report to SOE *and* to us whatever you consider relevant to the situation in Thailand, whatever that may be, but frankly, for the time being, I cannot imagine it happening.

"Go see Rutledge, he will get you sorted with uniform, press passes, food rations and the like.

"And he will give you the regulations you must — and I cannot emphasize this enough — you must abide by.

"Morale is everything in times such as this."

Lawrence nodded again.

"These are times that try men's souls," he murmured, half to himself.

Hewett looked up, surprised. "Very apt. Very apt indeed. I'd heard you are a good writer."

"Oh, not I, sir. Thomas Paine in *The American Crisis*."

"An American," Hewett shrugged deprecatingly.

"Actually, he was British. He also contributed to writing the French Declaration of the Rights of Man."

"Hmm. Bit of a turncoat, then, wasn't he?

"Right, off with you, mind you stick to those rules if you want to stay out of trouble, and good luck."

Being "sorted" by Sergeant Rutledge was not unlike the first day of school, Lawrence couldn't help thinking.

He was told where to apply to be issued with a uniform, there was another office that was to assign him accommodation — "it's not the blooming Strand, and you'll have to share," he was warned — where to collect food rations for the field, what transportation and sending dispatches arrangements were.

All in all, this uncomfortable feeling of being a new boy followed him throughout the day, and it was with some apprehension that he entered the bar of the Strand Hotel that evening, wearing his new, surprisingly not ill-fitting uniform.

As he expected, Darrell Berrigan was seated at a table in the dark, teak-panelled room, with two other men and hailed him with a cheerful "Hey Bangkok boy, sit down."

"No more of your beautiful cream linen suits, I notice."

"Lawrence here was the best-dressed stringer in Bangkok, weren't you, darling?" he added archly, and Lawrence was suddenly reminded that Berrigan always had a string of beautiful Thai boys in tow.

"Lawrence was – how do you Brits put it? – oh yes, our little bit of quality."

"This is Leland Stowe, and this is Edward O'Dowd Gallagher, known as OD."

Lawrence's nervousness only increased – he had heard Hewett mention the two names but had put them out of his mind, somehow incapable of believing that these two men, possibly the most famous journalists in the world, might actually be in Rangoon.

O'Dowd Gallagher was a reporter for *The Daily Express* and, after having covered the British Expeditionary Force's ill-fated campaign in France in 1940 and the wars in Spain and Abyssinia, he was most famously on *H.M.S Repulse* when it was sunk by the Japanese off the coast of Malaya.

After he was rescued, he published a last withering dispatch, headed "Singapore is Silent", excoriating the censorship imposed on the press there while the island was battered by Japanese air fire.

And Leland Stowe was one of the greatest foreign correspondents of all, a Pulitzer prize winner in 1930.

Lawrence had avidly read his coverage of the Nazi attacks on Finland and Norway, and just before leaving Kunming, had been told of a front-page article Stowe had written for the *Chicago Daily News* with a huge headline blaring "Burma Road Scandal Exposed", denouncing the corruption and inefficiencies preventing American Lend-Lease equipment from reaching the Chinese Nationalist forces.

"Gentlemen, I'm … well, at a loss for words," he stammered, still standing.

"That's a pretty bad start for a journalist," Gallagher drawled.

"Don't be nasty, OD," Leland Stowe said mildly, rapping his pipe out in the ashtray, "And you, young man, sit down. – I suppose you have words enough to order a drink? — Waiter, a whiskey, for my colleague here — and tell us how you made it out of Bangkok.

Easily, Lawrence recounted.

He took the train to Chiang Mai, providentially a day before the Japanese arrived, then, again providentially, from there an AVG pilot took him to Kunming, where he kicked around for a month, but got to know the pilots pretty well.

"I got a cable from AP ordering me here but had to wait over a week for transport and just arrived yesterday.

"What about you, Darrell?"

Berrigan cocked his head.

"Providence seemed to have played a big role in your escape.

"Or is providence another name for Gilchrist?

"You were pretty hugger-mugger with him, weren't you?

"Did *he* tip you off?

"I was wondering where you were, when you didn't turn up for that 'bury the hatchet' cruise the Japs invited us to.

"I was *not* hugger-mugger with Gilchrist, we're friends, and he's an old Oxonian too." Lawrence replied defensively.

"I went to see my elderly cousin in Chiang Mai, who'd been ill, then I heard about the invasion, and it was the British consul there who advised me to get out. Christ, you know that after what I wrote in Bangkok, the Kempetai weren't going to take kindly to me."

Strangely, he could feel his indignation rising, as if he had not, in fact, done exactly what Berrigan had described.

"And I actually left my wife behind in Bangkok, do you think that if I'd been tipped off, I wouldn't have taken her out with me?"

Berrigan laughed and raised his hands in surrender. "Cool down. Just kidding, just kidding!

"You didn't miss much on that cruise, anyway."

Lots of sake, lots of speeches of eternal friendship, the fellowhood of man in general and journalists in particular, then a lot more sake.

"After the first couple of hours, I couldn't remember a thing. Never want to touch the nasty stuff again in my life.

"When I woke up with a bitch of a hangover, the Japs were

in town and I was just about compos mentis enough to grab my things and hightail it to Hua Lamphong where I bumped into Standish, you know, the guy from the *Sydney Morning Chronicle*, we got on the first train North, then managed to cross into Burma with the help of some friendly Thai border officials."

"I heard about your feature on the Burma Road scandal," Lawrence said diffidently to Stowe. "I haven't had a chance to read it though, it took a couple of weeks for us to get the papers, and then only some – but I suppose you know that, having yourself arrived from Chongqing."

Stowe looked gratified.

"Oh? And how was what you heard received?"

Lawrence grinned in recollection.

"You were given a rousing toast, with a lot of whiskey and beer at Rose's."

All the flyers had cheered the fact that the American public was at long last being told what was happening to their tax dollars, with only Rose and Butch Carney looking peeved.

"Yes, I know about Madame Rose and her famous restaurant," Stowe nodded.

"But she is only one of the small fishes in the business, albeit one of the more colourful ones.

"What you probably didn't realize is that she has this thriving car smuggling operation, buys the cars in Rangoon, fills them with cigarettes and little luxuries like perfume, and cosmetics and marmalade – you know that the Burma Road is to be used only for essential goods and Lend-Lease materiel – drives the cars up the road as her own private property, then sells them at a tremendous profit.

"But at least, *she* doesn't steal any military stuff."

Gallagher lifted his head from his glass. "You got to know the pilots pretty well, you say? So, you're the "Unlikeliest angels" penman, I bet?"

Hand on heart, he quoted "*They were always our friends, they are now our allies*"?

Lawrence winced. "Afraid so, yes. But I... Well, Chennault loved it, anyway."

Gallagher guffawed, "Ah, just pulling your leg, mate. We've all had to do our own purple prose bits at times, and at least, yours has no byline.

"*I've* had to compliment the Governor on his cheerful demeanour, under my own name.

"Where're you bunking?"

Lawrence grimaced. "The YMCA, unfortunately. I dropped my bag there. It could be worse — my room is so small I shan't have to share, and I have a table — all in all, better than Kunming. I just hope the showers work."

"Oh, you poor innocent little thing! You should have insisted on a proper hotel, dear," Berrigan simpered.

He had snagged a room at the Strand, he said smugly, and Stowe and Gallagher had moved to the Rangoon Golf Club to be closer to Mingaladon airfield.

"That's where the story is, it's actually the only positive one we can write and it's also the only one people in the States want to read about, the RAF and the AVG putting on a truly amazing defence." Stowe explained. "Although, the Burma Road scandal was good at raising the hackles of your average American taxpayer," he added, somewhat smugly.

"Yep, and it's also a bid at another Pulitzer, admit it," Gallagher added with venom clearly heard under the cheerful tone.

Lawrence sipped his drink and listened to the talk, mentally making notes.

The two men who mattered, he was told, were General Hutton, the new commander of the Burma Army, and the Governor, Sir Reginald Dormand-Smith, but there was no point in requesting an interview with either.

Hutton had no time for newsmen and as to the Governor— "He has nothing useful to say. We call him Dormant-Myth or Dormouse-Smith — A nonentity," according to Gallagher.

"Way in over his head" in Berrigan's words. "He actually calls Japs 'those little blighters'.

"*And* he appointed his ADC, who *also* happens to be his daughter's fiancé, Tommy Cook, as head of press relations. Praise the good Lord that Hewett's his deputy and does all the work."

Stowe offered a more measured assessment. "He's only been here since last May, knows nothing of the country, and has no military experience, although it must be admitted he was involved in civil defence planning in England."

"Yeah," Berrigan sniped, "and look how much help that was."

The civil defence plan was a shambles, although an expert had been sent in from London —"one Richard de Graff-Hunter", Berrigan added, pronouncing the name in a plummy voice, "looks like a chorus boy" — but he'd arrived only last August, and nothing, nothing, nothing had been done to prepare the population for air-raids.

"When the bombing started on the 23rd, people just went out into the streets and watched.

"Over two thousand were killed, boom, just like that." Gallagher said. "Even Wavell, yes Percival Wavell himself, the Supremo of Allied Command in the Far East was caught, his plane had just landed in Mingaladon before the Jap bombers swept in, and he had to hide for over an hour in a slit trench by the airfield.

"Well then, the natives, those who survived, especially the Indians, they fled on foot. Can you picture that?

"Rangoon was turned into a madhouse.

"Thousands of people walking over a hundred miles, blocking roads, blocking the arrival of military convoys from the north?

"And would you believe it, the Japs sent big bouquets of flowers fastened to their bombs... What kind of people do that?"

What kind of people *did* do that? Lawrence wondered.

There was something disturbingly beautiful about the idea. Was it a tribute to those who were about to die?

Thankfully, the second wave of attacks on Christmas day was less deadly — people finally realized they needed to take shelter in the slit trenches that Graff-Hunter had ordered dug and our fliers certainly beat the Japs back.

Some of the refugees were returning now, as there seemed to be a lull in attacks, thanks to the success in shooting down Jap planes after the second attack and renewed RAF and AVG raids on Japanese airfields in Thailand.

"But what you've to understand, kid, is that the Indians — whom the Burmese hate, by the way — are vital to keep the port operations going.

"And Rangoon port is the only one left in the area, now that Singapore is doomed."

But there still weren't enough planes after the attacks on

Mingaladon — "the AVG have maybe twelve airworthy P-40s at this point, and that's with the reinforcements Chennault sent from Kunming, and don't get me started on the RAF — most of them are Kiwis, great guys, who are given completely outmoded Buffalo planes.

"And their commanders insist that they use the same tactics against the Japs as are used against the Germans, like there's only a single way to fight a war, and that way is the RAF's way.

"But the Japs are acrobatic fliers, and they can totally outmanoeuvre those clumsy, very aptly named Buffaloes." Gallagher growled. "I'm amazed those poor RAF pilots manage to shoot any down, which nonetheless, they do."

What was needed now was more troop reinforcements from India, and martial law, to impose stringent labour orders at the Port, and also to check the activities of Burmese fifth-columnists.

"There's a pretty large bunch of very political people here, students mainly, call themselves the Thakin, who believe Burma should be independent — and I can't say I blame them — and they see the Japanese as their ticket to freedom. Men like Aung San, for instance, and U Nu.

"They see what's happening in India, with Gandhi and the Quit-India movement. That kind of thing is contagious.

"The difference however, is that as I was saying, the Burmese loathe the Indians, whom they see as usurpers brought in by the British.

"So, they want *both* the British and the Indians out.

"Aung San was contacted last year by the Japanese and taken to train in Hainan with some thirty-odd young firebrands. They founded the Burmese Independence Army and are now, from what one hears, ready to join the Japanese army. But Military Intelligence here just poohpoohs the idea — I call them Military stupidity, myself."

By this point, Lawrence had pulled out his notebook and started scribbling, but Stowe shook his head.

There was no point in writing about that, it would never pass censorship.

"…and given the situation, I'm not sure it's a bad thing."

"What about the refugees? Human interest stories?" Lawrence asked.

Gallagher shrugged. "Human interest stories? About *natives*?

"Good luck with *that*!

"Nobody cares about the natives."

The only human interest aspect of this whole mess was the fact that the British in Burma, the burra-sahibs, were adamant about continuing their life as if nothing was happening here.

"Sleep-walkers among the bombs, I call them." Stowe added. "Their biggest problem seemed to be that they couldn't celebrate Christmas properly."

The British colonials were a pompous, self-satisfied group of people, intent on keeping the natives and other undesirables in their proper place, in the view of the three newsmen.

And that attitude extended even to the AVG fliers, who, admittedly, were a rowdy bunch given half a chance, which had led to pretty unpleasant scenes at the Rangoon Golf Club when the pilots appeared en masse, drunk, and determined to get even drunker.

Lawrence smiled.

He had seen the AVG guys at play and could well imagine them treating what he supposed was a venerable and stuffy institution like an evening at Rose's.

"Still", he mused, "criticizing them for not being able to celebrate Christmas or the New Year might be an angle, when you think of the privations of people in England trapped under the blitz, with just about everything rationed, and still, from what I hear, keeping good cheer.

"I mean, in England, they know that in the colonies, life is still pretty cushy."

"You do that," Gallagher retorted, and the censors here will be down on you like a ton of bricks.

"Morale, my boy, we must preserve the ever-important morale!

"Right, I'm going to hit the sack. Want to share a rickshaw, Leland?"

Stowe nodded as he relit his pipe, then stood. "One last thing though. You're going to need a gun.

"I know, correspondents mustn't be armed, yeah, yeah, we've all been told that.

"But Rangoon is a dangerous city, always has been, and the Burmese are pretty handy with a knife and would slit your gizzard for five bucks.

"So, get hold of one, it's not that difficult, just go to one of the Indian places.

"It'll cost you though, these days."

Lawrence nodded his thanks, refraining from saying that he already had one.

Berrigan seemed suspicious — clairvoyant? — enough, no point in giving rise to more doubts about him being nothing but an ordinary journalist — which he was, he reminded himself.

Until further notice, and possibly forever, he was nothing but a newshound like his colleagues, albeit less experienced.

He left the Strand Hotel with a last wistful look at the luxurious lobby — Berrigan, on bidding him good night had added that *he* had an enormous — "no scratch that, gigantic" — bathroom with enough hot water to drown in.

But at least, it was a short walk to the YMCA.

Stowe's words of warning had unnerved him, however, and as he walked the almost deserted streets, eyeing the shadows warily, he promised himself that he would henceforth always carry his gun.

Being a lousy shot mattered less, didn't it, if you needed to fire at point-blank range?

LAWRENCE'S DIARY
RANGOON, SUNDAY, JANUARY 11TH1942.

I finally managed to wrangle myself, as the Yanks put it, a room at the Strand, invoking in an exchange of cables with AP first the cheaper prices — the city receives no wealthy travellers these days, obviously, and the Strand is half-empty — the importance of preserving AP's prestige along with the need to keep tabs on my colleagues who are also my competitors, and heaven forbid I should be scooped while sitting in my austere but Christian room adorned with a cross on the wall and many, many, bed-bugs.

It is very strange, I exchange cables with AP having no idea who reads them, who discusses my requests, and who answers them. It is just "They", but who, indeed are "They"?

Actually, I didn't need to argue it at all, even with the lance-corporal, he who had warned me I didn't rate the "Blooming Strand".

He just yawned, had a sip of his tea and said, "Can't blame you, mate. Wouldn't stay at the bloody YMCA if you paid me."

I didn't bother to ask him why, in that case, he had assigned me a room there. I now understand that it is all part of the antipathy we correspondents seem to attract, and that he must have been rather surprised at my accepting it without a murmur.

Still very much the new boy yet, I need to rely on others to tell me where and how to submit articles for censorship and filing, although I have yet to write my first dispatch from here.

As to pictures, they must be developed before being sent, and one Wallace-Crabbe, of the press unit, is putting up a darkroom of sorts. I have no camera, so that does not concern me.

I went to church this morning, at the Holy Trinity Cathedral, not because I felt in need of spiritual succour, but to observe what Gallagher calls the Burma burra-sahibs and Stowe the "sleepwalkers among the bombs".

As I went in, the organ – quite a good instrument – was playing a muted Bach prelude while people entered, but there was none of the usual chatting, words of greeting, little laughs and checks on who's here and who's not, that I always saw before Sunday service at home.

Instead, the faithful exchanged nods or at the most some whispered words and sombre looks before taking place in the pews.

There was an expectant hush, followed by a collective sigh of almost ecstatic relief: His Excellency the Governor with wife, daughter and I suppose the fiancé, who is also HE's ADC entered, giving benign and reassuring looks right and left.

The organ switched to a triumphant hymn – I think, from my memories of school, that it was "Lift high the cross" –, while the Bishop, indeed lifting the cross high, led the procession to the altar.

The attendance was as I expected, the usual hatted and gloved ladies who sniffed into perfumed handkerchiefs – I suppose it must have been pretty smelly, with a massing of sweaty humanity – quite a few schoolteacher-cum-missionary types, unruly and fretting children, rather a lot of wealthy looking Chinese, of those who worship at all temples and religions just to hedge their bets, a smattering of men in uniform, but officers only, not the so-called 'other ranks' who must have their own church at their barracks.

My very recognizable war correspondent uniform – I seem to have been the only one there – drew a few disparaging glances.

I don't agree with Stowe, these are not sleep-walkers.

I scented true fear here, gallantly disguised, certainly, but would there have been such fervour otherwise, in the faces turned up to receive communion?

In other times, I am sure, ladies would have come to see and be seen, but would have spent the sermon reviewing plans for the day, a luncheon party at home or a curry at the Club, and men, dragged to the service by their wives would have been checking their watches and longing for the first stengah of the day.

Today, the Bishop's words were followed with avid attention.

His sermon was brisk and martial.

Our fighting men, the Empire, the forces of evil, the need to have faith in God and the role He fated England to play in the world.

From where I had placed myself, in one of the lateral pews, I could see the Governor's head bobbing in devout agreement.

The hymns were rousing and sung with ardour.

"From Greenland's icy mountains, from India's coral strand...", *"Jerusalem"* and of course, *"Onward Christian Soldiers."*

Afterwards, I took a rickshaw through the graceful, tree-lined avenues of this well-planned and laid out city, and despite the ugly piles of rubble and the bomb-scarred, gaping holes in many places, I couldn't help but admire the blend of classical and whimsical architecture, so different from higgledy-piggledy Bangkok, and having seen the Cathedral, decided it was only fair to visit the Shwedagon, the most revered Buddhist pagoda in Burma.

As usual, I found myself more moved by the worshippers than by the temple, although it is quite beautiful in its very shiny way.

I am always put off by the amount of gold in shrines devoted to renunciation of earthly goods.

But the women who bedecked the statues with garlands of flowers, the low chanting coming from inner chapels, the huge white smiles given me by little boys... all of that was familiar and soothing.

Then, feeling distinctly irreligious, I came back to the Strand to partake of steak and pudding. The menu put in front of me was written in French, and I almost burst in tears, thinking of Kate's embarrassment at such pretensions.

Stowe was summoned urgently to the Governor's office today — I imagine it was just after His Excellency returned from the Cathedral — and told to desist with his Burma Road scandal articles, of which only three have been published to date, to "avoid antagonizing the Chinese."

Stowe seems barely bothered by these, to my mind, infuriating orders.

"I've made my point," he says, "and from what I hear, it's already had some effect. The Chinese are cracking down on the smugglers and thieves that infest the Road, so…"

Oh, to be so experienced and detached, and not feel one has at any cost the need to prove oneself.

I cannot help feeling I'm an impostor, a little unimportant stringer from Bangkok, and that all these seasoned correspondents wonder what I'm doing here.

I don't know whether I imagine the looks I get when we meet for drinks and therefore keep as quiet as I can.

More correspondents are flocking to Bangkok, and are greeted with jokes and jests and questions about what they've seen or been through — they all seem to know, or at least to have heard of each other, and I have made a list to try and get their names and affiliations straight and not make myself look as uninformed and raw as I truly am.

Stowe, Gallagher and Berrigan I know, of course, but there's Wilfred Burchett, who's Australian, writes for *The Daily Express*, and, like Stowe, arrived from Chongqing, Roderick Macdonald, another Australian, from *The Sydney Morning Herald* and George Rodger, who is with the prestigious American *Life* magazine, and always has at least one camera hanging from his neck.

Rodger could be a subject from one of its issues himself, tall, curly-haired and handsome, with a movie-star quality to him.

You can imagine him as a fearless leader about to breach the Germans lines in the Great War, or as a pirate, dagger between his teeth swinging from a line to raid an enemy ship, and somehow, he looks better in his uniform than any of us do.

He is also soft spoken, and extremely friendly, and such is the prestige of *Life* magazine and the power of its publisher, Henry Luce, that everybody appears to defer to him.

He's great mates with Alec Tozer, of British Movietone news — Italian looking, short and dark, and always seeming to joke about everything.

The other newsreel man, Maurice Ford, from British Paramount, is far less approachable, at least to a tyro such as myself.

It appears everybody — well, at least, those who matter — have book contracts lined up to, as they put it, "tell the *real* story", that is what the military censors do not allow them to publish.

There was some surprise at hearing that I do not, but that is then put down to the fact I work for a news agency, not a newspaper.

I, of course, never admitted to the fact that it never had even occurred to me, when Stowe advised me on how I might proceed to ensure such a book deal, and expressed deep gratitude.

"Just make sure you don't scoop me, kid, okay?" he concluded.

Very slight risk of that.

Meanwhile, the Japanese army is advancing inexorably.

Manila was captured last week, and now the Dutch East Indies are under attack, Japan declared war on the Netherlands yesterday.

Kuala Lumpur fell today, while British troops are scrambling south towards Singapore.

I wonder sometimes if the two bomb attacks last month weren't mere distraction tactics, to keep the British army in Burma and prevent them from going off to support the troops in Malaya.

Might I write that?

If I did, would it pass censorship?

Probably not.

And, to quote Hewitt, nothing, still bloody nothing coming out of Thailand except for those blasted planes that sometimes buzz Rangoon at night and are chased away.

Of all my contacts in Bangkok, all the people I passed articles to, all those who read them, who expressed fear and despair or simply misgivings at the increasing Japanese presence and Phibul's policies, is it possible that nobody has tried to get some news out?

Did SOE actually *never* train *anyone* to use short-wave radio?

Or do they indeed live in such fear of Phibul's police and the Kempetai that they have all gone to ground?

I try desperately to not think of Kate, to wonder, to worry. But of course, I cannot.

It is easier at the Strand, as there is always someone there to talk to, and to exchange bad news with.

Gallagher just boasted that he managed to talk himself onto a RAF bombing mission over Bangkok.

I know — *I know!* — that the mission would have taken place anyway, but still cannot prevent a surge of sheer hatred when I think of it.

He says that the main damage was done to the wharfs and the airfield, and I realize that it was necessary, and will need to happen again. But I cannot stand him talking about it.

Tex turned up from Mingaladon, with Pete Petach in tow, saying he knew he'd find me here.

They were curiously subdued, or possibly just exhausted by all their sorties over North Thailand and French Indochina.

They are down to seven P.40s in Burma now, but claim they destroyed over twenty-five Mitsubishi Ki-21 bombers on the ground.

"Just like shooting ducks," they crowed. On the other hand, they say, the bomb damage on the runway still has not been completely repaired and it is still cratered and gouged out in places.

They gave me news of Chennault and Olga and Emma — Pete hopes they'll be able to marry next month in Kunming — and Tex gave me ten dollars from Olga for my warlord coat that she finally managed to sell back at the thieves' market, two dollars less than I paid for it. Keeping warm for over a month for two dollars was not such a bad deal.

It was with them, knowing they would not laugh at such naïve wonderings, that I was able to talk about something I have been puzzling about these past few days.

How can the Japanese manage not only to overrun such vast lands in so little time, but hope to keep control of them, given the sheer limitations of demography and national wealth?

Pete looked perplexed.

"I mean," I explained, "that although it is a densely populated country, it is a small country. Is all of the male population in the army? Is that even possible?

"And to produce such planes — 'amazing planes!' Tex chipped in — and warships, and guns and... Japan is made only of a few islands with no natural resources to speak of.

"It is not a wealthy country, in fact, many Japanese emigrated in large numbers to America and Brazil to seek a better life."

Pete reflected that one could say the same of Germany — "except that Germany has resources," I interrupted him to say. "Iron, coal, steelworks, chemical plants, a longstanding industrial and production history.

"Japan needs to import all of that, even oil, for petrol for their cars and kerosene for the planes. But yes, you're right nonetheless.

"How can Germany hope to gain and keep all of Europe?"

Berrigan would have swatted me away with a quip, and never would I have voiced anything of the sort in either Stowe or Gallagher's presence.

Tex shook his head. "You're right. Beats me.

"But you know what that tells me, buddy? It tells me we're going to win in the end."

Tex really deserves to survive this war.

TUESDAY, JANUARY 13TH1942

I have at last written my first dispatch, and gave it in for censorship, and by some miracle, as it was rather short and unobjectionable, and as I was the only one who had submitted anything today — nothing of note is happening here — it was vetted and filed.

I drew on the service at the Cathedral and a quick visit to the port yesterday morning where returned Indian stevedores were unloading military materiel and wrote along the lines that Rangoon prays and prepares.

Another reporter, Cedric Salter of the *Daily Mail* has just arrived from Singapore and says he escaped in his socks, hours before being taken prisoner.

The panic in Singapore is beyond description, he tells us.

TUESDAY, JANUARY 20TH 1942

Spent the week with the other guys touring Rangoon, being taken to the sites where more refugee camps are being built, listened to Hewett brief us cheerfully on the arrival of the 17th Indian Division, under one Major-General Smyth.

He stated that this was a much needed reinforcement, and taking a paper from his pocket and squinting at it, added that this Division was to join the 2nd Burma Brigade in Tenasserim, so as to control the border with Thailand.

"We've heard that already, Major, they've been here for a week," the recently arrived Dan De Luce, of *American Associated Press*, complained. "Give us a break, for once, and tell us something we don't know."

Hewett then shook his head with a good-natured smile and said that the hangars at Mingaladon were undergoing rapid repairs, but he refused, however, to comment on the fact that Indians have once more begun to flee north towards Prome to try to pass into India from there, or, of course, to speculate on labour conditions in Rangoon port with a depleted workforce.

What we did also hear, but from another source, a CBS radio broadcast, is that the Japanese have taken many British prisoners north of Singapore. Meanwhile, the 'Fortress Island' as it is now being universally called, is being battered by bombs from above and water and food are becoming scarce, while women and children are evacuated by ships.

Several have been torpedoed and sunk.

We all just sat in silence when the broadcast was over, not looking at each other.

At least, I think, this is something Kate was spared...

MONDAY, JANUARY 26TH 1942

A bombing air raid over Rangoon was intercepted in the morning by the AVG and all the planes were shot down, but later another formation swept over Mingaladon undetected and this time created considerable damage. We could hear the thuds and explosions from our rooms and took to the shelters, but Rangoon itself was spared.

Wrote a piece about the panic in the city, tempered it with faint praise about civil defence measures.

My second dispatch, but there is little chance it will be processed for censorship and filed as speedily as the first, which was published the day before yesterday in several British papers, and under my byline.

Gallagher has been giving me dirty looks since, but I have other things on my mind.

I sent my parents a telegram to tell them I am safe in Burma, and ask if they have, by some miracle, heard from Kate.

I received the answer today, terse as telegrams need to be, with prayers for my safety and Kate's, from whom they have no news.

I rage and rage at the lack of intelligence coming from over the border.

I finally broke down and went to question the pitifully inadequate Military Intelligence service here, even going so far as to tell the commanding officer that I am SOE Thailand but got nothing out of them.

All I was told, and I had already heard it rumoured – Stowe had it from the American military mission in Rangoon, a source I have no access to, unfortunately – but not confirmed, is that the Thai Ambassador to the United States, Seni Pramoj, whose banker brother, Kukrit, I met several times at Thip's house, has refused to communicate his country's declaration of war to the President, and is now considered an exile.

It was indeed ethical and brave of him, but was done from the safety of Washington D.C.

What is happening in Bangkok?

The Strand bar was full this evening, several more newsmen have arrived, and everybody is arguing about the safety or otherwise of Burma as a last line of defence, as it appears that Singapore is doomed.

Gallagher thinks Burma is next.

"Never," Berrigan replies testily. "How on earth can the Japanese invade both the Dutch East Indies – and need I remind you of how many islands that country is made of? – and Burma as well?

"A westward *and* a southward strike? While still in China, fighting the Nationalists?

"They have neither the forces nor the planes for it.

"Furthermore, US troops have just landed in Samoa. On how many fronts do you think the Japanese can fight?"

Stowe agreed with him, but Gallagher just shrugged, as usual.

"This place reeks of defeat, I've been in several fucking disasters, and this is going to be one. Mark my words."

He is looking increasingly unkempt these days, unshaven, his hair is too long, and his uniform is slovenly.

None of us correspondents strive for the spit and polish look, but still, he resembles some kind of vagrant. He waved for another drink.

"Anyway, I've asked the *Express* to recall me. I can't go on working like this, just churning out words to support the war effort.

"Is that a reporter's job?

"And when..." he turned to glare at me, "... news agencies ...," he spat out the word, as if it were some kind of insult, "...news agencies get their dispatches cleared before newspapers, well..."

There was such silence, I heard myself swallow.

George Rodger coughed slightly, and asked if someone could recommend a good restaurant in town.

Stowe looked Gallagher up and down coolly. "You're not getting recalled, OD, and you know it. Cut it out. Okay?

"None of us like working like this, but the kid's done nothing wrong, his piece was unobjectionable, it was well written if unoriginal, and certainly no worse than some of your own.

"He was the only one filing that day, and you know it."

So Gallagher picked up his glass, downed it, and the spat was over.

And Leland Stowe — Leland Stowe! — said my piece was well written and no worse than some of Gallagher's.

I have decided that faint as it is, it is praise nonetheless.

TUESDAY, JANUARY 27ᵀᴴ 1942

Yesterday's argument about Burma's safety is now so much nonsense and Gallagher's pessimism has been vindicated.

Five days ago — but for military secrecy reasons we just heard today — the Japanese attacked Tavoy, on the Tenasserim coast, south of Moulmein, making many British casualties among the 6th Burma Rifles, and captured reserves of high octane fuel.

Moulmein is under threat and Mergui is now cut off.

The 2nd Burma Rifles garrisoned there were evacuated by sea.

Of course, all requests to go and see the situation for ourselves in Moulmein were curtly refused, then, strangely, an hour later, we were told that a group of us could make the journey.

Roderick Macdonald, Dan De Luce, Maurice Ford and Alec Tozer for newsreels, Cedric Salter and myself, replacing Berrigan who has a severe malarial attack.

With a raging fever and through chattering teeth, Darrell made me promise I would share everything with him.

I think Stowe and Gallagher didn't apply because they've already seen so much fighting that they're just not interested.

We leave tomorrow, at dawn, it is to be a day trip only.

THURSDAY, JANUARY 29TH 1942

Have just returned.

It was a depressing sight, although our escorting officers tried to put the best gloss on it, saying that what seemed to be retreats were merely moves to more easily defendable positions.

"Still looks like a retreat to me," De Luce muttered, while Ford found himself shot at from across the river by Japanese troops that he was filming. "Bloody rude," he muttered, moving his tripod out of range, "interfering with a chap's work."

Civilians, British mainly, but also Indians and Chinese were crowding the road to Rangoon on foot, hoping for what?

That someone, somehow, would come to pick them up?

The British were indeed rescued by Lend-lease trucks sent from the capital later that day, but the others were left to trudge under that relentless sun on the dusty road, carrying packs and babies, and food.

Ambulances and jeeps carrying the dead and the wounded zoom past them.

We went briefly to the field hospital, doctors and nurses were working like mad. There seemed to be no shortage of medication or equipment from what my unexperienced eye could tell, just of medical personnel.

I felt embarrassed by Ford filming the wounded, even from

afar so as not to show their faces, so I tried to pitch in.

Held a basin for a nurse while she was cleaning a bullet wound on a Tommy's leg, and tried not to look at the blood.

My admiration for Kate has increased a hundredfold, and I told the nurse I was married to one myself.

"Oh, where's she stationed?"

When I said Bangkok, she just shrugged. "Probably safer there than here, I guess. Hold the basin closer, please, and you, corporal," she said to the moaning soldier who was clutching at her arm in his agony, "stop trying to feel me up. I know your sort, I do," and the man managed to laugh.

"Hey, Blondie, get out of the way," Ford bellowed, and I looked up, to see him trying to wave me out of his shot — it would seem that Blondie meant me. Then he looked through his viewfinder and changed his mind. "No, no, stay where you are, it looks good, the press pitching in."

The nurse cut in drily that she didn't give a fig how it looked, but she did need help, so I was to stay put and keep on holding the basin. When she released me, she gave me a quick kiss on the cheek. "Thanks, Blondie. Hope your wife makes it out all right."

It appears, from what was said by some of the soldiers we were able to talk to, that several of the Burmese soldiers deserted, either to just melt away into the jungle, or, more ominously, to join the BIA, the Burmese Independence Army, whose leader, Aung San, has arrived in Tavoy with the Japanese, and is recruiting combatants for his own force, promising them freedom at last from British rule.

Cedric Salter has been told of fifth-columnists who stretch razor wire across roads to decapitate soldiers riding in open jeeps and assured me it happens, but the military censors refuse to let that story get out.

Also, from what military intelligence was able to gather from aerial photographs, courtesy of AVG, is that the Japanese crossed the jungle-covered Tenasserim range from Thailand, with horses and elephants to carry and drag vehicles and weapons, much as the Kings of Siam and Burma did for centuries.

I know that area for having once or twice been climbing there and it is formidable.

I marvel at those people and still wonder how they are trained to perform in such impossible conditions.

I cannot help admiring — whilst fearing — such strength, but often ask myself if there are not among them, and there *must* be, men like myself, who prefer books and music to fighting, abhor violence and are just not very good at hating anybody.

If I ever were to write a book about this whole Burma campaign, that is what I would say, I think, and it probably wouldn't go down well.

TUESDAY, FEBRUARY 2ND 1942

The Japanese have taken Moulmein and will now be on their way to Rangoon if they cannot somehow be stopped.

The *somehow* is the word that we struggle to say.

"What's that Kipling poem about the road to Moulmein?" *Life* George Rodger asked mildly, fingering his cameras as we emerged from the terse briefing Hutton himself gave us before stalking out of the room and refusing to answer any questions.

"You mean the one where it says that *'By the old Moulmein pagoda, there's a "Burma girl a-settin ...?'* " Gallagher replied in a sombre voice. "Well, I'm not sure the temple bells are saying *'Come you back you British soldier'* these days.

"More like, 'Come you hither you Nippon soldier', don't you think?"

We all scramble like mad towards our typewriters and hope to be among the first to file.

TUESDAY, FEBRUARY 12TH 1942

The powers that be have reorganized the outfit dealing with us, the SPRO, the Services Public Relations Office — which apparently always was its name, but it is now being used systematically under its new head, Lieutenant-Colonel Foucar.

Apparently, Major Hewett, he of the cheerful smile and obfuscating manner can no longer deal with all of us, as there are more than thirty correspondents in Rangoon now, and as he said in his few words of farewell, he couldn't cope with "all you bloody..." Here, he seemed at a loss to properly define what we bloody things were so he ended somewhat lamely, "... bloody journalists.

"But Foucar's been one of you, so don't think you can pull the wool over his eyes or browbeat him as you did with me.

"Bye, chaps, and no hard feelings."

The first news Foucar gave us was that Generalissimo Chiang Kai-Shek had agreed to send in a Chinese division into the Shan States to prevent an attack on Burma from Northern Thailand, and on that same note, that US Army General Stillwell had been transferred to the CBIT and been appointed the Generalissimo's COS and CIC of the Chinese Army, and this was in line with the wishes of General Wavell, who, as we all knew, had been appointed by the PM to be head of ABDA.

"Sorry, Colonel, would you mind translating the alphabet for those of us who are not conversant with military abbreviations?" Dan De Luce asked with elaborate politeness.

"Ok, I know you chaps are ragging me because it's my first day, but I'll humour you," Foucar replied with a tense smile.

"CBIT is China Burma India Theatre, COS is Chief of Staff, CIC is Commander in Chief. You think you have that?"

De Luce was making a great show of writing everything down.

"Yes, I think I have it all, many thanks.

"Oh, no, what's ABDA?"

Foucar sighed and we all stifled laughter, which is amazing, because heaven knows there is precious little to laugh about.

"American-British-Dutch-Australian command. You *do* know what PM stands for?"

De Luce seemed to search his mind. "Prime Minister?" and Foucar rolled his eyes, but managed to keep his temper.

"Very well, then."

We were also told that Rangoon itself was to be fortified with the arrival of the 48th Indian Brigade, made up of three Gurkha battalions.

"You all understand that the order of the day is to defend the Salween River at any cost."

We nodded, we'd seen enough maps by now to grasp that.

He then reeled off a list of regiments that sounded like something out of Kipling's Kim, besides the Gurkhas we also heard of Baluchis, Pathans, Dogras, Jat, Punjabis, Sikhs, Gharwalis and Rajputs. I was writing them down as fast as I could, and feeling the strange fascination of those names.

"The Raj lives on..." Macdonald muttered behind me.

Finally, and given the arrival Mr. Aung San in Tavoy with enemy forces and the intent to bring aid and comfort to said enemy forces, several prominent members of the so-called Thakin group had been arrested for security reasons.

"That will be all, gentlemen, and if a press trip to the front were to be organized — and please note I stress the 'if' — then please apply for it at my office.

"Thank you."

"Well, well, old Vinegar Joe in Chongqing, that's going to be interesting," Stowe chuckled as we made our way out.

I must have looked puzzled, because he explained that Vinegar Joe was Stilwell's nickname, given, as one might guess, because of his filthy temper and acerbic tongue.

"Yep, sparks will fly," he continued with relish. "He and Chennault loathe each other."

Have been passed over for the trip to the front at Bilin river the day after tomorrow, which is a pity, because a famous French journalist, Eve Curie, the daughter of *the* Marie Curie, has just arrived in town, and of course, being a friend of Randolph Churchill and everybody else who matters in the world, she met with General Hutton and the Governor. She will go on the trip along with a couple of others, but she has been assigned her own officer escort...

Naturally, she is staying at the Strand and I met her as she was holding court at the bar; she is very charming and elegant and French and frighteningly intelligent.

She prefaced whatever she'd seen here with "naturally, I have just arrived and am only here for a glancing visit but..." and then proceeded to list everything she finds wrong with the situation, the racism and 'decayed snobbery', as she put it, of the British, the poor civil-defence organization, the lack of air support and transport links out of the capital and the subconscious defeatist attitude you sense as you arrive, which is hardly surprising, given the disloyal population.

"But, Madame," Stowe asked, "why should they be loyal?"

She threw her head back and looked at him.

She is pretty, but, as I remember my own French grandmother saying, "It is better to be chic than to be pretty – and of course, it is even better to be both." Eve Curie certainly is both.

"Indeed, Monsieur," she replied simply, "why should they?"

I must have looked mesmerized, because Macdonald nudged me in the ribs. "Get a grip on yourself, mate. Your tongue is hanging out."

I withdrew with him to stand at the long teak bar just to be out of the range of what George Rodger told us *Life* magazine had described as "those radium eyes".

"She's rather impressive, isn't she?"

Macdonald looked her up and down.

"I suppose. But she doesn't hold a candle to Martha Gellhorn, Hemingway's gal – or maybe ex-gal, can't never tell with him. Met them both in Hong Kong.

"Martha Gellhorn..." he added dreamily. "Now *that's* a babe."

WEDNESDAY, FEBRUARY 18ᵀᴴ1942

Singapore surrendered two days ago.

All those still inside the city have been taken prisoner.

How could this have happened?

I can still hear that SOE man Bill, or whatever his real name was telling me Singapore was impregnable.

And here, the battle for Bilin is being lost, we are told, the 17th Indian Division is being encircled by the Japanese 55th Division.

They are winning, they are winning...

We have been told that Rangoon is to be evacuated of all non-essential civilians within two days, and there is a scene worthy of Dante's Inferno down at the port where thousands are trying to buy their way on to an India-bound ship.

The price has deliberately been set far too high for most Indians, so as not to lose vital labour on the docks.

I have yet to hear anything more cynical.

I don't care if it doesn't pass censorship, I have to file a story on that.

THURSDAY, FEBRUARY 20TH1942

It would seem that correspondents are non-essential civilians, and we too are to be evacuated, but to Maymyo, a hill station about five hundred miles north, along with the Governor's services, and less essential civilians than them I cannot imagine.

Stowe and Gallagher have already decamped there, and will snag the best lodgings, of course.

I shan't be sorry to leave Rangoon, but in the past three months, feel I have been punted around like a bloody football.

It is the same, I realize, for everyone in times of war, but I constantly wonder, when Burma falls, what happens next?

Chapter XIX

With no military escort or interpreter this time, he just drove up to the hospital gates and parked his jeep inside, on the gravel driveway.

He was bearing two gift-wrapped packages, and almost ran up the steps to the second floor.

He then paused, scanning the signs on the doors, but they were written in French and Thai, so he opened the glass door to the covered porch and walked down its length, nodding to the few patients laying on the rattan chaises-longues, who followed him with anxious eyes.

What could a Japanese in uniform be doing at Saint Louis Hospital?

Belinda saw him first through the window of the maternity ward and immediately guessed who he might be.

Whatever he might be doing here, this man must be kept away from Kate at all costs.

She strode up to him briskly in her best Melanie manner and asked if he was looking for a new mother.

"A mother?" Akira replied in surprise. "No. What makes you think...?

"No, I'm looking for Doctor Sumet. The surgeon."

Belinda waved at his parcels, but her voice was chilly.

"It was your gifts, you see.

"And also, the fact you're about to pass into the maternity ward on this side. Surgery is behind you, you have to turn left at the central doors, not right, and ask the nurse on duty for him, he should be there."

Akira nodded his thanks.

"I also have this, for one of your colleagues, Nurse Fallon," he said with a tentative smile, showing the smaller of the boxes, tied in red ribbon.

"Is she around?"

"Ah…" Belinda tried her best to sound regretful. "I'm afraid she's out, for the day. Will you leave it with me? I'll see she gets it," she said, reaching for it firmly before he could protest.

"Thank you, Nurse… What is your name?"

"O'Grady. Belinda O'Grady."

He smiled again. "Pleased to meet you, Nurse O'Grady.

"I'm Captain Ken Akira."

Belinda gave him an arch look. "Oh, we all know who you are, Captain.

"It's not every day we get a Japanese surgeon with an important patient taking over our operating theatre."

She turned her head towards the ward, as if she had heard a cry. "Sorry, I'm needed, now, I'm afraid. Goodbye."

She spun on her heel and rushed to the room she shared with Kate, praying she would still be there, napping after a difficult delivery the night before.

Thankfully, she was.

"Kate. Quick, wake up," she whispered urgently, shaking her. "He's back. The Jap doctor."

Kate sat up, her eyes wide with terror.

"Was he looking for me?"

Yes, but not to arrest her. He had brought her this — Belinda showed the elaborately wrapped box.

"Looks like chocolates to me — I told him you were out for the day, so just lock yourself in here, stay hidden until he leaves.

"He also had something for Doctor Sumet. Just stay there and make no noise, all right? And don't eat all the chocolates without me."

Kate shivered and nodded. Before closing the door, Belinda gave her a long look.

"He seems nice though, doesn't he?

"I mean…" She shook her head in confusion. "Lock the door and only open if it's me."

Belinda shook her head again and straightened her pinafore over her dress before walking calmly towards surgery. Taking a deep breath, she knocked briefly at the door to Sumet's office, then poked her head in, "Ah good, you've found him," she said brightly, seeing Akira seated on the office's small couch.

Sumet was behind his desk, fiddling uncomfortably with his pen.

"I was telling Doctor — sorry — Captain Akira that unfortunately, Kate is out for the day."

"Yes," Sumet agreed. "I suppose she is. We have no surgeries scheduled today, so you see..."

Akira rose politely. "As I was saying to Doctor Sumet, I just came to tell him our patient is recovering. He'll never be able to walk properly, but he'll live and keep his leg."

He gestured towards the oblong box on Sumet's desk and grinned.

"It's just a small gesture of thanks — completely illegal genuine Scotch whiskey.

"You guys really saved my bacon the other day."

Sumet stared "Your bacon, doctor? I'm afraid..."

Akira laughed. "It's an American expression. It means — well, that you saved me from what would have been rather unpleasant consequences."

Sumet nodded. "Oh, I understand. I believe it's what is called a colloquialism, isn't it?"

He smiled self-deprecatingly. "You must forgive my poor old-fashioned English. I don't believe I've actually met an American before, you see."

Please, please, Belinda prayed silently. Don't overdo it.

Akira raised his hand to wave Sumet's apology away.

"Don't say that, your English is amazing. And I assume your nurses teach you Irish slang, don't they?"

Belinda shook her head. "We wouldn't dare, would we?

"Keep our slang strictly to ourselves, we Irish girls do."

Sumet rose and walked towards the door. "Well, thank you so much, Captain, both for the gift, and the good news.

"I'm glad we could be of help, but it was your skill that saved him — along with his good luck, of course."

Akira gathered his cap, looking a bit self-conscious. "Forgive me, I've been taking too much of your time. It's just that it's a relief to speak English, you know?

"In fact —," he turned to Belinda, "perhaps your colleague Nurse Fallon and you might accept to have dinner with me some evening?"

Belinda froze, her eyes darting towards Sumet then back to Akira. She swallowed and began to stammer, blushing. "Oh, that's most kind of you, I'm sure, but we couldn't, no."

She took a deep breath.

"You see, I'm engaged, my fiancé is interned in a prison here, and Kate, well... she's married and her husband was mobilized and she's no idea where he might be."

Akira raised his eyebrows.

"Our fellas are both English, Captain." Belinda added defiantly. "So, you do understand it wouldn't be proper."

"This awful war..." Akira sighed. "yes, I understand.

"I am the enemy after all.

"Good-bye, doctor, nurse. Thank you again."

He gave a very Japanese half bow and strode out of the room.

Belinda thought for a moment, then ran down the corridor to catch up with him and grabbed his arm. "Listen, Captain.

"I'm sorry, I mean, you are the enemy, but I think you're also a nice fella, and I just wanted to ask, if you can, if it's not too much, can you get me some news of Eddy?

"My fiancé? Please?

"All I know is that he is interned at the University. Edward Giles, his name is."

Akira looked down at her, frowning.

"Why wasn't he mobilized?"

"Oh, God love him, he's blind as a bat without his specs, he has flat feet, and a dicky heartbeat. Really not a threat to you people.

"But he means the world to me, and I worry, so please?"

Akira bit his lips, considering, and nodded, at last. He would do what he could.

Belinda rapped on their room's door and whispered, "It's me. He's gone."

Kate went back to the bed and flopped down on it. "What did he want?" she asked listlessly.

Belinda noticed she had not even unwrapped the package that lay, untouched, on the sheet.

"He just wanted to thank you both for," as he put it, "saving his bacon."

"The patient will live and will keep his leg."

Kate sighed.

Good, she had wondered about him. Although, was it right to be relieved?

"I mean, if he'd died, it would mean one enemy soldier less."

Belinda came to sit by her. "I know. But still... he was a patient.

"Would you have refused to assist in the operation, if you had been given a choice?"

No, of course not. Kate grinned, suddenly. "He actually said we'd saved his bacon? Lord, I haven't heard that expression in — oh, years."

"He actually did say it, and Sumet made a show of saying he'd never spoken to any Americans... He was great, all, you know, old-fashioned in a very English way.

"But guess what?

"Akira then asked us both to dinner."

Kate started. "You didn't say yes, did you?"

"Who do you take me for?" Belinda was offended.

"I said you were married and your husband was serving you didn't know where, and that I was engaged and that my fiancé was interned here. And then...

"Well, I just took the plunge and asked him to get me news of Eddy if he could.

"And he said he'd try."

Kate got up from the bed, and, paling, took a step back, as if to put distance between them.

"Oh no... you didn't... That means he'll be back, Belinda."

Then looking at her friend's stricken face and trembling lips, she fell silent.

"I have no news of him, Kate. I worry," Belinda sobbed.

Kate came back, and put her arm around her shoulders and hugged her.

"I understand. I would have done the same if I could get news of Lawrence."

Belinda sniffled, straightened herself and wiped her cheeks.

"Let's open these chocolates then."

She grabbed the box and tore away the paper. " Oh, no, look, it's little cakes. Well, chocolates, here — it would have been too much to hope for, I guess."

She picked one up and munched. "It's good, it has almonds. I think he's lonely, Akira, I mean," she added musingly.

"He said it was a relief to speak English. He's nice. Friendly-like, you know — well, normal. And not bad looking, either. You know, tall and he has a really nice smile."

She shook her head with an embarrassed laugh.

"Oh, just listen to me, what I am I saying? And about a Japanese fella to boot. But if he can get me news of Eddy, I'll speak English to him till the cows come home."

A brief note for Miss Belinda O'Grady was delivered to the hospital two days later, from Ken Akira.

It said that Edward Giles was in overall good health.

He had been there himself, to perform a general health inspection, and listened to Mr. Giles' heart; no problems, except a slightly irregular heartbeat.

There was an English doctor internee he had spoken to, who looked after all the inmates and, when necessary, requested medical supplies that were then provided, if available.

Living conditions were far from comfortable but not inhuman.

The note ended saying "It might be possible to have food and a message delivered, as the guards of that particular internment centre are Thai and not Japanese, and would be liable to render this service, against a small payment, of course.

"If you like, I might be able to get you a name, but I cannot do more than that, I hope you understand. You can reach me at the phone number below.

"Yours,"

"What will you do?" Sumet asked Belinda when she showed him the letter.

Belinda stared at him as if he were crazy. Of course, she would do it.

She just wondered which of the Thai hospital employees she might ask to be the go-between.

"It's not without risk." Sumet replied. "Khun Kate, what do you think?"

Kate shrugged, the answer was obvious.

If it were for Lawrence, she'd take the risk with no hesitation at all.

"When I was speaking of risk," Sumet said drily, "I was not only thinking of a risk for you, but for the go-between.

"Whose safety are you prepared to endanger?"

"Oh God and Holy Mother Mary," Belinda wailed, "of course. I wasn't thinking.

"But maybe — I don't know, Khop, perhaps?"

Nai Khop had two children, a wife and a mother he supported, was Sumet's response.

"Let me think, and in the meantime, call Captain Akira and get the name.

"You mustn't assume," he added thoughtfully, "that my people are heartless or dishonest because they'd want money to help.

"They are poor, and life is expensive in Bangkok, these days."

His hands tented below his chin, he reflected at length.

"No, I'll do it. Be sure to tell Captain Akira that.

"And keep his letter, by all means. If I get into trouble, he will know that he might as well."

As Belinda, weeping with relief rushed out of the office, he called Kate back.

"Don't let her get anything too bulky or heavy, please. Protein. Dried meat or fish, powdered milk would be best. Enough so that he can share with others.

"Also, soap. He'll need soap, certainly.

"You can find it all at Bangrak market.

"Go."

Belinda agonized before dialling. "What if someone else picks up? Someone who only speaks Japanese? How do I ask for him?

"And it might get him in trouble."

Kate was brisk. "If he gave you this number it must be safe. Just say you're calling from Saint-Louis Hospital."

"Yes, yes, you're right." She was almost trembling. "Here goes."

Akira picked up himself and sounded surprised when Belinda explained the arrangement.

"Doctor Sumet wants to do this himself? Is that wise?" and when told that it was to avoid putting a Thai employee of the hospital at risk, he sighed.

"He's a good man, your Doctor Sumet.

"I can tell you I got the name from the British physician, he himself suggested it would be a way to communicate when I said that Edward Giles fiancée's was asking about him, so I think it's pretty safe.

"The contact's name is Yong Siang, who has a liquor and spirits shop on the street behind the University.

"He's apparently easy to find, and he will know what to do with the package.

"Good luck, Belinda, let me know how it goes."

Sumet supervised the packing of the basket himself, checking to make sure nothing could be traced back to him, and asked Belinda to please be careful in the brief letter she had included. "It has to be as anonymous as possible, don't sign your name. He will know it is from you."

The following day was a Sunday, he had no surgeries scheduled, and it was his day off. He said he would take the tramway there, along Charoen Krung, early in the morning — "Be sure to wear a hat then, or they might not let you on," Kate said drily — and afterwards, he would go to watch the kite fliers on Sanam Luang, then pray at the Emerald Buddha Shrine.

His mother, who always complained about his lack of religious spirit, would approve when he told her.

"We can all use a few prayers I believe, in these times."

To his embarrassment, Belinda rushed up to him, and hugged him hard.

"Bless you for what you're doing. You don't even know Eddy."

The Thai surgeon smiled as he gently unfastened her clasp.

"No, but I know you.

"Mother Melanie would be proud of what you've become."

Belinda backed away, sniffling. "Bet you she'd find something to complain about, old scold that she is. Be careful."

As they watched him leave with the basket, Kate said wonderingly, that she had no idea he lived with his mother.

"Does he even have a wife or children? We know nothing about him."

Belinda shook her head. "All I know is that he will be in my prayers for ever, and that I will light candles for him at church tomorrow."

Sunday was endless.

Kate debated whether to risk going to see Thip, then decided against it.

The streets were always quiet on Sundays, and she would be noticed.

But she could at least phone.

Fon answered, as formal and courtly as ever. "Khun Kate, are you well?

"We think of you and the Khunying misses you. She is poorly, but do not tell her I said so. There is no news of Somchai, and she worries. Did you hear from Khun Lo?"

Nothing, she said and Fon sighed with her. "Please wait, I will get the Khunying to the phone.

"How are you, my dear girl?" Thip asked when she finally picked up the extension. She sounded breathless.

"I am well, and I miss you, but how are you?"

Oh... How could an old woman be when she had no news of her grandson, and missed the young people who had brought such joy to her life? There were tears in her warm voice.

Kate gripped the receiver in her hand.

"I miss you as well.

"Listen, why don't you come to the hospital for an examination?

"You sound breathless, and I don't like to hear that.

"Could you come and let us check you? Please?"

Perhaps.

She would speak to Pichit. He had been worrying about her, she knew. So yes, she would. She would try.

Kate hesitated. She hated to ask, but she must. "And when you come, could you please bring me some money?

"I'm very ashamed to have to — well, beg, I guess, is the word for it — but we are barely paid now, and Lawrence's bank account has been frozen, so... I'm really very sorry."

Thip hissed angrily. "It is I who am sorry for being a stupid old woman.

"Why did I not think of that before?

"I knew all foreign bank accounts were blocked.

"Of course, you must need money. I shall send Fon with some immediately."

She sighed again, but this time in exhaustion.

"And now, please excuse me, I must go to sit down. I am so very tired, you see. Goodbye, dear girl. I hope to see you soon."

Fon was not wearing his usual uniform of black trousers and white starched jacket when he arrived by samlo after sunset, carrying two hampers, looking like someone visiting a hospitalized relative.

He waited until they were alone before wai-ing deeply, and produced an envelope from inside his plain blue homespun shirt.

"The Khunying sends this," he said handing it over, "and food for your friends and you. It took time to cook the chickens, which is why I am late.

"She kept on hurrying cook, who said chicken does not know how to hurry in an pot."

"Thank you, thank you. And thank her."

He wai-ed again. "I am happy you look well, but you are too thin.

"And now, forgive me, but I must go back to be with her. She does not like when I away."

Kate gave him a teary smile.

"You really love her, don't you?"

Fon looked surprised. "She is my family.

"She is also my sister, but she is fifteen years older. My mother was a servant in her house, and her father... was also my father.

"Goodbye, Khun Kate. I will see to it that she comes to your doctors."

Two chickens, a cold spicy omelette that Thip knew Kate loved, a cake, mangoes and lychees and biscuits, three tins of sardines, a jar of marmalade, a tin of powdered coffee, and a bottle of orange squash. There was even a bottle of port.

Kate unpacked each item wistfully, remembering that she had taken all those luxuries for granted such a short while ago, and now she was looking at the food as greedily as Belinda, who was cooing in delight, "It really is Sunday, isn't it? I just hope Eddy gets his own tonight, or tomorrow. It's nothing as posh as this, though. Port, my Lord.

"I wish I'd thought of marmalade."

If it worked well, Kate suggested, as she put the chicken on a plate, it would probably be possible to do it again.

"You think?" Belinda asked excitedly. "Oh, I do hope so. And maybe he can send back a message.

"I'll go and get Bernadette and Rose, and tell them there's a feast waiting.

"We mustn't say anything about getting a parcel to Eddy, though, don't you think?"

Kate agreed. She was going to suggest the same thing.

The fewer people knew about it, the better... "And you know what?

"Let's not listen to the BBC, tonight. Let's take a break from bad news, for once."

It was difficult not to rush to Doctor Sumet when he arrived Monday morning, to behave as if nothing had happened.

Belinda was pacing the floor of the maternity ward, Kate kept herself busy in the surgical supply room, sterilizing instruments.

They crossed paths, exchanging meaningful looks, and when the nurses met for a morning coffee during a lull in their work, Bernadette looked at Belinda crossly. "You're as jumpy as a cat, and snappish as a crab. About to be your time of the month?" and Belinda shook her head in irritation.

Bernadette concluded disapprovingly that Belinda's mood was probably the aftereffects of the port they'd had last night, and Rose chimed that it took far more port than that to give her a headache.

It was lunchtime before Doctor Sumet joined Kate in the scrubbing room.

"Get Khun Belinda please."

It had gone well, surprisingly easily, in fact.

Yong Siang's liquor shop was on the street of the amulet vendors' market, and he had browsed there, looking around.

"In fact, I bought a Buddha amulet which I gave to my mother, which pleased her greatly, and I am in her good graces once more." He smiled as if in recollection of his mother's pleasure.

"It is not a very long street, so I quickly found the shop.

"I mentioned that his name was given me, and needed not to say by whom.

"He understood immediately, so I think am not the first to make such an arrangement.

"He said he would get the basket to your fiancé that same afternoon, there are less sentries on duty Sundays, and those who are there are still drunk from what he sells them Saturday evenings."

Belinda closed her eyes and crossed herself.

"Thank you. Thank you. And how much money did he want?

"Very little, considering the risk he takes. Fifteen ticals."

Belinda swallowed, then nodded.

"I shall get them for you now."

No.

Sumet wanted no payment. It was his duty as a Buddhist to assist those in need. "We call it making merit."

Seeing Belinda hesitate, Kate intervened.

"For this once, we both accept, with our deepest thanks. Truly.

"But if there is a next time, please let us pay. We shall take turns. Please."

Sumet shook his head again.

"No. You are nurses who have come from afar to help my people, in exchange for hardship and very little pay.

"I, however, am from a very wealthy family. I only work to cure the sick and because I enjoy it, not because I need to."

"But — still..." Kate stammered, "I received some money, yesterday, from Lawrence's friends, and lots of food, enough for a week, for the four of us, so..."

"Keep your money, Khun Kate. When your husband's bank account was blocked, you were treated unfairly.

"It is I who should thank you for allowing me to make merit."

Belinda eyes were teary. "Doctor, if I didn't know you would be embarrassed, I would kiss you.

"But just let me say, you're a lovely man."

Sumet laughed.

"Thank you. For your kind words, and for not kissing me.

"Now let us get back to work. We do not want Wanida scolding us for slacking, now that the patients are coming back."

It was true. Those who had been afraid of coming to Saint-Louis were now slowly returning, perhaps because the hospital was no longer associated with the politically disliked French.

Or perhaps also because they feared going to the hospitals and clinics the Japanese had taken over, although those offered free care, or because the free care was not trusted.

As an old woman told Kate, sniffing, "If it's free, how good can it be? And I do not like to be treated like a pauper."

When Kate reported this statement to Sumet, he smiled.

He and his friends had been spreading mistrust of Japanese

medical largesse for a few weeks, and it seemed to be yielding results.

But he was frustrated by the little they could do.

Although he himself, when requested to do so by Andrew Gilchrist of the British Embassy just before what he still considered the invasion of last December, had driven several opposition leaders to safety at his family estates in the North, giving them money and the false documents provided by some source Gilchrist had in Yaowarat, he felt he had not done, was not doing enough, and he found himself at a loss to find some means of resisting — spreading rumours about Japanese hospitals, while satisfying, was nothing more than an old gossip's weapon.

The Thai police, just like the rest of the people, lived in fear of the all-powerful Kempetai, and cracked down without pity on any form of subversion.

Even those who, before, avidly read the underground newspapers Kate's husband had contributed to — oh yes, he knew what Lawrence had done, and admired the young man's writing and bravery — well, those people now dared not even pick up the leaflets calling for resistance against the Japanese that were still being dropped at tram stops and near coffee shops.

Furthermore, there would be less and less of those leaflets. Several Chinese students who either wrote for or distributed them had been arrested, and nobody knew where they had been taken.

There were also disturbing rumours coming from the Western province of Kanchanaburi, brought to Bangkok by farmers who came to supply the markets, and by a monk from Wat Burana, who had gone to visit his parents near the city.

Some sort of camp, or prison was being built there, in the jungle by the bank of the Kwai river, and the monk's father himself had seen Japanese military lorries full of ragged farangs drive through his town.

Could the Kingdom, whose name was now officially, Muang Thai, or Land of the Free, be transformed into a prison?

The shame of it was unbearable. Why did Pridi, whom he admired, whom everybody admired for his moral rectitude, not do anything?

Yes, he knew the answer — Pridi was no longer in the cabinet, and now a politically impotent Regent, but still, he represented the King.

The King, whom all, save Phibul, revered.

Could not Pridi invoke the moral authority of the Crown to at least counter the worst of the Japanese hold on the Kingdom?

Sumet knew the people of Thailand were unhappy living under what was not Japanese occupation, but something very akin to it.

He could see it in their cowed look when an officer in putty-coloured uniform swept past with contempt in his eyes and a sneer on his face.

He heard it whispered amongst his friends, he knew that many of them silently cheered when it became known that Seni Pramoj, his friend since childhood, had refused to convey Phibul's declaration of war to the President of the United States.

He also knew that several of his friends' sons studying in America, had refused to return to Thailand, and furthermore Kukrit, Seni's brother, had implied that Seni was going to find a way to continue to fight for the Kingdom.

Kukrit knew this, he said, through one of the only eighteen young men who had returned — out of the several dozen who opted to remain in America.

This particular student claiming it was because his mother was ill, and he was afraid of never seeing her again.

They had argued constantly about politics on the voyage home, this youngster told him, debating whether Phibul had been wise in joining the Japanese, and thus the Axis forces, or whether it might not have been better to throw the Kingdom's lot in with that of the Allies.

"But you see," he had explained, "many of us experienced racism in America, we were called Japs or Chinks, or worse.

"And some thought it was treacherous to support France, who has been our enemy in the past."

As a rule, they attempted to avoid Phibul's two sons, Anan and Prasong who were also commanded to return, and who, for their part, had no choice but to comply.

"We did not want to speak with them because we felt that their father had no respect for His Majesty the King, and was attempting to replace him.

"And some of us loathed the idea of being allies of the Nazis.

"I think most of us who came home," the student finally confessed, "would have liked to stay and support Ambassador Seni in his plans to fight, but we were too afraid.

"I know I was."

Which form that fight might take, Sumet did not know, but if ever he were called upon to assist, he would make it his own.

When Lady Thip finally arrived at Saint Louis Hospital, she entered in majesty, in the chauffeur-driven Packard, escorted by Pichit, Busaba and Fon, who was once again bearing hampers.

Kate, who had been told of the appointment, was waiting at the main door, and was struck and worried by how much the old lady had aged in barely more than two months.

Thip was walking with a cane, Pichit holding her other arm, and the short walk from the car had left her breathless and pale.

"My dear, dear girl," she gasped, "what a joy it is to see you.

"No, Pichit, please let go of me, I want to greet Kate properly," and she stroked her cheek, checking her with still keen eyes.

"How have you been? You are thin, just as Fon told me.

"Not too many tears?"

Some, Kate admitted. Some, but she had promised Lawrence she would be strong, so she tried to be.

"Shall I get a wheelchair?" she offered, gesturing to Nai Khop that he bring one over.

"No," Thip said, just as "Yes," Pichit was saying, but she finally agreed with a sigh of relief to sit and be pushed.

She would first be taken to an examination room, and Kate herself would draw some blood to be tested, and measure her blood pressure, then, to see Doctor Sumet, Kate explained, he was a surgeon, but also a fine doctor and...

"I've known Sumet all his life," Thip interrupted with a laugh. "Pensri, his mother is a childhood friend, don't you remember?

"I told you at the wedding."

Kate smiled, she had forgotten.

"And here he is," Thip exclaimed with a delighted smile. "Nong Nok, how are you?"

Nong Nok? Kate knew that Nong meant young brother but Nok? Didn't that mean bird?

Sumet wai-ed deeply to Thip, then more briefly as was proper, to Pichit and Busaba, and seeing Kate's amused look, he laughingly explained that Nok was his nickname, only used by a very few people, thankfully.

"My mother called me that, because she said I chirped all the time, as a child."

"He did, he did," Thip confirmed. "Never quiet. And how is my dear friend Pensri?"

"As she always is," Sumet replied. "A tyrant to me, putty in the hands of my sister because of the grandchildren."

He took the handles of the wheelchair, and, nodding to Pichit, told him they could wait in the lounge outside his office, and that he would have tea brought.

"Now, Auntie," he chided her as he pushed her, "what is it that I hear from Khun Kate? You experience difficulty in breathing?"

Thip answered something in Thai that made him laugh, but he said that he would conduct the examination in English, so that Kate could take notes, and he would let her draw the blood sample. "I haven't done it myself in so long, I know I would hurt you and you would then go crying to my mother."

He listened to her chest, he took her blood pressure, and frowned, then took it again.

"Now tell me...," he said gently, and proceeded to ask her a series of questions, then sat back, and tented his hands, while she adjusted her bodice cloth.

"I'm not happy," he finally said. "Shall I tell you alone, or do you want your son and daughter-in-law here?"

"Alone." Thip grasped Kate's wrist and straightened herself. "I am a grown woman, as you well know."

"As I well know, indeed.

"Auntie, you are also a rather ill woman.

"You have a condition called heart failure.

"Your heart is not pumping enough blood, and that is why you are breathless.

"The urine and blood tests will tell us for sure, but I also suspect you have diabetes — actually, I don't suspect, I know, I'm just not sure how serious it is.

"Do you like sweets?"

All Thais loved sweets, she snapped back. Did his mother?

"She does," Sumet agreed, "and I try to limit them in her diet — but, but — *she* does not suffer from diabetes."

"Can you give me medication?"

"For the heart, I can prescribe nitroglycerin tablets when you get chest pain — the pain is known as angina, and the tablets will help.

"As to the diabetes, I'm afraid you will need insulin injections, once a day, at least."

Thip made a face and slumped, still grasping Kate's hand.

"I see."

"I will determine what dosage you need when I get your results back, and shall send over the insulin ampoules.

"Is there a nurse who can come to you?

"No, before you say it, Kate cannot. It would be unsafe for her, and for you.

"There must be some nurse living near you, Fon can make inquiries."

Thip sighed deeply. "Shall I live to see my grandson again?"

Sumet sighed as well. "I hope so. We shall do our best.

"Shall I call your family in now?"

Thip gave a defeated nod, and said not a word while Sumet explained the treatment he planned.

A quiet life, no exertion, such as stairs — might it be possible to move the Khunying's room to the ground floor, so that she would need only climb the veranda steps to return to her bed if — he corrected himself — whenever she left the house?

Pichit sat, stunned, and even Busaba looked shaken, but Fon nodded.

He would make the arrangements, there was the small drawing room next to the dining room that could serve. He would seek a nurse, he believed he knew of one. And he understood, absolutely no sweets, no sugar in her tea, no mangoes even.

"I'm so deeply sorry, Auntie," Sumet said as he pushed her to the waiting car.

"No, my dear Nong Nok, do not be. I shall be good."

"And look after Kate, she is very dear to me," she whispered as he helped her in. "It's strange, isn't it? That she could be dearer than my daughter-in-law? But she is.

"I never expected that, to find someone new to love, in my old age.

"Give my best to your tyrannical mother.

"She always was a bully, even when we were girls..."

Kate watched them drive away, feeling dejected.

"One more thing to worry about," she said to Sumet, who nodded and added that insulin was another worry. "It's imported from America, you know..."

It was difficult to get hold of, even at hugely inflated prices.

He gave her a meaningful look, and she winced.

"No, don't say it, please. Don't suggest asking Doctor Akira."

It might come to that, a gloomy Sumet replied. They might have no choice.

But he would do it in his own name, there was no reason for Akira to even hear of her relationship with that family.

No, there wasn't.

But somehow, Ken Akira was getting to be too important for them all, and she was scared.

How long before she actually needed to talk to him without wearing a surgical mask, and he heard pure Boston in her voice?

"Why should you have to ever talk to him?" Belinda wanted to know, munching on a fried prawn that cook had included in the hamper this time.

"Because... I don't know, it might just happen. You know, he turns up at the hospital unannounced, as he does, and the first one he bumps into is me.

"Oh hello, Nurse Fallon, how nice to see you. Oh wait, you don't sound Irish to me, aren't you from Massachusetts? Then what happens?

Belinda thought for a moment. "Well, you say you're just as Irish as he is Japanese."

Kate threw herself back onto the bed.

"That's not going to work."

"All right, then just ask him to keep quiet about it. You're doing no harm, you're just stuck here, he's a nice fella, he'll understand."

Maybe. And again, maybe not.

"You didn't hear him talk about the way the Japanese have been treated in the States. "

Belinda sighed, getting up from the floor.

"Come on, it's time for the BBC, let's hear what going wrong with the war today. I'll bring the port and some biscuits, all right?"

Yes, of course. They would probably need it to cheer them up.

The news bulletin was dire.

In Burma, Mandalay was under heavy shelling, after Rangoon had been abandoned to the Japanese who had also taken Batavia, the capital of the Dutch East Indies.

"Will they never stop?" Kate wondered, and held close to herself the precious secret that Lawrence was safe in China.

In England, more news of bombing of industrial centres, Malta was being battered by German and Italian aerial forces,

"Where is Malta?" Belinda wanted to know and Bernadette sniffed. " You know the Knights of Malta. I believe it's an island, near Jerusalem, isn't it?" – and in Berlin, Jews were now ordered to clearly identify their houses as Jewish.

"Why should they do that?" Rose demanded querulously. "Hitler has said he's going to kill them all, why make his job easier?

"It's like that in Ulster, you know, the Catholics and the Protestants all know where each other live, but at least the Catholics don't get rounded up.

"Not any more at least.

"Pass me the port, Kate, I think I need another drop. Many other drops."

And two days later, it happened.

It happened just as she always knew it would.

But in her worse nightmares, she could not have imagined why.

He was waiting for her, one afternoon, just outside Doctor Sumet's office, lounging in one of the armchairs, leafing through one of the out of date Thai magazines with their blurry pictures. He got up when he saw her, and took his cap that was lying on the table beside an empty teacup.

His smile was strange, she thought. Almost triumphant.

"Hello, Nurse Fallon."

She swallowed, nodded, and with her mouth suddenly dry, managed to say hello too.

"Can I have a word? In private?"

No, she almost whispered, attempting Belinda's accent, and failing. No, she was busy.

"You're not, actually.

"Miss Wanida says you've finished your duties as there are no surgeries today. And even if you were busy, it wouldn't matter.

"Next door, perhaps? That office there looks empty."

She hesitated, but he grabbed her arm, pushed her ahead of him into the room, dropping his cap on a chair, and closed the door.

Then he leaned against it, arms crossed, and looked her up and down while she kept her eyes down, to avoid showing how nervous he made her.

The blow to her face caught her completely unawares, he moved so fast, she had not seen it coming.

That was what she felt at first, surprise as she hit the floor, and then the shock, and the pain.

She picked herself up, and stared at him, and saw the other blow coming this time, and felt her head hit the wall.

She heard herself whimper, and pulled herself onto her knees.

"Shut up," he snarled, then he grabbed her arm once more and threw her into a chair.

He was leaning very close, she could smell alcohol on his breath.

"Why didn't you tell me you're American?"

She couldn't speak, she was feeling her lip swell, and her mouth was full of blood.

"Why did you tell me you're Irish? Why did you fucking lie? Why?

"Answer me."

Finally, she managed to regain her breath, and blessedly began to feel more anger than fear.

"I did not fucking lie," she managed to spit, "you just assumed I was Irish.

"And for that matter, I'm just as Irish as you are Japanese."

He reeled back at her words, and she mentally thanked Belinda for this suggested retort, watching him crumple on the chair opposite hers, his head in his hands.

"How did you find out?" she finally was able to ask.

He laughed, an ugly, nasty sound. "You'll never guess.

"It was Belinda's Eddy... yeah, funny, right?

"He asked about you and said it was comfort to know you were there for Belinda, that you always were nice, a little Boston kid who grew up poor and married some rich guy.

"Boston, I said? I thought she was Irish. Oh, no, well, Boston Irish, but she's a Yank all right.

"I don't even think he realized what he was saying, the poor jerk was so happy to get news of his girl.

"God, to think I bought the whole story, with Sumet saying in that British accent of his, 'I've never actually met an American...' "

"Oh no... Eddy..."

She must have said it out loud, because he laughed again and looked up at her.

"Oh yes, Eddy... and you know what?

"I was going to let it go, because, I said to myself, what harm can she do, so what if she's American, this goddamn war isn't her fault more than its mine.

"But you know what I found out today?

"My family's been deported, I don't know where, maybe North Dakota.

"My grandmother in Nagasaki was informed by the Red Cross.

"All of them, my mother, my father, my kid brother who's seventeen.

"My sister, her husband, and their baby. A suitcase each.

"My father's an ordinary guy, he has an insurance agency – he voted the straight Democratic ticket ever since he got citizenship, paid his taxes, we never went on the food lines even during the Depression, he put his son through college. And that's the thanks he gets."

She listened, appalled, getting even angrier – at those who had done such awful things, and at him, for seeking revenge on her.

Finally, she let her fury loose.

"So, you take it out on me. You needed to hurt an American, right?

"And because you're a coward, you choose the most defenceless one, instead of going off to fight."

She stood up, and faced him, her eyes blazing with rage.

"Go on, hit me again.

"I grew up in Boston, I know what guys do when they're drunk."

He shook his head, and wiped his sweaty face with both hands, then snorted a bitter laugh.

"You're right.

"You are the most defenceless one I could find, you're also the only one.

"And I *am* drunk, but I'm not a coward, I went out on a limb for Belinda, because I thought you were all nice people.

"I wanted to help, to – I don't know, help right a wrong.

"I wanted us to be friends. And by the way, you never thanked me for those cakes."

Hands on her hips, Kate managed a sneering smile. "And now, you're feeling sorry for yourself. Boohoo, poor you.

"Well, if you don't want to hit me again, go away, and leave us alone.

"And I apologize for not thanking you, but I don't like almonds, anyway."

He smiled again, suddenly. "You're very pretty when you're angry, you know. Even with that fat lip.

"And I don't know yet if I'll leave you alone.

"You're just going to have to wait and see."

He grabbed his cap, slammed the door, and she heard his footsteps all the way down the stairs.

She didn't know how long she stayed in the office, but it was getting dark, and the sun was setting when she cautiously opened the door, looked around to make sure she would meet no one, and made her way back to her room, wincing with pain.

Each step seemed to make her head throb even more, she appeared to have badly jarred her shoulder when she fell to the floor, and she dared not think of how her face might look.

There were no mirrors in the room that had before been occupied by nuns, but there was a washbasin, and she bathed her face gently, feeling each tooth with her tongue. None were broken.

That her lip was badly split, she knew, but she also realized there seemed to be a gash on her cheekbone. Was he wearing a ring?

She tried to think, to visualize his hand – yes, of course, those ridiculous class rings graduates were given by adoring families, and which they took such pride in showing off.

His had a red stone, she remembered.

Belinda thrust the door open, suddenly, still chattering to either Rose or Bernadette, and stopped, gasping, "Holy Mother Mary!"

Seeing Kate frantically gesturing for silence, she said in a careless voice over her shoulder, "No, nothing. Just stubbed my toe," and closed the door quietly behind her. Rushing over, she whispered fiercely, "He did that, didn't he?

"I knew he had come, Wanida told me, but nobody saw him leave.

"Why? How did he find out?"

She could not know, she could never know that Eddy was the one who had betrayed her.

"Exactly as I said he would." Kate managed to mumble behind the wet cloth she was still pressing to her mouth.

"How bad do I look?"

Belinda took her chin, and tilted her face to the light. "Bad.

"You're going to have a black eye, your mouth — well your mouth is a mess, but we know it's going to heal. It might take some time though.

"I don't like the look of that cut on your face, it could leave a scar. You might want to have it stitched. And that bump on your forehead looks nasty," she added, feeling it with tender fingers. "Anything else?"

Kate shook her head.

She fell on her shoulder but it wasn't dislocated, she could move. "It's painful, though."

He didn't kick her or anything when she was on the ground, did he?

Or... "Did he rape you?"

Kate tried to laugh, but it hurt too much. "It never occurred to me he would, you know? I think I disgust him too much for that. And no, he didn't kick me.

"He was drunk."

Belinda took the cloth and dabbed at Kate's bleeding cheekbone.

"Disgust doesn't stop them, love.

"But being drunk does, when you're lucky.

"Right. Wait here. I'll go get some witch hazel for your eye, and iodine and gauze. And I'm going to call Doctor Sumet, tell him to come over. I can't stitch that gash myself."

No, no, Kate begged. No, she wanted no one to know.

"You won't be able to hide for weeks," Belinda retorted, reasonably.

"We'll make up a story, that you were — perhaps knocked over by a bicycle — no, no, that won't work, we'll think of something

— but we have to have Doctor Sumet look at you. Is there anyone else you trust? No, you see?

"Just wait. Five minutes, all right?"

"You will say that you were attacked in the deserted soi next to the hospital by a drunken mob of Yuwachon who thought you were British," Sumet instructed her, while he put two stitches to her cheekbone, and one to her lip. "People can believe that."

He had not gasped, or even looked shocked when he saw her — Belinda must have prepared him for the sight.

"Khun Kate, I am so deeply, terribly sorry.

"And I am so surprised, as well. Why would he behave so?

"He did not give the impression of being a violent man."

Kate explained, in as few words as she could — speaking was painful, even with the local anaesthetic Sumet had injected near her mouth — about Akira's family being deported to some camp.

He needed to take out his rage on someone.

"And what about us?" Belinda demanded furiously, while she applied a dressing to Kate's cheek. "Eddy's been deported to a camp. He knows that. He knows how unfair it is."

He was drunk, Kate replied. He was too angry to think.

"He's probably ashamed of himself now, if he's sober, that is."

Belinda drew herself up indignantly. "No, Kate.

"You're talking like all those women who get beaten by their men and make excuses for them afterwards.

"Oh, my Paddy, they say, he's not a bad man, he'd just a drop taken, and he was so shameful afterwards, until the next Saturday pay comes and he does it again.

"Not you. You can't."

Kate raised herself on one elbow to swallow the sleeping tablet Sumet gave her with a glass of cold tea, then closed her eyes and shrugged.

She wasn't making excuses.

She never wanted to see him again in her life, and told him to leave them alone in the future.

Her mouth was numb now, and she found it difficult to shape her words.

"But he said he might, or might not.

"He said we'll just have to wait and see."

She closed her eyes, and tears began to seep out.

"I'm so afraid," she managed to add drowsily, then fell asleep.

Sumet and Belinda looked at each other in fear and dismay.

"What can we do?" Belinda whispered.

Nothing, was Sumet's discouraged reply.

They couldn't prohibit him access to the hospital, they couldn't refuse to assist in operations, and she, Belinda, in particular, dare not even show him an unfriendly face.

"Remember your fiancé..." − Sumet shuddered inwardly, thinking of the further horrific information he had heard about that camp near Kanchanaburi − "You would not want him transferred to some place with worse living conditions."

No, of course, Belinda whispered, crossing herself.

"I'll tell Wanida about the Yuwachon attacking Kate." Sumet offered. "That way, everybody will know in a matter of hours. And we shall pretend to Doctor Akira that we ourselves believe it.

"In the meantime, I think it best if you send no parcel to your fiancé. Let us make sure Akira does not extend his anger to us all.

"I will make inquiries, discreetly, of course, and find out if Yong Siang has had problems with the police."

He pulled up the sheet over Kate's shoulder and looked down at her, smoothing her hair. "It will be painful for her to eat. Make sure she has a mainly liquid diet − soup, mashed bananas, just like baby food."

Belinda snorted.

Where she came from, everybody knew how to feed a woman with her face bashed in.

For the next few days, Kate dozed, and daydreamed, of the one happy year she had with Lawrence.

The beach in Hua Hin, cocktails at the Oriental... watching the sunset from the sala.

She begged for a mirror, and Belinda had finally relented.

Staring at herself, Kate wondered if she really could be the same woman who had worn jade and diamond earrings and showed off her shoulders in a grey chiffon dress.

Would Lawrence even recognize her?

She barely recognized herself.

The bruise around her eyes had turned to a yellowish purple, her mouth was still swollen, but the bump on the forehead had receded.

She would not, could not think of what the coming weeks might bring.

Wanida came bearing a wreath of flowers and tearfully apologized on behalf of the Thai people for the shame those Yuwachon thugs had brought on them all.

"They could not have known of the good you and the Irish nurses have done for us."

Nai Khop produced a clear chicken soup with bitter herbs his wife had made specially. "It will make you recover, and help the pain."

Strangely, it did, and the soothing hot liquid was comforting.

Meanwhile, she waited, Belinda and Sumet waited, but there was no word from Captain Akira.

In time, the swelling receded, the bruises around her eye gradually vanished, and Kate was able to leave her room to have the stitches removed from her cheek, wincing with each stinging pull.

Sumet applied iodine to her face, and grimaced. "I did my best, but you will have a scar."

Kate shrugged. "It will be a memory.

"Has he been in touch with you?"

Sumet needed not ask who "he" might be. No, they had heard nothing. "As you said, he is probably ashamed, and rightly so."

She closed her eyes.

Perhaps.

And perhaps not.

The weather was burning hot, the sun relentless in a white, incandescent sky.

Tempers were becoming frayed, the nurses bickered amongst themselves, and snapped at patients.

Thip sent word that she would be going to Hua Hin to escape the furnace Bangkok had become, and could Kate perhaps come?

"Pichit has arranged for an ambulance to enable me to travel lying down. It would be easy to keep you hidden. Please say yes. Bring your friend, if the hospital can spare her."

"Yes, oh yes."

She yearned for the cool sea water, and to be free, if only for a week, from those hospital walls.

Sumet approved. "The police won't stop the ambulance

carrying someone from that family. I shall arrange it with Wanida, for you both."

The Packard travelling in front with Fon and luggage was stopped and papers checked, but the ambulance was waved through, and Kate and Belinda, their hair covered by their nurses' coifs were not noticed.

Lady Thip, smiling, listened to Belinda's excited chatter and Kate's quiet replies, and added only a few breathless words of her own, clasping Kate's hand in her gnarled and jewelled fingers, flinching with every bump on the uneven road.

They were held up, once, and waved over to the verge to make way for a long convoy of armoured cars and tanks, and Belinda's and Kate's eyes met, but they said nothing.

"This where I spent my honeymoon," Kate said nostalgically when they walked on the beach before sunset.

Belinda remembered how envious she was.

"I've never been to the beach here, can you fathom that?

"Eddy always said he would take me, I went and bought a bathing dress and all ...but, well...it never happened.

"Anyway, let's not talk about all that, all right?"

She waved towards the grey lines of Japanese ships on the horizon, cruising southwards, towards Java, or Borneo, or even Australia.

"And let's absolutely not talk about *that* either. We shall swim — actually, I can't swim, but I'll splash — and eat and sleep, and Lady Thip can tell us gossip of her younger days."

The nitroglycerin tablets were helping, Kate could tell, Thip no longer had those blue traces around her mouth, and submitted uncomplainingly to her daily insulin injection, and to the strict diet Fon was enforcing.

They had dinner with the old lady in her room, and listened to tales of growing up at the Royal Court — "Were you in line to be a wife to the King?" Belinda asked in titillated amazement, and Thip laughed her gasping chuckle.

No, it was more of a sort of finishing school, she believed it was called in England.

They learned how to cook very elaborate food, to dress, to behave, to embroider and how to move gracefully, to speak English. Even French, with Lawrence's grandmother.

"It was all about marrying well.

"It's always that, for girls, isn't it?"

And did it work, Belinda wanted to know, did she marry well?

"I was lucky," Thip sighed. "I loved him, and he loved me. He built the house to please me, in the English style, and although it was not in my taste, I never told him. I see him still in every room. He died too young, I had only one son.

"But the memories... He gave me beautiful memories."

When the week was over, and the ambulance had brought them back, Kate had begun to believe that her life, boring and restricted as it was, had returned to normal.

She was unpacking her bag, shaking out the sand from her canvas sandals, and caught herself singing *"The way you look tonight"*, the song she had danced to with Lawrence, on the Oriental's terrace, under the stars, remembering that he had crooned it softly in her ear, his cheek against hers.

She had just reached *"Never never change..."* when there was a knock on her door.

It was Wanida, who complimented her for looking so rested.

"I am glad to see you so recovered, Khun Kate.

"The hospital needs you, and you have done much for our reputation.

"In fact, I have good news.

"Captain Akira has asked you to come assist him for an operation.

"He wanted you three days ago, but I said you would be back only today, that you had gone away to recover from that terrible attack.

"He was most concerned."

Kate blanched.

"So — he did it without me, then?" she managed to stammer.

Oh no. Captain Akira said the operation could wait, that the patient was stable.

He would send a car for her tomorrow morning.

Chapter XX

The final evacuation of Rangoon continued for days.

Many of those civilians who were unable to get onto a boat, or the very few planes, or the overcrowded twice-daily rail service to India began to see Mandalay as their haven, and started to try to make their way there, by car or lorry if they were lucky – but most of them, mainly the Indians, knew better.

India was a long and dangerous march away, but in India, they had their roots, perhaps family who might remember their forefathers, and people who spoke their language and did not hate them.

The northern and eastern roads must at all costs be kept clear to bring in troops and supplies to the 14th Indian Army division fighting in the East, towards the Sittang river, so all the evacuees left Rangoon by the north-western route, even those who, like Government Services staff and press correspondents, were headed for Maymyo.

Long, never-ending columns of bullock-carts, but more often of men, women and children on foot, the elderly leaning on sticks, and all of them carrying pitiful bundles of what little food they had been able to buy or scrounge in the city that was becoming starved of supplies.

They advanced in swirling flurries of red dust, hardly ever stopping, not even raising their eyes from the person walking in front, barely moving aside to make way for jeeps and lorries and overloaded buses to get by.

The luck of the draw was that Lawrence was assigned to one of the last jeeps to leave the city, with water bottles full and several tins of sardines and a bunch of bananas. The Strand had not been able to provide them with more.

"Just look at those poor sods," Burchett said in an awed voice as they drove past the ragged, slowly advancing crowds. "The Brits brought them in by the boatload, promised them – well, I don't know what they promised them, but no doubt a better life.

"The Burmese hate them, the English despise them, and they're forced to walk back home with no food or water, or any arrangements made to get them to safety.

"That's the Empire for you, eh?

"Whaddya say, Larry? Your people big Empire builders?"

Lawrence wiped the dust from his face, and refrained from taking a gulp from his water bottle, to make it last, but also out of sheer shame for the fact that *he* had water.

"No, my father's a surgeon, actually. My mother's a judge's daughter, so... Not much Empire in the family business. You?"

Burchett shrugged. "I'm Australian, mate. Probably descendant of a convict. More of an Empire victim, I'd say.

"Hey, you ever been to Maymyo, Alec?", he asked Tozer who was riding in front next to their driver.

"The only ones who've been there, I think, are Stowe and Gallagher.

"Supposed to be nice. It's the old hill station isn't it? Should be cooler."

George Rodger, who was sitting in the back with Burchett and Lawrence stopped snapping pictures for a moment.

"I wouldn't mind cooler. Hey, have you seen what this guy is carrying?

"A bicycle with the back wheel missing..."

They all stared.

"Perhaps," Lawrence ventured, "he will need a bicycle for work wherever he ends up, and hopes he'll find a rear wheel there."

"Yeah, perhaps," Burchett replied, still turned back in his seat to watch, "or more likely that's all he owns."

The driver was forced to slow, there was a crowd ahead, and Tozer began to film. "What's happening?" he asked the driver.

"Sorry sir. Cannot go through." The Indian corporal was indignant. "I heard of this before, sir. Local police. They make people pay to cross into next village."

A woman, spotting the white faces in the jeep, pressed up against it, holding up her child, whose huge eyes were swarming with flies.

"Pani, pani..." she begged.

"She wants water," the driver explained.

"I'd got that," Burchett snapped. "Larry, George, your canteens. Quick."

The driver raised his hand. "Don't, sirs, please. We have not enough, and those who do not get, get angry. Please. Please.

"My orders are to get you safe to Maymyo, and we are only just in Prome ..."

Alec stopped filming and turned back to put his hand on Burchett's arm.

"He's right; they could tear us to pieces."

The crowd was slowly parting to let the jeep through, and the journalists were straining to keep their eyes ahead, away from the agonized faces and pleas for water and food.

Imploring hands brushed against the jeep's doors, and Lawrence bit his lips, hearing the low moans and the crying children.

An old woman in a bedraggled red saree was sobbing helplessly, bent over her black cane, clutching a tattered cloth roll to her sunken chest. Behind her, a small girl was holding the hand of an elderly man who appeared to be blind, so white were his eyes. Two barefoot toddlers were grasping her torn skirt, too exhausted to even cry.

"All right." Rodger opened his door. "There is, however, something we can do, and we're going to do it.

"Larry, Bill, come with me. Alec, you stay in the jeep and guard your equipment and my camera," he ordered, tearing it from around his neck, and tossing it into Alec's lap. "You fellows have your guns?

"Right. Keep them handy."

He strode ahead, with Lawrence and Burchett following, hands on the pistols inside their uniform blouse pockets. An old man knelt down to touch his forehead to Lawrence's shoes, whimpering "Pani, pani..." in a desperate voice. He shuddered, but could not bring himself to move, or lift the man to his feet either.

"What seems to be the trouble?" Rodger asked genially at the toll point, a ridiculous flimsy barrier of bamboo, where two Burmese policemen were strutting importantly in front of three men who seemed to be speaking for the refugees attempting to pass.

"Sir," one policeman saluted smartly.

"Sir," an elderly Indian with a hennaed beard and a dirty white skullcap, showing he had performed the pilgrimage to Mecca, raised his hands as if in prayer.

"...please, sir..."

"These people cannot get through if they do not pay toll for damage to road and fields," the policeman stated. "They steal fruit from trees. They foul water. It is one rupee per person to pass, and one anna per cup of water."

"Sir, we cannot pay," the elder appealed. "It is too much, some people have nothing left after paying in other towns."

Lawrence was standing behind Rodger, and he could feel the crowd pushing them forward, he could smell sweat, and unwashed bodies and despair.

"How much is it for us to pay?" he abruptly asked.

The policeman saluted again.

Oh no, there was no charge for them.

"Why, that's real nice of you." Rodger grinned, and looked around, to assess the situation, still smiling hugely.

"You guys cover me, Ok?" he muttered very low, pulled out his pistol and pointed it at the policeman, with Lawrence and Burchett drawing theirs and aiming at his colleague. The Burmese yelped, and a low murmur of panic swelled through the crowd.

"You are going to let these poor people pass through and let them drink the water from your river. Understand?

"Or I'll shoot you and blame the Japanese and my two friends here will write all about it their newspapers. We will wait as long as we have to.

"Understand?" he asked again.

The policeman paled, and nodded, and raised the barrier and people, chattering with excitement and relief, began to rush through.

"Hey, George," Burchett whispered, "how long do you want to wait? We haven't all day, you know."

Lawrence gazed at the toll barrier consideringly. "I think you need to wait just long enough for me to hack this to pieces."

He turned to the elderly Indian man who had followed the exchange with incredulous eyes. "Hajji, do you perchance have a big knife?"

The man smiled his understanding. "Not I, my son, but my friend has a kukri."

Lawrence nodded approvingly at the weapon. "Just the thing. In Malay, it's called a parang. Thank you."

When they climbed back into the jeep, Rodger leaned back into his seat and wiped his brow with a drawn out breath of relief. "That was fun."

Tozer gave them a round of mock applause.

"You gentlemen may not have realized it, but you may be the stars of Movietone News soon. I was filming the whole thing.

"Larry, that policeman thought you were going to decapitate him, you looked so fierce.

"If you had, of course, I would have cut that bit out.

"All done now, playing heroes? Can we go?"

Maymyo was indeed nice and verdant, with well-kept gardens and a lake, more churches than Buddhist temples and a cricket green in the town centre.

The houses, many of them half-timbered mock-Tudors, were fronted with trees blossoming pink and red and flower beds and bore names like 'Dunroamin' or 'Rose Cottage' and 'Larkspur'.

The temperature had dropped and they were all shivering.

"Looks like Devon," Rodger commented as the jeep drove up in front of the SPRO office.

"Feels like Devon too," Tozer replied, pulling on his army greatcoat, "if Devon were a day or two away from the Japs. Give me a hand with my sound equipment, will you?"

Briefing this evening at eighteen hundred, a Lieutenant Whittier told them, when they asked if there were any news.

Deputy PRO Wallace-Crabbe would answer their questions — "or not," Lawrence replied, drawing a frown from Whittier, who looked him up and down.

"I remember you from school, Gallet.

"Always a bit of a trouble-maker, weren't you? Well, we won't put up with that attitude here," before he continued his instructions in his peremptory voice.

Filing of dispatches could only be done from Mandalay, forty miles from Maymyo, but — but — first, they must be submitted for army censorship in Maymyo — "it's just a three mile drive, chaps!" — then to the civil censorship office — "but's that in Mandalay as well, so, rather convenient, what?"

In the meantime, here were their assigned lodgings in various guesthouses and hotels, and they were to consider themselves lucky to have lodgings and they were not to come to SPRO with frivolous complaints – the town was crawling with civilians, British and other, who had been evacuated from Rangoon, and were sharing lodgings or sleeping in tents.

"Yep," Rodger confirmed when they dropped him and Tozer in front of a guesthouse with petunias tumbling from window boxes and frilly curtains.

"Just like Devon. See you this evening.

"Find out where we drink, afterwards. Gallagher will know."

Lawrence and Burchett had been assigned Craddock Court.

"It sounds like one of those seedy places near Paddington. Or a cheap boarding house in Brighton." Lawrence had muttered on seeing the name.

"Ooh, bit of an elitist, are we?" Burchett asked.

"Eton, and all that? Was that the school the lieutenant was talking about?"

"Winchester, and Whittier always wanted to be head boy and never made it," Lawrence replied shortly. "I bet the place stinks of sprouts and yesterday's bacon."

It was beautiful, a stately white building with a deeply gabled, dark shingled roof, set in a park.

"If you think that's what it looks like around Paddington, you haven't been to London in a while," Burchett commented.

They found Berrigan and De Luce drinking in the bar.

"Is this the approved watering hole?" Burchett asked, collapsing in an armchair and ordering a gin and bitters.

"Nah," De Luce replied. "It's some other place whose name I can't remember."

"Candacraig, I've told you three times at least," Berrigan sighed. "That's where Stowe and Gallagher are staying, I think. Trust them.

"Have you guys heard the news?"

Lawrence shook his head. "There was a little twit of a Lieutenant at SPRO—I actually was at school with him, and he was already insufferable – who refused to answer questions, said Wallace-Crabbe would bare his soul to us this evening."

Berrigan raised his eyebrows at Lawrence's tone. "Someone's down at the mouth today. That little twit, as you say, couldn't talk because the news is just too bloody awful to trust to a junior officer.

"It's a rout. A bloody, mind-boggling, heart-breaking massacre.

"The Japanese have just destroyed the 17ᵗʰ Indian Army Division, they've crossed the Sittang and the road to Rangoon is now wide open."

Lawrence groaned, and slumped down in his armchair. "Oh no, not again... Are we ever going to win anywhere?

"What are the losses?"

De Luce closed his eyes, as if in pain... Bad.

The figures would be ... well ... Berrigan had heard that less than forty per cent had managed to retreat. So that would mean something like three thousand dead, missing, or captured.

Burchett pounded the table. "How do they fucking do it. How?

"It's like a curse."

He then got up, and raised his glass.

"Gentlemen.

"The 17ᵗʰ Indian Army, their gallantry and their fucking bad luck."

They all rose. "The 17ᵗʰ Indian Army Division, and their fucking back luck."

They sat again.

"And a pox on whoever did not relieve Smyth of his command," Berrigan added, raising his glass again. "The man is as sick as a dog, he's in constant pain, and incapable of thinking straight."

"So it's a pox on Wavell, basically?" Burchett asked. "Well, I'll drink to that too."

De Luce sighed his agreement, drained his glass then asked "Hey, Blondie, which side do you sleep on? We've been assigned the same room, but it's only got one bed — it's a huge four-poster, though.

"I guess they assumed we AP guys are one big happy family from both sides of the Atlantic."

Lawrence groaned.

"Just when I was starting to feel better about this place. I'll take the couch, if there is one."

De Luce shrugged. "Please yourself. Just so long as you don't snore.

"You guys want to drop your bags in the rooms, then we'll go to the briefing, all right? We have our own jeep for the four of us staying here.

"Who ever said SPRO was shabby?"

In his briefing, Wallace-Crabbe attempted to be reassuring, but his optimism rang false.

"No, the battle was not a defeat — The 17th Army Division merely drew back and regrouped — Fresh troops were brought in."

Questions came flying at him from all sides.

Was it true that it was a bloody massacre of the 17th Divisions?

"No, I would not put it that way —"

Then why the need to bring in fresh troops?

"Those lads had been fighting for days without respite, don't you think that they deserved a rest?"

"Was it to give them rest, or actually to replace those lost in combat?" De Luce demanded aggressively.

"And what about General Smyth's fitness to command?" Berrigan wanted to know.

Wallace-Crabbe rolled his eyes at that and, picking up his briefing notes, stated that there were many Japanese casualties — no, he was not at liberty to say if Japanese prisoners had been taken.

The good news was that the bridge on the Sittang river was successfully destroyed — "What about the rumour that many British troops were trapped on the wrong side of the river and had to swim back for safety?" De Luce asked.

"Where did you hear that?"

De Luce made a face. "We were among the last to leave Rangoon, and the first casualties from the Sittang were just getting in.

"Heard it there. They're also saying that the road to Rangoon is wide open."

Wallace-Crabbe flushed an angry red.

"Whoever told you that was either lying or did not have the right information — The Japanese *shall* be stopped on the way to Rangoon —," he sputtered and finally snapped. "Defeatist coverage shall *not* be tolerated.

"Why don't you chaps concentrate on the successful evacuation of Rangoon?"

"Yeah, Ken," Burchett retorted, "And the reason Rangoon

was evacuated, as well? Or would that be defeatist?"

"That would be Squadron-Leader Wallace-Crabbe to you, Burchett. We're not in the pub in Melbourne, now.

"As to the reason for the evacuation, it was, need it be said, because the security of the civilian population is paramount – and before any of you chaps bring it up," he added with a deadpan expression, "I have been instructed to say we are concerned with the safety of all civilians, regardless of race."

Jeers greeted that last statement, and Wallace-Crabbe merely shrugged, with a self-deprecating shake of his head.

"You've been told how and where to get your despatches vetted and then sent, haven't you?

"Then I think that's all for today, chaps."

The briefing broke up in a shuffling of chairs, muttered, incensed, expressions of disbelief and exchanges of rumours – "It *is* a rout I tell you" – "yes, but how can you be sure?"

"Heard it on the Japanese English language radio news program," OD Gallagher chimed in, and Berrigan nodded. "Me too."

"So you'd rather believe the Japanese, then?" Wallace-Crabbe had just joined their group, and stood easily, hands in his pockets, displaying none of the martial bearing and forced confidence he had shown on the improvised podium.

"Well, I'd rather believe anyone who's not lying to me," Berrigan retorted.

"Think you can do that?"

"Unfortunately, no," the press officer answered dryly, and walked away.

LAWRENCE'S DIARY
MAYMYO MARCH 2ND1942

Who knows how long we shall be able to stay here?

The Japs appear to be hot on our tails.

Rangoon, everyone now agrees, will fall any day.

Maymyo is crowded with refugees from Rangoon, some Chinese, quite a few Indians, but mainly English civilians, the Governor, of course and all his officials, teak-wallahs and jute-wallahs, local administrators and missionaries from little towns arriving with their families, who have all sought refuge in guesthouses or the several convent schools the city is famous for.

The outskirts of the town are covered with makeshift tent camps for the poorer Indians, and the smoke from their cookfires wafts over the chill breezes.

There is much muttering from the British escapees about wealthy Chinese and Parsi merchants from Rangoon who saw the writing on the wall, and arrived here before anyone else, commandeering rooms in all the best hotels. "Even Candacraig!" one lady seethed. "I mean, really..."

I spoke to a missionary woman who gazed at me with wide-open cornflower-blue eyes and professes she has no fear, "because God shall provide."

It is only her three children she worries about, because there is hardly any milk to be had, and food is so very expensive.

Neither she nor her husband had wanted to leave their town of Magwe — "how could we abandon these poor, poor Burmese souls to the godless Japanese?" but they were given no choice but to be evacuated here.

Of course, we are not allowed to write about that, only about the cheerful courage everyone is showing.

"Can't let our side down," is the order of the day, far more for me, actually, than for Dan who answers to the Yank side of AP, and can come up with headlines such as "Brit armour blasts through sun-baked plains to no avail" to report on a major tank battle that is now being fought at Pegu, with the British 7th Armoured Brigade and the 63rd Indian Infantry Brigade.

Crabbe-Wallace was publicly furious at him but privately agreed that whatever news filters, it is not good.

We were promised a trip to the front, but made to turn back by our accompanying officer because of safety concerns, and so must rely on hearsay, snippets given by the American military mission that was moved to Maymyo as well, and the universally detested Japanese radio English language news.

What was confirmed is that the 17th Indian Division was indeed defeated and almost destroyed at the Sittang bridge battle.

Rumour has it that one of Smyth's order to advance was

radioed in clear and that the Japanese of course heard it and were prepared for him.

General Hutton – he who had no time for journalists – has been replaced at the head of the Burma Army by General Alexander, who organised and oversaw the evacuation from Dunkirk.

He shall probably need to do the same for Burma... and Smyth has been officially fired, or so we hear, unofficially, from Wallace-Crabbe who veers between his stern, brisk and military style during briefings and a completely different attitude when we all meet for drinks at Candacraig, the palatial formerly rest house of the Bombay Burma Trading Company.

The only hopeful news is that additional troops of Generalissimo Chiang's Chinese army under the command of American General Stilwell are now being poised to come into the country to defend the Burma Road at all costs. Wavell had contemptuously turned down their assistance, Alexander is less proud and knows he shall need help.

Besides the refugees, Maymyo is also being overrun with ever more journalists, and because we are all always together, we snipe and snap at each other, over who files first – we take it in turns to drive to Mandalay, down from chilly Maymyo into the scorching plain, to have dispatches vetted by the civilian censor then sent via the telegraphic service, and whoever's turn it is then gets accused of favouring his agency or paper – or over, and more importantly, how and where we get out of here.

Stowe and Gallagher and a few others favour getting onto a plane to India, if and when there is one.

"Frankly, kid, the news here is done – it's another goddamn retreat, and I'm not interested in covering that again.

"The real story now is going to be India, now that Home Rule has been promised." Stowe told me, sucking on his pipe.

He and Gallagher have now reached a point where they detest each other, and barely talk.

Dan De Luce wants to try getting out northwards to China, and we have agreed, since we both report to Associated Press, that we should split and I take the route to India – but, as opposed to the seasoned and famous guys, I shall stay as long as possible – I need to prove myself, and if allowed, shall follow the British troops.

MAYMYO, MARCH 11TH 1942

Rangoon has now surrendered to the Japanese.

Two rather cocky Aussie correspondents, by name of Healy and Munday have turned up here from Rangoon.

They latched on to the 7th British Armour Division and witnessed the tank battle of Pegu by slipping the leash — whereas we from Maymyo were turned away — and tell us that the British forces' tanks were no match for the Japanese, which is when General Alexander gave the order to abandon Rangoon to its fate, but not before destroying anything which might be put to use against us.

The two journalists were there as well, and described the eerie sight of a city with empty, echoing streets, and the port and refinery ablaze lighting up the night sky.

I don't know where they went in Rangoon to see empty, eerie streets, because it differs wildly from what I was told by a Tommy from the 7th Hussars I talked to at Fraser's Inn (the 'other ranks' favourite place to drink — it's important to hear the experience of the ordinary fighting men, not just the lofty, supercilious views of officers who in any case are under orders to tell us as little as possible).

According to this sergeant, Rangoon was a madhouse, the prisons and insane asylums have been opened and the released inmates roam free in the city, looting and fighting.

As to the port, apparently, before it was set ablaze, the armoured divisions brought in from India were able to help themselves to tremendous amounts of Lend-lease materiel, and, added to this sanctioned looting, found a shipment of liquor and many soldiers got drunk as lords and were incapacitated for hours.

The zoo, too, was opened, and there are wild animals roaming the streets, including, it seems, an orang-utan who, in the sergeant's words, is said "to really be living it up."

He found that very funny. I, however, cannot help but feel for the poor beast who must be terrified by the noise and flames.

Meanwhile, the British way of life continues here.

Along with the other British correspondents, I was actually invited to a party (a party!!! Though it was not named as such — the invitation bore the description of the event as a "reception by HE the Governor") at Flagstaff House, the official summer residence and now General British headquarters, where we were served beer in iced silver mugs and givena jolly talk about keeping our side up through morale, etc.

Then, the hero of Dunkirk, General Alexander, was introduced to great applause, and he gave a rousing speech about King, country and Empire, and about how he is here to defend them all.

The missionaries looked quite moved, the press less so.

Flagstaff House is very mahogany and chintz-heavy, and I remembered my French grandmother, Julie, with her pitiless assessment of the decorative style of country houses she was invited to for hunting week-ends: "Fake-looking real Chippendale, good paintings badly hung and the smell of mothballs."

The numbers of the British military staff are overwhelming, one cannot but wonder why they are here rather than in the field.

Young officers of the Burma Rifles or other regiments in their best uniforms looked down their noses at us in our rather dishevelled ones.

I cannot tell if it is whether we members of the Press Corps are beyond the pale, incredibly vulgar (indeed some were heard sniffing that Cedric Salter was crass enough to bring up the subject of Burmese fifth-columnists in front of women, frightening the poor creatures), or just that they think us cowards.

Anyway, I realize I find American company more congenial, these days, perhaps out of loyalty to Kate – Kate!! I try and conjure up her smile, the sound of her voice and realize that I cannot. It is only in my dreams that she comes back to me intact – but more probably because since Kunming, I have become accustomed to their easy friendliness as well as their sense of efficiency and their realism about the threats we are all facing.

Also, they tend to not despise correspondents, they rather like getting good press – "Americans likes to know that their tax dollars are put to good use," as Dan said, "even when it's by the armed forces."

He and Berrigan have introduced me to some of the American Mission's men that I had no opportunity to meet in Rangoon, but in this small place, we are all thrown together.

A few stand out, one Frank Merrill, who served as attaché at the U.S. Embassy in Tokyo where he learned Japanese and then served in Manila with MacArthur.

He seems to have, as do I, this reluctant admiration for our enemy.

He does not hate them, and says he finds their civilization and culture fascinatingly cerebral.

"Japanese art," he told me dreamingly, "is extraordinary, in that what is visible only exists to enhance what is invisible, what is suggested.

"They worship transcendent beauty, impermanence, the fleeting moment.

"Samurai have been known to write poems about the fall of a cherry blossom petal."

Then he added, in a different tone. "Also, it's worth remembering that they value honour over life and all in all, they're pretty ruthless bastards."

We doubled at tennis at the Club the other day, and afterwards, we drank chilled pints at the bar, the sun was about to set, the banks of hydrangeas and rhododendron and the perfectly rolled lawns were fading away in the gathering shadows.

A couple of very proper blondes in party dresses were dancing with young officers to Glenn Miller's "Moonlight Serenade" that was playing on the phonograph and had it not been for the fact we were all here on borrowed time, it would have been perfectly idyllic.

Every Englishman's dream of life in the colonies.

Merrill looked around and said "You do realize, don't you, that whatever the outcome of this war may be, it will be the end of this way of life? The end of the Empire?

"Well of course you do.

"I'll have a whiskey, now," he added, waving to the barman.

"Empires fear they cannot last," he said, warming to his subject, "unless they expand, and expansion is their downfall.

"Look at the Romans, Napoleon, the Austro-Hungarians... Portugal, Spain...

"China and Japan only seemed immune to that mirage, because they were closed upon themselves, but they too became contaminated. By us.

"The Mikado shall cease to be a god, the Reich shall fall and crash and the British Empire will follow in some kind of worldwide snowball effect," he declaimed in an overloud and dramatic voice, probably due as much to the whiskey as to the subject.

No wonder we got dirty looks from the other drinkers.

MARCH 15TH 1942

Stilwell has arrived, along with several Chinese generals, but he is their commanding officer, being Chiang Kai-Shek's chief of staff.

One hears he speaks Chinese well, but I nonetheless wonder how that is going to work.

Meanwhile, those same Chinese generals and their divisions, according to Salter who got it from some staff officer at British Headquarters, shall be fighting under General Alexander.

It sounds like a great recipe for, as Salter said, a right royal fuck-up.

There is also a new colonel in town, one Wingate who has the reputation of being rather strange, 'a Bible-thumper' as Merrill described it, who has a project to create some kind of behind-the-lines force dubbed the Chindits. "Charismatic but a real nut. For some reason, London loves him. Personally, I'd give him a wide berth."

Apparently, he goes about naked, taking bites from a raw onion hanging from a string around his neck as he harangues his men, biblical-patriarch-like, and is seconded by a brigadier known as 'Mad Mike' Calvert.

The two, from what one hears, are merciless in training their men and managed to get themselves hated by the Gurkhas.

Best to avoid them.

MARCH 24TH 1942

Maymyo was bombed last night, for the first time.
We made for the slit shelters, huddling far too close for comfort against each other, children crying, mothers trying to hush them, the bells of the fire engines shrieking.

A moment of private hell, and I am ashamed to admit I was too bothered by the other people and the noise to be afraid.

The explosions shook the ground, and when we emerged after the all clear, several buildings were on fire.

Went to the railway station in the morning.

It was pandemonium, people pushing and shoving and

shouting, and there were many English women with children and babies in their arms, no men, of course, except for some elderly ones too old to fight.

How far they hope the train may take them is unclear – perhaps as far as Myitkyna, whence a plane might fly them to safety.

But some do still seem to believe that they will be sitting out the war in North Burma.

The English carry nothing but a small suitcase each and get jostled by the well-to-do Indians who have their belongings roped together and attempt to hoist them into overcrowded carriages.

The mood was defiantly cheerful, although I did hear a stout and haughty official's wife grouse about having to travel third class, but she was instantly quelled by some Red Cross matron, who just gave her hefty behind a push, and said "Set yourself there, love, and consider yourself lucky."

Some clambered onto the roofs of the cars, others were standing on the steps, clinging to the door sides, packages were thrown out of windows to loud and angry Indian protests that were laughed away.

Many of those who did not manage to get on board are too afraid to wait for another train – if indeed there *is* to be another train – and are preparing to hike their way to India, if no other transport is laid on for them.

One lady showed me the knapsacks she was filling with food for the journey, Horlicks and porridge and tins of sardines and meat, and then, she pointed to her two sons, who may have been eight and ten, at most.

"We've been trekking in the hills for the holidays, and Bill and Jimmy are quite good little walkers. How long can it take us, after all?

"A couple of weeks perhaps?

"It will be an adventure, won't it, chaps?"

I asked if she thought she would find milk on the way, "You know, for the Horlicks?" and she replied quietly that Horlicks is very nourishing even when eaten as a dry powder. Our eyes met, and I saw she is fully aware of the perils of her undertaking.

Wrote about it, stressing the courage and good and strong spirits, which do indeed force admiration, describing as I put it, the "best of British grit."

It was my turn to go to file down in Mandalay, and for once, I did not pause and admire the lovely sight of the many gilt pagodas in the plain, far too busy scanning the skies for advancing Zeroes, but all was quiet.

The airfield at Magwe was heavily bombed yesterday as well, destroying all of the RAF planes and quite of few of the AVG ones.

I hear that the AVG is about to withdraw to Loiwing, a Chinese airfield just the other side of the border from Lashio.

I hope Tex is still fine and flying.

Leland and O.D left by air last week, luckily before Magwe was destroyed, Dan is under instructions to adhere to the American forces if possible, so if they return to China, he will follow, and if not, will continue with them. If by some miracle, we are able to hang on to central Burma and advance from there with the assistance of Stilwell's Chinese Divisions, that is what he will do.

As to what I shall do, I don't yet know.

I have applied to go to the front at Toungoo, where the China 200th Division is fighting, and which is a battle Stilwell and Alexander have agreed to leave to them so as to enable the British forces to concentrate along the Irrawaddy.

MARCH 30TH 1942

Toungoo was another disaster, in no way attributable to the Chinese forces who were outnumbered, and had no air support, as opposed to the Japanese who bombed their positions aggressively and also used gas attacks.

I have nothing but admiration for the Chinese troops, who attacked, withdrew, regrouped and attacked again.

They are mere boys, most of them, poorly equipped, the supplies of food, munitions, and fuel that were to arrive by train were held up somewhere en route.

Stilwell, with whom I was able to spend some time at his headquarters in Pyinmana, blames Chiang Kai-Shek, who, he says, turns a blind eye to the rampant corruption of his generals, changes his mind daily, if not hourly as to the troops he agrees to throw into the battle.

He calls the Generalissimo "Peanut", and speaks of him with contempt.

"Would you believe that in the middle of this mess, with the Japs crawling all over us, he ordered that every four Chinese soldiers were to be issued with a watermelon to share?

"Can't you just picture them taking a break from combat, sitting on the ground and eating their goddamn picnic? Why not fry up a few chicken, while we're at it?

"And where the devil are we supposed to get enough watermelons to feed an army?"

Stilwell is assisted — or perhaps hampered? — by Chinese generals, Tu, Lin Wei, and Liao Yao-Hsiang who, according to Merrill, constantly wire the Generalissimo to have all of Stilwell's orders confirmed or stalled.

Merrill of course was there, and it is thanks to him that I was given access to Vinegar Joe, who looked me up and down, and told me to sit in a corner and be quiet.

Doesn't have much time for Limeys, he said, but if I could get the British to understand what was at stake in Burma, then it was worth his while to talk to me.

"You're the 'Unlikely Angels' guy aren't you?" he asked, and I was forced to admit it.

"Madame Chiang loved your article, she keeps on calling Chennault her chief angel," he replied with disgust, "but I guess that isn't your fault."

Afterwards, he took me in his jeep to visit the outer border of the front, and answered a few questions, and it was then that he vented his frustration with the whole command structure as it now stands. I quoted Salter's "right royal fuck-up", and he laughed and heartily agreed.

A bullet pinged my helmet.

Spent time at the field hospital manned by a Doctor Seagreave, an American Baptist missionary surgeon who enlisted in the U.S. Medical Corps.

Fascinating man, in his mid-forties, he was born in Burma and speaks Karen as well as he does English.

He is blunt, efficient, and dedicated, and, like Stilwell, has no time for niceties.

The makeshift wards were bloody.

And bloody, bloody awful.

The heat was atrociously high, the sun beating down on the metal sheet roof — "Thatch would have been better," Seagreave said ruefully, "but it catches fire like tinder."

I could not report on any of the details of the horrendous injuries and wounds in my dispatch — for morale purposes, soldiers are always cleanly injured, and receive immediate care, or if they do die, die instantly, — but the stench of spilling guts, gangrened limbs, excrement and vomit shall remain in my nostrils for my lifetime, I fear, as well as the sight of a pile of severed arms and legs, some still sporting watches or socks and boots, just tossed in a corner of the lean-to, along with rags and bandages sopping with blood and puss and bile, and already reeking to high heaven.

There were purposeful and bustling Burmese and Chinese female nurses whom Seagreave has trained himself, he says, and how they managed to keep working with serene and effective composure is beyond my comprehension.

I kept my mind on Kate to avoid swooning or vomiting at the sight of so much blood, thinking that if she could do it daily, I could manage for a couple of hours.

Finally managed to meet and talk with an American *Time* magazine correspondent, Jack Belden, who arrived with Stilwell from Chunking.

Another oddity, but aren't we all?

He speaks Chinese fluently, and is rather a loner, someone Conrad could have written about.

Tough guy, worked as a merchant seaman after university, then jumped ship in Shanghai and stayed on.

He makes me feel that I have known such a soft, sheltered, cossetted, easy life so far, but then, most of the journalists have that effect on me.

Now that Toungoo, the town Tex described as the best place in the world, has fallen, what remains is at any cost to defend the oilfields of Yenaungyaung.

If the Japs get hold of the oil, Stilwell said, Burma is over and done with, and nothing can then prevent them from invading India.

APRIL 9TH1942

Mandalay has been almost completely destroyed by a staggering air raid.

Over four hundred were killed, the streets are full of corpses and birds and dogs and pigs feasting on them.

There is no hospital left to tend to the many injured, and the moats of the Palace are full of bodies, men and animals alike stewing in a pink coloured scum.

Stilwell toured the city in a daze of horror, and Belden, Rodger, Berrigan and I followed in another jeep.

The telegraph office has been knocked out, which means we can only get our dispatches by air, from Lashio to Chunking.

Maymyo gradually emptying of its inhabitants, including troops.

Many are opting, like that hardy lady I interviewed, to walk to India, begging for lifts on the way, "before the monsoon sets it, because the tracks will be turned into rivers of mud", as one put it.

Rodger and Burchett are leaving tomorrow, by jeep, planning to make their way up to Myitkyna, then out through the Naga hills.

They have been pouring over maps and collecting assorted food from whatever is still available here.

Burchett asked Rodger how comfortable he felt at the idea of driving a jeep over bad roads, and Rodger answered casually that he'd have to find out – "I always take taxis."

We gave them a rousing send-off and George danced a very impressive "Boogie-Woogie Washer-Woman" with one of the British nurses, with everybody changing the first words to "Down in the jungle where nobody goes, there's Rodger and there's Burchett a-scrubbing their clothes."

Can't get the idiotic tune out of my head now.

APRIL 24TH1942

It seems to me that the Allied forces are much like bowling pins scattered out of the way by a careening heavy ball.

Yenaungyaung is lost, but at least the oil fields were destroyed by orders of General Slim, Alexander's second-in command.

The Japanese got the site, but not the oil wells, and it would take them years to rebuild, so neither will they get the oil.

And oil, from what I'm increasingly hearing, is what will win or lose us this war.

Alexander himself was surrounded and almost trapped on the battlefield, but General Sun Li-Jen rescued him with a small handful of men.

We hear, unofficially, that most of the Burmese troops under British command deserted.

Lashio is lost, Mandalay vulnerable, Stilwell is moving his headquarters to Shwebo, fifty miles north.

One of his Chinese generals actually managed to steal a train to get himself back to Chongqing.

We, all the correspondents, have been ordered by the British to evacuate to India "as best we can".

Berrigan, Dan and Munday are going to try their luck driving north then west with a jeep they managed to procure.

Dan and I agreed once more that we should split to cover two different sides of the story. "Providing," Dan said cheerfully, "that either of us makes it out, of course.

"So long, Blondie, see you in Calcutta!"

Belden has refused to obey the order, and is going to follow Stilwell.

If Vinegar Joe will have me, that's what I shall do as well.

APRIL 26TH 1942

My plans have been turned down both by Stilwell and AP.

Stilwell doesn't need an "extra hanger-on to feed" I was told.

I suspect Belden didn't want another correspondent on the trip, and leaned heavily on Stilwell to refuse me.

AP claims that whatever happens, Belden will scoop me for *Time* magazine, and that British readers deserve to know what is happening to "our boys".

Therefore, I shall get out with whatever is left of the Burma Rifles.

So be it.

Chapter XXI

Kate had not slept all night.

Belinda spent most of the hours before dawn huddled up to her, holding her hand in silence.

There was nothing to be said any more.

Doctor Sumet had come after sunset, and sat at the foot of the bed.

Yes, of course Wanida had told him, pleased to announce that one of Saint-Louis' surgical nurses had been requested by the powerful surgeon from the victorious army.

If she had any opinion on the victorious army's presence in Thailand, she had yet to voice it.

"She does not want to know," he said simply. "Like most of my people, she just wants to survive."

Belinda had suggested, then abandoned several possible ideas of escape.

Illness, taking refuge at Khunying Thip's house, at Doctor Sumet's house, fleeing to the country, but Kate had shrugged them off.

She would be found, she couldn't endanger either Thip or Doctor Sumet's family, and that is where she would be looked for first.

"No. I just have to go through with it, whatever 'it' is.

"If it is indeed to assist in an operation," Sumet offered hopefully, getting up to leave, "then Doctor Akira won't be drunk. He will probably behave more..." he hesitated, "... more honourably this time."

Maybe.

When Wanida, all smiles, came to rap at the door, Kate was ready, her uniform neat and starched, her hair pinned back and covered with the linen coif.

She leaned over to kiss Belinda.

"If I don't come back," she whispered, "try to get word to

Thip, please. You know she has all my possessions. And the jade earrings go to you, be sure to tell her."

Belinda shook her head.

No. No. No.

The car's driver opened the door for her and bowed, a strange courtesy, Kate thought, but after all, he could not know that she felt she was on her way to an execution, he was probably just a taxi driver in his civilian life and trained to look after his passenger.

She gazed out at the Bangkok streets, struck at how little they had changed, they were perhaps less busy than she remembered, but then, then, the car was driving along unfamiliar streets. What she did notice was that most passers-by averted their glance from the shiny khaki Japanese military car with its Rising Sun markings on the door.

She could not tell where they were going to once the car had taken the road out of the city, towards the airfield of Don Muang, but it soon was stopped by sentries, calls were made to persons of authority, gates were opened and then they were checked again, and finally, a young soldier with a disapproving look told her to get out and wait. "Here!" he pointed to a spot on the gravel, then opened a door and entered the building.

Wherever they were, it was neither a hospital, nor a prison.

It looked more like a sort of rest home, with neat lawns and borders of flowers, and bright bougainvillea bushes in pots.

The soldier came back, and nodded curtly at her, signalling she was to follow.

Kate gulped, and tried to breathe deeply as she climbed the stairs behind him, feeling the sweat gather and run down her hair, her neck.

She could smell familiar smells, ether, disinfectant, rubbing alcohol and camphor, and heard distant clinking noises, of metal and enamel and hushed voices, then a man's voice, moaning.

So, a hospital after all, perhaps.

She tried to pray with each step, "Holy Mary, mother of God...," but the words meant nothing or so little.

The soldier knocked at a door, then stepped aside to let her in, and she suddenly, strangely, perhaps because she had been trying to pray, she thought of being called in to Mother Felicity's office to receive one of her rare scoldings.

Ken Akira was seated behind a desk, and barely looked up until the door was closed behind her.

"Sit down."

She pulled the metal chair away from the desk, and the scraping noise it made on the tile floor seemed a screeching echo in the silence.

She was shivering and not just from fear — it was surprisingly cool, almost chilly inside the room. So, the Japanese even had air-conditioning, she thought with envious anger. Along with everything else they had.

Once she was seated, Captain Akira got up and stared down at her.

Setting her jaw, she forced herself to stare back, crossing her hands over her purse, to stop them from shaking.

"So," he merely said.

"So?" she replied, "What is this operation you need me for?"

He shrugged. "It couldn't wait, finally. I managed without you."

Good. She wouldn't be needed then, she said, rising.

"You might have avoided me this trip out here.

"I'm needed at the hospital."

He laughed. "That's what I like about you, Kate.

"You're plucky.

"Plucky, that's the word, isn't it, that they use for those movie characters, the plucky girl,?

"You know, like Carole Lombard or Katharine Hepburn?"

He paused and added thoughtfully, "Japanese girls don't tend to be plucky. It's not encouraged, you see. It's not feminine.

"Heroic, yes. In our movies, they're often heroic."

She just kept staring at him, until he finally said, "Come with me. There's someone I want you to meet."

She swallowed. "This is when you turn me over to the Kempetai, isn't it?

"Let's get it over with."

He laughed again. "We're not in a movie. Don't overdo this plucky act. Just come."

He took her down a long corridor, then opened a door to a very small and plain room.

A young man in pyjamas and a cotton dun-coloured robe was lying on the narrow iron bed, his face gaunt and unshaven, an unread newspaper on his chest, the radio playing some song in the background.

There was a branch of flowers in a glass of water on the windowsill, and some mangosteens in a bowl next to it, but the walls were bare, Kate noticed, whereas in every hospital where she'd worked, there was always a crucifix to remind patients and doctors alike that their fate was in God's hands. Well, she thought, I suppose they believe they make their own fate.

They're probably right, too.

The man looked up, startled, when he saw the Western woman come in behind the doctor.

Akira said a few curt words to him in Japanese, and turned off the radio, and the man said "Hai" obediently, sitting up against the pillow and nodding.

"Nurse Fallon, meet Lieutenant Watanabe.

"Well, actually, you've met before but you were focussing on his leg.

"We took off his cast day before yesterday."

He snapped an order, and the lieutenant pulled up his pyjama to show the long, messy scar that slashed his leg from mid-thigh to his shin, then mumbled a few words, looking earnestly up at Kate.

"I told him that without your help, he wouldn't be here. He said thank you.

"He also said that his father is ashamed of his behaviour and that he deserved to be killed, but his father too is grateful nonetheless."

Kate raised her eyebrows, and turned her eyes from the wounded man to the surgeon.

"You know that's not true. Tell him so. Tell him it was your skill, and Doctor Sumet's that saved his leg."

Akira shook his head with a cynical smile.

"I'd rather everybody believes you were instrumental as well. It will make it easier to ask for you to assist in the future. But it's nice that you should show such humility.

"We Japanese like women who defer to their men."

She came closer, and knelt by the bed, running her hand

down the red, swollen, tissue, and the man flinched.

"Does it still hurt?" she couldn't help asking, then bit her tongue.

What did she care if it still hurt?

Watanabe seemed to understand, and nodded, "Hai," then added something with a rueful, forced smile.

"It's the recovery, the walking exercises that hurt most now that the cast is off, but he hopes he'll soon be able to go back and fight America," Akira translated coolly. "Okay, let's go back to my office."

The few people they crossed in the hall — a middle-aged man with a white coat over his uniforms, a couple of nurses in immaculate, buttoned-up dresses with old-fashioned bonnets pulled low down on their foreheads — gave Akira a half-bow and eyed Kate curiously.

The nurses turned back to look at her, giggling, but Akira frowned and they scuttled away.

"So this is where you work," Kate said, once they were back inside his office. "I thought you'd be needed at the hospital, wherever that is."

He shrugged.

"I — well, I operate at the hospital, the more difficult cases involving important senior officers, that are sent from field hospitals, and that require more than sloppy emergency surgery. Mainly, I undo what harm was done.

"It's not that the field surgeons are incompetent, not at all, it's just that they work in horrifying conditions.

"Dozens of casualties arriving at the same time, extensive burns, gunshot wounds, bomb fragments, gushing arteries, amputations. You can imagine.

"Well, actually, no, you can't, and neither can I."

Kate cocked her head, unsettled, as she was the first time she'd heard him at Saint-Louis, by the familiarity and ease she felt when hearing him talk.

Stop, she told herself firmly. Remember what he did to you. You still have the scar to prove it.

"Why don't they send you to a field hospital then?" she demanded, with an edge in her voice.

He sighed and made a face.

"They won't send me to combat zones, although I did apply for it, because I'm not trusted, not really. Somehow, I think they imagine I might defect to the other side, given half a chance.

"They're suspicious of my American upbringing, although," he added bitterly, "the fact that my family was interned has improved my reliability in their view.

"They don't like my American past, but they love my American medical training.

"Anyway...

"This is not why I had you come here."

He rose from his chair, and paced the office, then took her chin and tilted her face to the light.

"You have a scar," he said, and added with a strange look. "I actually like the fact I've left my mark on you."

"What is does," Kate snapped back, "is make me remember what you are capable of."

He was drunk that day, he smiled, it didn't happen often.

He tugged at her coif to remove it, and dropped it to the floor, and unpinned her hair, letting it tumble to her shoulders and looked at it thoughtfully.

"I've always liked redheads," he mused. "There was this girl, in high school... Louise, her name was. Louise Barlowe. She was nice."

He walked over to the window and peered out, speaking to the view outside.

"Okay.

"This is how it's going to be.

"You are going to be available for me whenever I want you.

"You will assist in some of my surgeries — you might actually enjoy that, I think, you'll certainly learn a lot.

"But you will also spend the day or the evening with me whenever and wherever I say.

"I don't want to hear that you've gone gallivanting to the beach or wherever you were last week.

"Do you understand?"

Kate's hands clenched on her purse.

"Or?" she countered.

He turned back to face her, and spoke coldly.

"Well, for one thing, I know that you're American, passing

yourself off as Irish.

"For another, I also know who your husband is, and that he was wanted by the Kempetai.

"So far, the Kempetai itself doesn't seem to have made the link, probably because your marriage wasn't registered in Thailand, only at the British and American Embassies."

"Then how did you find out?"

"Eddy told me, remember?

"He even told me your husband's name. Lawrence Gallet. Journalist.

"It was easy to check."

Fumbling in her purse, she drew out a handkerchief to give herself time to think what to say and twisted it in her hands.

"My husband left me," she replied quietly, mentally asking Lawrence's forgiveness for the lie, and dabbed at her eyes for added effect, "and left me without anything, you also must know that."

Akira frowned.

"No, I didn't know. Belinda just said he was mobilized."

"She didn't want to advertise the fact that I'm ... what? A poor fool?

"I guess Lawrence may be mobilized by now, but he left before.

"He fled Bangkok without me, and I've no idea where he is."

War-time marriages, he mock-sighed. What did she expect?

Also, Doctor Sumet, her friend Belinda and herself were involved in helping British internees.

"You gave us the way to help," she replied furiously, "we have it in writing."

Ah, yes. He laughed.

"I was investigating on my own, you see, and once my suspicions are confirmed, I could have the good Mr Long Bang or whatever his name is arrested, and the doctor who is interned with Belinda's Eddy, and Belinda's Eddy himself transferred to a prison camp where, believe, the living conditions are far from comfortable.

"How long d'you think Eddy would last? I'd give him a week, at most.

"Doctor Sumet, I fear, is untouchable, his family is too well known here.

"But in any case, imagine the praise I'd get for discovering this conspiracy to help enemy internees... It would certainly improve my standing.

"You see, I've thought it all out."

She looked down at her lap.

"There's a word for what you doing, you know, and it's not a pretty one.

"Blackmail."

He moved as fast as a cat over to her, and grabbed her hair, twisting it to force her face back.

"It's not a word I'd care to use myself, and I advise you not to," he snarled very low, so close she could feel his breath on her cheek.

"Friendly pressure, perhaps, might be better."

She nodded, then waited till he had released her before giving him a vicious smile.

"I wonder if there's any one who might try to help your family being put under similar... friendly pressure...That would make things even, wouldn't it?"

The stinging slap to her cheek came as she expected, almost before she had said the last words, but it was not as violent as the last time, and she knew it would leave no bruise.

She got up from her chair and turned to the door. "That's enough. I want to leave, now."

"Ah, Kate, Kate," he chided her, "our business is not over. Take off your clothes."

No. She backed against the wall. No, she repeated defiantly.

"No?" he asked in a silky voice, walking up to her slowly.

Grabbing her hair once more, he forced her mouth open under his.

Eyes closed, her whole body braced against his weight Kate steeled herself not to fight him, to remain as stiff as wood. As ice.

She could not afford to make him angrier than he was.

Then he pushed her away with disgust — for her, for him? she wondered.

"No. You're right. I'm not in the mood for rape.

"You'll come to me of your own will."

She glared, her eyes wild.

"I won't."

"Oh yes, you will. You'll see."

Stepping back, he looked her up and down.

"That cheek barely shows, it will be gone by the time you get back.

"But the memory? It will linger.

"Not a word to Belinda and Sumet, you understand?

"Make sure they keep on sending parcels to Eddy, or I'll find out.

"Understand?"

She nodded dumbly, still astonished at the lightning changes in him.

"The car will take you back now.

"I'll let you know when I want you again."

She turned away, still half expecting to be grabbed once more, but he had already returned to the papers on his desk.

Snatching her coif and her purse, she schooled herself to breathe deeply, not to slam the door, not run down the stairs, to wait until she was in the car before she allowed a few tears to come quietly, and bit her lips not to give in to the sobs that were partly fear and partly relief.

She just wiped her cheeks and stared out of the window, and let his words play back, again and again, in her mind, and gradually, her resolution hardened.

She would go to him when he wanted, she knew, because she had no choice.

If she needed to pretend, if that were her only hope to see this war out, then she would pretend.

She would tell Belinda only a small part of what had happened.

Despite the relative safety of being Irish, Belinda remained vulnerable, because she was a woman, because she loved Eddy, and because Eddy was at risk.

Nonetheless, she needed to be told that Kate was to become, when all was said and done, Akira's slave.

If something were to happen to her, Belinda would best know how to explain it to Lawrence.

But someone should be told the whole story.

If only because, as Ken Akira had said, he was untouchable, and also, because she trusted him to keep a cool mind and measure the threat against them all, she would tell Doctor Sumet.

"He what?" Belinda gasped.

Eyes closed, leaning exhausted against her pillow, Kate wearily repeated Akira's bargain.

Her safety against her companionship.

"Well I never," Belinda sputtered. "The conniving sleeveen! To think I ever said he seemed nice."

"You're also the one who said you'd speak English with him till the cows come home," Kate reminded her with a bitter half-smile. "Well, that's what I'm going to have to do."

"Holy Mother, I do talk too much at times, and live to regret it," Belinda shook her head in despair. "Do you think it means we should stop sending parcels to Eddy, then?"

No, why should it?

"Remember what Sumet said?" Kate reminded her. "By telling us how to do it, Akira put himself at risk as much as us. You have his letter, remember?"

"Yes, that's true." Belinda exhaled, reassured.

"Let's start planning the next parcel, then," Kate suggested, "And put in that jar of marmalade we brought back from Hua Hin. He'll like that."

And then she added, taking Belinda's hand, rough and reddened as hers was by the many washings with lye soap and alcohol.

"You do realize, don't you, that it will be more than speaking English with him?

"You *do* know that?"

Belinda nodded in silence, grimly.

"You'll explain it to Lawrence if ... somehow... I mean, I don't know..."

"There'll be nothing to explain," Belinda answered stoutly.

"War is war, men survive as they can, and women do too."

Sumet listened gravely, without interrupting.

She spared him no detail, the slap, the order to undress, the threats against them all.

Once Kate had finished, he remained very still, eyes closed, his chin resting on his steepled fingers. When at last he spoke, the words seemed dragged out of a bottomless well of pain.

"A horrifying burden has been placed on you, Khun Kate, and I am powerless to help."

Kate laughed bitterly.

There was no help, except to keep living as they did, and perhaps to be more careful.

And to remember if ever Lawrence came back for her, and she were no longer there...

"I am going to say something that will shock you, perhaps.

"But much as I grieve for you, I also grieve for Captain Akira."

Kate mouth tightened.

"I wish I could have as much sympathy, Doctor.

"But I agree, if this awful war hadn't happened, he would be happily furthering his career in California instead of beating up defenceless women.

"As it is, he's trapped, and has trapped me with him."

And this prison camp that Akira had threatened Eddy with, did he himself know of it?

Sumet's eyes clouded.

Yes, unfortunately.

It was living hell for the inmates, who were all prisoners-of-war captured in Malaya, Singapore and Burma.

They worked in the blazing sun and the pouring rain, breaking rocks, with hardly any food and no medical care. Some of them had been described to him as walking skeletons. They were beaten and tortured, and the weakest were shot or left to die.

Villagers from nearby observed it in secret, and reported on what they saw through the network of temples in the area.

"Monks travel unhindered, still, and the news reaches us here in Bangkok.

"But you will forgive me if I say no more."

Kate raised both hands, as if to ward off the horrible image he had conjured.

She wanted to hear no more.

"We must keep Eddy out of that place, then," she shuddered, "but whatever I can do to help..."

Once alone, Sumet covered his eyes with his hands, feeling the agony of his powerlessness.

Was anybody somewhere in his country trying to combat the rule of Field-Marshal Phibul and the hold the Japanese had on him?

If so, he didn't know.

What he did know was that there were Thai armed forces marching into combat in Burma side by side with Japanese troops, in fact, one of his two Thai colleagues at the hospital had been drafted, and he himself was now expected to fill in for him.

His mother often spoke approvingly of one of her friends' sons, Charun Rattanakun, with whom he had often played as a child, before their studies had sent them on different paths.

Charun was now a Lieutenant-General, his mother, Khun Pensri, said with an admiring look, and was to head the army that would be invading Burma.

Kulap, Charun's mother was beyond proud — "perhaps even a bit annoying about it, as if having a son who is a famous surgeon were nothing."

From England where he was studying medicine, Sumet had heard about Charun joining in Khana Ratsadon and could still remember the envy he had felt at the courage and commitment of his childhood friend.

They still met occasionally at family functions, weddings, funerals, and the last time — it was for the funeral prayers of one of his aunts — they had spoken about the need to recover the territories lost to France, and Charun had gently chided Sumet for still working for the French hospital.

"I work for them, because they work for the poor.

"Don't you believe that those who have no money are nonetheless entitled to the best care?" Sumet had replied defensively.

"Ah, spoken as a good, true Buddhist," Charun laughed, slapping him on the shoulder, with perhaps a shade of condescension. "Well, I guess we work for all the Thai people in our different way."

Sumet sighed.

The papers were full of pictures of happy soldiers marching, Thai banners flying, but what the newspapers did not show was the dull, grim mood of the street, the lines to buy ever more expensive rice and vegetables, now that the Japanese appropriated the lion's share of the country's food.

But yes, he needed to admit, beyond the grumbling and the resentment, many Thais were cheering their army, their soldiers, the new, strong, martial, Thailand whose place in the world was by the side of the seemingly all-powerful, all victorious Japanese, defeating the white man come in from the west with gunboats, rifles and priests, and who for many years treated Asia as a land whose riches were to be exploited, and whose people were to be enslaved.

They were cheering the advent of a new order in the world, and a reversal — a correction, really, of the past, using the weapons the West had taught them to master, be they political theories, planes or machine-guns.

Sumet remembered his own elation when Pridi and Phibul and the other Promoters proclaimed the end of absolute monarchy and the advent of Khana Ratsadon.

But, despite approaches made by friends to join in shaping a new, more modern Thailand, he had kept out of the world of politics, content in the knowledge that he, too, was helping his country.

Well, he could no longer stay on the side-lines now, cutting and stitching and swabbing.

He needed to act, in his own way.

And to start, he would purloin from the pharmacy whatever drug or supply might be spared — anti-malarial and anti-diarrheal pills, perhaps were the most desperately needed — and contact the monks who might know how they could be smuggled to the living scarecrows in the hell of that camp near Kanchanaburi.

And brave, unfortunate Kate might be able to use Captain Akira's perverse but obviously powerful infatuation with her to get her hands on more.

From that evil, some good might come.

Chapter XXII

The monsoon rains had come, and flooded everything, turning whatever path or unmetalled road that may have existed into a river of viscous, red mud.

Lawrence kept his mind on his feet, as he struggled to lift each one out of the clinging, sticky sludge that came up almost to his knees, and kept his eyes on the man ahead to help lift him if he stumbled, or, as he had yesterday, and shuddered to remember, just push him out of the way, when it appeared that shivering and teeth chattering from malaria, the poor guy would not, could not, take a step more.

The rain came down in stinging, pelting bursts, Lawrence tried to tighten the hood of the oilskin cape he had been issued with before they had left Maymyo, two weeks — or was it almost three weeks? — ago.

He no longer wore his glasses when he marched, they were worse than useless as they always fogged up, and he needn't see much further away than the man in front.

He too shivered from what he assumed was malaria, he knew he had a fever, just from the way his mind circled in delirious whirls and he gripped the little pouch containing the quinine and opium and sulpha powder the SOE had given him in Malaya last year.

When they finally stopped at dark, he would find someplace hidden to dose himself, and smiled grimly, realizing that he had become, as they all had, nothing more than a selfish creature intent on his own survival.

So far, he had refrained from using his cache of medication, thinking himself somehow immune from the stealthy perils of the jungle and its hidden, lethal inhabitants, focussing instead on the more visible ones, the snakes, or worse, the tigers and bears preying on the weak, so weak, columns of men walking dazedly towards India and salvation.

Wild animals and disease weren't the only deadly hazards they had to deal with. Dacoits roamed the jungle, as silent and as pitiless as tigers, and sprang to attack and kill the hated British and steal the rifles from the soldiers and the gold and jewels the women carried twisted in a strip of cloth across their body.

For the groups fighting their way out of the green hell were not just made of soldiers, but there were also women and children, although, there were fewer and fewer children...

Some of those who died from dysentery and fever were left behind in scratched out shallow graves with nothing but a bamboo cross to mark the site, but others fell behind and simply vanished, and the mothers trudged forwards, bent with grief, carrying those who still survived, or chose to remain either in the few small towns they passed on the way, or in the evacuation camps the retreating army had hastily sent up, to nurse those who were still alive.

Like everything else in Burma, Lawrence reflected, relieved to note his brain was still able to think although his thoughts were an ever-repeating nightmare, those camps were ill-conceived, poorly equipped with little food and hardly any shelter, and embodied the "too little, too late" policy that had been the trademark of all the events that had brought him here, his shirt rotting on his back, his stomach growling with hunger and his guts wrenching from the poisoned water he drank from the muddy streams encountered on the way.

The column he had been assigned to walk with, the Burma Rifles, was under orders to continue to walk, no matter what.

No stopping for civilians, no sharing of rations, although he, and other soldiers, had often relented and either carried a child on their backs for a few hours, or given a handful of rice or strip of dried meat for a woman to divide up between herself and her children.

They had reached sharp, steep, mountain ranges, and scrambled up, clinging to roots, sliding down, shirts torn and bellies scratched and scraped by rocks, and doggedly fighting their way back up. The nights had grown colder and the rains as well.

"Where are we?" he asked the Lieutenant Foster, the officer who commanded his group.

"Buggered if I know," the man answered. "West of the Japs, I guess and closer to the Tamu pass, if these blasted mountains are anything to go by."

The man couldn't have been more than twenty-five, Lawrence thought, but he looked about fifty, gaunt, bearded, hollow-eyed, his hair grown long and matted — just like himself, he supposed.

"Then if we're close to Tamu, how long d'you reckon we'll need to get to India?" a sergeant chimed in.

The young officer shrugged. Depended on the mountains. On the rain.

"On how fast you fellows can walk, or how much time you spend squatting behind bushes."

And then, his voice dragging each word out, with transparent pain, he asked.

"How many have we lost today?"

"Twenty, twenty-five?" the sergeant replied, starkly. "Maybe more. Just have to wait, there were still some chaps climbing after dark, but... you never know, they might catch up. Or not."

The makeshift camp they had struck on a plateau just below the craggy peak was so wet, with water dripping from leaves, that it was difficult to keep the small fires going long enough to brew tea and cook enough rice for tonight and to be eaten cold tomorrow, but still, as opposed to the first week of their march in the plains and rice fields, with the thick cloud cover and dense canopy of trees there was no danger anymore of being seen by Japanese planes who dropped bombs on the retreating forces.

In fact, it had been some days since they'd last heard the ominous noise of the Kawasaki bombers above them.

After days of walking in the huge mass of tanks, jeeps, people, bicycles, native amahs pushing prams, bullock carts loaded with the flotsam and jetsam of life — sewing machines, clocks, furniture and mirrors — and hitting the ground to seek some shelter to avoid being strafed by Zero fighter planes, the order had come that they were to take a more Northern route, to try to reach the Tamu pass faster by passing through the Naga hills on a less travelled track.

Would it truly be faster? Lawrence wondered. And was it worth it, losing more men to the jungle than to the Japanese airplanes?

Foster doubted it as well, but had no choice but to obey.

"Fucking army," he muttered. "Ours not to wonder why.

Also," he added, "the powers that be claim there are so many cases of cholera in the column that however many soldiers are killed this route, it will be less than we'd lose to cholera."

A sobering thought, but Lawrence had stopped trying to get to know the men who marched with him, after Tony, a brittle little lance-corporal from Spitalfields who was an avid birdwatcher and animal lover and a Socialist, died in front of him, his body almost split in half by Japanese machine gun bullets from the sky, when he crawled out from the shelter of the bullock cart they'd dived under.

"Look. That dog there, that spaniel, someone's lost it. I've got to catch it before..."

He'd just grabbed the cowering, whimpering, dog when he was strafed, his guts spilling out, and blood pouring from a mouth still open to croon reassurance to the animal, who was killed in his arms.

Lawrence faced was splashed with blood — Tony's, the dog's? — and retched for an hour afterwards.

Or Welsh Peter Evans whom they'd left by the roadside, weakened and emaciated from dysentery and unable to take another step.

"Dunno why they sent me to ruddy Burma," he kept on saying, "trained for the desert I was. You see any desert here?"

Or young Sylvester from Birmingham, who had walked by his side for over a week, talking incessantly about how he would get an education, go to university when all this was over, "I swear I'll make something of meself, not end up in a smelting shop like me Dad."

His own great-grandfather, Lawrence had told him, started life as a smelter and made a fortune of it.

"Ye don't say?" Sylvester's eyes were shiny with hope. "Then imagine what I can do with an education!"

Sylvester fell from a ledge, broke his leg, and was left behind, with his gun by his side if the Japs got to him before any kindly villager did. They couldn't carry stretchers up these tracks.

No, Lawrence didn't want to make friends with any of them again, not even this ghost of a lieutenant from Oxfordshire via Sandhurst who was doing his utmost to keep them all alive, and knew the name and the story of all the soldiers he was charged to bring to safety, and jollied, threatened and urged them along.

Anyway, they couldn't talk, they kept whatever breath they had to climb, and walk, and slide and curse.

What instinct kept them going, he wondered.

It couldn't be hope of survival – he knew, they all knew, that they would most probably die at the next cliff edge or be unable to rise, racked with fever and drained by dysentery at the next stop. And he realized he, for his part, had stopped caring. He just went on, and on, because his body gave him no choice. Or perhaps, he thought at times, he was already dead, and this was the hell the priests of his childhood had promised all sinners.

When he dreamt, it was never of Kate or their golden days in Bangkok, but of Welsh Peter or Tony from Spitalfields bursting open a foot away from him.

And of food, the nursery food of his early days, and he woke longing for pudding and apple tart with custard and ate his cold rice and chewed on his dried beef with tears in his eyes.

They had no tents, but contrived to create some shelter by draping their rain capes across low branches and spread out their canvas ground sheets.

"What's the first thing you're going to do when we reach India, Gallet?" Foster asked sleepily, his head propped on his pack, and then continued without waiting for an answer, "Me, I'm going to have a huge whisky. Then a hot bath and a shave. But the whisky first."

Lawrence was removing the leeches on his legs by lighting twigs and applying them to force the blood-gorged horrors to drop off. The burns hurt like hell, but it was better than getting even more suppurating sores on his flesh.

He closed his eyes. "The same, I guess. And get hold of dry clothes."

The officer laughed shortly. "Yes, dry clothes.

"I always used to take dry clothes for granted. Now, as you heard, they're not even the first thing to come to mind."

The jungle night sounds were oddly familiar from those weeks of training in Malaya, but that didn't make them any more reassuring. The small fires would keep the tigers and bears at bay, but the mosquitoes buzzed close to the flames.

And although he found the climbing easier than most, never had he carried such weight, or walked in such razor sharp hills, or made his way under a waterfall by inching forward sideways on a slippery two-foot-wide ledge, his back pressed against the rock cliff full of jutting sharp spurs, or waded skidding and sliding up to his waist through swift, eddying, muddy torrents, his pack held high over his head.

The cliff ledge had cost them a mule, who'd plunged, howling with panic, into the rushing waters and they powerlessly watched it disappear, black head bobbing between the boulders and braying its terror until they could no longer hear it.

"And there go two weeks' worth of rice and bully beef" Foster just said despondently. "Keep going."

The two mules who had survived thus far and were laden with their radio — useless in such weather and with such tree cover — and spare ammunition, and the rifles taken from the soldiers they had lost on the way — whinnied gently when they were tied to a tree, but they were not pulling at their ropes or acting agitated at the scent of any predator.

So, for now at least, they were relatively safe.

He shifted to find a more comfortable position and ease his aching shoulders, wondering what he might jettison to make his pack lighter, but couldn't think of anything — he had no change of clothes only the torn and rotting uniform he wore, he needed his typewriter, Heaven only knew if he'd be able to procure one when — if — he made it to India.

The gold sewn into the lining of his survival pouch seemed heavier with each step he'd taken, and if this march were to last much longer, he would just throw it away. Much like the silver candlesticks and tea-sets he'd seen dumped by the side of the road by the retreating planters' wives along with feathered hats, high-heeled shoes and toys. So many toys...

Still, he'd hang on to that gold as long as he could, it would be invaluable if they needed to bribe someone — who? a Naga head hunter, perhaps? — he asked himself ironically.

When the morning light came, and if the rains eased a bit, he'd forage for something to eat — his jungle training had taught him that some ferns were edible, along with wild ginger buds or some bamboo shoots.

"Yuv'got to eat yer greens". The Yorkshire sergeant's voice came back to him.

"Other, you'se going to lose your teeth, got it, and get ulcers in your mouth, and those'll go sceptic and you die. Got it?"

He despaired of getting any one else to chew on a raw fern, but the mules, at least, would be grateful.

Day followed night followed day, and the rains relented at times, but too rarely, and with clear skies came the Zeroes, forcing them to take cover under the tall canopy of trees.

Lawrence discovered the foot rot he'd had for days had worsened. At the next stream, during what the soldiers called the "squits stop", he removed his boots to bathe his feet in the clear water, dried them as best he could in the pale sun and sprinkled some of his precious store of sulpha powder on the painful, oozing, cracks between his toes.

He couldn't afford to let the infection spread, not now, not when they were so close.

The malarial fever had not recurred, so perhaps the daily atabrine had helped, or perhaps it was not malaria after all.

The dysentery was perhaps the worse, though, and he ruefully tried to remember when he'd lost the instinct to try for some privacy and look for a bush to squat behind when his bowels turned to water — was it when he stopped minding when he saw the others helplessly shitting themselves in full view?

He was staring mindlessly at the water, just enjoying the feel of the sun and the firm dry rock that was his seat when the lieutenant came running, his ragged uniform flapping around his scarecrow body.

"We got the radio to work. We're about ten miles away, no more, but the Japs are hot on our tails, through the plains, with tanks.

"Get going, everyone!

"We've got to make it to Tamu before we get cut off."

LAWRENCE'S DIARY
JUNE 15TH 1942, IMPHAL, INDIA

I'd always wanted to visit India...

Here I am.

The last ten days have been a haze of relief and food and sleep, and they all seem to blur into each other, much as the days of marching did.

The last thing I clearly will always remember is reaching Tamu at last, the scenes of panic as the crowds were separated into groups — whites on one side, Burmese and Indians on another, every single man, woman and child in filthy rags, thin and ailing children crying, and everyone howling with rage and despair — and made to wait, while soldiers were marched through at double pace.

Looking back over my shoulder, I saw them trickling through, one by one and step by step, and wondered how many had died on the way.

Shall we ever know?

As we walked one way, we passed jeeps and tanks and troops on foot going the other, eying us with what could only have been terror, seeing what the Burma campaign has wrought so far.

The walk was interminable until we were once again divided.

"Officers, you've got jeeps waiting. Who're you? Press?

"With the officers, I suppose."

I would like to be able to say I did as Lieutenant Foster, who adamantly refused to be parted from those with whom I'd come this far, but I gratefully collapsed onto the seat of one of the waiting jeeps, with just a despondent and rather ashamed wave of farewell.

There was a stop at a town called Manipur, which was completely overrun with ragged and famished refugees, both Indian and English, and there were civilians to greet us — I learned later that they were planters and their wives, and also Indians, handing out clay mugs of tea and balls of sweetened rice.

Tea has never tasted so good.

In Imphal, there was some kind of makeshift tented camp, again not enough for even a fraction of the refugees.

The military seem utterly overwhelmed by the mass of the exodus from Burma, and, understandably, more intent on defending the border than on opening their arms to us.

I, as they say "was sorted" on arrival, handed a makeshift much-laundered but blissfully dry uniform and assigned a charpoy in an old school building taken over for the duration, the Johnstone School it is called. The students, one assumes, have been evacuated to someplace safer.

"You can give your dirty clothes to the dhobi," I was told with a sniff by the quartermaster, an Indian Army corporal when I was shown my room.

A dhobi, he added, as I clutched my new clothes and looked dazedly at the bed, the sheets, the ceiling fan, is the servant in charge of laundry.

He sniffed again. "Actually, I think it might be better if they were burned, don't you think?"

I realized that I must stink even worse than I'd imagined.

I stripped and dropped my mud and blood and excrement stained clothes to the floor, then sat on the bed, trying and failing to collect my thoughts. There was water to wash — though not hot, not the bath Foster dreamt of, just a vat of chilly water and a dipper. It was utter luxury.

And beer, ice-cold beer was available at the mess, to where I was told to get myself double-quick and then to HQ to inform whoever might be interested that I was still alive.

"But have a pint first. And some food."

The curry was made with some unrecognizable meat, goat, perhaps?

But it was hot, and it was delicious.

HQ was an exercise in averting chaos and failing, but somehow, I managed to get a harassed-looking female corporal to accept that I was a bona fide correspondent and to send a cable to AP, and then, as an afterthought, I also asked her to inform SOE Meerut that I'd made it to India at last.

"SOE, really?" she repeated with a broad Scots accent, pushing her spectacles up her nose. "Well, if you're sure..."

Obviously, I didn't look like her idea of a Special Operations Executive.

She refused, however, to let me send a telegram to my parents — no personal communications allowed. "We're swamped as it is," she admitted.

"But you can try the Post Office," she added helpfully.

"A telegram could get through."

And then I went back to my little cell of a room and slept for hours, repeating like a mantra, " I'm alive. I'm still alive."

Chapter XXIII

It was just a restaurant at first.

A messenger on a motorcycle delivered a note. "From Captain Doctor Akira," he managed to say in diffident English, with what Kate thought was a measuring and contemptuous smirk. "Needs nurse."

The letter was terse.

"Pick you up 8pm, for dinner."

"And that," Kate told Belinda in a resigned voice after unfolding the paper and reading it out loud, "is that."

But," she added, "if he thinks I'm going to get all dolled up for him, he's in for a disappointment."

Her only effort was to put on a clean uniform, without the pinafore and coif, her hair pulled back in a severe knot, and her face bare of make-up.

When he bounded up the steps up the hospital, he looked her up and down, frowning. "That's what you wear for dinner?"

The messenger said Doctor Akira needed a nurse, she replied coldly.

She was dressed as a nurse.

"Don't you have anything else to wear? We're going to a restaurant."

"No. Not really."

He pushed past her. "Where's your room? Let's see."

Sighing, she showed him the way, and watched as he went through her closet, pushing aside the two plain cotton frocks she used on her days off.

"These won't do," he turned back to her, annoyed. "Where are the clothes you wore when you went out with your rich husband?"

"Back at the house where we lived," she snapped. "I have no use for them now. Anyways, I didn't know this was a date.

"I thought you just wanted your pound of flesh."

He glared and took a step forward, and she flinched,

remembering the stinging slap to her face, and relented, teeth clenched. She must control her temper, she repeated silently, she must try not to anger him.

"All right. I'll borrow something off Belinda. Just wait here."

Belinda still had all those garish, printed frocks from her nights of dancing with Eddy, and rummaging through her friend's wardrobe, she picked up the bright green silk from Filene's.

How perfect, she thought. A cheap looking outfit from the days when I didn't know any better.

She returned to the room, and saw him lounging on her bed. He'd opened the drawer of her table and was reading her old letters from home.

"Who is this Mother Felicity?" he asked idly, as she stood there, staring at him in shocked and speechless anger.

"The nun who brought me up," she finally managed to reply, blessing her caution for having left Lawrence's farewell message with the papers in Thip's safe. "And how dare you read my letters?"

Just making sure she wasn't doing anything forbidden, he leered.

"No letters from hubby, I see."

"He left me, I've already told you, why would he write to me?" she answered wearily. "Would you get out, now, so I can change?"

He shook his head. No, he'd stay right here. "You can change in front of me, I'm a doctor, remember?

"That's a pretty dress, by the way. Goes with your colouring."

She turned her back to him, fumbling with the buttons of her starched uniform, and dropped it to the floor, then quickly slipped the green dress over her head, aware of his gaze, ashamed of her plain and serviceable bra and underpants, and furious with herself for feeling ashamed.

"You're very thin," he announced reprovingly. "You need to be fed up."

What I need, she dared not retort, is to be left alone, but she buttoned the tiny silk covered buttons, and finally turned back to face him.

He eyed her critically. "That's better. Now some make up? And let your hair loose."

She narrowed her eyes. "Yes, some powder, perhaps? To cover that scar you gave me."

He laughed gently. "That scar is useful, Kate darling, to remind you that you had better do as I say."

And then, with one of his abrupt changes that she found so disconcerting, he added, "Listen, this doesn't have to be a battle between us. There's enough war going on out there. Just see it as a date, like you said. Okay?"

She sighed. Okay.

When they were leaving, they crossed Belinda in the hallway, who gave Kate a wide-eyed, astonished look, but greeted Ken Akira with simulated friendliness.

"Any news from Eddy?" he asked her genially.

"Oh no, I think he doesn't dare send any, but we know he gets his parcels," she gushed. "All thanks to you. I'm ever so grateful, I am."

He smiled back. Well, he was first and foremost a doctor, and he didn't like to see people like Eddy who'd done nothing wrong suffer unfairly.

"I'll see if I can get my hands on something for his heart," he added.

Belinda stared at him, with sudden tears in her eyes. "Could you? Really?"

Perhaps. He'd try.

Belinda stood on tiptoe and kissed his cheek, while Kate gritted her teeth. How dare he use her love for Eddy?

"Kate, you look lovely. Have a good time," she called back to them.

"Oh, we will," he assured her. "We will."

The restaurant, thankfully, was none of the fancy ones, not the Oriental, or the Royal, just a plain, middle-class kind of place near the new Democracy Monument, where families went, and that served excellent Thai dishes and mediocre Western food.

She looked around. There were no Japanese, at least none in uniform, and she wondered out loud about it.

"Do you think I want to be seen eating out with you?" he asked in a dejected voice. "Like I said, I'm not trusted. But let's not talk about that now, all right. Just try to enjoy the meal.

"Speaking of which, I can't eat all that spicy stuff," he told her as he was perusing the menu.

"I'll just have a steak."

It wouldn't be very good, she warned him.

There was no frozen meat from Australia any more, it would probably be buffalo. Why not have a grilled fish instead? She could ask the cook not to use chillies.

He laughed. "Who might have thought that steak would be a victim of war? Tell you the truth, I'm a bit fed up with fish.

"I mean, I grew up on Japanese food, and I like it, but I miss a plain American steak, or hamburger. What about you?"

She could not help grinning. "Me too. The other day, Belinda was asking me what I craved, and I said a chicken sandwich. On white bread. And a Coke."

He closed his eyes in longing remembrance. "Yeah, a Coke and a sandwich at a drugstore counter.

"So tell me, why were you brought up by a nun?"

Once again, she felt unsettled by how comfortable it was to talk to him, to tell him about South Boston, the convent, her brothers.

It was strange, he was matter-of-fact about it, it wasn't like telling Lawrence who seemed to view her life as an exotic and romantic, if grim, story, and when he said, at the end, "You poor kid. But you were lucky to have someone take care of you all, someone who knew and loved your mother. And at least you were able to graduate high school, and go to nursing school after that," she felt that he understood what it was like to have overcome all those barriers, to try and make it out of poverty — Lawrence never could have, growing up so wealthy and spoiled and adored.

She was almost beginning to enjoy herself, or at least to let down her guard, when he asked, cutting his tough and overcooked meat. "So, what's the story with your husband?"

She put her fork and knife down and looked at him levelly.

"We met. We fell in love. Or at least I did. He just thought he did.

"But then, I didn't measure up.

"He's rich, he's educated, he could have married anybody, but there were very few single girls in Bangkok, and, I don't know, I guess he wanted me, and being the good Catholic girl that I am, he couldn't have me without marriage.

"So...

"Well, after a few months, I suppose he became a bit ashamed of me, I don't know which fork to use, or play tennis, or whatever rich girls are supposed to know. I think his parents were pretty mad, too.

"We began to fight – over everything.

"When the war came, it was a godsend for him.

"He just slipped away, saying he was going to visit an old relative up in Chiang Mai, and never came back.

"I knew, I could tell it was nothing but an excuse.

"I mean, he'd taken his passport, his typewriter, why would he have needed his typewriter if he was only going away for a few days?

"I never heard from him again."

Her voice trailed off, and she blinked away tears.

She was starting to almost believe the tale she was telling, and after all, some of it was true, wasn't it?

Had she ever really thought that she was good enough for Lawrence, and that his family would accept her?

She sighed.

"I stayed in the house where we lived, at first, with that Thai family. I think they felt sorry for me.

"They were nice, especially the old lady, Khunying Thip. I really like her, but she's sick, now, she has diabetes.

"We can get hold of insulin now, but if ever...? Do you think...?"

He nodded. "Probably shouldn't be a problem. We treat Thai diabetics at the free clinics with insulin, I can get hold of some."

She smiled her thanks.

"And what about you?" she asked. "I know you're from San Francisco, but what was it like, being seen as Japanese?

"In Boston, we were seen as Irish first, Americans second."

He nodded, and drank some of his beer – she'd kept to lemon juice, she knew she needed to remain absolutely clear headed.

"It was the same for us. At least you people speak English at home.

"When your parents go meet with your teachers at school, and you can see them struggling to be understood... and you have the feeling that everyone is making fun of them, it's tough.

"But otherwise, being a Nisei — that's what we call a second-generation Japanese — was okay, there were enough of us at school not to get picked on by bullies. And we all knew how to fight.

"And Japanese families' expectations of school performance are just so high that we were all really good students, and the teachers loved us."

He grinned suddenly. "Difficult to date, though.

"Nisei girls were totally off-limits — their parents don't let them go out — and American girls, well, that many didn't want to date a Jap.

"In medical school, however, it all changed.

"Nurses throw themselves at interns — sorry, don't make that face, I'm pretty sure that doesn't happen in Catholic maternity hospitals, but in teaching hospitals, you've no idea.

"Well, there were quite a few Japanese nurses, and every nurse wants to marry a doctor... So I had a pretty good time.

"Have you ever been to San Francisco?"

Kate nodded. She'd spent almost a week there, waiting to board her ship to Bangkok. "I was put up in a convent, everything arranged by the Sisters of Saint-Paul. But I managed to do some sight-seeing, take a trolley, visit China Town. The ocean looks so different from the Atlantic, so much — bluer, I guess. It's a beautiful city."

"Yes, it is.

"Of course, there are so many Chinese there that lots of people, we, the Japanese, I mean, we were lumped in with them, and they couldn't tell the difference. Even some of our teachers in high school."

He pushed his steak away, and made a face. "You were right, it's not very good. Never had buffalo before, and I guess this wasn't a young one.

"What's the matter, why are you looking at me that way?

She shook her head. "I was wondering what happens next."

He stared back.

What happened next was that he was going to take her back to his room and make love to her.

"I've rented a place off Sriphaya Road away from my barracks — we're not allowed to bring women back, and anyways, like I've said, I can't afford to be seen with a white girl."

"Make love to me," she repeated sarcastically. "Rape me, you mean."

He shrugged. That was up to her.

She sighed. "Listen. I enjoyed this dinner, well...

"Yes, actually, I did. But that doesn't mean I want to go to bed with you."

But she would, when she remembered the alternative, he replied calmly.

"You would actually give me up to the Kempetai? I don't believe you."

Ah, yes...

But was she willing to bet her life on it?

She sat back and crossed her arms. With a deep breath, she decided, as he'd just dared her, to bet her life on it.

"You said I would come to you. Make me want to.

"You know girls like me don't go to bed after a first date. Let's see how the second one goes."

He burst out laughing.

"With a corsage maybe?

"Not a chance, sweetheart...

"Let's get the bill and go."

Walking back to his jeep, he held her hand very tightly as if she'd might break away and run from him, and said nothing as he drove through the streets with jerky, abrupt stops to let late-night buses pass and finally pulled up to a shopfront house.

She looked around wildly at the people on the sidewalk gathered around a noodle vendor, but they all turned their gaze away from the man in uniform with his farang doxy, and anyway, she thought in despair, what could they have done to help?

His fingers dug into her arm as he propelled her through a dark doorway and up narrow steep stairs.

He fished into his pocket for his key, pushed the door open, then shoved her inside the damp smelling room.

In the gloom, lit only though the single window by the street outside, with flickering red and blue from neon lights, she could make out the shape of a bed and a couple of chairs and a table.

"Where's the goddam switch?" he muttered, feeling his way. "Ah, here it is."

With the dim glow of the single bulb hanging from the ceiling, it was even worse than she thought.

"Nice place," she sneered. "Is this the best you could do?"

He sat down at the table, and poured himself a glass of whisky from the bottle he had obviously brought earlier, along with a couple of glasses and a bunch of mangosteens.

"So. Plucky Kate is back I see," he replied in the same tone. "And to answer your question, yes, it is the best I could do. What were you expecting? The Oriental Hotel, maybe?"

She froze. Those words... "What were you expecting? The Oriental Hotel?" Lawrence's voice, gentle and teasing came back to her, and she backed away from this man in his hated uniform, who was stretching his hand out to her.

"Come here."

"No. No. I can't." Her voice rose to a shriek. "Don't you understand?

"I can't!"

When he grabbed her arm and twisted it behind her, she struggled, and pushed him off, and in her panic and rage, she could no longer feel the pull on her hair, and the buttons torn from her dress, when he threw her on the bed.

Writhing and scratching, she bit his shoulder, and for every blow to her face she tried to return one, still panting and biting when he covered her mouth with his to quiet her.

Then she gave up struggling because she knew it was useless now and she yielded to that kiss that was neither brutal nor painful, just the kiss of a man who truly wants the woman in his arms.

And God save her, her naked body was responding to his, and her body had become her enemy as well.

Sobbing quietly into the grimy pillow, she swatted his hand away when he tried to kiss the nape of her neck and slowly caressed her sweaty back.

He turned and sat up, laughing quietly.

"Well, that wasn't so bad, was it?"

"I hate you," she whispered.

He laughed again. "It didn't feel that way to me. It seems all you needed was a bit of rough courting. Let me take a look at your face."

She raised her head and stared at him angrily.

It would not be too bad, she could feel his slaps were only

meant to subdue her, and he'd avoided hitting near her eyes or her mouth.

"I bet it looks better than yours," she spat. "I'm just sorry my fingernails are so short."

There was a cloudy mirror on the wall and he went to look. "Thank God you're a surgical nurse," he admitted, fingering the scratches gingerly.

He looked back at her. "Don't ever do that again," he said quietly, but with an ominous note of warning in his voice.

Propped up against the wall, her arms crossed over her breasts, her hair tangled and her mouth swollen, she had tears streaming down her cheeks. "Just say you got yourself into a fight with an angry slut. You won't even be lying."

He laughed, poured out two glasses of whisky and handed her one, then sat on the bed as she sipped.

"Why are you so angry?" he asked gently. "I mean, it's not as if you committed adultery after all."

She shook her head.

"Just because my husband left me doesn't mean I'm not still married.

"And I told you, I loved him. I still do."

He shrugged. For all she knew, her husband had been killed, and that would make her a widow.

"And you'll learn to love me."

She closed her eyes. No, she swore to herself, she would not think of Lawrence dying. He couldn't be dead. She'd feel it, she was sure.

"Take me back now," she sighed.

He chuckled, and took the glass from. Not quite yet...

While they were inside, a monsoon rain cloud had burst. The side walk was drenched and puddled, the people had scattered and the jeep's canopy had leaked onto the seats.

He mopped the wet canvas as best he could after unlocking the door on her side and helped her in, and once again, she marvelled at his strange mix of cruelty and gentleness, roughness and good manners.

"How do you feel?" he asked as he drove down the deserted avenues towards Sathorn.

Sore all over, she retorted, trying to keep her bodice fastened with her hands. And how she'd explain the damage to Belinda's dress...

"It was her best, you know."

"Well, if I can get some heart medicine to her Eddy, I'm pretty sure she'll forgive me," he replied complacently.

Speaking of medicine... "Do you think you can get us some emetine? And sulpha powder?

"You saw how badly supplied we are."

The rain had started again. Eyes on the road, he nodded., and wiped the fogged up windshield with his sleeve. "And insulin, too?"

He slammed on the brakes. A roadblock manned by Japanese soldiers draped in dripping oilcloth capes appeared suddenly in the mist at the junction with New Road.

Orders were barked, flashlights were waved into their faces, and Ken rapped a reply. The insignia on his uniform was spotted, a cringing explanation was given with many bows, and they were bowed even lower again on their way, not, Kate noticed, without a leer at her torn dress and messed-up red hair.

"Military police," he grumbled. "There's some kind of bigwig staying at the Oriental, and they've cordoned off the street."

He gave her a wolfish grin. "Good thing I didn't get a room there!"

She forced a smile in response. "The medicines? Emetine, sulpha powder — or tablets if you have any? And the insulin? Please?"

Yeah, all right. He pulled up to the hospital, and leaned over to kiss her, but she shied away. "I don't want the watchman to see."

"Tell Belinda I'm sorry about her dress," he called after her.

Hurrying up the steps, she didn't turn back.

Belinda was dozing on Kate's bed, waiting for her to return, and started, fully awake in an instant, as her nurse's training had taught her. "Holy Mother, just look at you," she exclaimed in distress, sitting up. "What happened?"

Kate sat down wearily, clutching the torn dress to herself and shivering.

"Exactly what he said would happen."

Belinda came to kneel by her side, and gently parted the silk over Kate's breasts.

"Let me see — you're bruised, but not too badly. The arms are worse actually." she whispered, taking stock, and your face — she palpated it gently. "Does it hurt?"

Kate shook her head. Not too much. He was careful.

"He said all I needed was some rough courting," she muttered. "Can you believe that? Anyway, I gave as good as I got. He's going to need some explanation for the scratches on his face."

"Really? Good on you, love!"

She sat back on her heels with a smile.

"You really scratched him?"

Kate smiled back, triumphantly. And she bit him. Hard.

Belinda burst out laughing, and after a second, Kate did as well, hiccupping, and opened her hand to show the little silk covered buttons she'd picked up from the dusty floor of the room, "He said to tell you he's sorry about the dress..." and they both laughed till they cried, then Kate stated to sob, and Belinda hugged her close.

"Cry it out, love, cry it out. Was it awful?"

Kate lifted her tear-stained face with her smeared make-up to her friend.

"That's the thing... It was at first, and then.... It wasn't.

"What is wrong with me?

"Oh I'm a horrible woman, I'm doomed to hell."

Of course she wasn't, Belinda replied stoutly. "You can't control what your body wants, can you? I mean, when you're hungry, you eat, even if you hate the food.

"I think it's..." she hesitated, "... mechanical sometimes, somehow, even with women, despite what the priests and the nuns say. You just can't control it.

"I know what I'm talking about."

She gently rocked Kate against her, and her voice became softer and far more Irish, as she remembered. "There was a fella, oh well before Eddy, back home, in Ireland, and my Lord, could he kiss.

"He was a tinker, can you fathom that, he invited me to have a glass of cider at the pub where all we nursing students went, and we went outside and he had me up against the wall in the pub's garden, and then...

"I still get the shivers when I think of him.

"It's a blessed mercy it went no farther and that a friend came out looking for me. The next day he was gone, but I felt then I would have followed him to the ends of the earth. And I never even knew his name."

Kate let herself be soothed by her friend's voice and memories, gradually her sobbing abated and she lay down on her blessedly clean pillow and closed her eyes. "What time is it?"

Past two. Time they both slept. There was work to do in the morning.

"So you see," Kate finished telling Doctor Sumet about her ordeal, omitting only a few details, "I managed to get him to promise us more drugs.

"I thought we might use some, and perhaps you can get some to those monks you were talking about."

He looked around, instinctively, but the office was empty, as was the small waiting room outside.

"That was very brave of you, Khun Kate."

Not really, she shrugged. "I think he feels rather guilty, in his way.

"If he brings me drugs instead of flowers, that will make him less of a ... sleeveen. But it does make me some kind of a ... prostitute, I guess."

She gave him a wan smile. "I wanted to use a worse word, but I was afraid of shocking you."

The doctor sighed. He wished he could still be shocked, but alas, it seemed not.

He then put his hand on Kate's arm and said very low. "I want you to listen to me very carefully.

"You may continue to ask Doctor Akira for drugs, sometimes, but they are always to be used here.

"Do you understand?"

Kate frowned. But she thought...

"Those monks you spoke of, who report on that camp? Couldn't they manage to smuggle drugs in, well, not themselves, of course, but someone else?"

He shook his head.

She was to forget he ever spoke about those monks, please.

"If Doctor Akira perchance were to come check our pharmacy, I want him to see those drugs being used."

Kate kept on frowning, trying to work it out, then nodded.

"I get it," she whispered, "In your operation reports, and when you sign the pharmacy register for what you withdraw, you always write in an inflated amount or dosage to fool Bernadette and Wanida into thinking we're running low, and need to use the Japanese drugs.

"And you'll give our unused drugs to the monks or whoever. Is that it?"

He looked at her impassively and did not answer.

"You can't do it without me, you know," she said reprovingly. "I sign the operation reports too. Did you think I wouldn't notice?"

He allowed himself a brief rueful laugh. He expected her to notice and to close her eyes. And remain silent. Please?

"Okay," she sighed. "I understand."

She squeezed his hand. "Be careful. We can't do without you, you know."

He smiled at last.

"May I say the same to you?"

He watched her leave, her slim shoulders hunched as she walked with her arms crossed, hugging herself.

Poor girl.

Still, he could not believe for an instant that Captain Akira would betray her to the Kempetai, and whatever she managed to obtain from him would be useful.

It would be easy to get Nang Wanida to believe that the drugs were a form of payment for Kate's assistance during surgeries.

His mind dwelled for an instant on that unfortunate Japanese surgeon, whose divided soul was being tainted by the horrors of this war, and he pitied him far more than Kate, whose body was being sullied, but a body was but a body.

What misdeeds had Ken Akira committed in previous lives to find himself thus tried?

Tried and failing, he sighed. Well, there was little he could do for him.

Now...

How to get the anti-malarial and dysentery drugs to those who could smuggle them into that dreadful hellhole of a camp?

He needed to speak to the abbot of Wat Burana, he who had told of the horrors of that prison, but the approach must be made carefully.

In the meantime, he had a patient to see, the son of a family friend, Chamkat Phalangkun.

He remembered him from when Chamkat was a child, before he'd gone to school in England, and then, to his father's immense pride, on to Oxford, and all he knew of him was that upon returning to Bangkok shortly before the outbreak of the war, he'd fallen into disfavour for criticizing the Phibun regime in a student journal and had been rejected for a civil service appointment when he refused to disown what he had written.

He had heard, through his mother, that Chamkat had married and married well — his mother never passed up an opportunity to complain about her son's single status — "shall I die before you give me grandsons to cheer my days?" — and ushering in the slim, pale and be-spectacled young man, congratulated him and wished him happiness.

"What can I do for you?"

Chamkat crossed his hands and smiled. He had come only because his wife insisted, truly.

"You see, I have a burning pain in my stomach at times, and, well, my digestion... But it seems to trouble her more than me. She worries."

Sumet nodded. That was what wives did, he believed.

But this burning pain? When, after meals?

No. Between meals mainly, Chamkat said, and gasped, when, having undressed and lying on the examination table, Sumet prodded a spot with probing fingers.

"Tell me, how long have you felt this?

"Have you been under great stress recently — I mean, other than the stress of being newly married?" he chuckled, but he watched his patient with keen eyes, noting the chalky lips and the restless fingers.

Chamkat looked puzzled. What did he mean by stress?

Oh, nervousness, anxiety, worries...

He opened his mouth, closed it, then, "Can we speak English?" he asked suddenly.

"Of course," Sumet agreed in surprise.

The pains began shortly after he returned from England.

He had thought a first that perhaps it was eating chillies again, after all those years of bland food. But putting himself on a plain diet did not help, it only served to aggravate his mother who complained he could no longer eat like a proper Thai.

And the stress Doctor Sumet asked about?

"I suppose you know that I was refused entry into the civil service because of my political opinions. It seems everybody in Bangkok knows."

"Yes. I imagine that you must have been disappointed... and your family as well. But I must say I admire your refusal to withdraw that article.

"So is that when the pains began?"

No. It was before.

"I wouldn't have wanted to work for that man's government, anyway.

"But yes, my father was disappointed, although he did get over it once the Japanese arrived with Phibun's blessing."

"So the stress?" Sumet asked in a patient voice, wondering where all this was going, and why the sudden need to speak English.

"How do you spend your days?"

Chamkat hesitated, and his fingers twitched and pulled at the elastic of his drawers.

"I write. I read. I meet with friends.

"Do you know Louis Banomyong?" he asked suddenly.

Sumet raised his eyebrows

No, well, he knew Regent Pridi had a brother, but he'd never met him.

"Come to dinner, tomorrow, if you can," Chamkat said. "You'll meet him then, and you will perhaps see why I feel this stress you mention."

Sumet frowned.

"I'm not sure I understand you, but if I do, I'd rather not get involved."

Chamkat slipped off the table and buttoned his shirt.

Just one dinner.

Please. Actually, it was Louis who had suggested that he consult Doctor Sumet. The stomach pain was a perfect excuse.

"Yes, I know your family usually frequents a much more fashionable physician," Sumet commented dryly.

He hesitated, then feeling he was crossing a bridge from which he could never turn back, gave in with a sigh.

"Very well. I'll come. But, in the meantime, continue on your bland diet, and avoid fatty foods as well, coffee and do not smoke.

"I think you may have an ulcer.

"Cold water will help ease the pain, and I will prescribe Milk of Magnesia."

Clutching the prescription form, Chamkat looked deep into his eyes before wai-ing him deeply.

"Come. Please.

"From what we have heard of you, we think you actually do want to get involved."

Chapter XXIV

Lawrence woke up with a start when the train slowed to pull into Meerut, and the five British staff officers sharing his compartment began to noisily collect their bags. He rolled his head and shoulders to ease the stiffness, and put on his glasses to look through the grimy, soot covered window, feeling stale and dry-mouthed.

"Back among the living, are we?" a captain said. "We thought we'd have to get you out on a stretcher."

Lawrence managed a laugh. "I've been on a stretcher far long enough, thanks.

"Got out of hospital three days ago."

"Gippy tummy?" a lieutenant asked sympathetically — or was it condescendingly? "We've had a lot of that in our regiment among the newly arrived. Takes time to get used to the country."

Yes, gippy tummy — well, actually dysentery, plus malnutrition, plus malaria.

"When I got to Imphal last month, I thought I'd escaped unscathed, only to collapse in Calcutta."

Oh.

The officers looked at each other, than again at Lawrence, seeming awed and oddly respectful, although when they'd boarded the train in New Delhi, they had all but ignored him except for a quick disparaging comment about press correspondents who only saw the war through their camera lenses, which Lawrence had ignored, eyes closed from the exhaustion he could not seem to shake.

"You were part of the Burma retreat? We heard that it was pretty awful.

"Thought the press were evacuated early on."

Some were, Lawrence replied, getting his bag and typewriter case out of the overhead rack.

Many weren't.

Train stations in India were a chaos the likes of which he had never seen. Besides the ever-present troops in uniform, it seemed the whole of the population of the country was on the move, pushing and shoving, crowding the platforms, calling for porters to heave huge parcels wrapped in burlap and beat-up suitcases, women in purdah dragging wailing children, the tea-wallahs singsong chants barely audible in the overall din.

Throughout, military police were patrolling, scanning faces, hands on their batons ever at the ready, on the lookout for any sign of unrest.

Before being carted off to hospital, Lawrence had been told by Leland Stowe that the political situation of the country was uncertain, after the failure of the Cripps Mission, when Gandhi and his party, the India National Congress, had refused to support the Raj in the war.

Bumping into Stowe in Calcutta at the bar of the Great Eastern Hotel had almost felt like being reunited with family.

"What happened to you kid?" the American asked, putting down his pipe in concern before giving him a one-armed hug. "You look like death warmed over."

Four weeks of jungle march, with all that that entailed, Lawrence had replied briefly. Then Imphal, for a few days. He'd arrived in Calcutta yesterday.

"You, however, are, well... unchanged. That's amazing.

"Everything is amazing, actually. Clean sheets. Hot showers. Food.

"I'm still trying to get used to it.

"Where's everybody?

"What about OD? You look almost naked without him."

Stowe snorted. Hell if he knew. Last he'd heard, back in England.

"Seems he went all patriotic, and volunteered for armed service.

"As to the others...

"De Luce, Berrigan and Munday and Tozer made it through, driving the whole way, can you believe it?"

Lawrence shook his head. No, it seemed impossible.

"Well, they did. Got here sometime ago. They'll probably turn up a bit later.

"I hear Belden's back in China."

"Yep, Stillwell walked a bunch of them over the border as well, and didn't lose a single one, Jack says, although it was hell. He doesn't look that much better than you."

What about Rodgers and Burchett? They'd left Maymyo by jeep, driving North, a couple of weeks before, he, Lawrence, did.

They made it too. Drove and hiked through some pass through to Ledo.

"Claim to be the first white men to ever take that route and survive to tell the tale.

"Now, everyone is trying to get themselves to the Middle East. Seems to be the next big story, seeing that the Japs have Burma pretty much sewn up.

"Me, I'm going to hang around.

"I think the failure of the Cripps Mission and what Gandhi and the Congress party do next is going to be interesting. Anyway, I think American readers need to understand more about India, and how this war against the Japs isn't only to help you guys hold onto your Empire.

"What are you going to do?"

Lawrence rubbed his eyes, the lights were casting strange haloes and the overhead fan seemed to sway. The idea of doing anything next seemed overwhelming.

"I don't quite know," he admitted. "But I think I should stay as well.

"The Japs may well attack India now."

Stowe nodded. "Yeah, you may be right.

"Say, you're shaking. Shouldn't you be in sick bay?"

No, it was just a bit of fever. Nothing a strong drink couldn't fix.

And that was all he remembered, before waking up in hospital with a matron clucking over him, and Dan De Luce sitting by his bed, wearing a very new uniform, clutching a bunch of envelopes and what looked suspiciously like a bottle of local gin in a brown paper bag.

"Hello there, Blondie.

"We hear you swooned like a damsel down at the bar. Gave poor old Stowe the scare of his life."

And a very good thing he fainted too, the matron snapped.

He had no business being in a bar in the first place, with a fever of a hundred and four.

He should be drinking nothing more potent than plain sweet tea and barley water, he was dehydrated, and had dysentery and malaria and infected ulcers on his legs and she would thank the captain here to take that bottle back when he left, which should be very soon, because there was very little she missed and she would not put up with smuggling strong drink to her patients.

"Am I clear?" she demanded, arms crossed over her chest.

She might have been in her forties, with tight greying curls and steely eyes, and seemed totally impervious to the celebrated De Luce smile.

"Perfectly, especially as you are probably the first person ever to call me captain," he replied, before winking at Lawrence.

"So that's what those two silver things on my shoulders are. I'd always wondered."

The nurse huffed and flounced away, muttering something about cheeky Yanks.

"Am I a captain too?" Lawrence asked, struggling to sit up, his head spinning.

"Nah," Dan replied carelessly, "You're not important enough. Here's your mail, forwarded by AP, who sends best wishes for a prompt recovery."

"Really?"

"Of course not. They just want to know when you'll be fit again.

"They want a piece on your escape through the jungle, long on our — well your — heroic boys, short on blood and gore. You know the drill.

"I cabled back to say you were at death's door and to leave you alone.

"I retrieved your typewriter from your room, and managed to get you some new ribbons, just in case you feel like pouring your story out."

"Thanks, that was thoughtful. Not sure I'm up to it yet."

"Neither are those other guys," De Luce said, very low, looking around at the other beds in the ward. "But apparently, all of you are going to make it, that bossy nurse said."

Many men were bandaged, either heads, limbs, or apparently

all over, some were moaning quietly, others, those who could sit up were leafing through limp magazines, but most just stared in space, as if in amazement at being still alive.

"I walked by some other wards," he added, "yours is the best, for those who are expected to get out some time soon, I was told.

"So thank your lucky star you made it."

"I do. That's what I spent the first night in Imphal telling myself," Lawrence sighed, before taking his glasses from the bedside table. "There was a point at which I'd all but given up."

He looked at the envelopes — of course, none from Bangkok, that would have been too much to expect- but somehow, hoping against hope, there might have been one from Boston — and tore the letters open.

Two from his parents, conveying their love, worries, and little snippets of news from home. They still had heard nothing from Kate.

One was from his cousin Charlotte, who had signed up for service in the Royal Navy and was now a Petty Officer Wren, based in Portsmouth, and told him she had spotted one of his articles on the bombing of Mandalay — "We're all frightfully proud of you" — and that the family estate in Devon had been turned into a convalescent home for wounded officers.

"Papa is in the Territorial Army, and patrols the area with his gun, looking for Germans who might have landed in the woods, but actually trying to bag a pheasant for dinner, and Mama has taken to growing vegetables. They've carved a little flat for themselves in what used to be the housekeeper's quarters, and they're happy as fleas. Meanwhile, London is battered but very gay, and I try to get there each time I have a leave."

The last envelope contained a signal order for Gallet, Lawrence, SOE, to proceed to Meerut for re-assignment.

"Good news?" Dan asked, seeing Lawrence's smile.

Perhaps. Lawrence closed his eyes.

Hopeful, anyway.

So, here he was in Meerut, after an overnight, crowded, uncomfortable train journey to New Delhi, then a long wait to catch his connection, shifting his bag on one shoulder, his typewriter case on the other, buffeted by the crowds, confused by the noise, and feeling lost and discouraged, and completely abandoned.

He'd received a message informing him that a jeep would pick him up at the station, but there were a great many jeeps parked outside, and he had no idea where to even begin to look for the one assigned to him, when he heard a screech of brakes and a shout "Hey, Gallet, over here!" and saw an officer waving his bush hat.

Squinting against the late afternoon sun, he could even make out the face.

"Cumming? Stephen Cumming?

"Is that really you?"

He laughed in delight as he flung his bag onto the back seat and climbed in.

Stephen Cumming, a Scot lawyer who had worked in China, had trained with him at one of the jungle schools. He had a deadpan sense of humour and what had then seemed an inexhaustible enthusiasm for whatever competence they were assigned to master, earning him the sobriquet of "Volunteer Number One".

"Actually, the question should be, is that really you, Gallet?"

Cumming took his eye away from the road to give Lawrence a critical stare, then swerved to miss an errant cow that was placidly walking in the crowded street.

"I only recognized you from your hair and your specs. You look like a scarecrow. Or maybe it's just that uniform, if one can call it that...

"Are the press even allowed uniforms? What's the world coming to?"

Lawrence stretched out in his seat. The world was looking much brighter all of a sudden.

"I walked out of Burma. Got to Imphal late June. Then hospital in Calcutta. Though you're no beauty prize yourself, if I may say so. What happened to that lovely Scots complexion of yours?"

Cumming cackled.

"Walked out too. Got here in July. Obviously made of sterner stuff."

"No, it's just that you're such a slow walker."

They both burst out laughing.

"So what's happening here?"

Cumming swore at a dog that darted away from the jeep's wheels.

"You'll see. The boss is Alec Peterson, a Scot, therefore, essentially very good value. Lots of ideas, good ones.

"We're somewhat out of town, for obvious reasons.

"The digs are basic, but all right, I suppose. Former barracks from the last century. Better than what we had at training. And servants.

"And before you ask me, I have no idea what's in store for you."

Lawrence nodded.

He also knew better than to inquire what Cumming himself was doing, and looked as various sights were pointed out.

"This is the European cantonment, and we're passing the old Sadar Bazaar. There's another one, the Lal Kurti Bazaar.

"There are a few interesting temples, not that you're going to have much time for sightseeing."

The traffic was lighter as they reached the outskirts of the city, and the jeep drove through puddles that sprayed women walking in bright coloured saris with bundles on their heads and cows wandering by the roadside, cropping the few tufts of grass and leaves from low-hanging tree branches.

"It rained last night," Cumming said, "so the weather is fairly comfortable. Not the furnace that Delhi is these days.

"And here we are."

They were stopped at a gate by an Indian guard who checked Cumming's face and gave him a huge grin as he lifted the boom and the jeep pulled up in front of a low, thatched roofed, whitewashed building, with a wood colonnaded verandah running its length.

"Alec said to get you to his office directly we arrive. You'll settle in later."

How many times, since the war started, had he waited outside an office to meet with a man?

Bill or whatever his name was in Singapore, Chennault in Kunming, that press officer in Rangoon — Lawrence couldn't remember his name, and panicked suddenly, since his stay in hospital he'd had this strange blanks — Oh yes, Major Hewett.

He looked around.

This was not as impressive as mahogany and stucco-heavy

Rangoon, nor as strangely spartan as Kunming, or as dusty and derelict as the back room of the godown in Singapore.

There was an overhead fan whirring slowly, maps covered the walls, telephones were ringing somewhere, and he heard voices speaking softly in Hindi as people passed in the corridor behind, and a louder English voice telling them to hurry up.

But what there was here was this same feeling of purpose and efficiency and stress that he'd felt in Singapore, and Kunming — a feeling of mission.

He gave his name to an English sergeant sitting behind a desk and drinking tea, who looked up with a suspicious expression, as if keen to catch any impostor who'd managed to get by the guards.

"Yes. Gallet. Right," he grudgingly admitted after checking his name from a list. "I'm Gibbs. I do everything here, keep accounts, assign room, the lot. You better remember that."

Lawrence wryly nodded his promise to remember, then Gibbs snapped his fingers at a thin Indian dressed in a white kurta whom Lawrence hadn't noticed, perched on a high stool next to a steel filing cabinet, busily putting papers in binders with different colours, and sliding them into deep drawers.

"Get off your bottom, old son, and tell Mr. Peterson his visitor is here," and once the man had disappeared next door, confided in a low voice, "That's Ram Das. Not a bad chap, but lazy.

"Right, in you go," he added, as Ram Das beckoned from the open door.

Alec Peterson was a man with a high forehead, craggy features, and a big, jutting nose.

As he walked up to greet Lawrence, he peered at him under beetling brows, but his gaze was genial and his manner was that of a good headmaster — somewhat aloof, but friendly and interested.

"Good chap, you've arrived, after many an adventure," he announced with a slight Scottish burr.

"Was it not too awful being ordered here so soon after leaving hospital?

"Ram Das, bring us some tea, if you will, please. Sit yourself down."

It was not awful at all, rather a relief, Lawrence replied, sipping his milky and oversweet tea.

"I was feeling at a loose end, I think AP didn't really know what to do with me once I'd written that piece on escaping with the Burma Rifles — or at least what is left of them," he added.

Yes, Peterson had read that piece — "Everything goes through us, you know.

"Pretty harrowing, although I imagine you didn't even tell half of the horror that you experienced.

"But that description of your mule carrying the rice and bully beef tumbling off the ridge, and screaming as it was swept away...

"I bet that made it real for your readers."

Lawrence shrugged. Perhaps.

It was impossible to convey what a dreadful rout the Burma campaign was, and anyway, even if he'd been able to, it wouldn't have been published.

"What's happening now, really, at the border?

"I've only read the papers and listened to the BBC, and I know that they're censored."

Peterson grimaced. To put it baldly, it was bad, the Japs were pushing towards Manipur and Imphal, and there weren't enough troops in a fit state to hold them back.

Thankfully, the monsoon was slowing them down, and they were also getting bogged down in the Solomon Islands, after their crushing defeat at Midway, — "The Yanks seem to be getting their act together, at last." — so it meant that they were pretty strapped for men and matériel.

"And what about Thailand?" Lawrence asked.

Peterson looked down at his desk, where Lawrence's file was open.

"You have a wife trapped there, I see.

"There's nothing coming *out* of Thailand — and by the way, we refer to it as Siam here — but there might be something going *in*, at some point.

"There are quite a few Siamese students in England, and they have been organized under a Prince Svasti — do you know him?"

Lawrence shook his head. He knew *of* him. "He's a staunch arch-Royalist, I believe. Not very popular, therefore, in Thailand — sorry, Siam.

"I'm going to have to unlearn saying Thailand — it took me weeks to get used to the new name. I'm rather surprised they trusted Svasti, though. I guess they didn't have a choice."

Yes, well... The more promising of those students were to be trained at some point to be infiltrated back into their country. "Your knowledge of the country could be useful then. But it's all pretty tentative, at this stage, and anyway, it's not my bailiwick.

"I have other plans for you now, something you've shown yourself to be gifted at."

Lawrence smiled and sat back in his chair. "Propaganda."

"Precisely," Peterson smiled back, as if complimenting a very bright student.

"But not in Siam, not yet.

Here, in India.

"How much do you know about Indian history?"

Lawrence frowned. "What little I remember is from university. I did study history, but we focussed on European, or rather Western history, and what I know about India was more in the context of colonialism."

Peterson beamed.

"True, you're a Balliol man, as am I, actually – though I imagine we couldn't have crossed, I'm a good few years older than you.

"In my case, I knew very little about India, so I had to learn very quickly, once Mountbatten sent me here to do this job."

He looked down again, fiddled with a pencil, and started to doodle on the cover of Lawrence's file, then, realizing, hastily erased his scribble and blew the bits of rubber away, and raised his eyes once more.

"I expect that you've realized that India is a keg of powder waiting to explode."

Meerut was actually where the Great Indian Rebellion of 1857 began, which, once crushed, transformed what was a possession of the East India Company into a crown colony. "Which means we're not – how can I put it? – very popular, here."

"I remember that," Lawrence replied, "but surely, it's not limited to Meerut."

No, of course, but Meerut was a good case in point, Peterson continued in his professorial way, for instance, there was this – what could he call it? – trend, or movement among the population here, called the "Don't Move policy" which was to remain seated, in cinemas, during the playing of "God save the King".

"Harmless, I agree, but symbolic. And symbols are potent."

He cocked his head, a bit like a bird with very bright eyes, Lawrence thought, and was asked suddenly.

"What have you heard about the INA?"

The Indian National Army?

"It's not unlike the Burmese Independence Army, I suppose, fighting for self-determination and freedom."

Well, yes and no.

The difference being that members of the Indian National Army were recruited exclusively among Indian Army soldiers *and* officers taken prisoner by the Japanese, and organized under one Subhas Chandra Bose, who made frequent radio broadcasts encouraging Indians to rise up against the British and join the war, but on the Japanese side, so as to achieve independence.

"They're seen as heroes here, particularly amongst the more hot-headed youths, and even the Congress Party is divided about the position to adopt.

"Should they be called traitors or heroes?

"Add to that the fact that Cripps was unable to convince Gandhi, Nehru and the others to put their 'Quit India' movement on hold until the end of the war and you have all the ingredients for a general upheaval at a time when we need it least, with the Japs pushing at our border.

"There are been over a thousand instances of telegraph wires being cut, police and rail stations have been destroyed.

"Yesterday, Gandhi gave a speech in which he called for independence now, or to die trying. A proper call to arms, that was.

"It's not official, but what you'll hear within the next 48 hours, is that he, along with Nehru, and many Congress politicians are about to be arrested, probably for the duration.

"Which I personally think is a huge mistake, but nobody consulted me, obviously, and it will only lead to more unrest, which will need to be put down by troops that would be much better employed defending us against the Japs, instead of pushing the population to take the part of our enemies.

"So this is where you come in.

"We need propaganda material to be disseminated, by Indian agents, of course, throughout the bazaars, in the Indian papers, and rumours, well, you know what I mean.

"Anything we need to do to stop the people from actually

turning against us and welcoming the Japs with open arms."

Lawrence grinned. "It's Kim and the Great Game all over."

Peterson stood and came to clap Lawrence on the shoulder.

That was precisely what it was.

He was to try to get access to various Indian intellectuals and politicians, of all types, those who were pro-Raj, and those against, he explained as he walked Lawrence to the door.

"Your press status is the perfect excuse for you to talk to everybody and anybody.

"Listen to what they say, and see how we can best counter it.

"Pity the bigwigs are in prison, but you'll find others.

"You'll just stay here for a fortnight or so, so we can brief you on what we need and how we need it. Don't worry about how we use what you tell us, that's our problem.

"Now, if any of your correspondent colleagues wonders about where you were, just say you were recovering in the hills.

"I don't know, Darjeeling perhaps?

"One of those places.

"Just decide where and find out the name of a miserable hotel or guest house. I can't imagine anybody would check, but you need to be able to say, 'Oh, don't stay at the so and so, I was there, it's noisy, or uncomfortable, or whatever'.

"All right?

"And we'll try to get some flesh back on your bones, so the recovery story holds water."

He shook Lawrence's hand with a brisk "Off you go, now, Gallet," and Lawrence left the office feeling that he had just been dismissed by his headmaster at Winchester and sent off to do Latin prep.

LAWRENCE DIARY
MEERUT, MONDAY, AUGUST 17TH 1942

Back in harness, as it were.

At least I have a purpose, beyond writing about yet another catastrophic defeat, sugar-coating it so to not instil fear and discouragement on our side and delight on the side of our enemies.

Besides getting a refresher course in wireless transmission –

although, as I was told by my instructor, "you're not getting a set, so I wonder why we're both wasting our time here.

"That's the army for you, even though SOE ain't even the bleeding army" – I was put back to work on codes, which I've always enjoyed and 'Security in the field', which is fun because it's just like a spy novel.

Sobering, however, once I was told to never, never, never trust anyone but known SOE agents. Known personally to me, that is. And even then, it pays to be careful, and it's probably better to trust no one at all.

My instructor is obsessed by details.

"The boy who cleans your room, the dhobi who goes through your pockets before washing your trousers, the waiter at the restaurant who reads over your shoulder when you're scribbling notes waiting for your meal, even a fellow reporter – any of them could very easily be working for the Japanese. You've no way of finding out.

"Once you've sent us what we want, destroy everything you've written.

"You either use the codes we've taught you, but if by some stroke of luck you've contacted us through an Army or a Civil Government office, you don't just throw your papers in the burn basket

"Burn them. Yourself. Then crush the ashes. Scatter them."

When I said that sounded fairly funereal, he snapped back that those who didn't take such precautions might well find themselves guests of honour at their own funeral.

He was so threatening that I did not dare point out that I would not be handling major secrets, just giving impressions and ideas.

Oh well…

My crushing exhaustion seems to be gradually vanishing, and the doctor here says I'm on the mend. He gives me rather painful vitamin injections, and I'm told to fatten up, though the diet is so reminiscent of school that I often take myself to local restaurants rather than partake of boiled beef and steamed pudding with golden syrup – the Club, in the European cantonment, is reputed to serve good food, but is out of bounds for us.

Although I still get spells of intense fatigue, Peterson, like the headmaster he is in civilian life (I knew it!) refuses to let me indulge myself, and stoutly says things such as "nothing more restorative than making a schedule and sticking to it," or "early to bed and early to rise..."

I'm sure he is also a staunch believer in cold showers to control sexual urges, which to my dismay and embarrassment – and relief – are coming back.

I often wake up from erotic dreams – and they are not all of Kate – and find myself staring at women at the bazaars, although Cumming told me that the brothels there are to be avoided at any cost.

"Riddled with pox, or so they say. Anyways, brothels are off limits to SOE."

I'm just surprised they're not off limits to Army as well.

I sometimes spot a few females in uniform, Women Auxiliary Corps-India, or WACS (I), as they're known, and I assume they're very much in demand.

Furthermore, they're generally little memsahibs, daughters of senior officers in Indian Army regiments, and therefore, not to be approached by a lowly correspondent, but as SOE are forbidden from fraternizing with anybody else – "Why do you think we have this bloody, out-of-the-way compound?" the question does not arise.

It *would* be so nice though, just to spend an evening with a woman...

As I remember telling Gerald Sparrow, he who first got me involved in what I am doing now – and I shall be eternally grateful to him – I don't much enjoy being in an all-male environment, and I have spoken to very few women since I left Bangkok, except for those few missionaries in Maymyo.

However, in the absence of female company, I rather enjoy passing time with other SOE men here. I had already met one or two during our training, others are recently arrived from England. And although none of ever discuss what we do – and occasionally, one disappears without taking leave, no one asks where or why, and is replaced by someone else – it is a great relief not to constantly hide who we are and can freely exchange memories of what brought us together.

I recounted being targeted by the Kempetai because my name was on a list left behind in Shanghai by, I suspect, that Malayan plantation owner from Cambridge.

"Oh, him," I was told, though I had given no name. "He

bought it in Ipoh. He was organizing Communist guerrillas, and, by all accounts, was careless again.

"Thankfully, he was shot in an ambush."

Thankfully because he was killed before being made to talk. We drank to his memory.

MEERUT,
FRIDAY, AUGUST 21ST1942

I have been ferreting around to find out more about this group of Siamese students Peterson mentioned, and heard they were recruited into the Pioneer Corps in England – which, I discovered, is the only branch in which a foreigner can serve. I imagine they enlisted to avoid becoming interned as enemy aliens.

There is talk of sending them here, to Poona, to train before infiltrating some of them into Thailand – or rather Siam. I really must get used to the name again.

"It's all tentative, Gallet," said Dickie, one of the SOE I managed to pry the information out of, "and of course it all depends on what's happening there. And that we have no way of knowing."

Gnashing my teeth out of rage and frustration at being so cut off, and trying to understand why.

I cannot, will not, believe that all of a sudden, the country has become rabidly and massively pro-Japanese. It doesn't make sense.

Meanwhile, when I have the energy, I take myself to the bazaars, or bookshops near the university, and spend time drinking endless cups of sweet spiced chai at teashops wherever I see either young people congregating, or elderly gentlemen caught up in a game of chaupur and watch.

It's easy to just say I'm trying to learn the game, because there will always be someone who offers to teach, and a friend of his who scoffs at his skills, and buying tea all around makes for companionable moments.

What I've discovered is that religious animosity runs higher than I'd imagined, and, as one Mohti Lal put it, "It's not that we hate you British, young man.

"It's just that there's no more reason for you to rule us, than for us to rule you. But we shall not accept to be ruled by Muslims either."

I replied mildly that the friend he was playing, Ali Nazimuddin, who sports the hennaed beard and skullcap of a hajji was a Muslim, he shrugged.

"He is my friend, true. But does that mean that Jinnah and the Muslim League that Ali votes with can be trusted to govern in the best interests of us all? I do not believe that.

"They will favour their Muslim brethren, as, I admit, I would favour Hindus.

"When the time comes, let them have their own country, and us, ours."

"When will that time be?" I asked them both.

Nazimuddin shook the dice, threw, and moved his beehive-shaped piece. "When Allah ordains, and that will not be before the Japanese stop threatening us," he said equably.

Mohti Lal took the dice tumbler from him.

"But do you not agree that the Japanese would not threaten us if it were not for the British being here?"

No, was the answer.

The Japanese wanted their own empire, because just like the British, they were an island nation with no resources and wanted the riches of India for themselves.

I left them at that point, and told Peterson that hateful as it may be, pitting Hindus against Muslims may well be one of the solutions.

"While they're busy tearing each other apart, they may give us some breathing space to regroup and ready to get taking Burma back."

He sighed and shook his head.

"I know. It's a tricky tool to use, though.

"But another hateful thing — comparing the Japanese to us British and their need for an empire to exploit... That may well prove useful. Stick in my gullet though it may.

"I'll try to get some figures of Japanese wartime production, and have them trickled through to economics professors at universities here in India.

"If they can then spread them around to students..."

He took off his specs and rubbed his eyes, and I could see how red and tired they were. The man doesn't seem to sleep, whatever time of day or night, he's always at his desk, jotting down the arcane things I and others bring to him, and matching them with others.

He looked back at me and smiled, very much the headmaster in control, and told me I shall be leaving next Monday.

"Where shall you go?"

I'd already thought this out.

Delhi was where the story was. Then perhaps Bengal.

"I've a friend from Balliol there, who wanted to be a writer too.

"Probably as influenced by Tagore as I was by Malraux. His family is fairly prominent — his father is a lawyer — rather involved in politics, I think — so I think I could get some introductions to interesting people.

"There was another Indian chap, but he was a prince, we weren't really close friends, but I'm sure he'd talk to me. I think his ambition was to try for the Indian Civil Service. He would be easy to find."

"Splendid.

"And you're all better, I'm told, just keep on taking those malaria pills, and you'll be right as rain."

He also said he's leaving for Delhi himself, tomorrow, so we were to say our goodbyes then.

"And if by chance, our paths do cross in Delhi or elsewhere, of course, you know the drill — we've never met before."

Of course.

And now, I've packed, my uniform, and the change of clothes I have with me is clean and ironed by the dhobi, and as usual I check my escape kit.

The opium and gold were confiscated by Gibbs in his quartermaster persona, who counted out each coin and each little opium ball to make sure I hadn't used any without giving a precise accounting for it. But as I'd only used the sulpha and anti-malarial pills, I was in the clear.

He then told me grandly that I could keep the dollars and other bills. "Might come in handy, if you want to bribe a Yank."

And then he sent me on my way.

Enjoyable as these past weeks were, I'm eager to go, and feel as if I'm leaving school for the holidays.

Chapter XXV

The monsoon storm of the previous night had chased the clouds away, and the early morning sky opened silky and geranium tinted, with a cool breeze, birds chirruping madly and white squirrels jumping from the branches of the frangipani and banyan trees that lined Sathorn Road.

There was hardly any traffic yet, and not a Japanese military car in sight.

It might have been a normal peacetime day, Doctor Sumet thought as he parked his ancient Ford behind the hospital main building and winced at the screeching noise from the gearbox. If it were to break down, where would the mechanic get the spare parts to fix it, now that it was impossible to import anything from America?

Well, he shrugged, there were certainly old cars that could be taken apart and after all, a gearbox was not like a heart or a kidney, any one would work, he supposed. He refused to let worry about a piece of metal, useful as it was, spoil his pleasure today.

Yesterday, he had been to Yong Siang's shop to deliver the basket that Belinda and Kate had so lovingly and carefully prepared, and by now, this being his third visit, the liquor merchant recognized him.

Managing to simultaneously nod and give a slight shake of the head, he signalled that Sumet was to wait until he had finished serving the portly Chinese-looking man who wanted several bottles of herb-infused country gin and was haggling for a rebate.

Sumet looked around the shop.

Although Yong Siang was certainly doing good business, judging from the unopened cases stacked in a corner, the dark wood counter was covered with the grease stains of many sloppy meals, cobwebs clouded the window, and other goods for sale — cigarettes, fly-swatters and brooms, tinned food — were jumbled in big bins. Flypaper crusted with insects hung next to dried fish strung from a pole attached to the ceiling and their smell, mixed with camphor and mothballs, permeated the air.

Finally, Yong Siang escorted his heavily laden customer to the door, and locked it behind him then turned to Sumet with a relieved look.

He took the envelope of cash that Sumet slipped into his hand, glanced at it before tucking it into his shirt, grasped the basket and weighed it in his hand. Good, it was not too big nor too heavy.

Then he leaned towards the doctor and whispered that he had something as well — a much folded and grimy sheet of paper, that he showed after a quick look towards the window to make sure nobody was watching.

"For you," he whispered. "There is a guard who is the cousin of my wife's friend, and he does not like the job he does. But he wants ten ticals in return. Can you pay?"

Of course.

Sumet peeled two notes from his billfold and handed them over.

"He will not do it very often, but when he can…"

"Then I will pay," Sumet replied firmly. "But tell him he is not to endanger himself or any of the prisoners."

Yong Siang nodded.

He had already told the man the same thing. But life was hard and food was expensive … sometimes one had to take risks.

"There is a letter in the basket as well, I believe," Sumet added.

Yong Siang smiled broadly, showing an impressive display of gold teeth and his cunning face was suddenly transformed.

He was a scoundrel, no doubt, Sumet thought, but none-theless, in his own way, a helpful and compassionate man.

"It is meritorious to help those in need. The parcel will be delivered this afternoon, if I can."

Yes, it was meritorious to help, Sumet repeated to himself, but, he had to admit, also a pleasure. He imagined Belinda's delight, and took the stairs quicker than his usual sedate pace, impatient to find her.

He had good news and a letter from Eddy folded in his pocket, and his many other worries, for the time being, could wait.

Belinda grabbed the paper Sumet had handed over, clasping it to her heart and kissing it before she opened it.

She read, and two tears trickled slowly down her cheeks.

The girl had changed over these past months, Sumet thought, watching her.

Her hair had gone back to its original mousy brown, and she had long since abandoned her makeup along with the flighty, silly manner which so annoyed Mother Melanie. Although she still was prone to fits of unseemly giggles and irreverent remarks, she was now, in Sumet's mind, a fine, responsible nurse.

Yes, Melanie *would* be proud of her.

"Look, Kate, he hasn't signed it. Can we be sure he's the one who wrote it?"

Of course there could be no names, Kate objected reassuringly, for everyone's safety.

The two girls pored over the letter. It was short but the tone was determinedly cheerful.

"*My darling girl, thank you for everything you've sent, I know it cannot be easy, and I — or rather we, because you were so thoughtful to provide enough to share — are more grateful than you could ever imagine. We don't go hungry, we're fed buffalo and rice every day — not very good, so your tins of sardines and the marmalade were most welcome, my darling...*" — "You see," Kate interjected, "it has to be him, if he mentions the marmalade" — "*The guards are not unkind, and I believe, pity our lack of freedom, but of course, they are bound to obey rules.*

We are trying to grow some vegetables in the garden, and I exercise by taking long walks in circles around the grounds.

We've begun to put on plays for our entertainment, because the worse thing here is the boredom — and missing you of course.

So do not worry about me, please, and don't run any risks. Your safety is the most important thing.

I miss you and think of you every day."

"Lucky you," Kate sighed enviously. "I'd give anything to get news from Lawrence."

Feeling guilty at her own pleasure, Belinda hugged her. "You will. Sometime. I just know it."

"I don't know..." Kate shook her head. "I sometimes wonder if he's even alive. And if he is...," her voice broke, "And if he comes back, will I even be able to face him?"

"Don't! Don't think that, ever!"

Belinda had adopted her brisk and no-nonsense manner. "First of all, there's no reason you would need to tell him anything, and second, if you were to feel the need to confess..." she clapped her hand over her mouth — "no, I don't mean confess, you've done nothing wrong but try to stay out of the clutches of the Japanese police, I mean, if you well, need to talk — he'd understand, of course he would."

Kate was staring into the distance, looking unconvinced. "Listen Kate, what would Melanie say if she saw you like this?"

Kate laughed sadly.

"She'd say that I'm a fallen woman, that's what she'd say. She'd point out all the virgin martyrs who let themselves be put to death rather than be defiled by barbarians. I bet she'd have a whole list at the drop of a hat."

Belinda looked in despair at Sumet. He put his hand on Kate's arm.

"I don't think so.

"Mother Melanie always was — no, there's no reason to speak of her in the past tense — she *is* a very practical woman, and impatient with what she called ridiculous rules and conventions. I'm sure she would tell you that you'd have to do what is necessary to survive."

Kate tried to smile.

"Perhaps."

She shook herself, sniffling a little. "Just look at me, being selfish and spoiling your joy at Eddy's letter. Come on, let's get back to work before Rose and Bernadette begin to wonder what we're doing."

Yes, Sumet thought as he watched them walk away, Belinda's arm still hugging Kate close, and also before Wanida starts to suspect anything.

She was the sharpest — no rather, the most suspicious — of all the Thai hospital staff, and rightly so, he was forced to admit.

The hospital had become her life's work, and now that it was running more or less smoothly, she was not about to tolerate nurses illegally passing parcels to British detainees, or worse, one of her two surgeons secreting anti-malarial and dysentery drugs from the pharmacy to deliver them to a wat in the old city. How they were then to be smuggled into that dreadful prison camp, Sumet did not know, and did not want to know. He had vaguely heard mention of a vegetable merchant from Kanchanaburi who delivered the camp supplies, but had firmly put this bit of information out of his mind.

After all, had he heard correctly? Probably not.

And what would Wanida say at the idea of this self-same surgeon meeting in secret with plotters against the Prime Minister and the Japanese?

She'd no doubt have a heart attack, he thought with a grimace, reliving that dinner at Chamkat's house several weeks ago.

The Phalangkun family residence was in the wealthy area of Bangkok, the main house hidden by huge rain trees and palms.

He hadn't had time to admire the gardens, arriving as he did in a violent downpour, and was soaked taking the few steps to reach the covered verandah.

Shaking out his sodden umbrella, he gave it along with his dripping linen jacket to the clucking manservant who greeted him.

The gentlemen were waiting in the drawing-room, he was told, and shown to a large room, decorated with the usual clash of furnishings of an affluent Thai family who had embraced Western culture and habits — much like his own.

Lamps were muted by dark green tasselled lampshades, there were tufted velvet Victorian armchairs, oil paintings of thatched cottages hung on the walls beside a collection of photographs of Chamkat in school uniform, Chamkat graduating, Chamkat as a bridegroom in traditional Siamese clothes, along with a portrait of King Rama the Fifth, Lanna silver on the low tables next to what had to be Meissen shepherdesses and beautiful celadon dishes.

An old-fashioned wind-up phonograph and a new radiogram occupied a lovely golden teak console against the panelled wall.

There were only the two men in the room, Sumet supposed that Chamkat's young wife and his parents had been asked to take their evening dinner elsewhere in the big sprawling house.

Chamkat seemed even paler than before when he came with outstretched hand.

"Welcome, Doctor. I am so grateful you agreed to come.

"I would like you to meet Khun Louis," and a dark faced, fortyish man rose from his chair and smiled.

Sumet could see the resemblance with his illustrious older brother, whom he'd never met but knew from newsreels at the cinema, and countless pictures in newspapers and magazines.

"I am very pleased to meet you," Louis said softly. "I realize it was not an easy decision."

"I am pleased as well," Sumet replied. "I have long been an admirer of Luang Pradit, your brother.

"But you must realize I have decided nothing yet, I have just, as Chamkat suggested, come to listen."

Of course, of course, Chamkat cried effusively.

Khun Louis was well aware of that, "Aren't you?".

Louis sat down, and waited until the servant had left after bringing Sumet his drink before speaking again.

Yes, he was aware of Doctor Sumet's reservations, therefore, the doctor would understand if what he was about to say was more general than what he had hoped to discuss.

Sumet nodded, sipping his weak gin and bitters. Such precautions were normal.

Louis sighed, as if wondering where to start.

"You are acquainted with Andrew Gilchrist of the British Embassy?" he asked suddenly. "Yes, I know you are, I also know that you helped him out last December when he needed to find a hiding place for several young men before the Japanese Army entered Bangkok."

Sumet hesitated, but remained silent as Louis, apparently, was not seeking confirmation, just stating a fact.

"Well, you may be surprised to hear that the British and American and other diplomatic detainees are to be repatriated shortly, within a week or so. Including, naturally, Mr. Gilchrist."

"That is very good news for them, and for their families," Sumet replied in a neutral voice.

Yes, indeed. "But what might surprise you even more is that before boarding the ship that is to take them, Mr. Gilchrist is to be given a letter from... no, I cannot tell you at this stage... a letter conveying a message for the British authorities."

As he often did with his patients, Sumet waited, knowing that silence was the best way to encourage people to reveal what they were determined not to disclose, and, as he expected, Louis continued.

"This letter is the only way we have found to let the British know that not all Thai people are happy with the situation, and that Field-Marshal Phibul has taken us on a path we feel is dangerous for the future of our country.

"And that we are becoming organised to try and combat this

from the inside, but to do so, we need help from the outside."

At last.

This is what Sumet had always hoped for.

For the past year at least, he had wondered why Pridi appeared resigned to his exalted and powerless position.

Still, he felt he needed to know more.

"Organised, you say?" he repeated.

Yes. But Doctor Sumet must forgive him if he truly could say no more, pending some kind of commitment.

Sumet thought at length. "Why Andrew Gilchrist?

"Why not His Excellency, Sir Josiah? I assume he too is to be repatriated?"

Louis frowned reflectively, obviously not expecting the question.

He was not sure, but supposed it was because his brother, Luang Pradit — Pridi, that is — had a closer personal relationship with Andrew Gilchrist.

"Ah.

"Therefore, that letter was written by Luang Pradit?"

And when Louis acquiesced with an embarrassed smile at having revealed more than he wanted, Sumet sighed deeply.

Now was the time to commit, beyond his petty pilfering of the pharmacy and his delivery of parcels.

He had no choice, if he were to remain true to what he believed was his duty, as a Thai, and as a decent man.

"That is very good news.

"I have worried these past months at what I thought was your brother's acceptance of the situation.

"Just one last thing. What exactly was in that letter?"

Louis shook his head.

He had not himself read the letter, he just knew that it contained a necessarily brief description of a Free Siamese Movement, and included the fact that several provincial governors were part of it.

"For security reasons, you understand, it was neither signed nor gave any names."

Sumet's was aware his hands were sweaty, just like before performing a difficult surgery that might result in death.

Except the death, this time, might be his own.

He took a deep breath.

"I agree to join your group.

"Now tell me more."

Chamkat clapped his hands. "If there were still champagne to be had, I'd order a bottle opened!

"As it is, I raise my glass to the newest member of the X-O Group."

Both he and Louis stood, and softly, so as not to be heard by the servants, gave the traditional Thai cheer. "Chaiyo!!"

And then, Chamkat began his explanations: they met rarely, never as a group, so as not to give rise to suspicion, never with Pridi himself, except for Louis who was in an easy position to report to his brother.

He, Louis, who still lived in Ayutthaya, was a friend of the governor of the province, and reported on the general dissatisfaction of the population — mainly farmers — because of the high-handed way the Japanese commandeered their rice at rock-bottom prices and behaved as if they had rights over everything, including insulting elders and monks and assaulting women.

Furthermore, having been for centuries the Royal capital, Ayutthaya was for many Thai the spiritual centre of the Kingdom, and they also felt that Phibul was attempting, if not to abolish the monarchy, at least to make it some kind of old-fashioned, obsolete tradition of little importance.

"The governor is quietly sounding people who may at some point be in a position to help." Louis added.

"Louis is the treasurer of the Group. He's a businessman, as you know. And I," Chamkat announced, barely attempting to conceal his pride, "am the secretary."

Sumet smiled at his youthful enthusiasm.

"You are very young, but I believe you are the right person for the job. But tell me now, what are the plans?"

Louis and Chamkat glanced at each other.

The plan, Chamkat finally said, dropping his voice, was to spirit Pridi, along with several members of the National Assembly, out of the country, to form a government-in-exile.

"But of course, we cannot do this alone. We are hoping to contact Washington, or better still, London, to be helped in organising the escape."

How did they imagine it could be done? Sumet wanted to know. A submarine, perhaps?

Louis nodded. Yes, that was indeed a possibility. The likeliest one.

But to do so, someone needed to contact the Allies.

What they were thinking is that the someone might be Chamkat, who would travel to China, where, as they knew, the Americans were operating.

It would be a difficult and perilous endeavour, taking the smugglers' route. And an expensive one.

"There will be people to bribe along the way."

"So you would like me to help with money," Sumet concluded. "Yes, I can do that.

"I was afraid you might want me to engage in sabotage of some sort, for which I see myself ill-equipped."

They all laughed at the idea of the sedate and dignified surgeon laying sticks of dynamite near Japanese barracks.

"No, no sabotage at all, for the time being." Chamkat smiled.

"The important thing is to lie low, to pretend, as we all do, as we know you yourself do, that our main concern is living as best we can in this city that we feel is not longer ours.

"To be quiet, to meet only socially, and very rarely at that.

"But we will be grateful for your financial assistance, you understand, in cash or even better, gold."

Sumet shrugged. It would be easy, he thought, to buy gold from one of the many dealers in Yaowarat. The Chinese were great believers in putting their assets in gold in times of trouble.

He reached over and firmly removed Chamkat's glass from his hand.

"I understand now why you said you felt stress in your life.

"Come see me next week, I will have what you asked for.

"And in the meantime, as I told you, do not drink alcohol."

The following week, Chamkat returned to Saint-Louis, received the promised pouch of coins and Wanida was delighted at having a new patient from such a prominent family, little realizing that pale and wan Chamkat Phalangkun seemed to walk out with a heavier step than when he had arrived.

Once he had taken his decision, Sumet at long last felt at peace with his conscience, and was surprised to realize he no longer worried for his own safety.

The gold transaction had been done as discreetly as such operations always were, no questions asked, and even had there been, well, who could blame prudent Doctor Sumet for wanting to safeguard his assets in such uncertain times as these.

Anyway, whom did he have who might suffer if by misfortune he were to be arrested, besides his mother who, in any case, preferred his sister?

No one.

The weeks went by, the monsoon clouds ran across the skies in huge grey pouring billows, and everyone was waiting for Loy Krathong, the full moon festival which marked the end of the rains and the arrival of cool weather, when hopeful little rafts of flowers were set afloat on the river, to carry away all the bitterness and sins of the year.

But there was still almost a month to go, and as always, in the rainy season, mosquito-borne diseases such as dengue and Japanese encephalitis spread, and there were cases of cholera in some overcrowded areas of Bangkok.

Infant mortality rates had increased, and at the hospital, wards were getting crowded.

They sprayed the wards with insect-killing chemicals, they ensured the nets over the beds were always carefully tucked in, and so far, all of the cases they had had were manageable. But Sumet knew that could change from one day to the next.

His own mother had come down with a bad case of dengue, and the dreaded "break-bone fever" had kept her in bed, sweating and moaning with painful joints and a frightening high temperature. But at least, it did not evolve into the often deadly haemorrhagic form, and she emerged overcome with fatigue and more snappish than ever.

"They don't make ladies as tough as this anymore," he told Kate.

And by the way, was it not time for Lady Thip to come by for a check-up?

Kate blanched.

No, not now. Please. Next week, maybe?

"Look at me."

Yesterday, she had come back from one of her meetings with

Captain Akira with her mouth bloodied and bruises on her cheek and around her swollen eye.

"He was drunk again," she just said, resignation in her voice. "Some officer made a slighting remark and questioned his loyalty to the Emperor.

"So he takes it out on me.

"It's awful, he's like two different persons. Sometimes he's almost nice – or in fact really nice, and he seems to care about me – and at others, it's as if he were trying to punish the American in him by hitting me. And I'm so dumb, it comes as a surprise."

It was true, she had not expected the violence the night before, the last few times he had summoned her, he had been gentle, considerate, and at times, she was able to forget his other, unpredictable, side.

Their evenings now followed a pattern, almost as if it were a real relationship, not something the war had forced upon her.

He picked her up, they had dinner in quiet, out of the way places, then he took her to his dingy room and then he made love to her.

It was no longer rape, probably because she had learned to be compliant – but her body, she needed to admit, now welcomed his, and when he ran his lips down her neck, she shuddered and pulled him closer, listened to the endearments he whispered into her hair and desperately tried to remember making love with Lawrence – and failing.

"He is a man divided against himself, it makes him very angry, and he is to be pitied more than blamed," Sumet replied sadly. "But of course, nothing excuses his violence."

He examined Kate's face carefully, then gave her a reassuring smile. She wouldn't need stitches this time.

Good. That's what Belinda thought.

"She's so furious that I'm afraid she's going to give him a piece of her mind someday, and then what might happen? But when she gets mad..., well you know her. She's the only one who dared speak up to Melanie." Kate said.

"I told Wanida and the others that I'd slipped in the stairs and hit my face against the bannister. They pretended to believe me."

She paused and added, a steely note in her voice, "I got some drugs out of him, anyway. He feels so guilty afterwards, I could probably go to their central pharmacy and help myself."

No, no, no, she must be cautious. "Don't ask for too much. What if his superiors start to question him about the missing medication, and begin to suspect him?

"I'm sure they are as cautious in checking their stores as we are."

"All right," she shrugged, then hesitated. "Doctor? Can I ask?", then stopped, and turned away. "No, it's nothing, I don't want to bother you."

"You never bother me."

But she had already walked off.

With Belinda, she was more forthcoming that night in their room.

"I think I'm pregnant."

"What?" Belinda shrieked. "You think?"

No. Actually, she knew.

"I've missed two periods now, my breasts feel – I don't know – weird.

"I kept on telling myself that perhaps it was nothing – listen to me, a nurse, who thinks missing two periods could be nothing – but this morning I was nauseated and barely managed to make it out of the ward to throw up.

"Yes.

"I'm pregnant all right."

She managed a bitter laugh. "Just what Mother Felicity said would be my fate if I stayed in Boston, black-eyed and pregnant. Didn't need to go so far, it happened just the same. It's like a curse."

Belinda sighed and sank back against the pillow. "I always was afraid that might happen. Weren't you?"

"Of course. But somehow... I thought it couldn't," Kate answered wearily.

"I'm so stupid, I'd always heard that babies were conceived in love... You think I'd have known better."

She plopped herself down on the bed, wrapping her arms around her knees.

"You don't know how often I dreamt of having Lawrence's baby, we talked about it, but we knew – or rather I guess, he knew – that it would have to wait.

"We had chosen names, if you can imagine. Julie if it were a girl, Michael for a boy."

"What are we going to do?" Belinda said in a matter-of-fact voice, and cocked her head at Kate. "Listen, I know it's a mortal sin, and all that, but... you don't want to keep it, do you? "

Kate shuddered.

Of course not. "Do you think that Doctor Sumet...?"

"No harm in asking," Belinda replied briskly, and scratched her mosquito-bitten leg.

"Bloody mosquitoes. Bernadette swears that lemongrass oil works a charm, but just look at me."

"Stop scratching, you're making yourself bleed. Here let me put some alcohol on it, otherwise it will get infected."

"Yeah, and I'll get scars, and never be able to wear sheer nylons again!" she chortled in her old impudent way, then suddenly burst into tears. "Oh, Kate, do you think we'll be wearing nylons again someday, and go to the flicks, and lead a normal life?"

Kate gathered her to her, tears running down her face as well.

"I don't know, honey, I don't know. But we're going to try."

Sumet refused, his pain at doing so twisting his heart. He could not, as a Buddhist, take a life, even one as unformed as that.

"But there are herbs, that you could find in a Chinese pharmacy. I believe it's effective, but it is not without risk, and in any case, will make you very sick.

"The child in your body fights back, you know.

"And I believe it is as grave a sin for your religion too, akin to murder.

"Could you not consider...?"

What? Having this baby by a man who had raped her and threatened her, and then give it up to lead what kind of life?

Or keep it, and when the war was over, present it to Lawrence?

"I would rather kill myself." Kate said finally, her eyes blazing.

Sumet sat back in his chair, and crossed his hands.

"Captain Akira is a surgeon as well. Ask him.

"He will need to betray his Hippocratic oath. It would be his punishment."

Kate got up and looked down at him, her red hair flaming in the morning sunshine, the very image, Sumet thought, of one of the avenging furies of Greek myth.

Her smile was cruel, and instead of appearing beaten down, as she had in entering the office, she now seemed intent on revenge.

"Of course. You're right. If someone has to do it, it should be him!"

Belinda had carefully kept the note Ken Akira had sent all those months ago, with his telephone number, and when he answered, his voice was warm and teasing.

"Miss me already, darling?"

"Well, you could say that. I need to see you, tonight."

He laughed.

"It's what they always said about you straight-laced Catholic girls. Once you get going, you're insatiable. See you tonight, late. I have an operation scheduled at three."

"Don't pick me up. I'll take a samlo. I don't want people to talk."

"Who cares what people say? It's going to rain, you'll get drenched."

"I care."

"Suit yourself, sweetheart."

He was lounging on the grimy bed cover, but his eyes were not bloodshot, Kate was pleased to see, there was no whisky on the table, and instead, a little bunch of pink orchids.

Instead of feeling touched, she felt even angrier than before.

How dare this man pretend at times to treat her like a girlfriend, and at others like a dog he could whip at will?

He eyed her and said, "Your face is still pretty bruised. I'm sorry," then added with a satisfied leer, "Obviously, this hasn't put you off.

"Well, aren't you going to undress?"

Kate stared back, her face and tone grim and unforgiving. "Not tonight.

"I have something to tell you.

"I'm pregnant."

He paled, sat up, and bit his lip.

She waited, the finally snapped.

"So? Say something."

He shook his head. "I don't know what to say."

Kate sat down on the bed, her anger spent.

"Didn't you think it could happen?"

He shook his head again. "I didn't give it any thought, to tell the truth.

"Did you?"

Kate began to laugh bitterly. "God, men... Even doctors...

"I'm a maternity nurse. Of course I knew it could happen."

He rose from the bed and began to pace the room, thinking out loud.

"The thing is... we're not allowed to marry, we're only allowed to — well, I think it's called fraternize with, you know, prostitutes."

"The thing is," Kate replied dryly, "I'm not allowed to marry either, being married already.

"And I'm not going to keep this baby. So, what are you going to do about it?"

He sighed.

"The free clinic can perform D and C's, I know, but they're butchers. I won't let that happen to you."

He sighed again. "I'll do it myself, at your hospital."

"You must be crazy. No. Not at Saint-Louis, with everybody knowing about it," Kate spat. "Somewhere else."

"I'll find someplace."

He sat on the single chair, and looked at her. "I'm sorry. I really am.

"For what's about to happen, and what happened before. You deserve better."

He rubbed his eyes, then sagged down, his head between his hands.

"I wonder what my parents would think of me now. They brought me up right, taught me to respect others, and now...

"But I was just so lonely, so lonely..."

Without answering, Kate got up and went to the door. She was not about to listen to his self-pitying, maudlin ramblings.

"Let me know where. But I want this taken care of this this week."

"So he'll do it?" Belinda asked, then smiled nastily. "What price the Hippocratic Oath now?"

"Well, what about you?" Kate teased.

With the end of that nightmare of a pregnancy in sight, she felt bubbly with relief, almost elated. "A good Catholic nurse, advising me to have an abortion?"

Nurses didn't have to take the oath, Belinda replied happily, munching on one of the last biscuits from Thip's latest hamper.

"And friendship trumps oaths. So there.

"I'll come with you, and tell that sleeveen what I think of him."

She would do nothing of the sort, Kate told her firmly. And whenever her path crossed Ken Akira's, she was to remember Eddy.

"Love trumps revenge.

"Promise?"

Belinda made a face.

"All right. I promise."

It was a private clinic, somewhere off Naret Road.

When consulted by Kate, Doctor Sumet said it had a fairly good reputation for cleanliness.

"And of course, whatever else he may be, Captain Akira is a skilled surgeon," he added. "But Kate, one last time, are you sure..?"

Kate lifted her hand to stop him.

She was sure and wanted to hear no more.

"I've had you booked in for ablation of ovarian cysts," Akira told her, when he met her at the entrance..

"This kind of operation is illegal here, and nobody's fooled... but they're not going to report a Japanese surgeon.

"We'll put you under briefly. I don't like to use chloroform, so I'm using sodium pentothal and ether.

"You've had no food or drink this morning?"

Kate shook her head in exasperation. "I'm a nurse, remember? I know about anaesthesia."

"Of course. Sorry, habit. What did you tell the hospital to explain your being away?"

"That I was going to assist you in for several operations, and that I would probably be away overnight."

She showed him the bag she was carrying.

"That's why I took my uniform."

He nodded. Good thinking. But she would need a couple of days rest afterwards, how could she arrange that?

"I'll say I got food poisoning from the stuff I was given to eat. I'm sure everybody will believe that."

He sighed. "Give up the plucky act, Kate. I'm no happier

about this than you are."

She sighed as well. "Let's just get it over with."

It was strange being a patient lying on the table, waiting for it to start, looking up at the strong overhead light.

So this is what it's like, she thought, the helplessness, the metal clink of instruments being prepared, and this fear that somehow I may die.

I know what the risks are. I've seen women die from abortions. I might bleed out, and Ken won't be able to stop it. I might not wake up.

And if I don't... Well... who cares really?

I do, she told herself furiously.

I do, I want to live, I want to be back with Lawrence, I want to study medicine, maybe. I want my own life again, and I won't be made to feel guilty about destroying this life that never should have been.

Ken's eyes behind his mask were reassuring, and he explained, as he did to all his patients, that she would feel something cold when he gave her the injection, and he was about to put the ether mask over her face when she pushed it away, and mumbled, feeling her body and mind becoming heavy, "Why didn't you ask me to assist you in other operations? You said you would."

He raised his eyebrows and he must have been smiling, she saw his eyes crinkle. "I will." And then the world, mercifully, faded away.

When she came to, he wasn't there.

There was just a sullen Thai nurse, who mopped her forehead, then held an enamel basin when she vomited. "Doctor called away," she said. "Back tomorrow, maybe, before you leave."

And maybe not, Kate hoped.

Her whole body ached, she was cramping and bleeding, and the waves of nausea wouldn't stop. She knew it was due to the ether and would pass, but knowing made it no easier to cope.

The nurse returned with a cup of herbal tea that smelled of ginger. "Drink. Stop vomit," and holding up Kate's head none too gently, forced her to swallow.

Ken was right, she thought, nobody was fooled. That nurse was probably as good a Buddhist as Doctor Sumet, and considered her a murderer.

Well, had it been at Saint Louis under Melanie, she would quite simply not have been admitted.

She longed for release from the pain, she longed for Belinda, for someone who cared. She couldn't even muster longing for Lawrence, desperately ashamed of herself as she was, she just wanted to forget these past sordid months of fear and confusion.

Oh, just get me back to my own room. Let me sleep, Holy Mother, I'm sure you understand why I had to do this. Let me sleep.

The following morning, another nurse brought her tea and a banana, and Kate was amazed to find herself so hungry.

The nausea had vanished, but she was still sore and a bit dizzy, and dressed slowly, fumbling with the buttons on her dress.

There was a knock on the door, and Ken Akira entered, looking...what? Kate wondered. Embarrassed, ill at ease? Sorrowful, perhaps?

He sat on the bed, and took her hand. "How do you feel?"

She was not about to complain to *him,* —"All right. I'll live," — and let her hand lie lifeless in his, and after a moment, he let go.

"Good, because I have to tell you, that was my first ever D and C.

"I mean, I've seen it done, I knew what to do, but God, was I scared."

She smiled despite herself. "Thanks for only telling me now. I was pretty scared too."

"It didn't show. Listen, I can't stay. I've arranged for a car to take you back, but have something to tell you first.

"I'm going to be away, for several weeks, over a month probably, possibly even longer.

"I'm being assigned to visit field hospitals in the Philippines and New Guinea.

"There's a whole series of what in med school we used to call meatball operations that need to be corrected, and I'm going to have to do a few skin grafts on burn victims."

She couldn't help be interested. "Skin grafts? Have you ever done any?"

He'd done several, when he was an intern.

"It's tricky. There's a high rejection risk, and in tropical conditions, the possibility of infection... well, I don't need to tell you."

She rose from the bed, preparing to leave. "So, they now trust you enough?"

He made a face. "Possibly. Although, I'll not be anywhere near the front, and I'm sure they'll watch me like hawks.

"But yes, I guess, they're beginning to trust me."

He hesitated, and cleared his throat.

"There's something else I have to tell you. I didn't want to at first, but, you know, I may not come back, and ... well somehow, I owe it to you...

"There's news of your husband. He wrote something for English newspapers, apparently, he's a correspondent for Associated Press."

She froze, and paled. "How do you know?"

There was a kind of summary of the enemy press that tracked the progress of Japanese troops throughout Asia, published every month, and he had found an old copy in the waiting room of the hospital.

"Some dope of an officer left it laying around. Although, I'm not sure it was confidential, but personally, I'd never seen any of those reports.

"Anyway... He wrote about the bombing of Mandalay, that was late last May. So he is, or rather was in Burma.

"If he made it out, then he must be in India."

She had begun to shiver. It had never occurred to her that Lawrence might be anywhere other than China, still. So he had managed to get back to the English!!

Although....

They'd heard on the BBC that the retreat from Burma was a catastrophe, with thousands dying in their attempt to escape.

But she couldn't let Ken realize that somehow she had been following news on the radio.

"Why wouldn't he have made it out?"

Ken shook his head.

Most of the English retreated from Burma on foot, through the mountains, with the Japanese air force bombing and strafing them. "It was pretty horrible, I guess. The news I heard on the radio was gloating about it for days.

"And anyways, why are you so upset? He left you, didn't he?"

She felt so dazed with joy at the idea Lawrence was probably alive — press people were always taken care of, she was sure — that she'd forgotten her web of lies.

She took a deep breath to steady herself, and tried to sound mournful.

"Yes. He did.

"But I still love, him, I can't help it. I mean... I know it's over but..."

He took her hand again.

"And I love you, Kate, I can't help it either."

Her heart skipped a beat, and she felt as if he had slapped her again.

Oh God, would this nightmare never end?

She sat back on the bed, and tried to speak calmly, but her voice rose with every despairing word.

"You don't love me. Remember what you said? You're lonely.

"If you loved me, how could you treat me this way, threaten me, hit me, rape me?

"You don't do that to people you love.

"How could you not even care if I got pregnant?"

"How?"

He took both her hands and gazed at her earnestly.

"Listen to me. Those days are over. I know I treated you badly, and I'm ashamed of it.

"But I promise you, cross my heart — never again.

"And you won't get pregnant, I'll make sure of that."

He kissed her softly.

"I really have to go now, and your car will be here in a few minutes.

"Remember, take it easy for a couple of days.

"No aspirin for the pain, it could make you bleed more.

"I'll miss you, darling."

She heard his rapid footsteps running down the stairs, sat down again and ran both hands through her hair.

How could this be happening?

And then, she couldn't help it, she began to laugh so hard she cried.

Chapter XXVI

It has been a year since I've written anything in this diary.

I keep it well hidden in my bag's secret pocket, and the bag itself safely padlocked.

It's not that I haven't felt, at times, the urge to write for none other than myself, but... I have been reluctant to put on paper the events of my personal life over the past months, but I feel that as my life is once again about to change, I need to face and take stock.

I have been doing my job, or rather both my jobs, as best I can.

It certainly wasn't difficult to get people to talk to me about their views on the situation here in India.

It was actually more difficult to stem the torrent of words, at times invective, and certainly strongly held opinions, the most general being is that we British need to leave.

"And then, what happens?" I always ask.

Well then... answers differ, and run the gamut from, "Let us manage ourselves, and we shall do a better job than you" to "The Hindus (or the Muslims) will kill us all."

Which is why my messages to Meerut have always been, rather to my shame, along the "Divide and rule" line, which, I have no doubt, were then turned into whispered snippets about how the Japanese shall favour this group or the other, but also that the Allies were beginning to defeat the Germans in Europe, Stalingrad was a crushing defeat, Italy was being retaken by the Americans, and that the Japanese would soon be waging the war alone.

When the might of Britain and America was unleashed against them, on whose side did India want to be?

I also made much about the Japanese declaration of Burma's independence the first day of this month, and suggested that the Burmese, who were always known as foes of Indians, would sweep down their hills and savage the border provinces with Japanese support.

And because there is no logic to propaganda, thankfully, and one can claim one thing and then its opposite, I also suggested to Meerut that they spread the word that Wingate's Chindits seemed to be poised to retake Burma and that the Indian National Army renegades were redefecting *en masse* to rejoin their former comrades-at-arms, telling tales of Japanese racism and cruelty, of using INA soldiers to be mown down on the front lines, etc.

Well, *en masse*, is an exaggeration, but there apparently have been some cases.

I suppose this is how the stories of Belgian nuns being raped by German soldiers in the Great War were started.

Meanwhile, my official correspondent work continues, and I've been criss-crossing this immense continent to speak to the students protesting police brutality and arbitrary arrests, or to interview families of imprisoned Congress members, and most recently report on the horrors of the Bengal famine — earning myself a dressing-down afterwards by military censors who denied such famine existed. "Even the *Statesman* claims there are no food shortages, and it is published in Calcutta.

"And what is all this nonsense about a *cloth* famine?

"People robbing freshly dug graves to steal *clothes* off corpses? For their clothes?

"Have you gone quite mad?

"You've tried so hard to be sensational you've turned into a tasteless ghoul, Gallet. Anyway, Indians get cremated, not buried."

I mildly replied that it was true of Hindus, not Mohammedans or — and there are some — Christians. But that only served to enrage him to further.

"Don't you think all you sensitive little Oxbridge journalists should let local authorities decide whether it's a famine or not, and refrain from pouring oil on the fire?

"You see problems in food distribution, we see Indian inefficiency.

"You see shortages, we see hoarders, which an Indian tradition to push up prices."

Such was the official British position, as relayed to me by a sneering civil servant in a natty white linen suit.

Except that three days later the *Statesman* editor, Ian Stephens, published a series of photographs of famine victims several days running, and those made headlines all over the Western press, including in the United States.

The *Guardian* described the famine as "horrible beyond description."

When I asked Ian why he suddenly changed his paper's policy, he said he was sick of lying at the orders of his British owners.

Military press officers have come to hate me, which is, in a way, a badge of honour, although it meant that I was refused access to the front with the Chindits.

"Associated Press request or not, Gallet," I was told curtly, "we're not letting you and your defeatist Bolshy style of writing anywhere near the Chindits."

I cannot say I am sorry, as Wingate, he who marches around in the nude with a raw onion hanging from a string around his neck, and his second in command, Mad Mike Culvert, were once described to me by Merrill as "best avoided."

My "defeatist Bolshy" style of writing refers to the fact that I reported on the bombing raids over Calcutta last December and described them as "unchallenged."

"That is simply not true," some SPRO twit countered.

I was there, I replied, and saw no RAF planes.

But if he could give me the figures for the crews that went out to attack the Japanese bombers, I'd be delighted to publish a correction.

He snarled and ordered me out of his office.

Before the famine situation had reached the present apocalyptic proportions, and despite the bombing raids, I spent a delightful December in Calcutta, staying with Vikram, my poet friend from University. Alas, he has given up poetry under pressure from his father, has married a delightful young woman, and is being eased into the many family business interests.

The house is not unlike Lady Thip's in that was built as some sort of an Asian dream of a Tudor residence, and is set in an enormous garden, in what I can only assume is the most desirable area of Calcutta, far from the crowded unsanitary slums and busy bazaars.

As Tozer would have said, it was just like Kent.

I was made welcome, and introduced to many of their friends, who obligingly replied openly when I mock-naively asked what would most encourage the Indians to resist a Japanese invasion.

"I think...

"The fear of the unknown.

"We know nothing about the Japanese. They say they have our best interests at heart, but can we trust them?

"By now, we know you British well, and although we do not always trust you, we have learned how to deal with you, using the laws you have imposed here.

"The very same laws you have taught us," was Vikram father's very forceful views.

He adjusted his Congress cap to a more determined angle, and added in a warning tone, "As our own Mahatma has been doing, we shall now employ those useful lessons against you.

"Tell your paper that."

"The Japanese? Conquer us?

"They will never succeed, try as they may, because of the sheer size of the population and the country," a thoughtful lawyer said, "added to the fact we're quite unmanageable, with our different languages, religions, and castes."

But the British succeeded, I answered, with a smile.

"Ah, but you did not invade us in one brutal swoop.

"You seduced us, little by little, made us want to be like you, loved by you, and then, just like a cruel man with a new wife, once you'd conquered our soul, you enslaved us."

There was then a heated discussion as to whether the Indian soul *had* indeed been conquered, and I realized that there is nothing more pleasurable to Bengalis than an argument.

I could not spend my life going from hotel to derelict school to former barracks to being a guest here and there, and felt the need to settle somewhere, so I have rented a small furnished apartment in Delhi, taking it over from an Australian correspondent who was sent to cover the war in Egypt.

The furniture is a mishmash of Indian pseudo-Chippendale and utilitarian and ugly pieces. It's in a rather damp and aging building on a noisy street.

What with the war, prices are so high that I could afford no better.

I do not want to ask my father to arrange to have money sent, and I live off my correspondent's pay, which is no more than adequate. And in any case, the flat is sufficient for my needs, which I now realize, have become much less exacting after this past year.

Gone is the young man who demanded beauty as well as comfort — I have a table, chair, bed, and a bearer-cum cook who prepares basic food and sees to my laundry.

Delhi is the city where correspondents now congregate, because that's where most of the news is, though most of my old group have now moved on.

Dan De Luce was in the Middle East, as were George Rodger and I think, Alec Tozer, and are now covering the Italian campaign.

Leland Stowe is in Russia, or so I hear, and I read that Jack Belden was in Italy as well.

Nobody left to call me 'Blondie' except for Berrigan who is still in India, and we occasionally meet for drinks and swap stories but not scoops.

Burchett is in China, trying to get Chiang Kai-Shek to commit to an interview, but no luck so far.

And speaking of the Generalissimo, I bumped into Tex and a few other AVG men at the Great Eastern in Calcutta early last spring.

All of them very down at the mouth because the Flying Tigers, as the press had dubbed them, are now to be incorporated into the US Air Force.

They are going to be employed flying the supplies that Chiang Kai-Shek still desperately needs over "the Hump", that is the Himalayas, from an air base in Dinjan.

The flying conditions over those sharp, dizzyingly high mountains are hell, they say.

"Well, only five of us have accepted. Everything I tried to escape, now I'm back in the fucking army," Tex moaned into his drink.

"Yeah, and that means no bonus money for downed Japs," Bill Reed added.

Pete Petach and Red have married, and I also learned that Jack Newkirk, the pushy, brash New Yorker, was killed over Chiang Mai.

We drank to him.

"What about those who refused to be back in the Air Force?" I asked.

"Depends. Most are going back to the States. Some are fed up with India and China, and are going to join other units.

"Olga and Harvey have left already. You should have seen the amount of luggage Olga had! It looked like she'd looted all of Kunming."

My first friends of the war, scattered as well.

There is a new group of correspondents, but none with whom I have felt the kinship that developed in Burma, possibly because none of us here are in any danger except that of having a dispatch refused by the censors.

I am no longer the tyro, I have actually become what I used to long to be, someone experienced, someone newcomers turn to for pointers or information, and it is not the source of joy I once imagined.

Nonetheless, there are some friendly people with whom I spend evenings in the bar of the Cecil Hotel, and I still feel awe at their stories of the desert war, the blitz or the Russian front.

And there are women, too, among the journalists, and that, to me, was a novelty.

I see them toting their camera bags and lenses and exchanging mock insults with male colleagues, and they look as dishevelled as us — a far cry from elegant Eve Curie.

And among them was Sonia...

Before her, I am ashamed to admit that I engaged in several mindless affairs — Betty, a military nurse who was as lonely and lost as I felt, and Isobel, a rebellious WAC, daughter of an Indian Army major imprisoned in a German camp.

She was bright and amusing, utterly fed up with the attentions of the British officers who swarmed around her like bees to a honey pot, and thought a journalist a pleasant and interesting novelty.

But she was very much cast in the mould of the burra memsahib, and outside of bed, after a couple of weeks I began to be as bored by her prattle as she was by my talk of politics and the war, and we both were relieved when I went to Calcutta again to cover the ever worsening famine.

Which brought me to Sonia...

She was introduced one evening at the Cecil's bar. "Here's someone you'd like to meet, Sonia. Lawrence Gallet, AP, an old Asia hand who's done China and the Burma retreat.

"Sonia Tomara, *New York Tribune*."

Was she beautiful?

No, I never thought so, but as my grandmother used to say, she is better than that — she is elegant.

She is much older than me, but carries her years proudly, and when she smiled and began to speak in that husky French and Russian-accented voice of hers, she was irresistible — or at least to me.

She was born in Saint-Petersburg, and fled the Bolsheviks to Paris with her family, then moved to the States, came back to try and save her parents, and covered Hitler's rise and the invasion and the fall of France.

I never for an instant thought she might give a second's attention to someone as callow as myself.

We talked about India, and China, where she is to go next.

She has that rare quality of seeming to see and hear no one else than you, and I realized that since Kate, nobody had looked at me with such a tantalizing mix of interest and desire.

She is very French in a way, with all the sophistication and glamour that Paris gives women *d'un certain âge* despite her drab uniform, and her grey-streaked curls tumbled delightfully over her shoulders when she bent her head to have her cigarette lit. I saw her nails were polished bright red, and she wore pearls in her ears.

And when, dizzy from all the gin I'd consumed, I said I needed to get home, she quite naturally got up and said, "I'm coming with you."

I am sure I blushed, I am sure that the others watched us leave with an amused smile, and I'm sure that there was some muffled laughter, but I felt such lust I was beyond caring.

She is fearless, yet tender, funny and passionate, demanding and generous.

Did I love her?

Yes, in a way, I did, knowing all the while that this was to be nothing but an interlude of blissful release from all the ugliness of war.

When she left for China, I felt heartbroken, and at the same time relieved that I am still able to love.

It is nothing like what I felt — feel — for Kate, but she is now but a shadow in my mind, a dream of the more beautiful life I once led. I look at her picture, I stroke it with my lips, but... she is not real anymore.

For a few weeks, I held a real woman in my arms, there was a bottle of Chanel scent on the nightstand, lacy underthings drying on the towel rack, and she had draped a reddish scarf over the ugly bedside lamp.

I spent the following week or so in a daze of misery, smelling her perfume on my pillow, wondering what I was to become, and if I would continue to spend my time reporting on the fate of those, who I know, are far worthier of pity than me, and this only increased my self-loathing.

I am afraid I had far too much to drink, was belligerent even with Darrell Berrigan, and made myself utterly unpleasant.

But there are, as always, some merciful gods looking after me, and yesterday, I was ordered to report to an office which, I discovered, was Military Intelligence, headed by my old acquaintance Alec Peterson.

"You remember, last year you were inquiring about Siam."

I nodded, but felt my heart beating faster, as he shifted papers on his desk.

"Well, you are going to be pleased, I hope," he said. "There is a newish unit being set up under SOE, Force 136, to organize our behind the lines actions in Asia, divided by country into sections.

"The head of Force 136 is Colin Mackenzie, and, in case you had not already realized, he's the man you met with in Singapore."

Could that be Bill, I wondered, and asked if he had lost a leg.

Alec raised an eyebrow.

"Indeed. During the war, when he was in the Scots Guards. So you do remember him."

How could I have forgotten the man who'd warned me the Kempetai had my name, I wanted to ask, but said nothing, and just nodded, while Alec continued.

"Anyway, you would be sent back to Meerut, to S.C.S., Siam Country Section.

"They've asked for you."

I could say nothing, my mind was such a jumble of questions,

I knew not which to ask first.

He peered at me over his glasses. "Well?"

"What does it do?"

He shook his head.

"No idea, and even if I had, I would not tell you, would I?

"Your orders are to report to Meerut soonest. They need Siamese speakers urgently."

At last.

I could have cried with the sheer relief of it.

I was told that I was to be granted leave from AP – "Your behaviour these past weeks amply justifies it," he added, rather sternly, still very much the headmaster.

Is there anything these people don't know?

"I believe there are enough correspondents in India for your dispatches not to be overly missed."

I decided not to take offense, and just expressed my pleasure at finally doing what I had been trained to do, and took my leave.

When I left him, Alec was already reading another report.

And now, I am about to leave this flat. My packing was quickly done, I left an envelope with money for the bearer, and the landlord will have no difficulty in finding another journalist longing for someplace to park his typewriter and bottle of Scotch.

My illicit diary will be padlocked in my bag again, and I cannot wait to go.

MEERUT, 25TH OF AUGUST 1943

If anything, the train station in Meerut was even busier than when Lawrence had left a year ago, but by now, he was so accustomed to Indian crowds that he just pushed his way out to the front, and he heard his name called by a very young private with a thick cockney accent, ginger hair under his bush hat, a cheeky manner and who barely looked out of school, much less like a soldier than a boy in fancy dress. He was leaning against a jeep, smoking, and gazing around with obvious pleasure at the scene.

"You Gallet?" he asked with an impudent smile. "I'm Biggin, Charlie Biggin. I was told to look for a tall toff with specs. You're the only one who fits the bill. This is your ride."

Lawrence laughed, and threw his bag in the jeep.

"How do you tell a toff when we're all wearing uniforms?"

"Easy. I was training as a hairdresser, I can tell quality when I see it. Hop in."

Biggin chatted all the way to the same barracks Lawrence had been taken to last time, swerving smoothly between cows, beggars and bicycles, and obviously considered the typical chaos of Indian streets an enjoyable challenge.

"Love it here, I do. Been here three months.

"Love the weather, too, better than Delhi. Better than London, heaven knows, when it's not rain falling down on you, it's bombs.

"Ooh, look at that cow, she has a death wish, she does. Wonder how more don't get killed.

"You from London? Yeah, I thought so. It's that look you London gents have.

"Hear you speak Siamese?

"There're others like you supposed to be coming, they say."

He screeched to a halt in front of the barrier, raising a cloud of red dust, spraying the guard who swore at him angrily, then took off again, making the tyres squeal to drive the last hundred yards.

"I'm going to be a taxi driver if I make it through, I'm done with hairdressing. Well, here we are, go straight in."

"I'm sure London streets will be child's play for you," Lawrence replied wryly. "Thanks for the lift."

There was no Sargent Gibbs behind the desk in the front office to stare at him suspiciously, but Ram Das was still there, as emaciated and enigmatic as ever. He gave him a friendly namaste, and pointed at the open door, but a voice was heard booming, "Lawrence Gallet! Well at last! Things are beginning to look up!" and getting up from behind what used to be Alec Peterson's desk was someone he had last seen at the British Club in Bangkok, Peter Pointon, formerly of the Bombay Burmah timber company.

Lawrence gaped.

He never knew Pointon well, just occasionally exchanged a few words, because he seemed to spend most of his time either in Burma or up country, near Chiang Mai.

And whenever they had spoken, Lawrence was rather in awe of the man because of his age and also reputation — a war hero decorated with the Military Cross, a Cambridge graduate and a Siamese scholar.

He had always somehow felt that Pointon did not take either him or his literary ambitions very seriously and rather looked down on him as a character from an Evelyn Waugh novel, the fluffy aimless romantic who was "doing the East".

"Mr Pointon! I — I never — I'm at a loss for words," then spotted the single crown on the man's epaulette, and corrected himself, "Or rather, sorry — Major Pointon. I never expected to see you here."

Pointon smiled in greeting.

"I can't say the same, as I'm the one who asked for you, but I have to admit, I was rather taken aback when I heard you were SOE.

"Although, there is no earthly reason I should have been, you're the perfect recruit.

"Welcome to Siam Country Section of Force 136."

The door burst open, and a big burly man rushed in and enveloped Lawrence in an enormous bearhug.

"Our favourite journo!"

Lawrence disengaged himself to catch his breath. "Oh my God! Nick Nicholson!"

He shook his head in disbelief. "This is just like the bar of the British Club — next thing I know, Gilchrist will turn up!"

Nicholson's ruddy, honest, face beamed.

He had dropped a stone, at least, and looked far more impressive in his captain's uniform than Lawrence remembered him, mud splattered and raising a pint after rugby training.

"Not yet, but we're working on it.

"There's several of us here now — maybe this time we can finally get you on our ruggers scrum."

Lawrence mock-shuddered. "Not a chance. So Andrew made it out?"

Pointon intervened, to quell Nicholson's high spirited welcome.

"Sit down, please, both of you.

"Yes, Andrew was finally repatriated last year. You'll hear about it.

"You may also be surprised to hear that there's going to be a reunion of more old friends as the weeks go by.

"We're trying to get hold of all the Siamese speakers we can."

Lawrence sat. "So. Something has at long last come out of Thailand — sorry, Siam, I mean."

"Yes, please don't use the name Thailand any more. It was one of Phibul's decisions, so...

"But to answer you, something — we're not yet quite sure what, *has* come out.

"The question is now to understand what actually *is* happening.

"You know some of the people involved far better than we do, so we need your insights. What do you know about Chamkat Phalangkun?"

Lawrence thought for a moment. "The name Phalangkun is familiar, obviously.

"Chamkat rings a bell.

"I know I've never actually met him, I'd remember."

He frowned, racking his brain. "Wait! Isn't he the chap that got into trouble for publishing something anti-Phibul in some Thai students' newspaper?"

Pointon nodded. "It seems so.

"Anyway, this Phalangkun fellow appears to have walked — walked!! — into China with a message, purportedly from Pridi, confirming a previous message — which no one ever received — that there is a resistance movement in Siam, including the majority — he says seventy-five percent — of the armed forces including the navy.

"The idea is that Pridi wants to get out to lead the movement from abroad, possibly, I imagine, to join forces with Seni Pramoj — you know, the ex-ambassador of Siam to Washington — and declare a government-in-exile based in India.

"So Chamkat's instructions, he claimed, were trying to contact both the American and our governments to arrange this."

Lawrence sat back in his chair, digesting this information.

"Do we trust him, or see him as some sort of agent provocateur?

"Where is he now?"

Nick made a face. "He's in China, kept under wraps by the Chinese. That's just one of the complications."

Pointon intervened. "One of the other complications is that we're somewhat at loggerheads with the Americans as to Siam.

"As you know, we consider Siam an enemy country. After all, they declared war on us.

"The Americans, however, since Seni Pramoj refused to recognize and transmit the declaration, have a different attitude and are apparently prepared to consider Siam as an occupied country.

"The upshot is that, as Sir Josiah Crosby, our former ambassador to Bangkok, claims no knowledge whatsoever of any resistance movement in Siam, His Majesty's government refuses to attach any importance to this communication from Pridi – if indeed it does come from Pridi, which we at SCS believe it has."

"And what are the Americans doing?" Lawrence wanted to know.

"The Americans..." Pointon sighed.

They were playing their cards very close to their vest.

What was known is that, much as the British were, they were training a group of Siamese students organized under Pramoj for eventual infiltration into the country. "They call it the Free Thai Movement – whereas we call ours the Free Siamese Movement."

Both groups were being trained in India – the Free Siamese in Poona, the Free Thai in the Naga hills.

"From what I gather, they will then be sent to China, and thereon, if possible, into Siam."

"Well, shouldn't someone go talk to Chamkat, see if he's for real?" Lawrence asked.

"Although," he added, "I can't see Phibul choosing one of his known critics as a ploy, except the man is so twisted he may well have."

"Ah...," Pointon replied. "Which brings us to Prince Svasti, or Arun as he is known here."

"Svasti is here? And *he* is the one you'd send?" Lawrence was astonished.

Prince Svasti, brother to the last Queen, who had exiled himself in England with his sister and the King after the abdication, was an arch-royalist, an aristocratic and unyielding opponent of everything the Revolution of 1932 stood for, and presumably one of Pridi's most ardent foes.

He did not seem to him the best choice for a go-between.

Pointon's rejoinder was stern. "Arun is above all a patriot."

Yes, Prince Suphasawat Svasti was a known monarchist, but it was also he who had taken the initiative of organizing the induction of Siamese students into the Pioneer corps in Britain, and he had managed to overcome the reluctance and at times open hostility of the more left-wing minded of them.

He had, only through his personal influence and network of highly placed friends, managed to obtain an interview with the Prime Minister and emerged from it with a commission.

He was now a Major in the British Army.

And earlier that month, he *had* met with Chamkat in Chongqing — he knew him from when Chamkat was at Oxford — and was convinced Chamkat was a true representative of Regent Pridi.

"I sense a 'but'," Lawrence said.

"Indeed, but... Chongqing is...

"Well, Nick's description of it being complicated is an understatement.

"It's a Byzantine labyrinth of smoke and mirrors.

"The Chinese think they have the Americans in their pockets, and the Americans play along with that view, whilst imagining *they* are pulling the Chinese strings, who go along with the pretence, and so forth and so on.

"The Chinese, as Nick said, are more or less keeping Chamkat under wraps, and all we have to go on — I repeat, all — is Chamkat's word that there is some form of organisation; he calls it the X-O group, and claims that whatever he says is in Pridi's name because somehow he manages to communicate with Pridi from Chongqing by radio."

"So they do use radio," Lawrence interrupted. "Why on earth haven't they tried to contact us before?

"Don't they know how desperate we were for some sign?"

"Well, yes, that's one of the questions that shed doubt on Chamkat's story.

"We don't know why they haven't tried before, perhaps because they don't know how to reach us.

"Anyway, let me continue.

"As if you needed more twists to the plot, the person Washington sent to Chongqing as liaison officer with the OSS is Colonel Khap Kunjara, the former military attaché at the Thai embassy.

"You don't know of him?

"Well, his reputation is iffy, to say the least, he drinks, he chases skirts, he gambles — and that is confirmed by our own embassy in Washington — and suffice it to add that he was appointed by Phibul, who is a close friend of his.

"Seni Pramoj loathes him, and doesn't trust him one inch — which we were also able to ascertain from the very few contacts between our representatives and the Americans in Chongqing.

"Khap was the first to meet with Chamkat, and poisoned him against us, which in any case, wasn't difficult, because our own government considers him at best a somewhat deranged army of one and at worst an agent provocateur."

Lawrence was trying to tie the various strands of the story together.

"So you say, Chamkat is being closely watched by the Chinese, and but still met with an OSS representative — that would be Colonel Khap — and SOE — well, SCS — through Arun.

"We don't know what the Americans want, we don't know what the Chinese are doing with him. Right?"

Pointon nodded, while Lawrence went on.

"However, *we* still consider that there is an underground organisation in Siam, and plan our actions accordingly. Yes?"

"If only it were that simple..." Pointon sighed.

What Lawrence should bear in mind is that when Chamkat met Arun, he was violently opposed to assistance from the British, as he believed that their plan was to take over Siam after the war —"which is what Colonel Khap told him, and actually, what the Americans believe.

"Washington seems convinced that our sole aim in trying to win this war in Asia is to restore — and possibly enlarge — our colonial empire."

"Isn't it?" Lawrence asked ironically, and Nick barked a sharp laugh.

Pointon made a face.

"For some, including, it seems, Churchill, it probably is.

"For us, the only plan is to try to beat the Japs. What happens afterwards is politics, and we don't engage in that.

"To come back to Chamkat, Arun managed to reassure him somewhat, and Seni Pramoj has finally forked out the money to pay for his passage to the States, and the Americans have been leaning on the Chinese to let him go.

"They may yet, or they may not. Why they're so cagey about him is another mystery.

"However, what we do know is that the Chinese want the Siamese government-in-exile to be set up in China – and the Americans don't seem averse to that, strangely.

"There was one Miles, a US Navy captain, who was in cahoots with Tai Li, the head of Chiang's intelligence service and who does whose bidding, we don't know.

"Miles also appears to loathe us Brits, and told Grut in no uncertain terms that there would be no possibility of Free Thai and Free Siamese working together if he had any say in the matter.

"Furthermore, he claims that the OSS are about to put some Free Thai in the field in the coming weeks, which is madness itself."

Lawrence raised his eyebrows.

"It's worse than a Byzantine labyrinth, it's a tangle of snakes.

"So where does this leave us?"

Nick got up, clapped Lawrence on the shoulder. "Exactly as you said – we know there is an underground in Siam, and we plan accordingly.

"In good time, when we're ready, we put someone in the field with a radio transmitter, make contact, assess the situation.

"Come on, I'll show you your room, and then you can meet Arun, and talk to him, draw your own conclusions."

"What do I call him? Your Highness, or just plain Arun?"

"Major will do splendidly," Pointon replied dryly.

Lawrence rose, picked up his hat and typewriter case, looked around at the familiar office, the maps on the wall and the padlocked filing cabinets.

"You have no idea, no idea at all how very pleased I am to be here."

"Judging from how we ourselves felt when we were sent here, actually, we have a pretty keen idea. Doing something for Siam at last...," Pointon smiled.

"Mess at six, for a predinner pint all right?"

Lawrence gave him a snappy mock-salute. "Major, it will do splendidly."

He was greeted with good natured claps on the back and ribbed about fleeing Thailand in style on a plane, whereas, as one of the men Lawrence remembered as a beer-swilling, rugby-playing, dart-throwing bore put it, they had walked out through the jungle in Tavoy, "with just the clothes on our backs."

"Good to have you with us, Gallet," a loud, drawling, very Oxonian voice boomed at him, and a middle-aged Siamese officer in a well-pressed uniform with a major's coronet pushed past the rugby scrum.

"I am Suphasawat Svasti," he announced. "I believe we have friends in common. Khunying Thip and her son Pichit – I knew them – oh, it seems many lifetimes ago."

Lawrence smiled and nodded, comparing the man with everything he had heard of him.

Every inch the proud aristocrat, the prince stared back, with a challenging look. Yes, he seemed to say, I know what you think, but I am loyal to my brother-in-law, King Rama the Seventh, can you fault me for that?

"Yes, Major, Khunying Thip is a good friend.

"I would dearly like to have news, all the more so as my wife lives with her," Lawrence finally replied.

"Well, that's what we are all here for," Pointon, who had watched the encounter with uneasy eyes, stated quietly. "To finally get some understanding of what is actually happening in Siam. So let's all go in to dinner, and tomorrow, you can get to work."

Over dinner, Lawrence was also told of another group that were hand-picked by Nick in China, ten young Bangkok-born Sino-Siamese, who were being trained in Trincomalee to be infiltrated back in the country.

"We call them the Red Elephants, and the Siamese, the Whites.

"The idea, you see," Nick said, "is to get the support of the Bangkok business community, which of course is mainly of Chinese descent and who obviously must be suffering under Japanese rule."

Prince Svasti made a pinched, derisive face. "Personally, I think it's a mistake to employ them. They will have divided loyalties, and I think they will always favour China over Siam after the war."

"Major Arun, we haven't won the war yet," Pointon interrupted firmly. "And in the meantime, we need all the help we can get to do so."

What he was expected to do, Lawrence discovered, was his usual work of propaganda, but this time, aimed at the Siamese themselves.

Among the Free Siamese group being trained in Poona, some were not considered able, for various reasons, to be sent on missions into Siam, but were to broadcast anti-Japanese, anti-Phibul radio messages to the Siamese population.

"We're pretty sure that many Siamese listen. In fact, we know, from monitoring Siamese radio, that Phibul is attempting to contact Siamese students abroad, offering them a pardon if they return home.

"Two can play that game.

"So your job is to whip up distrust in Phibul, his Japanese allies, and everything they stand for.

"The war is turning against Axis forces, in Europe as well as Asia.

"Let them know, and let them realize what is at stake.

"Also, it seems you get along with the Yanks. If necessary, you will be asked to liaise with the OSS, if they ever agree to it."

Two weeks later, there was much excitement in learning the latest news from Chongqing.

Chamkat Phalangkun had communicated with Pridi again, and been told that another mission was on its way to China, headed this time by Sanguan Tularak, member of the National Assembly and a staunch Pridi ally.

"Therefore, we do know for sure a movement exists in Siam, and can now actually prepare to send people in," Pointon exulted. "Let's start moving from theory to practice, and get those lads from Poona to Trincomalee to get up to par with combat skills and radio transmission."

Prince Svasti — Lawrence found it difficult to think of him as Arun — intervened silkily.

"It might also be time, Major Pointon, to treat these young men with the respect they are entitled to."

Pointon sighed, but did not reply, and the Siamese aristocrat continued more forcefully.

"Yes, I know, I weary you with those demands.

"But so long as the Free Siamese members do not have their own uniforms, nor receive proper pay, nor recognition as the fighters you are asking them to be, I shall continue.

"Do you imagine they are unaware of the way the Free Thai are treated by the Americans?

"All that I ask is that they be given the same status as afforded by the OSS to their friends — or, in many cases, their relatives.

"Must they be punished because they chose your country — *your* country — to study rather than Harvard or Cornell?

"Is it not enough that they were forced to join the demeaning Pioneer Force as if they were criminals seeking redemption?"

Pointon sighed again.

"Major Arun, I know fully well what your position is, you have already made it clear. Many times.

"All I can say, once again, is that it is not in my hands."

"Then take it in your hands," Svasti retorted, and left the room in a huff, Lawrence watching his exit with a new, reluctant, feeling of respect for the man.

"He's right, you know."

Pointon shrugged. "Of course he's right.

"Just got to make London see that. Our masters have this... I don't know how to put it, really... resentment, perhaps is the best word, because Phibul declared war on us, and their ambassador in London chose to obey orders, whereas Seni, in Washington, chose not to.

"Just like those poor chaps chose to go to Oxford or Cambridge and the others to Harvard, as Arun was saying.

"Truly, the vagaries of fate hang on a single decision often made by someone else.

"But if we are to send them to risk their lives, and possibly bump into friends sent by the OSS, then we can't be seen as showing contempt for them, and reinforce all the prejudice they already have against us Brits.

"But it's an uphill battle, believe me.

"Meanwhile, tell me what you've got up to attacking Phibul."

Lawrence laughed happily.

"Seems we're getting under his skin.

"There's been a series of broadcasts from Bangkok by someone calling himself 'Constitutionalist' — yes, it's a strange moniker, but I guess it's meant to show the broadcasts are sanctioned by the highest levels of government — rebutting everything we ourselves have said in our own broadcasts, and claiming our speakers are pro-royalist renegades and warning them that they will be branded as traitors.

"Constitutionalist also alleges that the population of Siam fully supports Phibul's aligning with the Japanese.

"But obviously, if he needs to say so, well..."

Pointon smiled. "Good lad. Keep it up, then. And also..." he gave Lawrence a sheet of paper with a list of words, and combinations of words.

Lawrence glanced at it, then raised his eyebrows.

"I take it you want me to include these in the broadcasts?"

Yes, precisely.

A microfilm of the same code words and appropriate responses was going to be smuggled into Siam.

"Don't ask how, I'm not sure myself. Maybe some of those smugglers who seem to be able to flit around the area unfettered.

"Anyway, I will tell you which words are to be included and when, and Chamkat has assured Arun that there are short-wave operators at the Postal Services who can communicate by short bursts. They will answer using the same code."

Lawrence grimaced.

"Seems tenuous to me."

Tenuous was the best they could do at this stage, Pointon replied wearily.

Reports from Chongqing announced that Sanguan had arrived in China, with his wife and children, his brother, and Daeng Kunadilok, who was an official of the Foreign Ministry.

They slipped out of the country under the pretext of holidays in Indochina.

"How such a party managed to have anyone believe Indochina is a place for holidays these days is beyond me, but it worked," the SOE man on the ground wrote, "and Sanguan has announced himself as the president of the Committee for Siamese National Liberation.

"He was helped by some anti-Japanese French in Indochina, which is good news, as you may be able to rely on such help for getting messages through to Siam and future infiltration operations.

"Sanguan and his group are now en route to Chongqing."

There, however, the situation was increasingly unclear.

Chamkat once more favoured the British over the Americans.

No, he was giving in to the Chinese to set up the government-in-exile there. He had accepted a loan or rather, the promised mirage of one, from Chiang Kai-Shek, but still asked Force 136 for money, along with a diamond ring, which, he claimed, would be easier to conceal about his person, when coming to India to set up the Pridi government there.

It appeared he was engaged in a bidding war, and that although Chamkat was invaluable as a conduit to Pridi, he was proving irrational, suspicious, and altogether, the report said, "a veritable headache", because, perhaps, of his poor health, but more certainly because the poor young man was invested with greater responsibility than he could handle.

"Why", it concluded, "Regent Pridi chose him as an envoy, we can only wonder."

And then the news came.

Chamkat had died, suddenly.

"He's been poisoned," Svasti raged. "If not by the Chinese, then by Khap."

"No, he hadn't," Pointon objected, reasonably.

Sanguan had met him before he died, and Chamkat told him he had cancer.

"I met him as well, barely a month ago," Svasti snapped, "and he never mentioned it."

"How do you know he didn't just find out?" Pointon sighed.

They all turned away helplessly. They had no way of knowing.

But what they all realized was that the situation in Chongqing was even more lethal than they had ever conceived possible.

The following week, the SCS men left for China to reconnoitre the route the Red Elephants were to take to enter Siam from Yunnan and suddenly, for Lawrence, all the planning and preparing and training, all the broadcasts to Siam to garner support, were no longer some sort of pipe dream, a pretence they were trying to *do something* rather than sit back and watch.

It was real. It was happening.

Someone was going into Bangkok and would find out what was the true situation was.

Maybe not tomorrow.

Maybe not next month.

But someday soon.

Chapter XXVII

Ken Akira had been away for over seven months, far longer than he had said, and when the monsoon rains started and he was still not back, Kate began to think that perhaps he had been transferred to another area – or perhaps he had been killed.

At first, she just revelled in the peace of mind she felt each morning when she woke and realized she needn't fear any peremptory summons.

She went about her duties, and felt almost happy, checking on patients, assisting in operations, and, in the evenings, sitting on the tiled floor of the darkened pharmacy, listening to the BBC news.

The nurses whispered muted cheers with every further advance or victory of the Allies, and although they had never even heard before of many of the European cities or Pacific Islands where battles were being fought, they knew enough to realize that the Soviet victory of Stalingrad and the heavy bombing of Essen, the Ruhr and Berlin were marking a turn in the war.

Kate and Belinda even ventured sometimes out of the hospital grounds in early evening, to buy fruit at Bangrak market and once dared to sit by the river bank, sharing a bunch of mangosteens and watching the small boats ferrying people from one side of the rushing reddish water to the other. Although some did stare at the two farangs, none of the looks were hostile, and most women smiled.

But as soon as the sun went down, they hurried back through the back streets, avoiding Sathorn Road – when the city went dark, they had been told by most Thai orderlies, drunk Japanese soldiers roamed and the streets were unsafe.

Doctor Sumet no longer joined the nurses to listen to the radio – he seemed preoccupied, Kate thought, and though still kind enough to deal with parcels to be sent to Eddy, he appeared reluctant to chat with her.

When she had announced, last October, that Captain Akira

would be away, possibly for months, he just nodded.

Stung, Kate faced him defiantly. "Are you angry with me because I had that abortion? Is that why you're giving me the cold shoulder?"

"Cold shoulder, Khun Kate?" he asked, perplexed.

"Yes, cold shoulder," she retorted. "It means – oh, well, it means, that you're – how can I put it? That you're snubbing me?

"You never come to hear the news with us anymore."

He laughed gently. "Ah, cold shoulder. I thought it was a joint ailment.

"No, my dear, I am not angry with you – why should I be? – nor as you say, snubbing you.

"I am just busy at home – my mother is not well, as you know – and also, I do not want Wanida to wonder why I stay late at the hospital evening after evening.

"I do not want to get any of you in trouble if she were to come upon us in the pharmacy."

Kate frowned, unconvinced. "Is it because of what you do to help prisoners in that camp you told me about? Is that it?"

At that, he rose from behind his desk, and checked the corridor before answering, his voice low and serious.

No, he had stopped whatever help he had given there – it was too dangerous and he wanted her to forget anything she had heard from him, or indeed, from anyone else about that that horrible place.

"There is nothing that you or I can do about that.

"Please. I beg you to forget about it."

Kate nodded, somehow frightened by his tone.

But still – something was worrying him. She could sense it.

In May, when the rains had started again, Lady Thip made a visit to the hospital, with Busaba, and Fon bearing baskets, in tow.

She was no worse, she insisted, she just wanted to see Kate, and grasped both her hands with tears in her eyes.

"I have missed you sorely, my child," she wheezed. "and I so wish you could be with us at the house, as you were before. You look... too thin, and worried.

"Do you worry?"

Kate forced a wan smile, as she wound a tourniquet around

the withered old arm to take blood. "Yes, if course, though I try very much not to. But you know, I hate to say this, I worry about Lawrence less and less.

"It's been over a year now...." Her voice broke. "Longer than we were married.

"It sometimes seems nothing but a dream — him, the wedding, living with you — Your coming here reminds me that it wasn't."

She took a deep breath so as not to burst in tears, and busied herself with the syringe, watching as it filled with blood.

"There. It's done."

She wiped the wrinkled skin with an alcohol-soaked cotton.

"Do you have news of Sam? And where is Pichit?"

Thip looked away, her mouth tightened and Busaba shook her head.

Nothing.

But they had heard no news of Cambridge being bombed, so they hoped for the best. As to Pichit...

She made a face and glanced around, but they were alone in the examination room. "He is doing business with the Japanese, it keeps him very busy. And away from home very often.

"My mother-in-law doesn't approve, as you can see, and neither do I, really, but he says, what can we do?

"We have to sell the rubber from the plantations somewhere, and who else buys?

"But from what we hear, the war is going badly for them, so afterwards, I worry, what is —"

She broke off as Sumet entered the room smiling, and returned his wai.

"Auntie, Auntie, you do me great honour in visiting, and how are you feeling? Well?

"You keep to your diet?

"Has Khun Kate drawn blood yet? Yes?

"So we will know how your diabetes goes."

Thip gave him a withering look.

"My dear Nok, my diabetes is spoiling my life, but I believe it is helped by the Japanese who take all our sugar.

"There are no sweets for me to eat — or perhaps it is a lie Fon tells me to make me stop complaining.

"But you know, I am sure, about old ladies complaining."

Sumet laughed. "Yes indeed. My mother complains far more than you do, I am sure. But she's had longer practice.

"Now take a deep breath, I want to hear your heart and lungs."

He nodded reassuringly when he removed his stethoscope, and asked further questions. Sleep? Breathlessness or pain?

"Keep up as you are," he said finally as he pushed the wheelchair out to the courtyard and helped her into her car.

"Fon is taking good care of you.

"I will send over the medication when I check what insulin dosage you need.

"But you," he added, turning to Busaba, "I would like to see you some day this week to examine you thoroughly. I don't like your colour."

He looked down at her bare feet in her elegant sandals. "And your ankles look swollen. Make an appointment and come in the morning but take no food before."

It was true, Kate noticed suddenly. Busaba's lovely face was pasty under her makeup and seemed swollen. She ran the possible reasons through her mind. Kidneys? Perhaps...

But Busaba shrugged. She was fine, just sleepless nights. And the heat and rain were unbearable this year.

Kate grasped her arm. "Come. Really, you must do it. Come day after tomorrow, Thursday."

All right. Busaba shrugged again. "See you Thursday then," and the Packard made its way slowly onto Sathorn Road, waiting for a Japanese military car to race past, its Rising Sun pennant flapping wildly.

Sumet and Kate watched it go.

"What do you think?" Kate asked, finally.

Sumet shook his head.

"About Busaba? I was thinking some form of nephritis. Chronic, probably."

Kate nodded her agreement. That's what she suspected as well.

"It runs in her family, so it would not be surprising."

"You know that?"

Sumet laughed shortly. "My dear, there is very little about each other we old Siamese families don't know — unfortunately. For Busaba, the urine test will tell."

And Lady Thip?

"Not good. Her heartbeat is still very irregular, her pulse thready.

"And I'd be willing to bet her diabetes has worsened — indeed, how can it get better at her age?"

He sighed. "At least, there is no money problem to worry about for that family to afford insulin."

Yes. All the more so if the family's wealth, which rested on rubber, were in no danger.

Kate thought and decided to tell what she had just learned.

"Pichit is doing business with the Japanese, did you know?"

Sumet looked away, his face clouded. "I'd heard something, yes."

He sighed again. "People make choices, Kate.

"I have, Pichit has, you have. We cannot judge."

He turned again to look at her. "Captain Akira has been away several months now."

It was Kate's turn to look away. Yes, seven months soon.

"Sometimes, I hope he's been killed," she admitted, still staring at the gravel at her feet. "And then I feel awful. He's not a bad person, deep down, you know. But...

"I look at what he's done to me, and I don't recognize the person I am when he's here. You know... afraid, all the time, and a coward. I didn't use to be like that. I used to do what was right." Sumet put his hand on her shoulder to turn her back towards the hospital lobby. Who was she to decide, at this point, what was right? Was it right to live? He thought that in her case, it was.

And did not say that in his, what was right was perhaps to risk his life.

The news that Chamkat had reached Chongqing had finally reached the X-O Group, Louis Banomyong had told him during a seemingly random encounter at a wedding, but beyond the brief words, "By the way, our friend arrived," he was unable to learn more — just as well, Sumet thought.

But he was relieved to hear that Chamkat had survived the long and difficult journey, he had worried about the frail young man's health.

And now, what was to happen, he wondered.

Would Pridi manage to escape, and if so, what would it mean for those of the group left behind in Bangkok?

The Japanese secret police would scour the city to find all those who might have been involved, hunting down the slightest suspicion of any opposition.

Sumet shuddered.

He knew he had spiritual courage, but he suspected himself of being a physical coward, and did not know how he would fare if tortured.

And then, with an inner smile at his fears, he shook himself.

Pridi's escape would not soon be arranged, he suspected, and the winds of war were turning — it might never come to that.

Kate too was reflective as she walked slowly up to the maternity ward where a squalling newborn and two panting, moaning mothers in labour awaited.

She had not been completely truthful in telling Sumet she hoped Ken had been killed — although, there were moments when she felt that if he were never to come back, she could at last allow herself to think of the future.

More than his fits of dark, dangerous anger and the blows to her face and chest that left her cowering and whimpering on the floor, she feared that in one of his maudlin, drunken states, he might reveal her secret to another Japanese officer, who would be only too happy to arrest the dangerous American nurse, and possibly arrest him as well.

But another side of her — the stupid, stupid, disloyal, unfaithful side, she berated herself — had come to miss him, the nights with him, the touch and feel of him.

Felicity, Felicity, if you could see me now, she whispered. My mother's daughter in every way.

The truth of it was, if Ken Akira were to show up at the hospital doors, she'd open her arms to him.

Belinda was busy, supervising a young Chinese trainee nurse with frightened eyes and terrible skin who could not fold the towels to her liking, watching over a sweating and stoic woman who, by Kate's estimate, had several hours of labour to go, having a cup of tea and arguing with Rose about the way the pharmacy was locked.

"Listen, I know," she was saying, "you want us to lock both the pharmacy door and padlocks to the drugs cabinets at all times.

"I know that, I *know*, oh, Holy Mother, haven't you told me often enough, but what do I do when I've got my hands inside a poor woman and I need — maybe chloroform, maybe just ether, and I need it now, do you want me to fish out the key to my desk drawer from my pinny pocket, then give it to, say, gormless Oom here, and tell her to unlock it, find the two, not the one but two keys to the pharmacy door and drug cabinet, get out the ether, padlock the drug cabinet then lock the door, bring back... oh yes, note the drugs taken in your book, then go wash my hands after fishing the key from my pocket.

"Ooh, why bother?" she concluded airily, waving her hand in dismissal. "The poor woman's dead by now."

Rose was listening without a word, her head patiently cocked to the side. Everyone knew better than to stop Belinda when she was on one of her flights of indignation.

"Mother Melanie used to set out the necessary drugs for the day on the ward table," she finally said mildly.

"And don't I know that as well," Belinda retorted. "But you'll admit it's easier for any one with thieving on their mind to help themselves from the ward table than to go and look in the pharmacy."

"Sharper folds, dear, that's the way," she added for Oom, the trainee. "And go check on that mother there, she needs her face bathed don't you think?"

Oom gazed up at her, barely understanding English. "I go?" she asked.

"Yes, there," Belinda pointed at the labouring woman who was panting away, her face glazed with sweat. "Nam, water, all right?"

"Not to drink, to wash. Good, good, *dii!*

"I swear, I don't know how Melanie did it," she sighed, turning back towards Rose. "And I swear I don't know what the problem is, it's not as if there's been drugs missing, is it?"

"How would I know, you've not noted anything," Rose snapped back.

"Not today, because I note in the evening, before I leave," Belinda replied, furious. "Is there a day when I didn't sign out the drugs I've used?

"Is there?

"Show me!"

Time to step in, Kate told herself, happy to get away from

beating herself up with guilt.

"All right, both of you, stop it," she intervened in a peaceable voice. "We're shorthanded, we're overworked, we're tired, and the rains make us short tempered. That's enough.

"We're having a feast this evening, my friends brought me a basket, and it's very heavy, so I think there's port or sherry inside.

"All right?" she said again, looking at them both.

Rose, once rather stout, was still far from thin, but her face had lost her plumpness, her face was sagging and lank locks of greying hair escaped from her coif.

Belinda's face had become sharp and her grey eyes were shadowed with dark circles.

Rose turned away, and tried to smile. "I declare, Kate, if it wasn't for you, we'd starve on that diet of rice and fish we're on.

"I'd better go back, and, you," she added to Belinda, unable to resist a parting shot, "mind you keep that register up to date."

"Yeah, yeah, just keep on blowing your steam," Belinda muttered very low.

"And I'll keep on running my ward as I see fit."

Kate sat down and picked up a towel to add to the pile.

"Just listen to you," she smiled. "*My* ward? If Melanie ever comes back, let her hear you say 'my ward'.

"She'll hang you up by your thumbs."

Belinda didn't laugh.

She sat down next to Kate, still watching the labouring woman clutching Oom's hands and the new mother nursing her child, and rested her hands on her lap.

"I wonder," she finally said.

"What?"

"I wonder if she'll ever come back. I don't think so.

"I wonder if we'll ever get out of here, or if we'll spend the rest of our lives doing just this," she waved her hand to encompass the ward, but also the hospital and the rainy Bangkok sky.

"You know Kate, there are places where the world is still happening, where ... Oh, I can't explain it, but it seems to me we're just trapped in a cage, or like those toys you see sometimes, just doing the same thing over and over again, you know, like a soldier beating a drum, or a monkey clapping cymbals.

"Automats, yes? That's what they're called, I think."

Kate closed her eyes.

"I know what you mean.

"In Filene's store window, one Christmas, there was a Santa Claus mannequin, holding up his bag full of toys, and two children clapping their hands. Again, and again.

"My little brother Teddy got very upset, he thought it was the real Santa, and that he was jailed at Filene's for good. That's us. Just like Santa and those kids."

She shook her head.

"We've got to stop talking like this.

"We both know that something, somehow, is going to happen.

"The Allies are winning in Europe, and when they're through beating Germany, they'll beat the Japanese. It'll happen.

"It *has* to happen," she added more urgently, her hands locked in prayer.

"Eddy and Melanie and the others will get out, and Lawrence will come back."

But what she would say to him if he did, she didn't know, she thought despondently.

Belinda gave in to her urging and nodded, with a determined smile, "Yes, we'll get out, somehow.

"I know.

"But Kate? If we had to be locked up, I'd have much rather been at Filene's. From what you say, it sounds grand."

She sighed as she pulled herself out of her chair.

"Right. Time to get that woman's baby on its way, now, I think. Wish I knew how to hurry those little creatures along, I don't want to miss dinner."

Busaba came and submitted with ill grace to all the tests Sumet prescribed and did not even blink when told she suffered from chronic nephritis.

"Bright's disease, in other words," she dropped. "I thought as much. My mother and grandmother both had it."

She buttoned her tailored silk blouse. "I'll live."

"You'll live better if you abstain from salt," Sumet said.

Busaba rose from the chair and smirked.

"No sugar for one, no salt for the other. What a household we shall be.

"You're well out of it," she told Kate with an ironic smile, wai-ed Sumet and took her leave.

Kate watched her leave, her high heels clacking on the floor.

"What a piece of work, as Mother Felicity would have said," she commented.

"I still can't tell if I like her or not."

Sumet shrugged.

"All the women in her family are like that. It's not just nephritis she's inherited.

"But poor Pichit... I think it may be because I saw how unhappy he is that I never married myself."

The days passed, the rains cascaded down, and Kate began to wonder if Belinda might not be right, and whether as the war raged around the world, they were not in a forgotten country with a strange forgotten peace.

Then one day, around noon, Kate found an envelope on her desk, with a scrawled note inside.

"Meet me tonight if you can, after seven. Otherwise tomorrow. K."

"So he's back," Belinda said, in a cutting voice, when she was shown the paper. "I suppose you have to go."

Kate glanced at her, surprised by her tone.

"You think I shouldn't? "

Belinda shook her head irritably. "I think you have no choice.

"Unfortunately.

"Who knows what the man would do to you — or to Eddy, in fact — if you broke off from him. But I don't have to like it.

"And I don't like it that you seem almost happy to see him.

"He frightens me."

She turned away, still shaking her head. "I have to get back to the wards. I suppose I'll see you tomorrow then.

"Mind you don't get pregnant again."

Kate watched her walk away, then ran a few steps after her to catch her arm. "Please don't be mad at me, Belinda. Don't be like that. You know I'm just as trapped in this as Eddy is, somehow."

Belinda spun back to face her, furious.

"Don't. Don't even begin to compare yourself to Eddy. He's done nothing wrong!"

Kate froze, her face flushed to an angry red then blanched. "And I have?" she whispered finally.

"You think I've done something wrong?

"Just trying to stay out of the clutches of the Japanese, you think it's wrong? Weren't you the one telling me I had to do what was necessary to stay alive? Weren't you?"

They stared each other down for a moment then Belinda's shoulders finally slumped in despair.

"No. Of course I don't. Please Kate, don't mind me."

Her mouth trembled and eyes filled.

"I don't know what I'm saying any more.

"I'm just...

"So tired, so.. so very tired.

"I'm worried about Eddy, and I'm worried about you, and I'm worried about doing a proper job.

"Just like the other day, when Rose was accusing me of not keeping track of the drugs.

"What do I know about running a maternity ward, I'm just pretending to be Belinda the fierce when I'm still only little Bridget O'Grady from Coolock with her runny nose and her mended clothes and shoes."

She began to sob.

"I don't think I can do this anymore. Go on pretending."

Kate gathered her in her arms.

"I understand, honey, I pretend too." she crooned softly. "I pretend I believe things will get better, but I've no idea if they will.

"But we have to go on. And we can't fight, I need you. You're all I have."

Belinda sniffled, "It's not true.

"You have Lady Thip, and Busaba, useless as she is, you even have the sleeveen."

She rubbed the tears away with her fist, just like a child. "I'll be all right. I promise. I just needed to... "

Kate sighed, "Me too, honey," and they stayed for a moment, forehead to forehead, then Belinda released her, and lifted her chin with a resolute look.

"There. All better now.

"Go see the sleeveen, then, but remember. Mind you don't get pregnant again. Otherwise, I'll kill him."

Ken Akira was sitting on the bed in the dirty, musty smelling room, still wearing his uniform. He looked up with a faint smile when he saw her at the door, shaking her umbrella, and rose to take her in his arms.

"You're all wet," he laughed.

"It's pouring, outside, didn't you notice?"

"Maybe — I was just in such a hurry to see you.

"Oh Kate, Kate," he murmured into her hair. "You have no idea how happy…"

She let herself be held for a moment, then gently disengaged herself from his clasp, and stepped back to look at him.

He had changed.

His face was thinner, and darkened by the sun, there were some white hairs in the thick quiff that stood up from his forehead, but what struck her above all was his expression.

He looked — she searched her mind to try and define it.

He looked defeated, sad. There was nothing left of his usual cocky, slightly arrogant expression, his awareness of being a successful, skilled surgeon in a triumphant army, a man who felt he could bend a woman to his will…

"Long time no see," he finally muttered, self-consciously, his eyes shifting away from her.

"Long time, yes" she replied, "What happened?"

He moved away towards the table, to pour himself a drink from the dust covered whisky bottle he had left there, almost a year ago, and fished a pack of cigarettes and a lighter from his pocket.

She raised her eyebrows.

"You didn't use to smoke."

"No, I didn't, did I? Another thing that's changed.

"It's useful having cigarettes as currency. That's how I bribed one of your orderlies to put the note on your desk," he answered, with another half-smile, blowing smoke.

"I started smoking in hospital, just to relieve the boredom, if you can believe it."

So the surgeries were not as interesting as he'd expected, then?

"Well, this time I was a patient, you see."

He unbuttoned his sand-coloured shirt and pulled it away from his shoulder, revealing an ugly, thick, purple zigzag of a scar, from the collarbone down to his ribs.

She gasped. "How did you get that?"

"A piece of hot metal flying across the deck of the ship I was on, the *Surabaya Maru*. The convoy was attacked both from the air and by a battleship on the way to the Solomon Islands.

"I was told to go below deck, but I just couldn't stand the idea of being trapped if we were sunk. And then, we were hit. I was helping a sailor who was burned when...." He swallowed, took a deep breath and went on. "There were metal debris flying around us, and flames and smoke... Then something exploded and I was in the way. Whatever it was, it tore right through me, thankfully just missing my lungs and heart.

"I got other small pieces of shrapnel in my scalp."

He ran his fingers through his hair, and she saw a web of white scars.

"We were lucky. Lots of casualties, but we stayed afloat and were able to go on. The ship closest to us, the *Meiu Maru* was sunk. Thankfully, there was a good surgeon in Manila who repaired the worse of what the meatball medics did on board.

"I'd have lost my arm if not for him."

He laughed ruefully.

"Yep, wounded by Americans. Just when I was thinking that... "Well, never mind."

She looked in his eyes. "When you were thinking? And when you say, 'another thing that's changed', what do you mean?"

He sighed and stubbed his cigarette out in a grimy ashtray, then came back to sit on the bed again, pulling her hand to sit her next to him, and spoke looking at the wall.

What had changed was that he didn't believe in all this anymore, the war, the fight against the white man.

"Listen, I know the States aren't perfect, and I know my parents were locked up — I mean, I hate those who did it to them, but... they weren't massacred. As far as I know, they're treated as civilians. That doesn't make it right, but...

"The things I saw, in Shanghai, where I boarded the ship, then afterwards, in Manila... you can't imagine. And I can't talk about it."

It might help, she replied quietly.

He turned to stare at her. "No. You don't understand.

"I can't. Not after shooting my mouth in protest after seeing how the POWs were treated.

"It's not safe. For you.

"And anyways, trust me, you don't want to hear it."

He rose from the bed and took a wrapped package from the chair, half hidden under his still dripping oilskin rain cape.

"I got you this," he said shyly, offering it to her. "Go on, open it."

It was a thin satin kimono, in garish sunset tones of red and yellow.

"You like it?"

Of course, was her reply, thinking of the lovely dark blue dressing gown that had belonged to Lawrence, the feel of the heavy silk that seemed to represent all of those magical days and nights in the little pavilion under the frangipani trees.

She smiled.

Of course she liked it.

"Then put it on," and he watched her undress and drape on the slippery, shiny robe, smiling with pleasure.

"Beautiful. The kimono and you."

He grinned and pulled a foil packet from his pocket, with the embarrassed grin of a teenager, and held it up.

"See, I'd promised I'd be careful.

"Now come here, I've waited so long for this."

He was tender and gentle in bed, kissing her hair, her neck, and whispered how much he had missed her.

Eyes open, staring at the dust crusted fan and the blinking light from the neon sign across the street projecting itself on the ceiling, she just listened, saying nothing.

How could she tell him that at times, she too had missed him, but now that he was back, she realized his absence had been a blessed relief from fear and anger?

But he didn't seem to realize that although Kate's body responded to his, she murmured no endearments, her mind still on the feel of Lawrence's dressing gown on her bare skin.

When he was spent with a low growl and a shudder, she moved carefully away from him after drawing a sharp yelp and a wince when she'd jostled his shoulder.

"It still hurts. It probably will for a long time, but... I was lucky," he said again, sitting up on the pillow. "The nerves in my arm weren't damaged.

"Otherwise, goodbye surgery, hello dermatology...

"You've heard of this new miracle drug, penicillin?

"It really fights infection, far faster than sulpha powder.

"I was running a really high fever, and after a couple of shots—gone. Magic.

"I could barely believe it."

He propped himself up to look at her, then kissed her collarbone. "You're much too thin, I'm going to have to do something about it. How's Belinda?"

Much the same, she replied, just like them all. Tired, hungry, and overworked.

"And her Eddy?"

They supposed he was all right, but if he weren't how would they know?

"I'll find out for you."

He stroked her arm. "You'll see. I've changed. Things are going to be good from now on."

She couldn't resist.

"You think so?

"What happens when the Allies finish beating the Germans — they're bombing the hell out of Hamburg and Berlin and starting to win in Europe, you must know that? — and all of them throw everything they've got against the Japanese?"

He shook his head, and turned to grab his cigarettes.

"Nope," he said reflectively, the smoke a halo around his dark head.

"I don't know where you heard this, but I suppose you listen to the BBC.

"Don't worry, I won't rat on you.

"But I can tell you this, the Japanese will never give up.

"You have no idea how determined they are. Japanese soldiers would rather commit suicide before they surrender. That's what they're taught."

She got up from the bed.

"How stupid, how wasteful," she snapped, buttoning her dress.

He shrugged.

"I know. But that's the Western way of seeing it. The Japanese think it's noble."

Belinda was still awake, drinking tea, waiting.

"How was he?"

Kate sat on the bed and thought.

Different.

"Sort of beaten down. He's been wounded, and spent two months in hospital, then rehabilitation.

"He's a valuable surgeon, so they gave him the best treatment they have, I suppose. Including a new expensive drug called penicillin. Wish we had some.

"But for the first time, he was saying 'them' about the Japs. Not 'us'."

Belinda pursed her mouth.

"Pity he wasn't killed, that's what I think.

"But if wishes were horses, beggars would ride, as they say, so I guess I should just be grateful he's changed if he has.

"Though in my experience, they don't.

"Was he careful?"

Kate responded with a wry grin.

"Yes. Gosh, the conversations we Catholic girls have."

Belinda stretched and yawned. "Better have them than not. How else would we know? Had them in nursing school too, not that I ever got any use of it, but I remember some girls that did, and a very good thing, too.

"All the nuns taught us was how to help bring babies into the world, not how to stop them happening.

"*That* was a sin, they said, and made the good Lord and the Holy Mother weep.

"Makes *you* want to weep rather, it does.

"Bet you anything English nurses know a lot more than we do.

"Especially with the war on and all those randy soldiers around....

"Come on, get into bed. There's work to do tomorrow."

As the new year of 1944 of the Christian era dawned, Sumet's mind was veering between worry because nothing seemed to be happening and a rather shameful relief for the same reason.

He knew that he could not contact those very few members of the X-O group whom he'd met, but he wished that someone, somehow, would tell him how Chamkat's mission was faring.

Or that one day he would open the paper and read that Pridi had fled, endangering his good name but ensuring a future for the Kingdom, now that victory seemed within the Allies grasp, perhaps not this year but the next, with Germany who had lost all her foothold in Africa and Italy and Japan foundering in the South Pacific.

And at the same time, he knew that such an event would lead to tumultuous days for Thailand, and that a cornered army was all the more deadly.

Or perhaps, he thought hopefully, all that had been needed from him was the gold to ease Chamkat's way, and that the plotting was left in the hands of younger, less timid men...

But one cool morning of January, he was visited at the hospital by a quiet young man with distinctly Chinese features and expensive looking clothes, who complained of a nagging pain in the abdomen.

"There is this burning sensation in my stomach, especially after meals," he announced, although he had the well-fed, glossy look of perfect health. "I have this university friend, Chamkat Phalangkun, who came to see you for the same kind of ailment, and he said you helped."

"Indeed?" Sumet asked in a non-committal voice. "Do undress, and let me examine you."

He had never met the young man, who had introduced himself simply as Apichai. Was he part of the X-O Group?

Or was he just, as he had said, a friend of Chamkat's who had mentioned his doctor's name?

"Yes, he told me you diagnosed an ulcer, perhaps I have the same thing?" the man continued in English, stripping off his shirt and lying down on the table.

Sumet nodded, "Let us see," and probed the smooth, muscular abdomen.

"I have not seen Chamkat in some time, so I expect he is better," he continued as he pushed the sensitive spot under the man's diaphragm, without inducing any wincing or cry of pain. So, not an ulcer.

"Unfortunately, I have heard he died abroad."

Sumet raised his head, in shock.

He took a deep breath, and nodded again.

"I am sorry to hear it. Do you know what the cause of death was?"

Apichai shook his head.

"Some say it might be poison.

"You don't trust me.

"Good, it is better to trust no one.

"I was sent to let you know that Sanguan Tularak is on his way to China as well, with his wife. He feared for her if she were to remain.

"The plans for – the leader of our group, shall I call him? – to leave for India are still being prepared, but nothing can happen before March at the very earliest, I hear."

"Oh? Why?"

Apichai rose and started to button his shirt.

"That I cannot say. But if you were to provide the same kind of help as you have once done, we would be most grateful as this would help smooth some difficulties, such as asking people to turn a blind eye when the time comes."

Sumet sighed, went back to his desk and picked up his pen.

"Let me start filling this patient file. What is your family name?

Apichai smiled.

"Apicharat. Apichai Apicharat sounds good, don't you think?

"I made it up.

"My father demanded that I create a new name when I left for England, because he felt that it would be easier to…" – he hesitated, then again smiled, a bit nastily, Sumet thought –"yes, to make my way when returning to Thailand if I were somewhat less Chinese.

"He wants me to have a career in politics, or become a senior civil servant. So as you see, I am beginning my career in politics now.

"My father is very well-known in the Chinese community here, and you would perhaps have heard of him but never met him."

"I see."

Sumet scanned through the names of bankers and rice millionaires, sons of Teochew migrants who had arrived in Bangkok with nothing but the shirts on their backs and a limitless capacity to work and save and work some more, and whose fortunes were as recent as they were dizzyingly spectacular.

Names that were pronounced, if they were ever said out loud at all, with a sniff.

Apichai was right, his own high-born family didn't frequent such people.

"May I ask who sent you? It is always useful to have a referral."

Apichai, rose and went to the door, opened it to check no one was behind, then came to sit down.

"Besides Chamkat? You still don't trust me, do you?

"Our mutual friend Louis, then.

"May we count on your help, now?"

Sumet smiled in return.

Yes, he would help.

"By the way, I don't think it is an ulcer. Gas, probably. Bland diet."

Apichai burst out laughing.

" What a humiliating ailment! I shall return next week, to see if the bland diet is effective."

His hand on the door to leave, he turned back.

"By the way, do you listen to the radio? There are interesting programs broadcast from India. Well worth listening to. Very encouraging."

Sumet smiled.

He knew, yes. He too enjoyed them greatly.

Once again alone in his office, Sumet rose from the desk and went to the window, gazing at Sathorn Road and its endless traffic. He sighed deeply.

So, Chamkat, that young, brave man had died.

Could it have been his ulcer that ruptured, and bled him to death, or had he, Sumet, been mistaken, and were the stomach pains the symptom of something yet more serious? Gastric cancer?

Had he not been too hasty in his examination, intrigued as he was by the meeting Chamkat had offered?

He would never know, and there is very little he could have done, if indeed it were gastric cancer, barring an operation which in England might have been successful.

Not in Bangkok, not these days.

At least, Chamkat died with the knowledge that his mission of bringing Pridi's message to the Allies had been accomplished...

And now, Sanguan Tularak had left for Chongqing as well.

Strange that his disappearance from Bangkok had made no waves. How was it managed?

A member of the National Assembly couldn't just vanish unnoticed.

Or was it noticed, and was the dreaded Kempetai secretly investigating?

Well, nobody could think him involved, keeping far away from the world of politicians, he had personally never met Sanguan, one of Pridi's longest allies, who had been a rising star in politics up to the moment when Phibul had wrested the Prime Ministership for himself.

From what he knew, Sanguan was himself the son of Teochew migrants. That certainly explained the connection with Apichai.

Despite his sadness at Chamkat's untimely demise and regret for perhaps not having diagnosed him properly, he could not help but grin, thinking of that cheeky and self-assured young man. He would go far, he was sure.

And he had been the bearer of doubly welcome news — the plan to spirit Pridi away was still on for later in the year, and all that was required of him was more gold, which he could well afford to donate for such a cause...

So, he thought, March... could he himself arrange to disappear for a while then?

No. It would look suspicious.

Better wait it out, when, and if — he reminded himself of the all-important *if*, it happened.

And in the meantime, there was very little he could do except be a good doctor and a friend to the people who worked at the hospital.

Wanida was struggling as best she could with a dire financial situation, and the increasing difficulty in obtaining drugs and medications. All pharmaceuticals now came from Japan, and he believed they were adequate, but there was the vexing problem of dosage and wondering if the translations in Thai on the labels were accurate.

Nang Lek, the accountant, for her part, spent many hours trying to obtain the best, lowest prices for food and supplies, but it meant that patients were either fed rice gruel and fish, or that their families had to provide anything else.

He himself had informed Wanida that he would work for free as long as necessary, but the other Thai doctor was not wealthy and needed his fees.

And then, there were the nurses...

Captain Akira had returned several weeks ago, Kate had informed him, a man for whom witnessing war at first hand had stripped him of all of his aggression and certainties.

At least, she had not come back from seeing him with bruises on her face.

"But he keeps on claiming he loves me," she said wearily. "I try to say it's an illusion, and that I still love Lawrence, but he just won't listen, and tells me I'll end up loving him. I won't, I can't... but I don't hate him... Well.. not anymore."

Doctor Akira should be careful about voicing his feelings about the war, he warned her. His American past would never be forgotten.

"He doesn't just have an American past," she replied in a dejected voice. "He's kept his American passport. I tell him he's crazy, but he thinks it might save his life someday."

Sumet templed his fingers under his chin and considered what he had just heard. The passport would more likely have him be shot as a traitor if it were to be discovered about his person.

"Would he entrust me with it, do you think?"

Kate shrugged. "I'll ask him. Perhaps."

But Captain Akira had refused, after sputtering furiously at the news that Kate had revealed the existence of his American passport, and had only calmed down when she reminded him of all Sumet had done to shelter her and help Eddy.

"You can trust him."

"It's not just a matter of trust.

"If I need it in a hurry, I won't have time to get hold of it."

"So be it," Sumet told Kate. "People make choices. "

She threw her hands up in frustration.

"How," she demanded, "how can you just keep on saying, 'people make choices' when you know perfectly well that he's making a crazy one?"

"Do you know the Buddhist and also Hinduist concept of

Karma?" he replied.

"It's complicated, but to make it simpler, choices have consequences on our fate.

"Yes, I know you want to interrupt and say that precisely, his choice may have possibly harmful consequences. But it is his choice, his fate, and we don't control them.

"He may be right, and his passport may save his life at a critical juncture.

"He may be wrong, and it could turn out to be his death sentence.

"I'm just trying to explain to you why I can offer to help, but that it is incumbent upon him to accept my help or not, because he will have to live with his decision, not I."

She listened with an annoyed face. "I don't understand at all."

He smiled. "Ah, you are from the West and you are young..."

He smiled again, remembering the way she had stormed off, muttering "I don't understand Karma, but I understand stupid, and this is stupid!" and opened the glass doors to the surgical ward, to check on a patient whose hand had been mangled in an ice-crushing machine. He might need to amputate if the infection didn't abate.

Kate had mentioned the miracle drug given to Captain Akira, and he wished he had some of this new penicillin, that was only in the early research stage when he was still a medical student.

Still, sulpha could well be effective.

Kate was sitting at her desk at the entrance to the ward, updating the patient's file. "He still has a high fever," she whispered, "but there's no trace of gangrene as yet."

Good. They had a couple of days to see if the man's body could fight.

Kate hesitated, then asked "Would you mind checking on Belinda?

"She has a fever as well. She couldn't even get up this morning."

She led him to the room, while he asked on the way whether she'd nausea or vomiting.

"I don't think so." She stopped before opening the door. "You know what this reminds me of?

"The flu."

Influenza was unusual at this time of year, and he'd not heard of an epidemic but still, it was possible.

Belinda was lying on the twisted sheets, her body drenched in sweat, her breathing stertorous. She was barely able to open her eyes when he touched her burning forehead. He didn't want to bother her with a thermometer and he could tell it was at least 104, if not more.

He pulled up the chair next to the bed, and asked gently where it hurt.

"Everywhere. Hands, legs, and oh... my knees... and head," she moaned.

"That's why I thought of the flu," Kate explained.

He pulled the sheet away and drew up her old and often-mended nightgown to palpate her spleen.

No, not enlarged, so it was not malaria.

He drew the garment back down, noting the torn lace with a twinge of pity, and ran his hands down her thin legs, noticing the scratched mosquito bites around her ankles.

She began to thrash around, "Cold, I'm so cold," she repeated, so he covered her and motioned to Kate to switch off the ceiling fan, resting his hand on her hair to smooth away from her face.

"Kate is going to stay with you, but first, she'll get you some hot tea and something to make you feel better. And you must drink plenty of water throughout the day, all right?

"I will come back in an hour to see how you feel."

In the corridor, Kate could see he looked concerned.

"It's flu isn't it? I thought so."

Maybe. But the shivers indicated the fever was still going up, and that seemed rather high for an ordinary influenza.

It wasn't malaria, in any case.

Kate shook her head. No, they were both careful to take their quinine pills.

"I was thinking of dengue. She has mosquito bites," he said frowning.

Kate frowned as well.

"Dengue. Break bone fever. That's what your mother had. It's serious, then."

Yes, it was.

"There's nothing we can do, however, but keep her comfortable and try to bring the fever down with aspirin. Bring her sweet tea.

"Stay with her, I'll look after the surgical ward, and if I need help, I'll ask Bernadette.

"She has a few days of this, but she will improve."

Later the first day, the aspirin helped, and she was able to sip broth and tea, and let Kate sponge cool water over her, and even be moved to a chair long enough to allow her drenched sheets to be changed although she wasn't able to stifle her moans when she was eased gently down again, shifting her legs carefully.

Sitting up in bed, she held her cup with trembling fingers, and Kate finally had to hold it for her, encouraging every mouthful with low murmurs.

"There you are, honey, just a bit more. Please. For me. For Eddy."

But Belinda finally pushed the cup away. "I can't. No more."

The next day the fever was still high as high, and she was sluggish, speaking nonsense, as if lost in an unpleasant dream.

The third day Belinda's body was covered in a strange red rash, and blood ran from her nose and mouth.

Sumet grimaced.

It was the haemorrhagic form of dengue, the most dangerous one. "Do you think you could call Captain Akira? Perhaps that drug of his might help if he is able to get some."

Captain Akira was not available, she was told on the phone, but she could leave a message.

When he called back, he sounded annoyed. "Don't call me anymore, it's raising questions. What's the matter?"

But when she explained Belinda's illness and the need for penicillin, his voice changed to concern.

"I can't get you penicillin, it's as controlled as gold here.

"More so, in fact.

"Not sure it would help, either.

"I don't really know tropical medicine... But whatever you do, don't give her aspirin, it will make her bleed. "

Kate gasped. "Oh God... We have, we've been giving her the maximum dosage every day, and she has blood coming out of her mouth and nose and she's covered in a rash."

"Shit," he muttered. "Well, stop, then. Cool baths to bring down her fever. I'll come by this evening."

When he arrived, Kate greeted him joyously. "She's a bit

better, she can hold up her head. Come see."

Wanida, Nang Lek, Rose and Bernadette were hovering around the bed, straightening the pillows, pressing cool towels to Belinda's forehead, and even managing to get a weak laugh out of her.

She raised her bloodshot eyes when she saw Ken leaning against the doorjamb, and turned her red and blotchy face to Kate. "What's he doing here?" she asked in an unfriendly voice.

If he noticed, he didn't show.

He came to crouch by the bed, and Sumet shooed all the women back to work, promising a full report later.

"Hi Belinda. I've come to see how you are. Kate and Doctor Sumet are worried about you."

She closed her eyes. "They should be. I'm going to die, aren't I?"

Kate gasped, but Ken just chuckled.

"Die, from a little bout of break bone fever? You? Of course not.

"Can I touch your face and throat?"

"You can do what you want. You always do, anyway, don't you?" she replied tartly.

"Kate is right, you are better, back to your old bossy ways, aren't you?

"Now, I'll listen to your heart.

"By the way, Eddy is fine, I saw him last month. So don't worry about him, OK? Ah, that got me a smile. I knew it would."

He listened, he felt the glands on her throat and groin, and took her pulse.

"All right, I'll let you rest now.

"You're going to be fine.

"Just a few more days of aching joints – it really hurts, doesn't it? That why they call it break bone fever, you know. Then all of a sudden, you'll feel much better."

She glared at him.

"No. I'm going to die. I know it. I'm Irish and I have the eye."

Kate snorted in annoyance. "Stop being so dramatic. I'm Irish too, and I know you'll be fine. So there."

Ken smiled down at her. "I'm going to side with Kate. You'll be fine."

Kate came to drop a kiss on her forehead. "I'll be back in a moment. Behave, all right?"

In the corridor, Ken was no longer smiling. "It's not good," he told Sumet.

"Her neck is stiff, her heart is irregular. What's her temperature?"

When told, he shook his head.

"Not good," he said again. "It might be turning into encephalitis. No —" he raised his hand, "don't ask me for penicillin, it wouldn't be effective. But I'll get my hands on some adrenalin ampoules, to be injected only if you feel she's at risk of cardiac arrest.

"I have to go back now. They're a lot more careful about checking my comings and goings, but I'll try to be back tomorrow.

"You call me," he told Sumet, "you, not Kate, you, if she falls into a coma."

Kate was standing there, her hands clasped before her mouth, paralyzed with fear.

No. It wasn't possible. Not strong Belinda the fierce, as she had once described herself. Not Belinda who had brought her to the British Club that evening. Not Belinda, closer and dearer than any sister.

Ken shook her gently. "Listen, don't panic yet. And don't show her how worried you are. You're a nurse, you can do it.

"I really have to go.

"Bye, darling, doctor." He kissed her briefly, and she didn't even notice, just stared, in a trance-like state of fear and misery as he ran down the stairs.

At midnight, Rose rapped on the door, and brought Kate some tea.

"Get some sleep, now. I'll stay with her. How is she?"

Kate looked up, her red-rimmed eyes deep pools of despair.

"Much the same. The fever hasn't broken. She keeps clutching her head and moaning."

"So, encephalitis, then," Rose sighed.

She took the chair that Kate left her, and pulled out her rosary. "I'll pray for her, as I'm sure you have."

Kate shook her head. It hadn't even occurred to her.

The next day, Belinda began vomiting, and couldn't even keep water down.

She was confused, called for Eddy, and grabbing Ken's hand

when he came in the late evening, whispered endearments to him, pressing it against her burning cheek.

Kate sat by the bed, crying quietly.

"What do you think?" Sumet asked.

Ken looked at him. "I think what you think. Tomorrow, she'll be in a coma. Then... a day, two days... She may still pull through. But..."

"She's dehydrated. You haven't the equipment for intravenous infusions, do you?"

Sumet shook his head sadly. Ken sighed. "I'll try and spirit some out tomorrow – if I can. No promises."

Belinda woke as the sun was rising, her forehead cool and all her confusion gone.

She groaned as she tried to lift herself up, and Kate woke with a start, stiff and puffy-eyed from crying most of the night.

"What is it, honey? Do you need something?"

Belinda tried to swallow, her lips were chapped and crusted with dry saliva.

"Here, drink some water. Little sips now. That's it. Some more."

She eased herself back on the pillow. "That was good.

"Kate, I need you to promise me something."

"Anything, honey. What do you want?"

Belinda swallowed again, bringing out the words with effort. "I want you to be me."

Kate gave a little sob.

The confusion was back... Her hope had shot so high, feeling the cool hands clasping hers when she was holding the glass to her lips.

"No, Kate, listen. There's not much time, I know it. We don't have time for you to cry. When I go..."

"Where are you going, silly? You're staying right here in bed."

"Will you listen to me?"

Belinda's exasperated voice sounded so much like her old self that Kate almost laughed.

"I'll be dead by morning. I can tell, I feel the life is just... leaking out of me. Take my passport and have me buried as you. You'll be safe then."

"No. NO. I won't have you talking this way. It's just your fever, you'll be better by morning, you're already better."

Belinda's hand felt like nothing but bones as she clutched Kate's.

"That's all I can think about. Maybe I'm wrong, and maybe I'll make it. But if not, promise me. Please."

Kate had tears running down her face. "I promise.

"But you'll see, we'll go dancing again someday, and wear sheer nylons, and eat cakes, lots of cakes.

"I'll take you to New York, we'll eat pie at the Automat.

"And Filene's. We'll go to Filene's basement and buy the place out."

Belinda closed her eyes and smiled, holding Kate's hand, quiet now that she had her promise.

"Filene's. Yes. That would be grand."

They buried her in the blue silk dress she had worn at Kate's wedding, and the temporary marker bore the name of Mary-Katherine Fallon.

The sky was clear and almost cool, and Father Perroudon, who had never taken the time to know any of the nurses by name, extolled the virtues of kind and devout Mary-Katherine, who had come from so far to help new mothers at Saint-Louis Hospital, not even realizing it was much kinder Belinda who was put in the ground of the old Catholic cemetery on Silom Road.

Wanida agreed with the scheme, once Sumet had explained the danger to Kate, under one condition.

That there should be a letter written explaining what was done, and why, and that letter should be kept safe, for after the war.

"The girl's family will need to know."

Sumet nodded. "And you may need to prove you are still alive as well," he said to Kate who since the moment Belinda's hand became cold in hers, had not shed a tear.

"Wanida will report it to the Red Cross, your family will be notified."

"I don't care," Kate just said dully. "I don't care about anything."

Sumet also said that Lady Thip must be made to believe it.

Kate started, shocked out of her misery. "Oh... No. Please, no!"

Yes. Sumet was inflexible, as was Wanida.

"The only people who can know are the Irish nurses and us. And Captain Akira.

"The hospital staff won't realize anything, they have no idea whose passport is whose.

"But remember Pichit is working with the Japanese. He can't be told you're still alive. One slip and..."

"But what if Lawrence comes back...?"

"I will give the letter to Lady Thip to keep in her safe. I will say it was your last letter to him. When he returns, she will give him the letter, and he will know."

All right.

After all, what did it matter?

Lawrence wouldn't come back and she would live all her days here in Bangkok, trapped like a mannequin in a shop window, endlessly clapping her hands at nothing.

Chapter XXVIII

Lawrence sat on the long verandah outside the low building that housed the SCS offices, and watched the monkeys playing, or rather fighting he thought, swinging from branches and scampering with angry chatters away from sticks thrown by guards as soon as one approached the open jeeps parked under the jacaranda trees.

He had left his desk to be alone and clear his mind, away from the arguing inside.

Their most promising operation, dubbed "Prichard", which was for a submarine to rendezvous in December with Siamese resistance on a on the beach in Hua Hin and deliver men, weapons, and short wave radios, had failed.

Army Signals Station in Calcutta monitoring broadcasts from Bangkok "thought" they may have heard the appropriate responses agreeing to the rendezvous, or perhaps it had just been static?

But they hadn't been following that carefully, there was a war going on, did Meerut realize that? And Wingate's campaign signals from Burma took priority.

Prichard would go ahead, anyway, Pointon ruled. They couldn't leave the resistance on a beach sending up flares, now could they?

The submarine waited for several days then was forced to turn back.

And now, another attempt was to be made, an airdrop this time, code named "Appreciation".

Peter had put his teak logging-days knowledge of the hills northwest of Bangkok to use, and decided on a fairly deserted area, but which would afford a not too difficult journey to the capital, once the team had landed. Aerial photographs seemed to show that there were no villages nearby, but a good drop zone had been cleared by logging several years ago, allowing a safe landing.

Lieutenants Khem, Deng and Dee were selected, trained in parachute jumps, claimed their readiness to leave the fleshpots of Calcutta and begin to bring the war to their country.

They could only carry their own weapons and a shortwave radio, plus money of course.

Sanguan and Daeng in Chongqing had given whatever information they possessed of Japanese garrisons in the area, so everything appeared ready, or at least, as Peter admitted, as ready as they could make it.

But...

Lawrence had not been involved in the planning, he had no voice in the final decision.

However, when hearing "Appreciation" described on the day before the final green light was to be given, he was uneasy, and said so.

How would these men travel inconspicuously to Bangkok, by bus, or by train? Would villagers not be suspicious, with unknown, manifestly citified youths, suddenly appearing in their midst, to hitch a ride to the nearest station?

"They'll have to split, obviously," Pointon replied in an irritated voice. "Having agreed on when and where to join up later."

"So," Lawrence continued, "What's their story going to be?

"They have to account for their presence in the area, somehow.

"What about the currency? Has anybody checked whether the Japanese have imposed a new kind of baht bills?"

"Yes, we have," Pointon snapped back, "and they haven't."

Svasti intervened.

Villagers wouldn't dare interfere with these men, once they were told of their mission.

"But they mustn't tell anyone!" Lawrence cried in exasperation. "That's a ticket to the Kempetai."

Tom Hobbs, a recent arrival, was looking doubtful.

"Gallet has a point," he ventured.

Pointon swirled back to stare at him, his eyes blazing.

"Do you have a better idea? Does anyone?

"Anyway, Gallet is in charge of propaganda, not operations," which was when Lawrence decided to leave the room.

The door opened behind him, and Pointon came to sit by his side, puffing on his pipe.

"We can't just leave those lads stewing in Calcutta, you know," he finally said mildly.

Lawrence took off his glasses and wiped them on his shirt, nodding. He knew.

"And you realize we can't just sit out the war here in Meerut, waiting for something to miraculously come out of Siam, we have to do *something*."

Yes. But still...

Pointed interrupted him.

"They'll be dropped tomorrow night."

Lawrence got up. "Fine. I'll just go back to propaganda, Major, then, shall I?"

"No. Sit. I have something else in mind for you."

He leaned back, his eyes on the monkeys. "We're going to have to do some re-organizing here in Meerut."

His heart in his mouth, Lawrence sat down again.

He was going to be sent back to reporting, to punish him for his lack of faith. He knew it. "Listen, Major, I wasn't questioning your judgement, in there, I was just..."

Pointon smiled. "You were, though.

"And you were right to. I need to hear all possible objections before deciding, but then, I have to decide.

"But that is not what I wanted to discuss.

"You may have heard, or not, that Arun is leaving, he's going back to London.

"Heaven knows, he's been agitating long enough to be able to get back and further himself as the only one who can talk to Seni Pramoj about what will happen after the war — doesn't Seni somehow remind you of De Gaulle?

"They both want to carve roles for themselves...

"I suppose that's what happens when wars seem about to end, men pop up and start jockeying for position. Happened under the Romans, and I assume the Greeks too."

"But this war has yet to be won," Lawrence countered. "The Japs are putting on a pretty aggressive show in Burma, although they seem to be losing ground in the South Pacific."

"Over-extended. Yes.

"And resistance in Siam is vital, to make sure we can somehow harass them when they regroup back there.

"Hence Appreciation." More thoughtful puffing.

"Why did I tell you about Arun leaving?

"Can't seem to remember. It has nothing to do with you. I was just struck by how quiet life will be when he's not around challenging me every step of the way.

"Tell me, you get along with the Yanks, don't you?"

Yes, he did. As a rule, he rather liked them.

"Good. Because you're going to liaise between SCS Meerut and the OSS.

"Detachment 404, Kandy. Ceylon.

"That's where you're going.

"Ah, you're interested, I see."

"Yes, of course, but why me?"

"Because you probably know Bangkok as well as any of us, and you know the Siamese much better — none of us has lived with a Siamese family of that class. You're to give field advice for a plan being hatched — I can't tell you yet, you'll find out soon enough — no, don't thank me, it wasn't my idea.

"Mackenzie's actually, he says Stillwell spoke highly of you.

"Vinegar Joe was surprised to hear you were SOE.

"Where did you meet?"

Lawrence grinned.

"Burma. I interviewed him in Mandalay after the bombing, and we toured the field in his jeep.

"I just missed a bullet, it dented my helmet. I didn't even flinch, I was so surprised. I think he liked that.

"So, we're friends again with OSS?"

Pointon smiled sourly.

"The fact that we needed to look high and low before thinking of a journalist with known American sympathies to represent us might be your answer. However, since Miles — you remember, the US Navy captain in Chongqing who hates us Brits — was fired by OSS thanks to your friend Stillwell, things have been going somewhat better."

"When do I leave?"

As soon as possible was the answer, but it would take several days to days to get the necessary orders through.

"You'll be briefed on the mission in Delhi first. Mind you behave yourself while you're there. Keep away from the Cecil, we don't want you running into your former colleagues."

Private Biggin drove him to the station a week later at his usual breakneck speed.

"See you've been promoted, Captain," he mentioned slyly when Lawrence threw his pack in the back of the jeep and climbed in. "Tell me if you'd rather sit behind, in style like."

"Charlie, nothing escapes you, does it?

"Of course I don't want to sit in the back. It's a temporary rank, to make me look important."

"So you're not a real captain, then? Good. Was afraid you'd go all grand on me.

"I'll get you there in time for you to have a beer before the train, and maybe, if you like, I can get a thermos of coffee and some sandwiches made for you at the station restaurant. You're going on a long trip, I hear."

"Really? And where did you hear?"

Biggin grinned.

"I do a little this or that at the daftar, that's what they call the office, y'know. Helped Ram Das to type your orders.

"What do you say to your packed meal?"

"Charlie, you'll be wasted as a taxi driver. Become the concierge at the Ritz, that's your career."

"You think so, Captain?"

He dragged the word out luxuriously. "Concierge... Have any connections at the Ritz, then Captain?

"No? Pity, that. I'll look into this concierge business meself then."

LAWRENCE'S DIARY
MARCH 25TH1944
ON THE TRAIN TO CALCUTTA

I have just left Delhi station, and by some miracle, I have a single berth to myself.

No one is going to Bengal, it seems, at least not tonight.

Quite extraordinary what the rank of captain can achieve in

easily securing what I used to fight for with my lowly correspondent patch.

Pointon was very clear in telling me this was not a promotion, it was temporary and only for show.

"We want the Yanks to think we're sending someone equal in rank to those you'll be dealing with."

He peered at some official list. "There's a Captain Smith. Probably not his real name.

"Although... his first name is Nicol. Nobody would make up such a daft first name for himself, would they?"

Poor Pointon. There were still no news from the three chaps on the Appreciation mission when I left, whereas by his calculation, they should have been able to report by short wave by yesterday at the latest.

Everything seems to point to them having been arrested.

Perhaps the radio was damaged during the jump. Perhaps they are waiting to reach Bangkok, he says, clutching at straws.

And perhaps the Kempetai have them already, but nobody dared say so.

Sitting at the window, watching the hypnotic landscape of India go by, endless plains with the occasional column of peasants back from the field, the women's saris flickering like flames against the setting sun, little villages with but a few lights to brave the night, and waiting for my bed to be made up, I realize it has been many days since I've thought of Kate except as a beautiful memory of being young, happy, in a world at peace.

I cannot imagine her now. I try and try to conjure the feel of her skin against mine, the sound of her voice so present in my dreams before, and she is nothing but an elusive sense of happiness. Nothing comes, no sense of whom she might be now.

I fear I have lost what she was, but there is no feeling of death and yet no feeling of life. Her picture is just that now; a picture.

He reflected on the three days he had spent in Delhi.

What was being planned, he was told, after signing a number of documents binding him to the strictest secrecy — "Yes, we know you're SOE but this goes much higher" — was arranging the escape of "Codename Ruth", someone so exalted that he would hear the real name only in Kandy.

There was a three-man planning committee, he was there only to provide such technical details as were needed.

His counterpart on the American side was one Nicol Smith, "you'll get along with him, he's one of you daft Asia hands," said the martinet of a major who kept on walking around his chair and suddenly bellowing his next words into Lawrence's ear, making him jump. Lawrence had disliked him on sight.

And then he was treated to a long and confusing lecture on the rivalries between OSS Chongqing and Force 136 Delhi, the nefarious influence of General Tai Li —"Chiang Kai-Shek's Himmler" — over Colonel Khap of the Free Thai in China, and Sanguan and Daeng's respective roles in a future independent Siam.

"Independent, but under British influence, remember that," the major stressed, witheringly, smoothing his little Errol Flynn moustache.

"And it's all very well to be friendly with the Yanks, but don't forget whose uniform you're wearing, Captain."

The last word said ironically.

He was then allowed to give his half-hearted salute, and taken down the hall to see Colin Mackenzie, also known as CMK, head of Force 136, and the man whom he'd met in Singapore years ago, and who then had called himself Bill.

Mackenzie rose to greet him with a genuine smile. "The scribbler!

"So we meet again. Come in and sit and have some coffee. You must need it after the China lecture.

"The good major has something of a bee in his bonnet about Chongqing — rightly so, I believe, but he can be somewhat wearing."

Lawrence took a chair, and a cup, and admitted he didn't really understand the situation there — "Oh, don't worry about that, nobody does, really," Mackenzie chuckled — but also why he might need to understand it.

Not so much needed to understand, but remember... Mackenzie paused thoughtfully.

He had changed but little since the derelict godown in Singapore, though his thinning hair was now all white and his face had new creases and lines.

He still looked like a kindly judge in an American film, perhaps, and his manner was as professorial and deliberate as ever, as if he had all the time in the world to discuss the war in Asia with such an unimportant agent as himself.

He pointed to the map behind him.

"Here, China.

"Here, Siam, with nothing but Jap-occupied French Indochina between them.

"Siam, as you well know, has a large Chinese population, who've been treated unfairly in the past twenty years. Yes?

"French Indochina wants its independence after the war. You know that, I know that, everybody but the French know that.

"It's basically something China can ensure if Ho Chi Minh and his friends play their cards right. Yes?

"Now, Siam?

"Why do you think the Chinese want Pridi's government in exile in China, and not in India?"

He swivelled back to face his desk and had a gulp of coffee.

"Just things to bear in mind, as well as the game the Americans might be playing, to ensure their influence in Asia against ours.

"Now, tell me about yourself.

"Read any philosophy lately?"

Lawrence shook his head. The Burma retreat had knocked any philosophy out of him for a while, except perhaps discovering it wasn't the intellectual support it promised to be when one was hungry, ill, and desperately frightened.

"But tell me, if you can. From what I've just gathered, Codename Ruth is Pridi, isn't he?"

Clever lad.

And the reason they were acting so hastily to get him out now was because they were forcing the Americans' hand before they agreed to give him up to Chongqing, which was what Miles and Tai Li were apparently cooking up between them, before Miles got on the wrong side of Stillwell and Wild Bill Donovan and got himself fired.

"I'm... I'm astonished," Lawrence muttered as he rose to leave, still stunned to hear it confirmed that Pridi was Ruth.

The Regent of Siam was working for the Allies, whereas the country had signed a pact with the Japanese, and he actually had a codename...

Pridi, whom he had researched so thoroughly for that stillborn book of his... But to think about it... yes, the quiet courage, the ability to hide his true self in plain sight...

He shook his head in amazement.

Of course, the Siamese twins...

A move from one leading to the opposite from the other.

Phibul was a Japanese ally, so Pridi acquired an SOE code name...

Of course.

Mackenzie thought he was still referring to China.

"Aren't we all, at such brazen show of American self-interest?

"But it's not your concern, what we need from you is everything you can tell our friends about Bangkok, and even more importantly, Hua Hin.

"Off with you now, and Godspeed."

Speaking with Mackenzie is what brought on all this heartache about Kate.

How I wish I had been more forceful in following his advice and getting her out. She would now be in Boston, studying medicine, I have no doubt, and we could write to each other, instead of wondering if the other is still alive.

I encountered Mountbatten as I was leaving the building,

He did not give me a second look, of course, as I, and everyone around me, flattened ourselves against the edge of the courtyard to let him and his entourage sweep through.

I wonder if *he* understands the China situation?"

APRIL 2ND1944
KANDY
CEYLON

What a heady experience American wealth is, even in war time.

I was greeted at the airfield by a lanky, slouching private chewing a cigar, who drawled, "You're Captain Gallet, right?

"I'm Bruneau. Known as French — Notice I knew to say your name, 'cause I'm from Louisiana, that's why they call me French," and whisked me away in a new, shiny jeep to a camp of big khaki-coloured tents, with signs carrying mysterious initials, and dropped me in front of a one with "ADM HQ DET 404" on the sign in front of it.

That I could understand.

A woman sergeant was seated at a desk typing — the desk new, the typewriter new, I noticed enviously — and lifted her eyes, giving me an all-over look and wrinkled her nose. Obviously not impressed by either me or my rank.

She had blond curls in the kind of hairdo Belinda favoured for special evenings, and fresh lipstick.

"Captain," she just said, and showed me a chair with her chin.

So I sat, picked up a dog-eared *Stars and Stripes*, the military daily paper, and read the headlines. And waited.

"May I just ask..?" I finally ventured, but she cut me off.

"Don't ask me anything. Captain Smith will be with you."

As if he were waiting just behind the flap door of the tent for his name to be spoken, it opened, and an immensely tall man entered, taking off his bush hat.

"Captain Gallet, I presume?" he asked with a grin. "Nicol Smith. Welcome. Betty here been showing you around?"

Betty gave a flouncing toss of her head.

"Nope, I don't work for you, you're Detachment 101," and went back to her typing.

I was amazed at her cheek, I couldn't imagine anyone in Meerut, not even irrepressible Biggin dismissing an officer, but Smith just laughed.

"Don't mind her, I think she's got her heart broken too many times by one of us guys.

"Come on, I'll show you your tent. You're bunking with me, by the way, hope you don't mind. "

I assured him it was fine, and fell into a friendship just as easily as I had with Tex.

After the tent — huge, with two of what Smith calls cots and I learned in India to call charpoys — he took me to, as he put it "chow down", words I hadn't heard since Kunming.

Over hash-brown potatoes and fried eggs and beans, we agreed to use first names, and he told me a bit about his life travelling and exploring — he was shipwrecked in the South Seas, adopted by a tribe in the Amazon, drove the length of the Burma Road and just spent a year in Vichy France.

It's very much a "Boy's Own" sort of life, seemingly impossible for one man to have done all that in less than forty years, but, somehow, I believe him.

He brought over the Free Thai agents from the States and is now based in China, training them to be infiltrated into Siam when the time comes (Aha! The China connection, I thought when he said that...).

He very much likes the agents he brought over, he finds them intelligent and brave, and also very good company.

I felt rather inadequate in talking about what little I have achieved thus far — Oxford, one book yet to find a publisher, war correspondent — but he was flatteringly awed by my account of the walk out of Burma, and impressed that I should speak Siamese.

"Listen, I know our services don't see eye to eye about — well, actually about anything, really, except the need to win the war," he finally said over straight bourbon in steel mugs in our tent.

"But there's no reason for that to have anything to do with us. We're not negotiating, thank God, we're just providing input for Operation Uddingston."

I burst out laughing.

What an appalling name.

He agreed and we toasted to that.

Met the negotiating team, Major Scofield and Colonel Heppner for the American side, and a special envoy of Mountbatten himself, Captain (Royal Navy, therefore much higher up than me) Garnons-Williams.

Garnons-Williams just said to me briefly, out of the corner of his mouth, like a gangster in a bad film, "I've no time to monkey around with these chaps, I've just come to force the issue that we're doing the retrieval, understand? You're to give them the details later."

Smith and I cooled our heels in the anteroom, only going in when called, I to discuss the beach in Hua Hin, and what I knew of the golf course, (very little) and Smith I don't know what about, but I can safely guess it deals with getting Pridi out through China, taking the same route as Sanguan and Chamkat.

Over lunch, we were joined in the mess tent by a most fascinating and intimidating woman, Cora Du Bois, an anthropologist who has spent most of her career in the Dutch East Indies and self deprecatingly claims to know nothing of the area save the island where she did her research.

She is head of R and A SEAC — Research and Analysis South East Asia Command.

They love speaking in initials here, it reminds me of the press officer in Rangoon being teased by Dan De Luce. I guess it is a military trait, and heaven knows you cannot escape the knowledge you're in the Army here — anthem played morning and evening, then the flag is raised and lowered with a bugle call, and all freeze and salute.

I cannot imagine that kind of ceremony in Meerut, which compared to here, feels like a strange but benign university.

Salutes are snappy, ranks are given, although there is a quite extraordinary familiarity between officers and other ranks.

Sergeant Betty, in particular, has not warmed to me but Anna, a pert, brunette New-Yorker explained that Betty thought she was engaged to a British airman who then revealed he actually was married.

"So she doesn't much like you Brits, see."

I assured her that being married myself, to an American, and not about to hide it, I presented no risk for unit morale.

Besides Cora Du Bois, who is an oddity at such a high post, there are many women around, typists, secretaries, nurses and radio operators, and despite their uniforms, they look stylish, very groomed, and even the plainest has more suitors than she can handle.

Nicol is leaving tomorrow — there will be no escape from China, SOE has carried the day, with British Catalina sea planes and submarines in the region whereas the States have none, but I am to stay on to continue to provide my knowledge of Hua Hin.

I was making every effort to write in secret, but wonder why I bothered, here everybody seems as intent to chronicle events as my erstwhile colleagues from the Strand Hotel were.

Still, I shall refrain from including any details of the project, as opposed to, say, Scofield, who angrily takes notes during dinner, pushing his glasses up his nose as he brings his forkful of beans to his mouth.

"It's the only way I can bear the frustration of this useless exercise. Personally, I believe it will never happen," he told me quite candidly.

And speaking of dinner, I shall be going there now, I cannot seem to get enough of the food here, so different from the diet of Meerut with its eternal steamed puddings or the greasy curries.

I have had steak, yes, steak, arriving frozen from Texas, and ice-cream.

Every effort is made to ensure the morale of the fighting boys. Last night, there was a screening of the recent film, *The More the Merrier* with Jean Arthur.

Once again, officers and enlisted men mingled and joked with each other, there were no separate rows of seats. Unthinkable in the British Army, when I remember Burma before the fall...

Nicol claims I shouldn't judge all US bases by what I see (and eat) here, and that soldiers in the field more often than not subsist on what he calls K-rations and much-thumbed porn.

There was no steak that evening, but something far less appealing, called turkey loaf, but still far better than anything Lawrence had tasted in Meerut.

Anna, the New-Yorker, came to sit by his side, as apparently, she had no prejudice against the British, and a red-headed man with crosses on his collar points shyly asked if he might sit next to Nicol and put his tray down opposite Lawrence.

"Sure, Padre, join us," Nicol said, pushing his tray aside to make room.

"This is Captain Gallet, our guest from SOE."

The chaplain swallowed nervously, and looked at Lawrence with strangely familiar grey-green eyes.

He coughed, then gave an uncertain smile as he sat down.

"Yes... er.. Hello, Captain Gallet. Lawrence Gallet, right?

"I heard you were here and I wanted to meet you.

"I'm Father Francis Fallon, and I think I'm your brother-in-law."

Nicol sputtered with laughter, "Talk of a coincidence," and Anna clapped her hand to her mouth, her eyes turning from the priest to Lawrence, but Lawrence could say nothing.

He just looked back, dumbstruck and smiled slowly.

"You're her brother," he finally said. "You have her eyes."

Francis nodded, biting his lips, watching Lawrence laugh happily.

"I... I – don't know what to say.

"I'm so happy to meet someone from her family...at last..."

Francis looked at him searchingly, frowning, then stretched out his hand to grab Lawrence's wrist.

"Can we talk outside? Please."

Lawrence frowned. "Why?"

"Not here. Please."

The dining tent seemed to spin.

Lawrence's heart slowed and felt about to stop, his tongue suddenly seemed very thick, too heavy form the words he was afraid to say, his lips could not move.

Francis rose. "Come with me."

Nicol rose as well, his face concerned, "You need help?"

Francis stopped him with his hand. "Later."

Outside, there were a few stray dogs, and sentries walking around, and the scent of frangipani, and Lawrence could only listen as Francis told him, the Red Cross, she died in January, of encephalitis following dengue fever...

"We had no idea how to contact you. I thought you knew until I saw you smile."

No. No, not Kate...

"So that was why...," he whispered.

"Why what, my son?" Francis asked, then mumbled, "Sorry, habit.

"Why what, Lawrence?"

"Why I could no longer feel her.

"I tried, and tried, but she just... she just wasn't there..."

"She's in a better place," Francis murmured consolingly, his hand on Lawrence's shoulder but he was pushed away.

"Of course she's not! How can you believe all of that claptrap?

"She's gone, she died alone, she's in the ground and you talk about a better place?

"How dare you?" he shouted angrily.

"I dare because that's what I believe," Francis replied, his voice even.

Nicol appeared out of the darkness, holding his bottle of bourbon and three stacked metal tumblers.

"I think we might need this," he said, handing a full measure to Lawrence –"and let's get you a chair."

Anna had put two and two together, he explained, she knew the chaplain had lost his sister... so...

"Drink."

No. Lawrence was shaking his head blindly, he wanted to run, he wanted to scream, the idea of alcohol made him retch, but all he said was "No. Back, to the tent, not here."

Francis had his arm around his shoulders as they walked, each step careful, focussing his mind on putting one foot ahead of the next.

They piled pillows behind his back so he could sit up, staring at them without seeing, seeing what?

A pair of jade and coral earrings, the glow of her hair in the moonlight in Hua Hin, the cheap dress she wore at the British Club, that first night.

"I have a wife," Nicol finally said in a far way voice, "whom I've have not seen in in over a year, and I cannot imagine... I would want to howl."

"I want to howl," Lawrence replied dully, and gulped his drink. "I want to die."

Francis had taken out his rosary beads. "I don't suppose you might want to pray, instead," he offered, his smile trembling.

"But you might find it helpful to know I've been remembering her in my masses, every day since I heard.

"And you shall both be in my prayers."

He rubbed his short red hair.

"I wondered whether it was the right thing, the charitable thing to go see you... if you hadn't heard.

"But then, if you had, I thought you might need a brother.

"You've lost Kate, but you have a brother..."

Lawrence didn't answer. He didn't need a brother.

He needed Kate.

Francis stayed by his bedside most of the night, talking in a muted voice, telling him about Kate as a child, "so determined, always, like our mother.

"But then ... well... After she died, Felicity, bless her, stepped in, but Kate kept the kids together, working at the convent as a maid during the summer, to help pay for their room and board. And Da...," he hesitated, "he's not a bad man, but the drink... That's why I left as soon as I could, to go to the seminary."

He stopped, and took a gulp of bourbon.

"Look at me, talking about the drink.

"You know what I liked best about the seminary at first — it was the quiet.

"I'm not sure I had the calling then, I just wanted another life. But the Lord touched me, and I knew I was in the right place.

"How did you meet?"

So Lawrence told him, about the British Club, and their separation, and how he always knew something was missing when she wasn't around... and that he went to wait for her at the hospital after hesitating for weeks...

"I was afraid she might have met someone else, I was afraid she was still angry with me."

"She could be fierce when she was angry," Francis said. "Just like our Mam."

"She was, but she married me anyway."

"Do you have a picture?"

His eyes misted when he was handed the snapshot, the only photo of Kate Lawrence had slipped in his bag when leaving Bangkok.

She was leaning against the balustrade of the Oriental's terrace, laughing, her head was thrown back and her jade earrings caught the light.

"She looks happy."

"She was. We were...

"... we were so happy, my God, so happy...

"And then... I wanted to make her leave, before the war broke out, but she wouldn't go.

"I blame myself, and I blame her, and I blame those blasted nuns at the hospital who made her believe she was needed.

"No one needed her as much as I..."

The following morning, he rose bleary-eyed and tight-lipped.

He still had a job to do and presented himself at the meeting tent.

"Listen." Scofield and Heppner headed him off at the entrance.

"We know. Smith told us.

"We're all more than sorry, but we really need you to keep on briefing us on what you know of Hua Hin, if you think we can land two Catalinas instead of one, and how Ruth can get himself and his family down to that beach. Think you can do that?"

Yes. He took a deep breath. Yes, of course he could.

For another three days, he listened with no interest to the different scenarios being presented, he objected when he thought the plan would not work, he stressed his belief that only one, not two Catalinas could possibly make the run undetected, and that Pridi's entourage would have to be limited to a small group.

He said the hot season, starting these very days actually, was best to justify a trip to the beach, and all the while his mind was on the bleak future ahead, no reason to get back to Bangkok, to imagine her when he opened the big gate to Thip's house, running through the garden to be caught in his arms, covering his face in kisses.

He listened to the demands that Pridi had made through Sanguan, and advised against accepting them all — "There will be no room for family *and* entourage, not with one plane.

"I understand that the Japanese will swoop down on the advisors if they're left behind, so perhaps consider evacuating them by submarine a day earlier?" — he answered all the questions, but he felt strangely split in two.

Half of him was in the room, the other... with Kate. But try as he might, he couldn't conjure up her face, only perhaps, her smile.

And her eyes... he had recognized them right away when he saw Francis.

He barely started when he heard that there was no question, in anyone's mind, to give Pridi the status of a head of government-in-exile, and felt only mild disgust at the future division of the spoils happening before him.

Francis walked him to his jeep when he left, and before saying goodbye, took out his camera.

"Do you mind? I'd love to send your picture back home, and I think Felicity would want one too. She was devastated, Maura wrote, when she was told.

"Kate was the closest thing to a daughter that she ever had."

Corporal Bruneau took a snap of them both posing in front of the gently waving American flag. "Say 'Cheese'."

"Why?" Lawrence asked, startled out of his trance-like misery.

"Oh," Francis was flustered. "… it's supposed to make you smile."

He couldn't bring himself to smile, though, staring ahead beyond the camera at the swaying palms and the empty, empty blue sky.

When Francis hugged him, and whispered, "God keep you, brother," he hugged him back, dry-eyed, unsmiling still, then turned his back, and got into his jeep.

At Meerut station, Biggin was there, and chattered away as happily as ever, pretending not to notice that Lawrence was staring at the road, and not even flinching at one of his more daring skids, but Lawrence knew that somehow he'd been told – Kandy had probably wired Meerut – from the tender way he took charge of his pack and the sidelong glances he was giving him.

It was only when he was unloading his pack from the jeep that Biggin mouthed that things had not been going well here either.

"Lost Appreciation, they did. Don't ask, it's better. Major Pointon's been beating himself up over that one."

Pointon looked up when he rapped on the door then rose and came to him, too embarrassed to venture any gesture, just shifting his weight from foot to foot, clutching his pipe in his fist.

"My dear fellow. I'm so desperately sorry."

Lawrence managed a pale smile, feeling it strange to move his face muscles this way – he had not smiled in ten days.

"I won't say anything more. I'm sure you couldn't stand it, from someone who didn't know her…"

"Right, then," Pointon finally muttered ineffectually when Lawrence remained silent, "well, I suppose you should know that Appreciation was a failure. We think.

"The monitoring of Siamese news bulletins hasn't spotted any mention of arrest of foreign agents, but…

"So we're sending Appreciation II in next week. No, don't look at me like that, man. There's no choice."

Lawrence shrugged, then pulled a chair to him and sat.

He had given the matter thought during the long hours of travel back to Meerut, and although he knew he would be turned down, he wanted to try.

"Major, I want to be included in the training of active agents."

"For the field?" Pointon choked, "You, blond haired, blue-eyed, taller than any Siamese? Because I suppose," he added deprecatingly, "that it's not Germany where you want to be sent, although you'd fit right in.

"You're mad.

"I understand that you're grieving, but getting yourself killed won't bring her back, you know.

"Whatever field training you got before the war is perfectly adequate for what you're doing now, and I won't let you apply for more."

Lawrence set his mouth and bit out his words.

"I am not mad nor am I a fool.

"I didn't mean being sent to the field now, but later when we have a reliable foothold.

"I have many Siamese friends in Bangkok, I could be hidden in a temple, easily. Or in Yaowarat, where the Japanese don't go, for sure.

"I know the city much better than any of you.

"Nicol Smith from OSS will go in when it's time, and he barely knows Bangkok. Why shouldn't I?"

Pointon shook his head firmly. No.

Lawrence sighed.

"All right, I thought as much. Then instead, I want to go back to being a correspondent.

"You can pull some strings with AP, can't you, to get me back in and invent a story to account for my dropping out of sight all these months?"

He could but he wouldn't, Pointon said finally.

"You are needed here. Here where we need Siamese speakers and people who know the country inside out.

"Kandy sent a glowing report of the intelligence you gave.

"So no, I won't pull a single string, and I want you to remember there's a war going on, which will not be won by having you senselessly killed in the field or by following your friend Stillwell throughout Burma, but which you might contribute to winning just by what you do here.

"Understand?"

Lawrence looked down at his joined fingers, crossed so tightly they were white at the knuckles and spoke very low.

"I understand.

"But I'm bored with what we do here, it used to be — I don't know... fun, for want of a better word, but I can't stand it anymore.

"Sending ill-prepared agents on ill-prepared missions, playing mind-games with broadcasts.

"In Kandy, I felt I was doing something worthwhile. Not here. Not anymore.

"Find me something useful to do."

Just keep on doing your job, Gallet, he was told.

When the time came, he might be assigned something else.

Appreciation II happened as did as its predecessor.

The three-man team was dropped in the teak-covered hills close to the drop zone of Appreciation I — Pointon was still adamant that it was the safest area — and then vanished with no trace and no sign of life.

SCS held its collective breath and waited, in vain.

Pointon tried the "No news is good news" saw as often as he dared, but he was alone in doing so.

In May, he gave the go ahead for operation Billow, a Catalina sea plane infiltration on the Southern Siamese coast of four men from the Red team, the Siamese of Chinese extraction.

Their mission, besides attempting to establish contact with the movement in Bangkok, was to recruit a team of saboteurs — the Reds were assured of the help of many of their community suffering under harsh Japanese rule — and to destroy the railway line linking Singapore with Bangkok.

The men were seen paddling to the shore.

Then nothing.

A month later, news broadcast on Siamese radio revealed that two teams of traitors, Siamese men all of them, had been parachuted into the country by enemies of the Kingdom and were held in custody, having been interrogated by the Japanese.

Another team had attempted a beach landing, two of its members were killed, including its leader, a renegade Sino-Chinese.

Mackenzie in Delhi was beginning to doubt the very existence of a resistance movement in Siam, and the Foreign Office repeatedly confirmed its total distrust in anything that Chamkat, Sanguan and Daeng had claimed, and questioned the usefulness of the work done by SCS – all the more so that the codes, working methods and very intentions of SOE had probably been revealed to the enemy.

In such conditions, it seemed likely, therefore, that Operation Uddingston to get Pridi out of Siam would not go through.

Pointon went around for weeks locked in a thundery mood, almost silent but for snapped rebukes when something was not to his liking, and very little was.

Official Siamese news now included dire warnings against parachutists of enemy forces, attempting to achieve what had never been done before, enslave the Kingdom into the British Empire.

But the people of Siam cherished their freedom, the broadcasts claimed, and would never surrender!

"Well, so much for that," Lawrence said in dejection, dropping the mimeographed sheet just received from the monitoring section in Calcutta.

"Whatever we do seems doomed."

Vic Wemyss, a more recent arrival, who had been a mining engineer in Phuket, was still perusing the report, translated by two of the Free Siamese members who were unfit for active duty.

"Phibul really seems to gave gone off his head," he commented with glee. Listen to this. He wants to build a new capital in the jungle near Petchabun and a so-called Buddhist city in Saraburi.

"Talk about insane plans – how much will it cost?" he shook his head in mock wonderment.

"He'll probably ransom the Chinese in Bangkok to pay for it," Lawrence replied sourly.

"Yeah, possibly. Unless, of course, the war ends before he can continue to bleed the country white.

"At least the news from Burma is good, at last."

It was.

Earlier in the year, the Chinese in Yunnan had defeated the Phayap Thai Army at Xishuangbanna, consolidated their positions and pushed the Siamese back over the Burmese border.

In the west, little by little, between them, Slim with the Indian XV Army Corps, Stillwell, heading the Chinese troops he'd retreated with from Burma – and now in command of the Chindits since Wingate's death in a plane crash last March – had not only repulsed the attempted invasion of India in Imphal and Kohima, but gradually begun to push the Japanese back inland, harassed deep behind their lines by the light, fast, extremely effective unit called Merrill's Marauders, named for their leader, Frank Merrill, he who had spoken to Lawrence of his admiration and respect for Japanese civilization.

"Wish I could be there," Lawrence said resentfully, remembering the heady feeling of excitement and urgency he had only got a taste of in Mandalay, following Stillwell up to the front.

"Bet you don't, really," Vic countered, putting his feet up on the desk and tilting his face back to feel the fan-cooled air.

"No, I do, really," Lawrence insisted, filing the report in a folder and looking down at his desk, feeling an intense sense of nostalgia for those terrible days in Burma when he was surrounded by friends and still believed he would someday be reunited with Kate.

"I met all of them in Burma," he went on. "Stillwell — well, I grant you, he can be a real son of a bitch, Sun Li, his top commander, he's incredibly brave — and Merrill, who's the best of the bunch, I think.

"He actually speaks Japanese, and he knows how they think. He's a genius."

Wemyss wasn't impressed.

"You and I speak Siamese, mate, doesn't make us geniuses."

Lawrence snorted. "How true.

"All it's done is get us here, planning how to send yet more young men to be slaughtered."

Wemyss cocked his head towards the door.

"Don't let Pointon hear you say that, he'll have your guts for garters."

"He knows how I feel."

Lawrence picked up another report and tried to concentrate on what the official news from Bangkok revealed of the soaring prices of rice and other necessary foodstuffs for the mood of the country.

Anything, even work as dry and boring as this, anything to keep his mind off the emptiness of his life.

He had written the necessary letter to his family and received loving and concerned letters back.

"I so regret I never met your Kate," his father wrote, and his mother, besides saying she prayed for Kate's soul every day, attempted to console him with the knowledge that she had probably been surrounded by his friends Lady Thip and her family in Bangkok and concluded *"I know she thought of you till the end."*

Even his cousin Charlotte had taken the time to pen a few hurried words.

"I am sure you are doing some top-secret and important war work, as am I (ha-ha! Do you know anybody at all who might trust me with a secret?) and I do hope that it somehow serves in keeping your thoughts away from your wife.

I'm also sure everyone is telling you that time will heal your grief, because they said it to me when Dickie, the man I was going to get engaged to, was shot down over France last year,

They, whoever your 'they' may be, are right. It does.

Believe me.

Life does go on.

When all this is finished, and for us, it appears it might happen in not too distant a future, you'll take me to the Ritz and tell me all about Kate, I'll tell you about Dickie and we'll cry in our cocktails and feel much better for it. Although of course, London is taking quite a beating these days, so the Ritz may no longer be standing. But we'll find someplace else."

It was the only letter that somehow helped.

He put all the letters away with Kate's picture.

He couldn't bear to look at it now and kept it in his locked bag, along with his diaries.

The following week, the reports from Burma listed yet more advances.

Merrill's Marauders had taken and were holding the airfield at Myitkyna, but elsewhere, the monsoon rains had begun and the advances were slow, though the Japanese were suffering, if possible, more than the British or the Americans, their soldiers captured on the battlefield were ill, emaciated and starving — at least those who let themselves be taken.

Pointon, who still seemed to not have recovered from his black mood following the failure of the three operations, read from dispatches sent by Delhi, recounting how the retreating Imperial Army mined the fields and when they ran out of mines, dug deep pits with a grenade-equipped soldier inside each.

When tanks and troops advanced, unsuspecting, over the pits, the soldiers exploded their grenade, and themselves with it.

Japanese losses, judging from the bodies left on the battlefield, were tremendous.

"Well, that's rather good news," someone ventured, "For us."

Pointon gave him a bleak look.

"You think so?

"For me, it shows me what they can do when they're desperate."

There was at last an American bombing raid over Bangkok, and although, because of heavy monsoon clouds, the port and Hua Lampong train station were spared, the railway yards at Makkasan were hit and two buildings — which turned out to be, according to Siamese official radio news, a Japanese military hospital and the Kempetai headquarters — were destroyed.

The celebration was muted at SCS — they could not help but wonder what else had been hit in the city, which was still, to all of them, very much their home.

The news of the landing in France was a blessed relief, and instead of parsing the news broadcasts from Bangkok with yet more of Phibul's bombastic announcements, they huddled around the radio to listen to the BBC, swearing at the static, and twisting their fingers nervously or biting their lips, following the first days' advances, their minds far away from the hills of Meerut or the steamy banks of the Chao Phraya.

Awed by the description of the tremendous firepower thrown against Germany, they were picturing the relentless battles, on the misty beaches and in the damp and green hedgerows of Normandy.

At dinner, tears in his eyes, Pointon offered a toast in South African sherry, the best liquor the mess could offer.

"I give you our gallant brothers in France, whether they be British, French, Canadian, or American.

"Gentlemen, the Allies, may God favour their battle."

Just a few days later, when it seemed certain that the Allies would not be thrown back into the Channel, Signals Division in Calcutta contacted SCS with an excited but perplexing message.

Both Appreciation teams, who had by now been considered as probably dead at the hands of the Kempetai, and whom Pointon was still mourning, had made contact.

"They're held in jail," Pointon said, his voice trembling. "They — actually, it was Khem, the head of Appreciation I, or at least his shortwave transmission, from jail, if you can fathom that! — they claim they are protected by the head of Police, General Adun, who refuses to turn them over to the Japanese.

"They are safe, they are well, and they have been joined by the two surviving members of Billow.

"Yes, I know —," he raised his hand to quell the sudden clamour of exclamations and questions — "how much trust can we put in this?

"Signals Division obviously replied, asking for all the code security checks.

"Khem confirmed. There is no doubt it was indeed he who was transmitting. But...

"We all know what it possibly means. Was he transmitting under duress?

"Do the Japs now have our codes?

"That, of course, is what London is going to conclude, and instruct us to pay no attention to the message.

"I, however, intend to reply that we just have to see what happens, and play along with it."

He closed his eyes briefly. "And for my part, I just thank God they are alive."

Further messages arrived fast and frequent.

General Adun had informed Regent Pridi of SCS's intentions, as conveyed by the men in his possession.

Pridi instructed him to keep them safe and out of Japanese hands. For the present, there was little more he could do.

London was withering in its assessment of Lieutenant Khem's credibility.

"General Adun is not seen as a reliable opponent of the Japanese, but as a diligent military officer who will always execute orders given.

"As to Lieutenant Khem, methinks the chap doth protest overmuch," was one of the views expressed.

"Either none of them had any intention of working for us, just wanted to get home, and surrendered as soon as their boots hit Siamese soil — how else can one explain the speed at which they were apprehended and are now in police custody?

"Or else they were indeed captured as spies, and broken by the Japanese, who now dictate all this nonsense.

"Ignore."

Pointon acknowledged, and confirmed his intention to ignore. However, he did not specify that what he would disregard was this latter instruction.

"We have to go on responding. If they are stooges of the Kempetai, let them believe we have been fooled. It could be useful, if only to pass along false information. If not, well... we shall find out in due course. But we can't afford to remain silent."

Bangkok, for long so silent, was now an almost daily source of information.

The SCS team, barely recovered from its excitement at having made contact with Appreciation — for what it was worth, of course, as they kept repeating like a mantra — was shaken by what was heard on Radio Bangkok news.

Prime-Minister Field Marshal Phibul Songkram had resigned, ousted from power by the Parliamentary Assembly, because of two votes he had attempted to force through — the founding of a new capital city near Petchabun and of a Buddhist city in Saraburi.

"God, if we only had champagne! "Nicolson called out." Can't face that sweet sherry again, we'll have to celebrate with beer."

"I'll believe when it happens," Wemyss muttered, but still, at mess, they raised their glasses to Pridi, and to Phibul's foolishness which had caused his downfall.

"Doesn't mean the Japs are going to relax their hold over Bangkok," Pointon warned them all, damping the elation.

"If anything, they're going to be even more suspicious."

The team spent hours listening to the radio, alternating between the slow progression of the Allies in France, the confusing, piecemeal snippets from Radio Bangkok, and Khem's transmissions from deep inside his jail.

The name of the new Prime Minister had not yet been announced, and from what both SCS and the Siamese monitoring group in Calcutta were able to put together, Phya Phahol — he who had been one of the forces behind the coup of 1932 — might be chosen.

"Phahol?" Lawrence was astonished. "He's a least a hundred years old."

"Don't talk rubbish," Pointon snapped. "he was young enough to spearhead a coup, what — twelve years ago? — and now you think he's in his dotage?"

Lawrence shrugged. "Well, not really. But as far as I knew when I left the country, he wasn't in good health."

Then, it was Thawi Bunyaket, but before they could rejoice — Thawi was a known Pridi ally — it was no again.

Phibul was going to be appointed Prime Minister once more.

"Well, it's happened before," Pointon was dejected. "I suppose we should have expected that."

Wemyss threw down the report. He knew it along, hadn't he said so?

Then the name of Khuang Aphaiwong finally was announced, first by Khem and then confirmed by Radio Bangkok.

"Never heard of him," Wemyss grumbled."You, Gallet?"

"Yes. He's the man who cut the telephone lines during the coup. He was head of the Telegraph Department."

Yes, yes. Pointon closed his eyes, thinking. That's why the name was familiar.

There was still not that much known about him, and very little revealed from the news bulletins.

"Let's cross our fingers, and see."

Analysing and cross-matching items from the government sponsored news in Siam, the long winded and grandiloquent Constitutionalist communiqués on Radio Bangkok, and other, seemingly irrelevant, items, such as the sharp rise in the price of rice and oil, was a painstaking and possibly error-fraught exercise.

But added to the — perhaps purposefully misleading — transmissions from Khem, it began to give a fairly clear idea of the situation, all the more so as Khem was becoming increasingly outspoken in his announcements.

The Co-Regent, Prince Aditya, had refused to accept Khuang as Prime Minister.

Phibul, still Commander-in-Chief of the Army, might well march on Bangkok.

It was said that troops had been pulled back from the Burmese Shan States now under Siamese control. Why, if not for that?

Kuang had gone to the Lopburi garrison, where Phibul was now residing, to beg him to refrain.

Khuang had had to borrow a car to get there, Khem went on gleefully, as Phibul had driven away with the Prime Minister's official vehicle.

"Nobody could make that up," Lawrence commented with delight. "It has to be true."

From over a thousand miles away, he felt as if he were in the streets of the capital, imagining the anger of housewives faced with a sudden doubling of the price of food, the muted conversations in coffee shops, the hopes of so many.

And above all, he tried to guess what Pridi was doing.

Finally, it was official.

On July 31st, Prince Aditya resigned from the Regency Council, and the National Assembly had voted Pridi sole Regent, and Khuang Prime Minister.

Khem broke the news, Radio Bangkok confirmed and Constitutionalist had gone off the air.

Pridi had won.

The Royal Government of Siam was now entirely made up of his allies.

"Well, it looks promising," Pointon smiled, and Lawrence thought that only in Siam could one have such a situation: whilst still allied with Japan, the Kingdom was now headed at the highest level by men chosen by Codename Ruth, OSS agent.

But once the frenzied excitement of the past month had died down, while the others were busing themselves analysing, considering then rejecting plans to send another team in, or test Khem by feeding him false information, or devise arcane means to contact Pridi himself, Lawrence found himself jaded, at a loss, almost bitter.

It began with the realization that Operation Uddingston would now have to be scrapped.

Well of course it would, Pointon said dismissively. "We're not about to get Codename Ruth out when he's so much more useful inside.

"Besides, what's the point of having a government-in-exile, when you can have a government in situ?"

Yes, of course.

But... Although no one had ever suggested that Lawrence might be on the team sent to Hua Hin, he had somehow always assumed that his knowledge of the seaside town would make him indispensable.

And now, all he was left with was the task of devising yet more ways of inducing the Siamese people to loathe their Japanese allies, whilst supporting their new government.

He just couldn't bring himself to care anymore.

The ceaseless arguments over such or such minister — "Admiral Sinthu Songkhramchai, at Defence ... reliable or not, pro-Japanese or not?

"Well, obviously, not pro-Japanese, don't be daft — Phya Phahol, is back without portfolio, what could that mean?" — exasperated him, and although he knew, yes, he knew, that the work they were all doing was important, he no longer believed he could contribute to it in any useful way.

He increasingly spent evenings in the poky room he shared with Wemyss, prostrate on the rough sheets under the creaking fan, reading whatever the inadequate library could provide, detective novels, Western tales of derring-do, Walter Scott and Shakespeare, and drinking far too much gin, alone, or else, against all orders, strolling the bazaars, hoping against hope that something, anything, might happen to put an end to this unbearable life, and again, drinking too much gin.

The SCS team had learned to avoid him outside work hours, and even Biggin had begun to dodge when he saw him in the courtyard.

In the first days of August, a message announced the long-awaited arrival of Andrew Gilchrist, and Pointon left for Calcutta to take part in his briefing.

When both arrived back in Meerut, Andrew's honking laugh preceded him to the mess, where he greeted Lawrence with a long, searching look, and then hugged him briefly.

"You see, laddie, we meet again, just as I promised.

"What can we get drunk on?"

There was only beer, local gin, and a disgusting sweet sherry, Lawrence replied.

"Gin, then, I suppose."

When Gilchrist considered Lawrence had imbibed enough, he leaned towards him and said very low. "I'm desperately sorry about Kate. She was a rare woman.

"What I can tell you is that by the time I was repatriated, she was not interned with the other Americans, that, I know for sure. Some were repatriated on the same ship, and I asked.

"So if she escaped being rounded up during the first months, there's every reason to expect that she continued to live safely with Lady Thip.

"For whatever it's worth, I thought it would comfort you to know that."

Lawrence didn't answer, just stared ahead, as Gilchrist went on, "Pointon's worried about you. You probably know why... well..

"We both agree you need a break.

"Take a few days off, go walking in the hills, or — as our American friends so charmingly put it — go get laid in Delhi, or, here's an idea, go to Agra and see the Taj.

"Whatever you do, snap out of this mood you're in, because we need your knowledge of Siamese politics.

"So get out of here, and come back prepared to work.

"It's an order."

Lawrence took five days leave, his first in a year.

Andrew was right.

He was heartily sick of Meerut, SCS and everything to do with it, and knew, if he didn't manage to somehow dispel the anger and misery that simmered in his mind, day after day, he would not be able to go on much longer.

He had no intention of spending hours on a train, so, with Biggin's help, he borrowed a jeep from the pool and drove to Agra.

LAWRENCE'S DIARY
AGRA
AUGUST 28TH 1944

The Taj Mahal, as the story goes, is a shrine to the memory of a beloved wife.

Just what I needed.

Of course, I should not have seen it first in the glaring afternoon sun, it just seemed... well, like its pictures, and I wondered what made it so famous, apart, of course, from the possibly apocryphal love story behind it.

The whiteness of the marble seemed to reverberate inside my head, I was pestered by beggars, fortune tellers, souvenir sellers and urchins, and bothered by the smells — cow dung and worse — and the heat.

Of course, my mood, never good these past months, was not improved by driving on Indian roads, avoiding military transports, lorries, bicycles and cows.

I should have taken Biggin with me, instead of just slipping him twenty rupees to have him turn a blind eye to a jeep missing for four nights.

I registered at the Imperial, deciding if I were to be court-martialled for the theft of a jeep, I may as well spend my last free days in luxury.

Of course, luxury is a relative concept and in wartime, I was not expecting much and not much is what I got.

Still, the shabby grandeur is comforting, my room is large, the mosquito net intact, and the bathtub immense. And the bliss of not hearing Wemyss' snores....

My tea was served in a silver pot and the tablecloth was darned but very white.

There was a piano player, tinkling slightly out of tune Cole Porter numbers, and the turbaned waiter looked straight out of Kipling.

It was a bittersweet moment, the nostalgia of by-gone times that probably never should have been, and were so obviously to be no more.

I was thinking of what Merrill said all that time ago in Burma about the demise of the Empire.

This war has changed the world, I fear — and somehow...

No, I do not fear, I feel that some things have begun to be righted.

But there are yet many bloodbaths to come.

That is what I fear.

I returned to the Taj as the sun was setting.

The minarets seemed to whirl in the air, the marble shimmered against the orange sky and both were reflected in the canal along which I walked, undisturbed except for some whispered offers of delights I can too well imagine, and which added to the enchantment rather than spoiling it.

And somehow, in the shadow of this monument to love, I came to accept my loss, and feel lucky that I had those perfect months with Kate. I told her I had met her brother, I relived every lovely, thrilling moment, and I silently made my farewell.

Afterwards, I sat on the verandah and drank gin and bitters keeping an eye out for any correspondent I might have known in a previous existence, for instance Berrigan, trying to think of some story to account for my year-long absence from AP.

I actually would very much enjoy seeing him but I expect he is in Burma with Slim's advance.

But thankfully none, nobody, just English officers and their dissatisfied, sniffy wives, some American service men with pretty young women out of uniform who giggle excitedly, gape at the emaciated pi-dogs fighting with crows for trash, the wandering bony cows, and simper coyly at being called memsahibs.

Only this afternoon, they would have annoyed me, but I now feel.. what?

At peace, I suppose.

I don't know what the future holds.

But I know somehow there is a future.

Chapter XXIX

The Allies invaded France, and on the same day, Lady Thip died.

Doctor Sumet was by her side, and had been visiting her daily for the past week.

"It is over," he said, downcast, greeted at the hospital gate by Kate.

"Her heart gave up. No, do not cry, please. She would not have wanted that."

The bathing ceremony would be that same evening, and then the funeral rites and prayers would take place at the house every day for the next week.

"Normally, in such a family," he went on, his heart grieving at seeing her tormented, pale, face, "the cremation would be held a month or more later. But in these times... Pichit decided to not wait any more than necessary."

How were they both, Kate wanted to know.

Sumet sat down heavily behind his desk.

Pichit was... he opened his hands, unable to find the words to describe the broken, guilt-ridden man he had left crying quietly by his mother's bed.

"He blames himself, because she worried so about him. As to Busaba, who can tell?

"She is not well, though, and since her face and legs have become so swollen, she never goes out anymore, she does not want to be seen.

"And Fon... He did not leave her room, he slept on the floor by her bed. I think he would have preferred to die himself.

"She was his sister, did you know?"

Kate nodded, sobbing.

With Thip gone, the last link with Lawrence had been severed. And she was alone...

"What we Buddhists believe," he said, trying to console himself as well as Kate, "is that we shall be reborn, according to our merits.

"Lady Thip shall surely be reborn to an ever better life, and shall perhaps be reunited with her husband, whom she loved most dearly.

"Do Catholics not also believe something similar, but only on Judgement Day?"

Kate turned away. She didn't know what she believed any more.

She had been officially dead for five months now, and had spent the first weeks crying unconsolably, realizing that since she had lost her friend, she had also lost her name, and any future that she might have as the wife of Lawrence Gallet.

Lady Thip had taken the news very badly, Sumet reported miserably.

Why was she not told, she would have rushed to Kate's bedside, she should have been there to hold her hand, how could Sumet not even think to telephone?

"Of course, what with the worry about Somchai, which I think, she bears with greater difficulty than Busaba and Pichit, it was a blow.

"She asks if she could have done more, perhaps, to help...

"But I said nothing could be done in such cases, and that until the last hours, we had hoped for a recovery."

"Wouldn't it be possible just to tell her in confidence?" Kate begged.

Thip could be trusted.

No.

If Kate Fallon were to disappear, she needed to disappear for everyone.

Ken Akira had been dumbstruck when he was told of Belinda's last plan, and then, he couldn't help but laugh and she glared at him angrily.

"Sorry, forgive me, but it's so perfect. It's crazy, but it can work.

"Of course. Belinda was a genius, poor girl.

"Who besides Sumet knows about this?"

Rose and Bernadette, the two Irish nurses, of course. "They don't like it, but they understand, or at least, they say they do.

"Wanida, the hospital administrator. Nuch, the accountant.

"That's it. The other staff keep on calling me Kate, but they have no idea I took Belinda's identity. They barely speak English, just a few words.

"None of them were at the funeral, so...

"And Father Perroudon has never bothered to learn our names..."

Her voice faltered.

Mother Melanie had written a lovely letter from the convent where she was interned, addressed of course to Belinda, trying to comfort her for the death of her close friend.

"*I asked to attend the funeral, but permission was not given,* − 'Oh, Lord, I never thought of that!' Kate exclaimed, horrified − "*so I retired to the chapel and thought of you every step from the chapel to the cemetery.*

"*I pray for Kate morning and evening, but I know that she has been welcomed into the blessed arms of our Holy Mother, and I want you to try and remember, please, that although she died very young, she knew great happiness and love.*"

"Whereas, Belinda never did, really... I don't know how I'm going to be able to do this," Kate sobbed.

"And some day, if I ever get away from here, I'll have to face her family and tell them."

Ken made a face and nodded.

It would be hard. And the later Belinda's family knew, the better for them.

"But I can't help admitting it's a relief, for me.

"Military Security is watching me closely − I know that pretty soon, they're going to want to know all about my girlfriend..."

Kate shuddered.

"Will I be interrogated?"

No, no reason, now that she was officially Irish... "but if it happens, just show them her passport.

"You didn't exactly look alike, but who looks like their passport photograph?

"And what about Eddy?" he asked. "Military Security might find it strange if I go make another visit there, but I could swing it, I think.

"I wouldn't much like having to be the one who tells him, though."

No. Eddy should not be told.

Sumet had his head in his hands and looked down at his desk

despairingly when Kate asked, trapped by the spider's web of lies that enveloped them all, and he himself most of all since he had signed the death certificate.

"No," he said again. "And we must go on sending him parcels. He must go on believing, for his sake as well as yours, that Belinda is still alive."

Kate looked away, embarrassed. The thing was, she wasn't sure she could afford to send parcels any longer.

"Lady Thip used to send me some money, with the baskets that Fon brought.

"But now that I'm supposed to be dead... And everything is so much more expensive..."

Sumet was brusque. She wasn't to worry about that, he would buy what was necessary.

And, he added, she was to stay in her room tomorrow morning.

Busaba had an appointment and Kate must not be seen.

The cool weather of winter passed, giving way to the throbbing fiery skies of March and April, and Kate learned to lie low, to sign her pitifully meagre wage slip with Belinda's name and to grieve alone.

She missed Belinda, oh how she missed her — far, far more than she missed Lawrence who was now but some dream with as much reality as a fairy tale future.

Lady Thip sent a basket — "For Kate's friends," — a few days after the funeral, but Kate knew there would be no more, and doled out the biscuits sparingly.

They still listened to the BBC, and the news from Europe was so encouraging that Rose and Bernadette began to make plans for when the war was over.

"How can you?" Kate snapped. "Just because the Allies are winning, it doesn't mean the Japanese won't.

"They'll probably kill us all before they kill themselves.

"They won't surrender, you'll see."

The others exchanged glances, and Bernadette sniffed that Kate seemed to have inherited Belinda's temper along with her name.

A few days later, they heard, eyes widened with horror and disbelief, the reports of the Bataan march as told by ten escaped American prisoners who had managed to make their way to safety.

"So that's what you were talking about," Kate told Ken, during one of their increasingly rare meetings.

Yes, he replied quietly. That and Shanghai.

During the Holy Week leading to Easter, Ken was called away again, to Burma, then returned to Bangkok a month later.

He was somber, and when Kate entered the room, she saw that he must already have had enough whisky to make him flushed and irritable.

Standing at the foot of the bed, she looked down on him.

"I can see — actually I can smell — the mood you're in. Shall I leave before you start hitting me?"

He shook his head silently, and made space for her to sit down.

"No. I'd be happier hitting myself, though, if I could."

"What's the matter?"

He barked a biting laugh.

"Apart from the war, the hundreds of guys dead, Japanese, Americans, yes Americans in Burma, imagine that, and Brits, the horrible, grotesque casualties, guts spilling out, bayoneted chests, hands blown off by grenades and legs blown off by mines — nah, what could be the matter?"

Not only had he been forced to do the most appalling surgeries — in a tent, with an oil lamp hanging above, no ether, no disinfectant except for alcohol splashed over gaping wounds making the poor guys scream, and be held down while he cut, or stitched or amputated.

"But you know what the worse was?"

He had been called to the field commander's tent, because an American POW had been taken, and for once, allowed to live.

"Usually, they just bayonet them to death, so as not to waste ammo — I know what you're going to say, so don't bother.

"This guy, they wanted to interrogate him.

"So they asked me to translate."

Kate closed her eyes.

"You don't have to tell me..."

Ken sat up, and spoke very low, his head in his hands.

"I shouldn't, but ... I have to tell someone, and I know enough now not to protest the way I did in Manila.

"Anyway... The guy was wounded, pretty badly.

"I promised him morphine for the pain if he would talk. He

just kept repeating his name and his serial number.

"So he was taken outside and bayonetted in the chest, and I was sent back to do surgery."

He gulped down some more whisky.

"You know what I've been thinking?"

"How everything comes down to luck. If I hadn't been in Japan that winter, I would've been drafted, sure, but on the US side, and maybe I could have done something for my folks.

"If...Goddamn bloody fucking if."

Kate bitterly picked up his monologue.

"Yes, and...If you hadn't come to do that surgery, if Belinda hadn't asked for your help, if you hadn't talked to Eddy, you never would have found out I'm American, you never would have threatened me, and Belinda would not have taken my identity and I wouldn't be in this awful situation.

"I'm dead but I'm alive.

"Can you imagine what it feels like?"

He would have known she was American as soon as he'd heard her speak without a surgical mask, he replied wearily. And anyways...

He looked up at her, his face bleak.

"Kate, I think we're losing."

"Who is 'we'? "she retorted icily. The Japanese? Oh, so you've chosen?"

He lay back, balancing the glass on his stomach.

What did it matter now? When the end came, all they would know is that he was wearing a Japanese uniform.

"The Americans will put me in a camp, unless they shoot me, as a traitor, of course.

"Or maybe before it's over, I might be ordered to commit hara-kiri."

"Don't joke about it."

"I'm not," he smiled bitterly. "Although I doubt it would be ordered, I think it would be left up to me to decide if I can bear the dishonour of surrendering.

"I've actually heard some guys discussing the possibility.

"You know, we have swords to go with our dress uniforms, not as sharp as a scalpel, I guess, but they would do the job."

She lay down next to him, took his hand, and they both stared up at the slowly revolving fan.

Goddam bloody ifs.

In early June, Sumet had just returned home after spending an hour at the bedside of Lady Thip, listening to her increasingly laboured breathing.

"I'm afraid it won't be long, now," he had told Pichit who flinched and looked away, his eyes filling with tears. Fon had paled, and even Busaba's bloated face looked shocked.

He had driven home in a solid curtain of rain, wondering how he could prepare Kate, and looking forward to a drink and an evening at home, by the radio.

He had just settled down to listen to Radio Bangkok propaganda while the servants were still awake, and then the BBC when he was sure of not being heard, when the telephone rang.

It was an unknown voice. "I am General Adun, the head of Police. I am very sorry to disturb you on such an evening, but I require your services."

"Do you?"

Sumet's tone was cool, to cover the instinctive fear that gripped his bowels and slowed his heart.

"Yes. I have several patients in need of care."

"Do you not have your own police hospital?

"They're competent there, from what I know."

Adun spoke impatiently.

Yes, the doctors at the Police Hospital were competent, but Doctor Sumet realized, did he not, that the hospital also served as a Japanese military hospital?

"The patients are rather important, and your name was suggested by Louis Banomyong. Can you come to the central prison? Now?"

It was almost ten, it was raining — surely it could wait until tomorrow, Sumet objected, playing for time.

"No, it cannot, I am sorry."

What did it mean? Had the X-O Group been discovered, and had Louis been forced to give names?

What could be held against him? He had given gold, yes, but otherwise, he couldn't think...

What was happening? Had the time come for him to be tested?

He knew very little about General Adun except that he had been Deputy Prime Minister under Pridi several years ago, and that he had the reputation of being ruthless.

He put together his medical kit, looking lovingly at his office, bidding farewell to all the objects he had accumulated there, the framed covers of *Punch* magazine, the surgical textbooks from over a hundred years ago, the Sawankhalok pottery pieces on the shelves...

Shaking himself, he said firmly, "Beautiful as they are, these are but objects."

He considered, then rejected, writing his mother a letter — saying what? — then left the house, his head lowered against the beating rain.

The sentries on duty must have been informed, because as soon as he rolled his window down to give his name, he was waved though, his car was taken to be parked, and he was hurried along sinister, grey-painted corridors with single bulbs hanging from the ceiling and a strong smell of drains and creosote.

The sentry knocked on a door, and stepped aside.

This is where his life might turn, Sumet thought, and entered.

A man seated at a table where there were still the remains of a meal rose to greet him. He recognized General Adun from his picture in the papers, a saturnine, forbidding presence.

"You have come," he said, wai-ing, "I am grateful. Follow me."

He unlocked the door behind him, which opened into two more corridors, and turned left, Sumet wondering all the while whether it was customary to express gratitude at a someone who might be arrested.

The general unlocked two rooms, that Sumet by now realized probably were cells.

There was a young man, lying on a stained matrass, tossing and muttering.

"He was captured in the south, the bullet was removed, but..." the general said apologetically. "Can you do something?"

Sumet grimaced, and crouched by the bunk, probing the proud flesh oozing pus.

"I can debride and clean it, and do what I can, but..."

An idea struck him. "You say the police hospital is also used by the Japanese army?"

Adun nodded, nonplussed.

"Then can you get penicillin from the Japanese doctors? I know they have it."

"It will cure him?"

It was his best chance. But what excuse would he give?

Adun looked down on him haughtily.

"I am the head of police. I need no excuse."

Then he was to get some by tomorrow morning.

When he was done attending to the man, with Adun serving as nurse and handing him the ether, alcohol, sulpha powder and gauze bandages, he rose, easing his aching back.

"Who is he?"

An agent, sent by the English, Adun replied as if it were the most natural thing in the world. "There are several more next door whom you might help."

"I have brought the doctor," he announced.

Four young men looked up, two from playing cards, one from a chair where he was leafing through a magazine, and one from the narrow bunk bed fastened to the wall.

Sumet looked at all of them, frowned, then he turned to one who had risen with a wince when he entered.

"I believe I know you, don't I?"

The man smiled shyly, tugging on his homespun blue shirt.

"Yes, Doctor, you do.

"I'm Puey Ungphakorn, I used to teach your nephew, at Assumption College, and gave him private coaching in French at home. That's where you met me, several times.

"Then I received a scholarship to study at the London School of Economics. But in this group, I'm known as Khem."

Four more young men entered, and Khem then introduced him to all, all members of a team sent by the British to contact the resistance movement in Bangkok.

"We were parachuted into Chainat province, but we were seen by villagers, arrested and brought here, with our wireless radios.

"Thankfully, General Adun was able to protect us and keep us safe."

They had, he went on to say, been questioned by Japanese security, but with the General present so they were not mistreated, and managed to get them to believe they were all students trying to get back home.

He had sprained his ankle while landing, and it still was swollen and painful.

Sumet knelt down to examine it, and saw they there were also festering sores on his leg.

"Yes, they also kept me chained by the same ankle, when I was in jail. I fear it got infected."

He had probably broken a small bone in his foot, Sumet said, cleaning the sores, but by this time, there was nothing much he could do about that.

One man had his arm in a sling, and another a nasty gash on his cheek, with blood still seeping.

"The village headman called me a traitor to Field Marshal Phibul."

While Sumet worked, stitching the gash, disinfecting and swabbing, he listened to their story, all of them in high spirits, telling about their days in England, and how Prince Svasti had encouraged them when they were inducted into the Pioneer corps, — "Prince Svasti? Really?" Sumet exclaimed.

Really.

Most of them were mistrustful of him at first, but when he offered them the possibility of joining a group to be trained as agents for SOE, they had all followed him enthusiastically.

"You have no idea how we were treated in the Pioneer Corps.

"It's a sort of a military outfit for enemy aliens who happened to be In England when the war broke out.

"We were with Italians, and Germans, and Russians...

"They had us cleaning latrines, and peeling potatoes, and digging trenches...

"And we were all students, in economics, and engineering, medicine or law."

There was even a prince of the Royal family in their group, who had been subjected to the same demeaning treatment.

So when Prince Svasti appeared and offered them the chance of fighting with the British for their homeland... They had all jumped at it.

"We keep on trying to contact our command in India, but so far, we've had no luck," Khem said. "I guess they've given up on us, but someday, they will be tuned to our frequency and hear us."

Sumet straightened from his crouch after checking another man's ankle sores and looked down at them all.

"I admire you all greatly," he said. "Truly, you will be the pride of the Kingdom."

Adun rose as well. "Yes, well, we have yet to win. Come, Doctor.

"I shall get the medication you spoke of — just write down the name here, please.

"Will you come back tomorrow night?"

Sumet considered.

He needed to ask Ken Akira about the dosage of the precious penicillin.

There was Lady Thip, about to breathe her last, and his hospital duties. And there was also the constant threat of being noticed by the Kempetai. What might happen to him if he were to be caught treating British agents, albeit in prison?

And then he shrugged all those worries aside. There was a brave young man with his life in the balance.

"No, telephone me as soon as you get it. It cannot wait.

"I will come immediately."

Adun walked him back to his car.

"I am grateful, Doctor," he said once more, and Sumet shook his head.

No, he was more grateful, for being trusted. For being able to help.

And hunched over the wheel, peering through the condensation and squeaking windshield wipers, he drove off into the rainy night.

Later that night, the dark was rocked by loud explosions, and the sky was full of the rumble of heavy airplanes, circling above the dense cover of monsoon clouds.

Kate was shaken from her bed by the noise, and she ran from her room, only to be stopped by Rose, who was on duty in the wards.

"They're bombing us," the Irish woman cawed shrilly. "What should we do? Where should we put the patients?"

Kate couldn't think, so loud was the roar from above, and she felt the wide planks of the floor trembling under her feet.

"I... I don't know," she stammered. "I don't think.. there's

465

nothing we *can* do. None of the beds have wheels..."

Oh Lord, she thought, why, why, why, weren't any of the beds equipped with wheels, as they were in her training hospital?

Why hadn't she ever thought of that?

She heard her gasping voice, as if from a distance. Bernadette arrived as she was wringing her hands, trying, desperately trying, to come up with an idea, any idea.

"It wouldn't be any good," Bernadette said curtly "There's nowhere to shelter them. Let's just go in and try to calm them down. And pray."

They spent over an hour, fleeting from ward to ward, moving from bed to bed, holding down the thrashing new mother, who had her child against her breast, and was howling hysterically, soothing the old lady dying of liver cancer, who was as motionless as a statue, but keening like a banshee, easing the man with carbuncles back into his bed, soon joined by the Thai nurses and the night watchman who came to help.

Suddenly, there was another explosion nearby, the windows shattered, sending glass shards flying through the ward and Bernadette fell to her knees, rocking back and forth, crossing herself wildly as smoke and dust filled the air and the ceiling fans began to swing crazily, along with the overhead lamps which then flickered and went out.

Kate shuddered, and hunched between the wall and the bed she was clinging to, covering her head with her hands.

More dust fell in little puffs from the ceiling, but the floor stopped thudding beneath her. There was a clanging of bells from the fire engines racing down Sathorn Road, but they kept on going, passing the hospital.

Finally, she crawled out over the broken glass to the verandah to see if the fire were nearby, and pulled herself up, grabbing the wood balustrade and pushing aside smashed tiles fallen from the roof.

"Come back, you fool!" Rose was frantic, cowering against the wall, her coif at her feet and her hair tumbled over her face.

Kate licked her dry, dust-caked lips, coughed to clear her throat, and swallowed. "No, it's all right," she manged to call. "There's a fire, but not on Sathorn Road, I can see — I don't know, some red in the sky, not far away, towards the river... but I don't hear the planes any more.

"I think they've gone. Are you okay?"

They were.

Some glass had landed on the beds, but the patients were hiding under the sheets, their heads covered with their pillow. They were all hushed now, even the newborn infant was quiet, suckling his shaken mother who was crying quietly.

The nurses set about clearing the debris, shaking the covers free of glass, and the night watchman appeared with a broom.

"It's a miracle," Bernadette finally declared, surveying the dusty room.

Doctor Sumet burst in as the sun was rising — "I had to wait for the all clear siren," and Wanida had arrived from her home on Chan Road, clucking and fussing and professing relief at finding her hospital largely untouched.

But when she saw all of the broken windows she burst into tears. There was no more glass to be found in Bangkok.

The following day, Lady Thip died, and at the central prison, General Adun welcomed Doctor Sumet with three vials of penicillin and the news that the Allies had landed in France. He thoughtfully watched him inject the precious medication, asking whether this would cure the man.

"I hope," Sumet sighed. "It's his only chance, now. It might be too late, however, but... well, as I said, I hope. Try to make him drink plenty of liquid, sweet tea, broth."

It would be done, Adun, said, but Sumet could see that he was preoccupied.

"Our Japanese friends are very nervous," he confided, walking down the grey and damp corridors, "and rightly so, I assume, as the Germans will probably soon be defeated.

"But they claim they are fully able to wage the war alone in the East against the Americans *and* the British, and win."

"Do they just say that, or do they actually believe it?" Sumet wondered, half to himself.

"Oh, they believe it," Adun replied with certainty. "I think they are wrong, but they believe it. But in the meantime... It will make our life more complicated."

During the evening receptions for Khunying Thip's funeral rites, people talked of little else, cautiously, of course, ready to break off any comment — about the war, the bombs that scarred the city only two days ago — more than a thousand killed, and rumours that all children were to be evacuated, but where to? — the bedraggled and bloodied Thai Army limping back from Burma, or what appeared as Phibul's increasingly fragile position...

Had Sumet heard about this plan to build a Buddhist city near Saraburi?

Of course, one could not be against returning full importance to faith, but still... did anyone believe Buddhism was less revered than in the old days?

But behind the polite, careful words, there was none of the belligerent calls for the greater respect for Thailand which only Phibul could ensure, and that Sumet remembered from only last year, or the assertive claims of greater Asian fellowship and the need to recover all of the lands lost to France.

No, what Sumet heard was worry, about the future, about day-to-day living, prices going higher daily, and imports from Japan — and many necessities could only be imported from Japan, nowadays — were scarce, given the attacks on the convoys in the Pacific, and everything, everything, everybody said, cost up to five times more than last year.

"Even here," he overheard a woman muttering, grabbing a sweetmeat with a thin jewelled hand, "look, the food is not what it would have been two years ago."

As he had hoped, Kate had smiled — she smiled so rarely now — when he described the funeral customs and the reception, every evening, which was more of a social occasion than a gathering to grieve together.

"It's kind of what we do," she remarked, "at our wakes. Except the men get drunk, and sometimes there are fistfights, and singing.

"It's not sad, not really."

She had sighed and turned away. "I wish I could go to Lady Thip's wake, though."

Sumet sighed as well, as he stood by his mother who could not, somehow, hide a look of victory on her wrinkled face.

"I'm three years older than Thip was, and I'm still here, and I survived a bad case of dengue last year," she was saying to Pensri, the mother of one of the generals who had led the Thai Army attack on Burma and who was now, it was said, heading back to Bangkok with his forces begging for food along the way.

Pensri nodded, her hands clutching each other and looking around nervously, as if she expected to be blamed either for her son's defeat or for the fact he had partnered with the Japanese in the first place.

"It is time to drive you back," he finally said firmly as his mother was launching into an involved description of her ailments, and guided her to the door, pausing to bid farewell to Busaba, who had remained seated throughout, her swollen legs hidden by a long dark paisin, and her lovely face impassive under her make-up.

Pichit looked distracted, and worried, and rightly so, Sumet thought, if he were involved in business dealings with the Japanese army.

Well, he would certainly go on adding to the family fortune for the time being, and afterwards... who knew what might happen after the war?

Fon was hovering nearby, keeping an eye on the servants passing platters of drink and food. "She was a very great lady, and loved you dearly, as her brother," he told the butler, who tried a smile, but seemed unable to answer, his eyes glittering with tears as he wai-ed deeply.

"I have prepared a basket for Khun Kate's friends at the hospital," he finally managed to say, "I think the Khunying would have wanted me to do that," and he vanished towards the kitchen and returned with a hamper.

"The Khunying was very grieved at poor Khun Kate's death.

"So her friends can remember her."

Kate was not forgotten, Sumet assured him, shameful for his lie.

As he drove, he listened with only half his mind on his mother's chatter, about the guests, all those old women, to think they had been children together, poor Pensri, who used to be so proud of her general of a son, and who had lorded it over the others, about the food, so disappointing, but what could be done in these times? And must he really return to the hospital?

Anyway, it was a strange business, Thip befriending this farang girl, whom she had loved more than her own daughter-in-law, grieving for her as if she were family.

It was dark, and rainy, and surely the basket of food could wait.

It couldn't, he finally snapped.

Just because she had plenty to eat, still, even in these difficult times, must she forget those who didn't? And when his mother, cowed into silence for once was mutinously looking out the window, he just stared at the empty streets mindlessly, enjoying the quiet.

As he expected, the three farang nurses were sitting on the floor in the darkened pharmacy, following the Allied advance in France on the BBC. They turned pleased faces to him when he entered and even Kate was smiling, he was gladdened to notice.

"You've heard?" she asked. "It seems as if they're finally moving away from the beaches and towards Paris."

He settled himself crossed-legged next to her. Yes, he knew.

"And here is a basket, sent by Fon, to remember Khun Kate."

Kate pushed it away. "It sickens me, to have them all believe I'm dead."

"Well, it doesn't sicken me," Rose retorted, pulling it to her and opening it,

"We all need to eat. So get over yourself, and remember Belinda wouldn't thank you for just starving yourself.

"Now eat something, and listen to what's happening in France instead of feeling so sorry for yourself. You're alive. Think of all those poor young men, who are dying on those beaches. Yanks as well…"

Kate sighed, accepting a chicken wing, and her eyes filled with tears.

For all she knew, one of her brothers may well be in Normandy, shivering in the rain, afraid, wounded, thinking of home. Teddy, or Joe Jr. or Francis, with only his cross as a weapon…

"Oh, in the name of the Holy Mother and all the angels," Bernadette snapped. "Just shut up, now, will you?"

Kate ducked her head, gnawing on her chicken, and sat shivering against the wall, as Doctor Sumet leaned towards her, asking in a whisper if she had heard from Captain Akira.

"No, not in over a week. Why?" she replied, surprised.

Doctor Sumet looked down at the floor, twisted his fingers, and told her haltingly that in the bomb raid, the main Japanese military hospital had been destroyed.

Kate closed her eyes.

"Oh. I... I see," she just said.

Of course, Sumet stumbled on, wondering how she might take yet another loss, even of someone whom she feared and cared for, it seemed, in equal measure. They knew nothing yet, and had no way of finding out, he said. So all they could do was wait.

"Well, if he's been killed, I officially died for nothing then," she whispered back grimly. "No Kempetai looking for the American..."

She didn't know, he repeated urgently. So ...

"You know what, Doctor?" she finally dropped in a low, bleak voice, her head in her hands. "I'm past caring."

He rose to go, laying a consoling hand on her shoulder.

"Don't think of people dying on the beaches," he murmured. "Think of them winning, instead. Because they are."

He was very tempted to go by the prison, but thought it wiser to wait until he were called by General Adun, who would best know when he might not attract attention to himself, or to the agents.

These were times when he missed having a wife — he chuckled ruefully, knowing no wife would have agreed to share his austere and monastic life...

And no woman had ever given rise to the thrill he had been appalled to recognize all those years ago, one night in London, and which had led him, in his horror and self-loathing, to swear off any form or manner of intimacy.

But still, it would be nice to have some company other than his difficult and demanding mother.

So he reluctantly started his sputtering old Ford, and drove back towards the river and his empty, silent home.

When he was next called by General Adun, he found all the agents ebullient, in a state of high excitement. Contact had finally been made with SOE Meerut, Khem told him, his voice burbling with relief.

He had tried every day, at the allotted time and on the allotted wavelength, to raise some response, and finally, finally, it had happened.

"They're probably suspicious, after all these weeks, and must think we've been turned by the Japanese. But they will come to realize, I'm sure..."

And only two days ago, a group of four more agents, but sent by the Americans this time had been brought to him, coming from China this time.

"Did you all know each other before?" Sumet asked, checking the scrapes and minor injuries the new arrivals had suffered on their way.

The young men looked at each other, and shook their heads guardedly.

"Well," Khem finally stated, "some of us knew some of them but here, at home, before we went abroad to study. But..."

One of the American-trained agents picked up his sentence. "But, when we were being trained in India, we were kept well apart and never allowed to meet, even those of us who had relatives being trained by the British."

"Why?"

Sumet looked at Adun, who just shrugged, as mystified as he was.

"In the States, Colonel Khap was told to be wary of the British, because they want to colonize us after the war."

And did any of them believe this?

All the men looked at each other again and finally, Khem spoke again.

What the British wanted would be very different from what the British might achieve when the war was over.

"Could you get some information for me?" Sumet asked Adun, once he had checked on the well-being of all the hidden agents.

He wanted to know if a Japanese surgeon, Captain Akira, had been injured or worse when the military hospital was bombed. "He was friendly to me, and it was he who told me about the penicillin."

Adun shook his head.

He didn't want to attract any more attention by asking unusual questions. Getting hold of the penicillin had already been difficult enough.

"I didn't realize it is so rare and precious, and needed to insist, which I think raised some Japanese eyebrows. I said it was for a wounded nephew.

"Also, I think it best that we be discreet now, and that you come only if there is an emergency.

"And now, you should go. I don't want you to get stopped by the Japanese military police, there are only so many people I can protect."

The next week went by, with the BBC reporting on further advances after hard-fought battles in France and Italy, and a crushing Japanese defeat at sea near the Mariana Islands, and, after a three month siege, the final end of the battle for Imphal, at the Indian border.

General Slim's 14th Army was now pushing the Japanese back towards the Chindwin River, and inflicting tremendous losses.

But there were also news of horrifying new weapons, the V-1s, rained on London, obliterating whole neighbourhoods and killing thousands of people.

The newsreader's voice was somber, describing the ambulances rushing through the night, the blazes lighting the London sky, the plight of the homeless sifting through the ruins, but also the courage and the good cheer of the men, women and children huddled in the underground Tube stations, breaking out in song to cover the noise of the explosions and the scream of the sirens.

"We shall not be defeated," was the message endlessly repeated, while Kate, Rose and Bernadette listened in stunned silence.

"Still," Rose finally said, snapping off the radio, "it does seem as if the Allies are winning on all fronts, flying bombs or no. I wonder how long it will take here..."

Kate did not answer, and pushed herself wearily up from the floor.

Yes, it did seem as if the war were finally being won, but no, she did not think anything would change here. Why would it? she wanted to shout.

Things would just go on like this for years.

The absence of news from Ken Akira also worried her.

Well... as she told Doctor Sumet, it wasn't so much worry, not yet — after all, he was absent fairly often, on the front in Burma, or elsewhere... but... if something were to happen to him, she wouldn't be told.

"And if something were to happen to him?" Sumet asked gently.

It was war, after all, and on the front, he was exposed, not as much as the fighting men, but...

Kate shrugged helplessly. "I don't know..."

She no longer hated him or even feared him, she did not love him, but she cared for him because he was now the only one who cared for her, with Belinda gone.

"He was my only link, somehow, with the States.

"Isn't that strange?

"He's the enemy, but the States is still home for both of us.

"I could talk about it, with him, oh, silly things, food, movies, songs that were popular then, and he understood...

"And also," she finally admitted sadly, "he's all I have ... Now Lady Thip has died," she added, biting her lips, "If he has died too... there is no one left."

Sumet nodded.

"Well, you know what they say," the surgeon tried to be reassuring, "no news..."

"Is good news, yes," Kate cut in sharply, turning away, her eyes full of tears. "But they're wrong, aren't they, those who say that?

"Look at Belinda's parents. They probably think all is well with her.

"No news is just waiting for the bad news to catch up with you."

Chapter XXX

The first telegram, the official one, was routed through SOE London to Calcutta and Meerut, and he was called into Gilchrist's office, and quietly told the news.

The family house destroyed in the recent waves of V-2 bombings, both his parents killed, their bodies found in the ruins, so there was "no hope, laddie, none at all.

"You'd best believe how desperately sorry for you we are, but we all have to go on working now, you know that, don't you?"

The second telegram, Andrew said, had actually arrived two days before, but Pointon and Gilchrist had both decided to sit on it and await confirmation, if any — telegrams these days were always bad news.

It was from his Aunt Sophie and reading the words he could almost hear his aunt's high-pitched, trembly voice.

He dropped it and just sat and stared at Andrew, his unseeing eyes very far from the cool blue of Meerut's skies visible through the window.

He imagined the twin columns surrounding the front steps reduced to rubble, the bay trees in their white boxes splintered and covered in dust.

He had seen the newsreels showing the gaping slashes in the fabric of London's landscape, huge holes cratering the sidewalks, crumpled buildings, smashed roof slates, stones, plaster and shattered glass, furniture and bodies scattered onto the streets, and firemen attempting to douse the flames spurting up from broken gas pipes.

Alongside, indecently intact houses, and yet a bit further, the nonsensical half-destroyed ones, rooms opened to the fog and rain, exposing pathetic patterned wallpaper, and lamps lying next to bookcases spilling their contents on ruined carpets, and miraculously, chandeliers still swinging, intact, from ceilings.

There was the feeling that somehow, it was inevitable... Why, how, would his parents have escaped, when everything else in his life had been destroyed?

Was there any other family beyond his aunt, Andrew asked in sympathy, trying to get a reaction out of him, any reaction beyond the empty, faraway blue eyes.

Lawrence absently looked upwards, yes, an uncle, a few cousins, on his father's side, his mother was an only child — as was he, he dropped, almost casually.

"Well," he finally announced, pulling himself from his chair. "I suppose I should get back to my desk."

"Wait, laddie."

Andrew put out a friendly hand, "I know I said we have to go on working, but I didn't mean you have to get back to it right now.

"It's a shock. Take a minute, and just curse the Germans, or the gods — or something."

Lawrence shook his head, his face still void of any expression.

He had not seen his parents in... he paused to think... more than seven years, now, and for the last five, he had steeled himself to receive such news as this.

"So, somehow, I guess I was ready."

Gilchrist nodded, with infinite pity.

"I hear that's what everybody says at first, at least until it sinks in..."

LAWRENCE'S DIARY
MEERUT, FEBRUARY 2ND 1945

I am numb with... with what?

I am numb with the numbness which is another word for grief, I suppose, but it feels in no way like the all-consuming pain and misery and rage which engulfed me when I heard of Kate's death.

Whilst desperately sad, it feels expected, as if I knew somehow I would never see my parents again.

I tell myself I am alone now, and a part of me answers that I have been alone since I learned of Kate's death.

What I find most difficult is the idea of the house no longer being there, all the little things I am trying to remember, the smell of wax and copper polish when you entered, the creaking, uneven step going up to Father's study, the secret and forbidden drawing I did on the wallpaper behind the chest of drawers in my room, and, in what used to be the nursery, the loose skirting board, revealing a secret compartment in the wall, where I hid a map to the treasure – some coins, I think, and a cheap paste earring found on the street – which I buried in the garden when I was ten.

I was unable to cry for Kate, I am unable to cry for my mother and father, but that treasure in its tin biscuit box brought me to tears.

Pointon called me in his office before dinner, and shifting from foot to foot, gave me his usual inept sympathetic talk.

I know he means well, but do wish he would refrain.

MEERUT, FEBRUARY 9TH1945

Andrew has ordered me to accompany him to Calcutta tomorrow, announcing that in the absence of operations where either he or I might be useful, we are about to take Operation Lucifer several steps further, and although I am not cheered – I believe I have not felt cheerful for a year – I welcome the change.

Whose brainchild Operation Lucifer actually *is*, his or mine, neither can remember, but both trace it back to our frustration when told that hundreds of thousands of propaganda leaflets in Siamese script we had laboured over for weeks, were quite simply to be destroyed, because only Force 136 organisations operating from Ceylon were authorized to make air drops over Siam.

Fine, Pointon replied, we'll ship you the leaflets, you drop them – but no, again, because air drop propaganda materiel must be prepared by either Political Warfare Division SEAC based in Kandy, or by Political warfare Executive based in Colombo, both organisations, Pointon told us, trembling with rage, who had no one to write in Siamese and furthermore, no one with any idea *what* to write.

And then an official news report from Bangkok mentioned the extreme shortage of matches in the country and I suppose we just looked at each other and one of us said that a matchbox wasn't a leaflet, was it, and the other muttered that a short message in Siamese, such as "Hold fast, we are coming!" wasn't really propaganda, was it? More like statement of fact...

It was just a bit of mischief, at first, a "What if?" to spite the ridiculous regulations, but gradually, the idea grew, and grew... And thus was Operation Lucifer born.

We are now to try and achieve the go-ahead for production, having commissioned a rather fetching label of a kinnaree holding a thunderbolt and the words "Death to the Japanese".

It is strange that after these two years of feeling that Siam Country Section was some sort of poor and embarrassing cousin, labouring somewhat on the fringes of the war, now there are at least ten agencies competing for future influence, and as Gilchrist says, "That's just us Brits", as the OSS have as many, if not more, which is a ridiculous duplication of intelligence, manpower, and material.

I actually heard him tell visitors from Mountbatten's team that pretending the Yanks didn't exist would not make them magically disappear.

There are over two dozen of our agents in Bangkok, some have been in, met Pridi and left again, bringing back vital intelligence, the most useful being that as we, who know and like the Siamese have always thought, the country is chafing under the Japanese and the most upsetting is that there are dreadful prisoner of war camps, where men are worked, starved and beaten to death.

We had always suspected it, after hearing of the appalling treatment from those who managed to escape in the Philippines, but it is now confirmed.

CALCUTTA, FEBRUARY 14[TH]1945

Lord how I hate dealing with the army!

I am so angry I could spit. We have been informed we need to pay duties on matches. No, there are to be no exceptions, even for a war propaganda operation.

CALCUTTA, FEBRUARY 25TH1945

Thank the gods of war for all the victories in Europe and the Pacific, otherwise, I truly would despair.

Eastern France is free, Belgium almost, and Dresden has been bombed to smithereens, which should appal me — thousands of civilians killed — but somehow fails to, because the newsreels of flattened, blackened, smoking buildings, at the cinema here, were followed by the most gut-wrenching, sickening pictures of prisoner camps liberated by the Americans and the Russians.

Except these were not camps as we thought we understood that concept, these were slaughterhouses, designed for systematic and efficient killing of millions.

The Nazis seem to have achieved hell on earth, gassing the luckier of the prisoners, Jews most of them, immediately, and starving, working, torturing and experimenting on the others.

The gates opened on living, walking skeletons, barely able to hold themselves up — so no, I was not even moved by the destruction in Germany — I thought myself above the spirit of revenge, but am not, apparently.

Next to me, Andrew was retching uncontrollably.

The Yanks have taken Iwo Jima, with considerable losses on both sides, and are about to regain control of Corregidor in the Philippines, the Burma Road has been re-opened when Slim took Ledo.

Yes, the war is close to the end, and in all likelihood, shall not last beyond the summer.

Meanwhile, Andrew and I fought like wolves to have our little labels pasted on to matchboxes and encountered tremendous resistance — did we realize there was a war on? Matches? Indeed? At whose cost? Who was to drop them, etc, etc.

Finally, a friend of a friend who works for the Swedish Match Company dealt with the printing and pasting, and I blithely used Andrew's name in signing various invoices to be presented to SOE Kandy.

We tested the packages by throwing them from the sixth floor, and yes, they broke, but without scattering the boxes. We shall make the wrapping stronger, and in any case, they should fall on softer ground than the pavement outside the office building.

CALCUTTA, FEBRUARY 25TH 1945

All we needed was a friendly pilot to release our parcels of matchboxes from his bomb bay, and suddenly, one appeared. He had had his flight cleared but his bombing mission cancelled, and asked if perchance we wanted something dropped over Siam.

Did we ever, I replied happily, and rushed our several jeep loads of matches to the airport.

KANDY, FEBRUARY 28TH 1945

I am replacing Andrew who has been hospitalized with jaundice.

The present project is to prepare the insertion of a team of saboteurs because the powers that be were planning an operation codenamed Roger — a military operation, no less, at long last! — but in an area where precisely we had no agents whosoever.

Typical army, Andrew groused before collapsing.

Security here is headed by some ruddy-skinned, tiny-moustached, hatchet-faced despot of a captain named, improbably, Winsome, who hails from the world of insurance and therefore hates diplomats, journalists and intellectuals. He rather admires engineers, so Wemyss finds favour in his eyes, but despises the rest of us who tinker up in Meerut with bits of information about matches, the price of cooking oil and the mood on the streets of Bangrak.

He has big signs on his wall saying "Your best friend is a spy who hasn't been turned yet" and "Anyone can be bought, if the price is right, so what's yours?"

He is also in favour of random searches in all lockers, packs, etc, so my diary shall be cached away in the secret pouch of my bag — only those who did the Malaya jungle training were issued this model and know how to find it — and although Winsome may think a lot of himself, he didn't train in the jungle — he is afraid of spiders.

Remembering my journalist friends from Burma who all had a book project up their sleeve, I know I may someday want to remember all of this, including operation Roger and the agents — codenamed Priests — but shall just note the exasperation all of us from SCS feel, when we try to convey our certainty that the whole country, or almost, is in league with us against the Japanese, whereas South East Asia Command insists on seeing the Siamese as enemies who must be crushed.

MEERUT, MAY 9TH 1945

Victory in Europe, at last!

Germany surrendered, Hitler committed suicide in his bunker, and there were fireworks all over London last night, with Big Ben ringing as it hadn't in six years.

Ever since Andrew emerged, bone thin and yellowish from six weeks in hospital, there has been a dizzying series of news, for once, all of it good.

As he is not allowed any alcohol, we take it in turns to raise then drink his glass.

Agents come and go into and out of Bangkok with amazing ease, and are given protection at the highest governmental level — I hear that Nicol Smith is there now — and somehow, the Japanese seem increasingly irrelevant — although Pointon warns us daily against the danger of complacency.

We are winning everywhere, and although the Japs do put up a brave and completely desperate effort, it is a matter of weeks, or at worst, months, but of course, they do inflict considerable damage against our land and even more so, naval forces with their suicide pilots crashing themselves onto our ships.

And speaking of pilots, our matches, according to Bangkok, are a huge success — therefore, after threatening to court-martial us for illegally spending military funds, SOE Kandy wants to repeat the operation.

If someday I have a child and he asks, "Father, what did *you* do in the war?" I shall answer, "My son, I made matchboxes and dropped them from planes."

Chapter XXXI

It was a month now since the two power stations had been bombed, and Bangkok was getting used to living without electricity.

No lights, no refrigerators, no ceiling fans – and worse of all, no pumps to bring water to the taps for those who could not afford a generator and the fuel to supply it, so people congregated around communal water points just as in the old days, and grunted and heaved working the heavy cast iron handles to fill jerrycans with the mercifully still functioning hand operated pumps.

The laundry building of Saint-Louis itself had been hit in the last wave of air raids, and the last of the windows were broken in the blast, but nobody was injured – probably because there were no more patients.

How could they treat people with no clean sheets or bandages, no proper lighting in the wards, no fans, no water to wash?

Of course, the first few days, they removed shards of glass, and painted iodine onto cuts, but now... even that simple first aid care was beyond what Saint-Louis could offer.

Although the watchman remained in his little hut by the gate, the Thai nurses all had homes they could go to and left, so Kate, Rose and Bernadette cowered alone in the big, silent building, cooking their own meals from what little they could buy at the market with what little money they were still paid.

Doctor Sumet came by almost daily, sometimes with a basket of fruit, once with a live chicken which Bernadette, to the others' horrified astonishment, casually dispatched with a practiced twist of the neck.

But the days were long with nothing to do but filter and boil water and no place to go and no radio to keep them informed about the war.

The war... It was almost over, soon, soon, Sumet kept insisting, although how *he* knew was more than Kate could understand, and anyway, she no longer believed him.

Last year, when Pridi had come to power and Phibul retired petulantly to an army base in Lopburi, Sumet seemed to believe that things would change, that the Japanese would soon be driven away, but nothing happened, except for Kate crying as she remembered Lawrence first telling her the story of Pridi and Phibul in the lovely sala on the river.

Wherever he was — if he was still alive — she hoped he had heard the news.

"This," Rose declared one morning, as she was boiling the water brought by the watchman, "is what it must be like in limbo."

"Don't be blasphemous," Bernadette chided her sharply.

"Where's the blasphemy?" Rose retorted. "We're trapped here — not really suffering, but spend our nights crouching outdoors praying we won't get killed by a bomb, and our days trying to eat and wash, and all the time waiting, waiting, without really knowing for what."

While Bernadette sniffed, Kate scoured their single pot for cooking rice and did not bother getting involved, staring at her bare feet splashed with dishwater.

Far from blasphemous, limbo seemed exactly right to her, and she remembered Mother Felicity trying to explain it to her, and finally coming up with something a twelve year-old girl could understand: "Limbo is boredom for all eternity."

Was dear, kind, strong Belinda in limbo? Surely not, there must be a special place in heaven for those such as her.

And what about Ken Akira, who had died, almost a year ago when the military hospital was bombed, what was his fate in the afterlife?

His memory troubled her.

She could not help missing him, although at times she felt a malicious relief at no longer having to fear his moods and his anger — but most of all, she felt pity for a soul as lost and confused as he.

A week after the first bombing raid, a Japanese officer with the Medical Corps insignia on his shoulder drove up to the hospital and, with a click of his heels, demanded to see the "surgeon and Irish nurse", then formally announced in stilted English that Captain Akira had been killed in the cowardly American bombing of the military hospital.

"I know he come here often, " the officer added with a knowing look at Kate, who had blanched and clasped her hands with a gasp.

"We were always grateful for his help," Sumet replied quietly. "I considered him a friend. We both did," he added, glancing at Kate, still standing silently, but tears streaming down her stony face.

"Yes. He my friend also. But a traitor, perhaps. You knew?"

When the officer went through Ken's effects, he said, he had found his American passport.

Sumet sighed. "I knew he was born in America. But he was bitter about the way his family was treated."

"Yes," the Japanese replied. "Maybe he think that passport will save him if we lose the war. But maybe, it will be worse for him. So maybe, not traitor. I burn passport. He my friend."

"So sorry for news. Goodbye."

He bowed and turned away.

"I suppose the gods were merciful to him," Sumet murmured finally, "they spared him the ordeal of betraying or being betrayed by one of his two countries."

Kate shook her head. She didn't think there was such a thing as a merciful god.

That evening, as the sun was just setting, Kate heard the familiar coughing noise of the surgeon's old Ford and came out to the front steps to greet him, surprised at the second visit in one day.

"My dear, I have bad news — no, no, not Lawrence, I know nothing of him — no, it's Pichit. He was killed yesterday, murdered, at one of the rubber plantations in the South."

Kate felt her way to one of the miraculously remaining rattan armchairs on the verandah, stifling a whimper with her fist. So many deaths, too many...

"Why — how?"

Sumet shrugged, his lined face showing that he, too, was exhausted by the past months of strain and uncertainty.

"His cooperation with the Japanese made him many enemies. He was targeted, no doubt, by the anti-Japanese guerrillas, it could not have been robbery, he still had his wallet and watch, Busaba said... The Japanese military police is investigating, but of course, they will find nothing."

"Poor Busaba," Kate sighed. "All alone, now, in that big house."

How was she taking it?

"With Busaba, who can tell?" Sumet replied tersely, taking a seat next to her.

"All she said to me was that she had warned him time and again against doing business with the Japanese Army, as if somehow she was taking comfort in being proven right.

"But they never were the closest of couples."

"At least, Lady Thip did not live to see it," Kate finally said sadly.

He was always very kind, he never seemed to mind us living there... Well, of course, he spent so much time away... "

Her voice trailed off.

"Are there to be prayer services at the house all week again?"

Sumet rose, and smoothed a crease in his shirt.

No, there was to be no ceremony at all, the cremation, he believed, would be held tomorrow or the next day at some temple in the South, and Busaba would not go.

She claimed to be not well enough, which was true, and to fear being assassinated as well, which was ridiculous... or was it? Who could tell?

"He'll leave all alone, poor man, more or less as he lived."

Two weeks later, when the May monsoon rains were starting and the throbbing white skies of the dry season were replaced with roll upon roll of dark clouds, the watchman arrived in high excitement, his four jerrycans sloshing water out of the wheelbarrow.

The Kempetai were evacuating the beautiful old house they had commandeered on Sathorn Road, a block up from the hospital.

"*Yippun pai, pai, pai leew* !!" he crowed in jubilation. The Japanese are going, they're gone!

Could it be true?

None of the three farang nurses dared go and check for themselves, but what they could see were dozens of Japanese military cars and motorcycles whizzing down Sathorn towards the port of Khlong Toei.

Kate took her bowl of rice and dried fish to the bench in the shade and watched, just as, over four years ago, she and Belinda had watched the Imperial forces arrive. This time, there seemed to be fewer pennants.

"No, no, go inside!"

Sumet exclaimed when he came the next day and found her by the gate, gazing with a belligerent look at the convoys speeding past. He grabbed her arm, and marched her through the garden and up the stairs, shaking his head in concern.

"And please, please be careful!

There have been cases when they shot at people who were cheering when they saw them leaving. Yes, the Japanese are moving forces in great numbers to defend Okinawa, I hear, but there are still quite a few soldiers in Bangkok, and many more in the provinces where the prisoner camps are, and all of them are very angry."

He turned to face the three nurses, and the worried scowl on his face gave place to a smile.

"But this is not why I came. I have very good news. Germany surrendered two days ago. The war in Europe is over."

Rose yelped and Bernadette kissed her rosary then both crossed themselves with prayers of thanksgiving, but Kate just stood there, still looking sceptical.

"Is it really true? Not just a rumour? How did you find out?"

It was true. Friends of his had a generator at home, and so could listen to the radio, Sumet replied carelessly. They had called with the news, as, amazingly, the telephones still worked.

A reluctant grin was finally spreading over Kate's face.

"Now that the Germans are beaten... It will be over soon now, it has to be," she murmured. "The Japanese can't hold out alone much longer."

Bernadette had tears running down her cheeks.

"And we shall be able to go home, then."

Home... What did the word mean to them? A village in Derry for Bernadette, with a church, very green hedges and softly falling rain, a noisy street in Cork for Rose.

In Dublin, Belinda's parents were no doubt praying that their daughter would return soon. Kate shook her head to chase that idea away.

And for her, where would home be?

The little pavilion by the river, if it still stood, once Lawrence came back to her.

But what if Lawrence were dead?

She realized that for months now, in the back of her mind, she had been accepting that it might be true.

If Lawrence were dead, where would she go?

Back to the States, once she had her real identity back?

No, she would not think of that now, she couldn't.

Sumet was thoughtful as he walked back to his car.

Despite the absence of radio, news was spreading in the city, and the people knew not what to expect, realizing, or some of them at least, that Thailand would not come out unscathed of the upheaval peace would bring.

Would the Kingdom not seem complicit once the truth about the horrors of the prisoner camps came to light, once Phibul's craven surrender to the Japanese were known?

And would the cornered Imperial forces not take revenge on the people who they now knew had turned against them?

Pridi, it was said, was confident that the last year of his clandestine cooperation with the Allies might save them all, but Adun had his doubts.

Sumet shook his head.

A young policeman he had spoken with at the prison said that the Thais should all be praying the Lord Buddha to give them a golden tongue.

"Because otherwise," he added ruefully, "I don't know how we will explain all this."

It would not be an easy peace.

He turned back to wave at Kate, who was watching him leave from the verandah.

He did not hear the crack of a shot, he just felt a blow to his back, and fell face down on the pavement, but when Kate who had rushed to him, was cradling his head in her arms, calling for help then wailing with despair, he managed to smile despite the blood pouring through his mouth.

"Peace," she thought she heard him say "Peace."

Chapter XXXII

The war was over!

Listening to the BBC summarizing Emperor Hirohito's broadcast of the official surrender of Japan, Lawrence found he was less jubilant than still shattered by the news of the unimaginable destruction wrought by the two atom bombs.

"Of course, he surrendered, poor sod," he muttered half to himself amidst all the cheering in the mess. "What choice did he have?"

Gilchrist came to sit next to him, bringing a large mug of beer, and sat back, contemplating the celebration.

"Remember when the war was declared?" he asked. "The evening at the British Club?"

How could he forget, Lawrence replied in a morose voice.

"It was just like this, men drinking beer and slapping each other's backs, and claiming it would be over in a month.

"Who could have imagined the horrors that would be unleashed on the world?"

Gilchrist raised his mug, drank deeply and wiped the foam off his mouth.

"Yes, well, it's not over yet, you know.

"French Indochina up in arms, the Russkies beginning to crawl all over Asia, the Yanks trying to beat them to it. This is when it becomes interesting.

"So, I ask you, do you want to stay on and go back?"

Stay on, as in SOE? Lawrence asked cautiously. And back, as in Siam?

The answer to both questions was yes.

They needed Siamese speakers in Bangkok very soon, to see how relations could be repaired, and to counter the influence of the US, who were aching to have another foothold in the East.

So?

Lawrence flushed, then paled. "I don't know. I just don't

know. I'm afraid of what I'll find there."

Gilchrist nodded. "By the way, Arun has had a bit of bad news. You remember, in May, a group of agents landed near Nakhon Si Thammarat, and a local plantation manager raised the alarm and was killed?

"Well, he was actually the owner, your friend Pichit, and it seems he never raised the alarm.

"He was executed by one of the local agents, and, Arun claims, it was more business rivalry than politics."

Lawrence winced. "He was a nice man. Maybe weak, and spoiled by his mother, but I liked him."

"Yes, well..." Andrew said again. " Don't dally too much before making your mind, but remember, we need Siamese speakers, and you probably need something to do, and somewhere to go to, don't you?"

Yes. He did. But first, although he dreaded the idea, he should go back to London, to deal with... things.

Gilchrist grinned hugely.

"I'm sure that can be arranged, we need someone to go brief the Foreign Office on the Siamese resistance, the silly buggers there want to treat the country as a former enemy — granted, they did declare war on us, but now Phibul's out of the picture..."

Phibul would never be out of the picture as long as he drew breath.

Lawrence was convinced of it.

"You'll see, he'll find a way to wriggle out of it, saying the only choice was to yield to the Japs to spare the people. He'll claim to have behaved like a hero.

"And many will believe it, you know."

Gilchrist made a face.

"Yes. Which is why we have to bolster Pridi's hold over the country and that means not imposing martial rule over Siam. Otherwise..."

LAWRENCE'S DIARY
DELHI, MONDAY, AUGUST 27TH 1945

I fly to London tomorrow, and wonder at what I shall find.

I suppose I can stay with my uncle John in Chelsea, if his house still stands, and then... what?

I've no idea.

I shall report first to SOE on Baker Street on Thursday, then to the Foreign Office, and somewhat fear I shall be fighting a losing battle.

I'm told that the powers that be are toying with the idea of turning Siam into a quasi-colony — which, let's face it, we've been trying to do for the past century.

The only bright light on my horizon is the drink at the Ritz my cousin Charlotte promised me.

LONDON, FRIDAY, SEPTEMBER 14TH 1945

How grey, battered and cheerfully defiant London has become.

How friendly, when I remember it as a city where one avoided smiling in the street for fear of being thought mad.

How impoverished the people are, still living on tiny rations, their clothes tattered and mended and worn... and how free and forward the women have become.

"It's the Yanks," Uncle John said despondently, over bad port in his dusty and threadbare study.

"They've ruined any sense of decency we had, came in here with their bloody stockings and chocolate bars and lack of manners, and driving proper girls crazy.

"Ruddy rape of the Sabines it is, carrying off the women of England. Your cousin Charlotte, for one, and her mother, my silly sister Sophie, seem for some reason to think it's wonderful."

And that's how I found out that Charlotte is going to marry one of those bloody Yanks and move to Chicago as soon as Lieutenant Mike Colehart is demobilized and can return to his life as a lawyer.

Aunt Mary nodded in her usual austere way.

Just let some Yank try and take away either of her two daughters,

Rosemary and Grace, and she'll give them what for, her stern look seemed to say.

Poor people.

Their oldest son, Edward, was shot down over the Channel, and Peter, their youngest, burned over half his body when his ship was sunk and exploded.

He is still in hospital, awaiting another painful skin graft and in the meantime struggling to get back the use of his right hand.

"Still," Uncle John said stoutly, "he's alive, and can carry on the line, the doctors say."

I pity them, but barely recognize them.

And I'm quite sure they barely recognize me.

Charlotte too, has changed, she is no longer the annoying schoolgirl I remember, or the giddy debutante Mother wrote about.

And she is the only person who spoke of Kate to me, and did so with compassion and understanding.

I would like to believe that Uncle John was too afraid of stirring emotion — after all, he barely mentioned my parents - but I cannot help thinking that he would not have welcomed a working-class Irish-American into the family.

Hard to believe he is free-thinking Julie's son.

I return to Delhi tomorrow, and then... Bangkok. Siam.

Andrew has already arrived and sent a teletype saying I am expected.

I cannot sleep, I have not slept since I was told that at last, at last, I shall return to where I was most happy.

What shall I find there, I wonder.

Perhaps a shadow of who I was.

PART III

Chapter XXXIII

A bird screeched.

Wondering if he had dozed off and if this room were yet again but a dream, Lawrence opened his eyes, breathed deeply, and stared around to convince himself that yes, he was back.

Home – or at least, the closest thing to a home he had known since starting university.

Flying down into Bangkok yesterday, he gazed at the deadly mountain ranges of Burma, and when those were behind them, at the placid silvery rice fields of the central Siamese plain and remembered how he had escaped the city almost four years ago.

When the plane began its descent, he was struck at how untouched the city seemed with the many gleaming spires of the Palace and the temples, and it was only when it circled closer above Don Muang airfield that he could see the bomb scars near the port and Hua Lampong station, the grey empty spaces glaring and ugly like missing teeth.

Trembling with excitement and also nervousness, he left the ramshackle wooden airport building with many signs in Japanese still posted on the walls and doors, and found that, as promised, there was a driver waiting for him, a blonde, languid twentyish WAC(I) corporal in a creased and sweaty uniform, who gave him a half-hearted salute, as if she were used to driving a much better class of officer.

"Might take us some time to get you to your billet," she warned him, fanning herself with a tattered map. "Can't make head or tail of this place. Sir," she added as an afterthought.

Where was the billet, Lawrence asked.

Some school. Assumption College it was called. But getting there was a headache.

"I know where it is. I'll drive."

She shot him a sideways glance, then laughed as she passed him an envelope... "Suit yourself. Major Gilchrist said that was what

493

you would do. But you want to read this first. From him it is."

Lawrence laughed. "Major is it now? All right."

Andrew had written in haste.

"You're at Assumption, for your sins. Oriental is a mess, the Japs destroyed as much as they could before leaving. Come by the office as soon as you arrive."

The office was the British Embassy, virtually unchanged since Lawrence had been there all those years ago, to make out his will, he seemed to remember.

"Yep, it stood here untouched and also undusted," Andrew told him briskly as he walked him to his old room. "Which is in its way a mercy, I suppose.

"It could have been vandalized.

"Listen, we've a bit of a flap on.

"There's a Siamese delegation in Kandy negotiating the Kingdom's post-war status with SEAC, but it seems the Foreign Office is intent on humiliating the Siamese as much as possible.

"As we expected.

"Mountbatten is trying to force through an agreement linking military with political aspects without consulting the Yanks, and as we've got over ten thousand troops in, and another ten thousand due over the month, Pridi isn't in much of a position to object, not really.

"Meanwhile, next door, the French are about to be ousted from Indochina and Chiang Kai-Shek is breathing down the necks of all the Western powers in Asia."

Lawrence sat, and looked around at the dusty pre-war files on the shelves, and at the makeshift bed pushed against the wall. "So what do we do?"

"That's where I slept for six months when we were locked in here," Andrew said, following his look. "Never thought I'd be back, really.

"Well, to answer your question, we're on standby here, waiting for things to decant, or rather for the Yanks to put their collective foot down. Before that, lots of talking needs to happen. So in the meantime, we're assisting in the evacuation of POWs.

"It's not easy, I warn you."

He paused and swallowed, and his eyes stared, unfocussed, at something Lawrence could only guess at.

"Bad?" he asked.

"Worse than bad. Unimaginable."

Then Gilchrist appeared to shake himself back to the present.

"Go see the quartermaster – he's on the ground floor – to collect some money. You'll need it, things are expensive, not that I imagine you'll need to buy much, but ...

"Listen, as I said, sorry about billeting you at Assumption, but it wasn't my choice. If you can get your old digs back, that would be a boon to us all. Beds are scarce, here.

"And," he added slyly, "speaking of beds, I advise you to consider the luscious Leslie, your driver. She has a preference for ranks above captain, but as you're rich, you might pass muster."

Lawrence snorted.

"No thanks.

"I'll go by the house tomorrow, it's too late, now...

"What about you, are you going to look up old lady friends or will you enjoy the privileges of being a major?"

"If I were, laddie, you'd be the last one I'd tell, you're just too handsome. By the way, Nicol Smith is in town, still, and asked about you."

The following morning, Luscious Leslie had driven him to the Lady Thip's house, drumming her fingers impatiently on the dashboard as he slowly got of the jeep and walked up to the gate, and zoomed off even before it opened.

She had better things to do, it seemed, than wait for a lowly ex-journalist to deal with his memories, and hesitate and gaze at the wooden gate without daring to ring the bell.

But finally, finally, he had.

And it was opened.

There was a gentle knock on the door which opened a crack and Fon's soft voice asked "Khun Lo?"

Lawrence started, called away from his dazed remembering of times past. He put down the little notebook he had stopped reading, and looked around, almost unable to believe that he was back in this room, unchanged and full of ghosts, Kate's, Lady Thip's, Pichit's and yes, his own.

"Khun Lo, Lady Busaba is awake, and is very happy to hear that you are here. Can I tell her you will join her for coffee?"

Busaba...

Beautiful, beautiful, unhappy, imperious and thrilling Busaba whom he had thought he loved for a few weeks, and whose lust had fed on his own.

He took a deep breath, bracing himself to talk of all those who had died, and perhaps worse for the poor woman, of Sam, her son, of whom nothing yet was known.

He smiled at the anxious, patient face of Thip's faithful servant, he who must miss the old lady most of all.

Of course. Just a moment, to make himself presentable.

Fon looked critically at the worn, shapeless uniform.

"There is a tailor, nearby, who could perhaps take in one of your suits," he offered.

Later, Lawrence smiled as he ran his fingers through his hair in front of the mirror, realizing that despite the ghosts, he was feeling at peace in this room where he had been happy.

Later. Next week.

Busaba rose to her feet from the divan on the verandah, making fluttering, flustered gestures with her hands, to avoid perhaps, having him come too near or to kiss her cheek.

"Lawrence," she said in her breathy way. "Look at you. So unchanged. So... so young. And me... an old woman, a widow now, and ugly."

He sat next to her in one of the big rattan armchairs he remembered so well, the cushions now faded and worn, and looked across the garden at the river then turned to her.

She never could be ugly, he smiled.

And indeed, she was not ugly, but she had lost her otherworldly beauty, and he was shocked at the change.

Her face was puffy, there were grey threads in her chignon, and her swollen, reddened, fingers seemed strangled by her heavy rings.

"Busaba... I was so sorry to hear about Pichit. And Lady Thip, of course."

His voice caught. "It was like losing a member of my family. Like losing my grandmother."

Busaba sighed.

"Yes. She loved you too. More than she loved me, certainly. As much as Pichit, almost. As to Pichit, well... He..."

She took a deep breath. "You will hear it no doubt, so I may as well tell you myself.

"Actually, you are lucky to find me in Bangkok, I came back only ten days ago, I went to Hua Hin for three months, after the... after Pichit was killed, to avoid the rumours and all of the hypocritical sympathy.

"You know what Bangkok is like, I couldn't face seeing anyone."

She swallowed, and continued. "Pichit was collaborating with the Japanese, he was selling them rubber, so the Seri Thai guerrillas took revenge on him. Or so it is said. But it's not true.

"I believe it was a neighbouring landowner who hopes to buy the plantation cheaply from me, now.

"But I will not sell. Not as long as there is a hope that Sam comes back.

"I will hear soon. I know it."

She looked at him, her eyes welling, her voice beseeching. "There's no reason, is there? For him to be dead.

"Is there?"

He took her hand. "Yes, you will hear. Very soon. Of course you will."

They sat in silence for a moment, while Fon busied himself around them, pouring coffee, offering dry biscuits.

Then Busaba steadied herself, and took her cup. "And you? Your family?"

Dead, he said simply. The house was bombed earlier this year.

With those new flying bombs, there was no time to go to the shelters, or perhaps they just ... he spread his hands helplessly... they just didn't want to go down into a Tube station and spend hours there... Who could tell?

"But they were together, and that's a comfort, I guess."

"I guess," she replied wearily. "And you lost your wife, of course, poor Kate... She was always very kind to me when I saw her at the hospital — she moved there, after a while, to avoid being picked up as an enemy alien.

"They were rounding up the farangs, for months, you know, after the war started."

She shook her head and sighed.

"Doctor Sumet said it was very sudden, and that nothing could be done."

She raised her head, suddenly, struck by a thought.

"Oh, of course. Fon asked me to tell you.

"She wrote you a letter, at the end. It's in the safe, with her passport, her jewels, and your bank book, I think... Although, my mother-in-law had to give her money, your account was closed, she said."

She called out to Fon, her manner brisk and commanding, as it was in the old days. "Get the papers Khunying Thip put in her safe for Khun Lo."

And once Fon, nodding, had left, she leaned towards Lawrence. "Can you believe my mother-in-law gave him the combination, but not me?

"Well, he opens the safe when I need something, and when I'm up to it, I'll go through everything.

"Not that there's much, only her jewellery and a few old letters, I think." Her voice trailed off.

Fon came back with a small packet of papers and a leather-covered box, and Lawrence rose to leave.

He wanted to be alone to read Kate's last words.

Was Kate's friend, Belinda, still working at the hospital? he wondered. He wanted to see her, she was with her till the end.

Busaba frowned. "The bottle blonde? I suppose so.

"If Sumet were still alive, he'd know, of course — Yes, he was killed, two months ago, in front of the hospital, actually. I was told some Japanese soldier thought he was rejoicing at their defeat.

"Anyway, I assume that nurse is still there, although the hospital was hit in February and had to close, but I can't imagine where the nurses would have gone."

She stretched out her hand.

"Will you be here for dinner?"

He paused at the top of the steps. "I think so. I must go now. Excuse me."

He was suddenly in a hurry to leave her, her sadness and her anger, and the envelope in his hand was making him tremble.

Back in his room, he sat, opened the jewel case, and stared at the ruby ring and the jade earrings, picked up her passport and leafed through the red booklet, gazing at her picture, so serious, so sad-looking.

It must be done, he must face it, so finally, steeling himself, he took the envelope and saw that it had been addressed in an unfamiliar hand, and teeth clenched to ford away tears, slit it open, and removed the sheet of paper it contained.

Disbelieving, he read, then again, and again, and suddenly rose, feeling very cold, and paced the room, then read the letter a fourth time.

He rushed out to the gate, bellowing to the guard to find him a samlo, then, not waiting, ran down the soi, and finally managed to flag one down, stammering the address, then shaking with nerves, not looking as they passed the shops of New Road, twisting his fingers and reading the letter yet once more.

If this were not a sick, evil joke, and why would it be, then, then... there was every chance Kate was still alive...

In front of Saint-Louis hospital the garden he had known crowded with refugees was overgrown, the wooden gate sagged on its hinges and sorely needed paint, the entrance was deserted, but he noticed nothing.

He raced up the stairs, calling out, "Kate, Kate? Are you here? Is anybody here?" tearing through the empty wards, then opening doors to rooms, and stopping suddenly.

A single bed was unmade, with a plain nightgown crumpled on the pillow, and two cotton dresses hanging from hooks on the wall, and a brush and comb on the bed stand, next to a picture of an elderly couple.

Someone was still living here.

He opened the doors to the next two rooms.

Here the bed was neatly made, there was a rosary on the bed stand and nothing more.

The last one was empty, except for a single garment hanging in the wardrobe, a bright green dress, and coming closer, carefully, silently, as if trying not to disturb a sleeping ghost, he fingered it, noticing the missing buttons, the torn neckline, and remembering.

Belinda's dress, the night he met Kate.

But Belinda was dead, if the letter were true...

He heard a noise behind him and turned.

It was a wizened little man wielding a hammer, a watchman probably, who slowly lowered it and looked at him questioningly.

"The nurses? Khun Kate?"

The watchman stared back at him, astonished. "Pai."

Gone.

Where, where?

The man shook his head. He didn't know.

"I can tell you."

A middle-aged woman's face appeared in the doorway, her hair scraped back in a bun. She had sagging cheeks, as if she had lost weight, and her eyes were ringed in grey circles.

"I know you, don't I?" Lawrence said uncertainly. "You're... one of the maternity nurses."

"I was. Yes.

"Sister Bernadette Byrne. Now, general nurse. I work at the military hospital, taking care of the poor men from the Jap prison camps."

She cackled, a drawn out, bitter sound. "Not much call for maternity nurses, now, you see. And I know *you*...You're the rich husband."

She pushed past him and came to sit on the bed. "I came back to get a few hours' sleep. This used to be her room you know."

She looked up and cocked her head, her eyes unfriendly, her hands slack on her lap. "You've come back for her. Well, that's what she always hoped for. And now... Pity you're too late.

"She's always been the lucky one, hasn't she?

"Marrying money. Melanie's favourite. Sumet's favourite. Trained for surgery. First one out. Always special.

"And now, after all she's done, you came back, and I'll bet you'll find her and forgive her and she can just forget about it all."

He didn't understand, and didn't want to try.

"She's alive then. Where is she?"

"Oh yes, she's alive, that one, it would take more than a war to kill her, so. Belinda is dead, but *she's* alive, all right."

He glared at her, his voice rising to a shout, "For the love of God, tell me, where is she?"

Bernadette leaned her head against the wall, and closed her eyes.

"At sea, somewhere. Who knows?

"Actually, Rose might.

"She'll be back soon, if you want to know that badly."

He nodded curtly and turned to leave, but she called after him.

"She's not what you think, you know.

"She was a Japanese officer's tart.

"Oh, she never said, she always pretended he came to help—and it was always, oh, Captain Akira came to assist Sumet in an operation, and oh, Captain Akira gave us some sulpha powder, and this and that, but make no mistake, Rose and I always knew.

"She was his tart."

He spun back to face her. "No, not Kate. Never. If she ... she had a reason."

Bernadette sniggered. "That's what Rose says, but I know better. And even so...

"Think of the martyrs. So what if he was going to turn her over to the Kempetai?

"The blessed Saint Agnes and the blessed Saint Joan — they died rather than let their bodies be sullied...

"But not her, cat in heat that she was."

She seemed to run out of venom, and linked her fingers as if in prayer.

"Listen to me, Bernadette Byrne," Lawrence came to tower over her, and spoke very slowly and clearly. "You're deranged. It may be the war.

"But I'm sure you've always been a bitch."

He sat on the front verandah, and waited and waited, his mind churning.

She's alive. She's a tart. A Japanese officer.

And gradually, after Bernadette's rant, the letter left for him began to make more sense, the grave danger Kate faced having been recognized as American by a Japanese officer...

She's alive. Think about that. Only that.

A jeep stopped in front of the gate, and a woman got down, wearily, her head drooping with fatigue, but she turned and called "Thank you" to the driver, who responded "Pleasure, Sister. Pick you up tomorrow, then."

She came up to the steps, spotted Lawrence and stopped, surprised, then smiled. " You've come, so. I wondered when you might.

"Do you remember me?"

"I do. You're Rose, you were at our wedding."

Rose hesitated. "And do you know…?"

He stared back, his face frozen. "Yes. I met her brother.

"The Red Cross told the family she was dead. So I believed it as well.

"Where is she? That madwoman — Bernadette — told me she's gone."

Rose took the rattan armchair next to him, and rubbed her back, before easing herself against the cushion.

"She is. She left on one of the first ships repatriating those poor men.

"She'll probably reach England in three weeks. She was intending to go see Belinda's parents, I know, to tell them. Bernadette…"

Lawrence turned to her, and grabbed her arm.

"I don't want to know, do you hear, what Bernadette accused her of, I won't listen."

Rose put her hand on his.

"I wasn't going to say anything about Kate, just that you can't pay Bernadette too much heed…

"She's gone funny here. We all have."

And why, why had she not gone by the house to recover her passport, her papers, everything? he demanded. Why?

She had, Rose replied quietly. The house was empty.

Oh God! Lawrence struck his forehead. Of course.

Busaba was in Hua Hin, and the doorman didn't know her.

"I have never seen her cry as she did when she came back, not even after Belinda and Sumet died.

"She kept saying that she never could be herself again and that she had lost you forever."

Lawrence looked down at his clenched hands, his vision was blurry with tears.

Too much, too much had happened today. He could no longer think. All he knew was that Kate was alive.

"Rose, do you know the name of the ship?"

The huge mass of the *HMS Orion* pulled slowly into the dense fog, followed by swerving, cawing seagulls and Kate, leaning on the railing, shivered as she sniffed the cold air.

It felt like Boston. It even smelled like Boston.

The voyage back had been slow, with stops in Rangoon and Colombo then Gibraltar to disembark some repatriated POWs who became too sick to be treated on board, and squalls in the Bay of Biscay, and banks of mines left in the Atlantic to be avoided.

Kate had struggled with seasickness, and huddled on her bunk, trying to block out the sound of the seven women with whom she shared a cabin built for four.

All of them been interned in camps in Malaya and cried or shrieked at nights, and during the days several sniffed at the Irish nurse who had escaped the hardships they had endured, and a couple of others just stared, empty-eyed, at the grey metal bulkhead.

But at last, the coast of England, and many of those who had come on deck to watch the arrival broke into song, "Rule Britannia" and "God save the King".

A lieutenant from a Scottish regiment came to stand by her and watch the shore come into sight.

"Good old England. It's a beautiful sight, not as beautiful as Scotland, of course, but by God, I never thought I would see it again. Or see my girl."

"Yet here you are," Kate said gently, "and on your two feet. Your girl will be so happy to see you."

"Would you be?" he asked, looking sideways at her.

He was scarecrow thin, and had lost most of his hair and teeth, and his face was misshapen by a broken cheekbone.

"Of course. You're alive, that's all that will matter to her."

She shivered again, and he slipped off his jacket, brand new with shiny buttons, procured in Gibraltar.

"Here, Sister. You've no coat."

She smiled. "Thank you. For a few minutes. Down in my cabin, I have a raincoat one of the nurses gave me in Bangkok." And where in Ireland was home for her, he asked.

She shook her head. She really didn't know.

There was a brass band playing in the cold drizzle, and the regiments did their best to march proudly down the gangplanks, nurses rushed up, assisting those who could still walk and bringing up wheelchairs for those who couldn't and Kate heard a woman scream, "Andrew, Andrew, it's Mum, I'm here!" and felt tears of envy come to her eyes.

Once again, here she was, standing on the side-lines of other peoples' happiness with no idea where to go next.

She was told on the boat that her best bet was to catch a train to Liverpool, from there a boat to Dublin.

When all the repatriated men were off, she picked up the small case with her few belongings, a photo of Belinda to give to her parents and the thin sweater she was given in Singapore, tied a scarf over her hair and walked slowly down to the wharf, feeling the sway of the waves still in her legs. The drizzle was now a downpour, and she could feel the cold rain trickling down her neck.

He had been waiting for over two hours, propped against a wall, watching the pitiful procession of the men hobbling down, being helped into ambulances and thinking of those he had left behind in Burma.

What were their names? He couldn't remember.

And then, he saw her.

There was no mistaking that determined tilt of the head, or the hint of red hair under the awful scarf. She was looking straight ahead, and he was about to call, but he didn't want to startle her.

She would see him.

Then she looked his way, her pale face going a ghostly white, seeing the man, taller than most, with corn-coloured hair dripping over his forehead, his hands in his pockets, who was watching her with a quizzical smile through misted horn-rimmed glasses.

He walked to her, pulled a red booklet out of his pocket and said the words he'd rehearsed for the past three weeks, ever since he had received Andrew's blessing to leave and he'd boarded the plane to London, but his voice came out strangled and hoarse, not light and gentle as he'd intended.

"I believe you've lost this, Mrs. Gallet. You might need it sometime soon."

She put her case down and leaned against him, and he saw the thread of a scar on her cheekbone, and stroked it with his thumb, feeling her shuddering, silent sobs.

"Come, I'm taking you home."

"Home?" she asked. " Where is that?"

He pulled her arm through his and walked her towards the grey city.

"I'm not sure really. But I expect we'll know it when we're there."

Bibliography

Bansal, Ben, Fox, Elliott, Oka Manuel *Architectural Guide Yangon* Dom Publishers, Berlin 2015

Buchan, Eugenie *A few planes for China* ForeEdge 2017

Charnvit Kasetsiri *Studies in Thai and Southeast Asian Histories* The Foundation for the Promotion of Social Science and Humanities Textbooks Project, Bangkok 1979

Crosby, Sir Josiah *Siam: the Crossroads* Hollis and Carter Ltd, London 1945

Direk Jayanama *Thailand and World War II* Silkworm Books 2008

Duckett, Richard *The Special Operations Executive in Burma Intelligence Gathering In WWII* Bloomsbury Academic 2017

Gilchrist, Sir Andrew *Bangkok Top Secret* Hutchinson of London 1970

Goodall, Felicity *Exodus Burma : The British Escape through the Jungles of Death 1942-1943* The History Press 2011

Greenlaw, Olga, Ford, Daniel *The Lady and the Tigers: The Story of the Remarkable Woman Who Served with the Flying Tigers in Burma and China, 1941-1942* CreateSpace Independent Publishing Platform 2011

McLynn, Frank *The Burma Campaign Thailand and Japan's Southern Advance 1940-1945* Vintage Books, London 2011

Pridi Banomyong, Chris Baker *Pridi by Pridi* Silkworm Books 2000

Reynolds, Bruce E. *Thailand's Secret War OSS, SOE, and the Free Thai Underground during World War II* St. Martin's Press, New York 2005

Reynolds, Bruce E. *Thailand and Japan's Southern Advance 1940-1945* Cambridge University Press 1994

Rodger, George *Red Moon Rising into Siam* The Cresset Press 1943

Smith, Nicol and Clark Blake *Underground Kingdom* The Bobbs Merrill Company, Indianapolis New York 1946

Sparrow, Gerald *Land of the Moon Flower* Elek Books, London 1955

Stowe, Judith A *Siam becomes Thailand: A story of* Intrigue University of Hawaii Press 1991

Strate, Shane *The lost Territories : Thailand's History of National Humiliation* University of Hawaii Press 2015

Terwiel, B.J. *Thailand's Political History — From the Fall of Ayutthaya to Recent Times* River Books 2005

Tuchman, Barbara W. *Stillwell and the American Experience in China* Macmillan 1971